IN THE GENERAL'S HOUSE

Jan 10/07 —

For Sacha and Mike —

all the Best!

*"It's a pleasure to read fiction so obviously steeped in fact
and so gracefully revealing the indomitable character
of the human spirit . . ."*
    –Joe Collins - BOOKLIST, The Journal of the
                                American Library Association

In the General's House

&

Other Stories

By

Philip J. Albaum

Res Gestae Press

SANTA BARBARA, CALIFORNIA

1993

To Pufi,
my gorgeous Hungarian wife,
who brought serenity, beauty,
and a touch of real class into my life.
She made everything possible.

Published by Res Gestae Press
A division of the Res Gestae Foundation, Inc.
Post Office Box 5401
Santa Barbara, California 93108

LIBRARY OF CONGRESS CATALOGING-IN-PUBLICATION DATA
Albaum, Philip
    In the general's house and other stories / Philip Albaum.
        p. cm.
    ISBN 0-9619708-0-4—0-9619708-1-2 (pbk)
    1. World War, 1939-1945—Fiction. I. Title.
    PS3562.U594I5 1992
    813'.54—dc20   92-22736
                                                               CIP

Contents

Preface 7

I. Hitler and His Trusted Colonels 11

II. Kriegie Diary
Chapter One —   What A Difference A Day Makes .. 35
Chapter Two —   The Long March to Prum 50
Chapter Three —   To Prum and Beyond 62
Chapter Four —   The Panzer Captain's Quest 74
Chapter Five —   Gerolstein and
                     The Orient Express 82
Chapter Six —   The Train Yard At Limburg 91
Chapter Seven —   To The Elbe and Beyond 100
Chapter Eight —   New Year's Eve 105
Chapter Nine —   Getting To Know the Brits 109
Chapter Ten —   A Bit Of Blighty 120
Chapter Eleven —   "We Bring You The Griff" 129
Chapter Twelve —   The Passing Of A President 135
Chapte Thirteen —   A Night To Remember 142
Chapter Fourteen —   The Cossack Ponies 150
Chapter Fifteen —   Life Among The Russians 160
Chapter Sixteen —   Link-Up At The Elbe 167
Chapter Seventeen — Farewell To 12B—Then A Look
                     At The Dark Side Of The Moon .. 175

III. In the General's House

Chapter One — Sonya's Nightmare 187
Chapter Two — The Eight Of Krondorf 195
Chapter Three — Bismarckstrasse No. 79 207
Chapter Four — The General's Wife 217
Chapter Five — Return Of The Candy Man 225
Chapter Six — Weisskopf In Charge 233
Chapter Seven — A Real Friday Night Dinner—
  One Day Late 241
Chapter Eight — The *Pistolentasche* 249
Chapter Nine — Frau Von Hesselmann's
  Lonely Vigil 254
Chapter Ten — Sonya At Rest 260
Chapter Eleven — The Man From Borodino 265
Chapter Twelve — Peace, It's Wonderful 273
Chapter Thirteen — A Walk In The Park 282
Chapter Fourteen — Sergeant Kagan Returns 290
Chapter Fifteen — Going Home 296

IV. Requiem for Father and Son

IV. Requiem for Father and Son 305

Bibliography 333

List of Illustrations/Maps

The Battle of the Bulge 10
A Kriegie Odyssey 34
Krondorf – May 1945 186
Viktor Wulf's Final Journey 304

Preface

THE STORIES CONTAINED IN THIS VOLUME are a mixture of history and fiction. They were inspired by what was seen and experienced by the Author during the Second World War, during the Battle of the Bulge and then in the months immediately following, as both a prisoner of war, and as a newly liberated American POW in Soviet-occupied East Germany, until the end of hostilities on the European continent in May 1945. Certain recollections and impressions across a chasm of almost half a century can oft times remain vivid and true, yet one must accept the inevitable evanescence of old memory. Fiction serves as a flimsy garment to clothe inadequacies in the recall of distant events and characters whose outlines have been dimmed by time.

To authenticate and broaden the historical parameters, recourse has been had, when necessary, to the voluminous scholarly reportage which is readily available on the general subject of these writings. Within these pages, with the exception of major historical figures who appear and are so identified, and whose careers and deeds, and misdeeds, have over the years become well documented, all other characters are fictionalized composites, and any resemblance of such to actual persons, living or dead, is unintended and purely coincidental. Care has been taken not to compromise the privacy of any actual persons, living or dead. Toward this end, the names of characters, place names, and such things as unit designations have been fictionalized where deemed appropriate and where such does not unreasonably diminish the historical message.

All of the numerous characters herein, whatever their nationalities and loyalties, were actually, in one way or another, victims of the war and the Nazification of Germany during the Hitler years. As I have mellowed and matured, and reflected over the years, I have come to the opinion that, except for the prime movers and shakers, those who operate entirely of their own free and untethered will, in the massive human collisions of history, such as occurred in both the military and non-combatant arenas of the Second World War, there are really no good guys or bad guys—only victims, both the innocent and the guilty, caught in a spider's web of evil, and inexorably bound to remorseless destiny.

Hitler and His Trusted Colonels

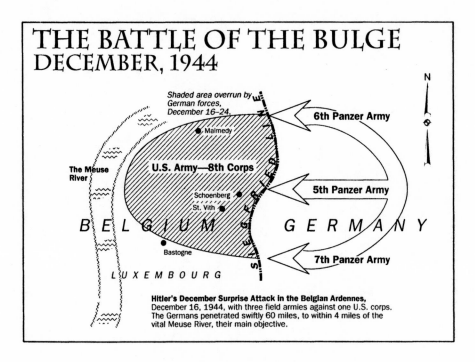

THE BATTLE OF THE BULGE
DECEMBER, 1944

N

Shaded area overrun by
German forces,
December 16–24.

6th Panzer Army

Malmedy

The Meuse
River

U.S. Army—8th Corps

5th Panzer Army

Schoenberg

St. Vith

B E L G I U M

G E R M A N Y

Bastogne

7th Panzer Army

L U X E M B O U R G

Hitler's December Surprise Attack in the Belgian Ardennes,
December 16, 1944, with three field armies against one U.S. corps.
The Germans penetrated swiftly 60 miles, to within 4 miles of the
vital Meuse River, their main objective.

Hitler and
His Trusted Colonels

1944 WAS THE YEAR when Adolf Hitler came face to face with the issue of his own mortality. It was in this sixth year of the war when he was compelled finally to fight a defensive ground war on several fronts, on opposite ends of the European continent, with his adversaries gaining one victory after another on all the major fronts.

In June the Anglo-American land, air, and naval forces, under the leadership of General Dwight D. Eisenhower, executed a brilliant and spectacular landing and deep penetration on the German held coast of Northern France. Ike had proved that Hitler's Fortress Europa was no longer immune to massive invasion from the sea, and that such amphibious operations could penetrate Hitler's coastal defenses and move inland to threaten the entire German position in Western Europe.

The landings in Normandy and the events of the summer that followed had proved conclusively that the Führer's string had, at last, run out—and that he was, in fact, on borrowed time.

Facing calamitous reverses on all the military fronts, Hitler was to become obsessed with the writings of two classic nineteenth-century Prussian military theoreticians, both of whom had in their time been prolific advocates and molders of modern German military philosophies.

The one, Count Alfred von Schlieffen, had warned in his

writings that the greatest potential peril to German national viability would be posed by an enemy, at this time the Anglo-American land forces, who, moving from the West, might be approaching within striking distance of the Rhine barrier at the western approaches of the Fatherland; as distinguished from an attacker moving on Germany from Eastern Europe. Schlieffen's premise was that any peril approaching from the East, now represented by the powerful Soviet armies then surging westward, could be more easily managed and delayed because the vital German organs and nerve centers were not so readily reachable from that direction. Hitler subscribed wholeheartedly to Schlieffen's thesis.

The other revered theoretician implicitly credited by the Führer was the attack-minded General Karl von Clausewitz, whose classic admonition to military planners was: "A swift and vigorous assumption of the offensive . . . the flashing sword of vengeance . . . is the most brilliant point in the defensive!"

In the late fall of 1944, while a suffocating blanket of doom hung over all of Germany, and a full generation after Schlieffen's death, the Führer had suddenly come to embrace Schlieffen's theories as crucially relevant to his own immediate situation, while Clausewitz's doctrine of aggressive warfare had indeed always been the shining beacon which lighted the Führer's way.

The Führer accordingly decided that his monster tanks, the 60-ton Tigers and the even more heavily armored King Tigers, most recently proven of limited effect against the hard-charging Russians in the eastern territories of Russia and Poland, were now to be redeployed and unleashed against the American Army, which was spearheading the Anglo-American drive against the western defenses of the Reich and indeed coming within striking distance of Germany's vital Rhine River defense line.

To the great dismay of his senior generals, most of whom he had recently come to distrust and dislike intensely, Hitler proceeded to strip his Eastern Front forces of much-needed manpower and tanks in order to be able to strike out sharply at the

Anglo-Americans in the west. Clausewitz and Schlieffen notwithstanding, the top-ranking German officers—including the venerable Field Marshal Gerd von Rundstedt, nominal commander-
in-chief in the West—were aghast at this vast expenditure of
critical resources on this contemplated speculative venture in the
tangled and mountainous terrain of the Belgian Ardennes. Moreover, this massive strategic shift to the offensive was to occur at
precisely the time when the Reich was faced with a desperate last-
ditch defensive effort on both the Western and Eastern fronts.

Ironically, despite the disastrous German setbacks on all fronts
during the past summer, and the general loss of confidence in
Hitler's management of the war, there were some unmistakable
signs that the Führer's star was, incredibly, in the ascendancy. Fate
had, after all, reached out and saved him from the deadly bomb
which some dissident generals had so recently set for him in his
headquarters on July 20 of that year. While suffering some painful
wounds, the Führer had escaped without serious harm and without
any incapacitation. Many "defeatist" and "traitorous" German
officers, including field-marshals and generals, would pay with
their lives, often in the cellars of the Gestapo, for that bungled assassination attempt.

All this was to be followed within a matter of weeks by the
great German victory in Holland in late September when an entire
British airborne division was trapped and annihilated while two
top-rated American divisions, the 82nd and the 101st Airborne,
were successfully held at bay taking heavy losses. That decisive
confrontation around the Dutch town of Arnhem had sealed off
the Allied advance into Holland and guaranteed the continued integrity of the vital Ruhr industrial region for the Reich. British
Field Marshal Bernard Montgomery, tragically miscalculating the
resiliency of the German military machine, had placed his
paratroopers inside a German pocket. Montgomery would stand
helplessly by as his prized Red Devils, Britain's premier airborne
troops, were liquidated by a German Army that had earlier been

written off by Allied Intelligence. The psychological and morale dividends for Germany were incalculable.

And now, inveighed the German Führer, why not strike out with all power at an American force, made up in large part of green troops freshly arrived from America, and which seemed for the moment to have lost its direction and initiative? Hitler would excoriate the "doubters and defeatists" and tirelessly proclaim to the faithful that five years of unremitting warfare had not inflicted any irreversible damage upon the German war machine or its supporting economy, and that the Allied leadership was deluding itself in its hopes for an early or easy victory.

In fact, there was a new and inexhaustible labor pool of millions of slave workers recently brought "on line" by the mass deportations of "undesirables" from Hungary and other occupied satellite countries. Many of these people, though characterized as "enemies of the state," were well educated and easily trainable as semi-skilled labor. They knew that it was "work or die." They were obviously cheap and very manageable—no vacations, no pensions, no relocation problems. Truly a remarkable strategic asset in wartime.

And as for military manpower, here, also, Hitler was hardly hurting. Numerically, his armies were actually at peak strength at this late phase of the war, although he had had to stretch the age limits for new inductees. The new replacements were both younger—as young as sixteen—and older—up to age fifty-five—than their veteran comrades.

True, the twenty- and thirty-year-old classes, the prime combat ages, had earlier been drastically depleted in Russia, in North Africa, in Italy, France, and elsewhere. But the teenagers out of the Hitler Youth were fresh and eager replacements in the front-line ranks, while the oldsters at the other end of the age spectrum could perform those military chores in close-up support roles which did not require the same degree of youthful commitment and vigor.

And Hitler could at this time take further comfort from the

economic statistics. In industrial production of military goods of all categories, all the figures were up; very encouraging, despite the incessant Allied air strikes against the factories and the national transportation network. The bomb damage could be swiftly and painlessly repaired by the rich supply of slave labor, which also made possible the physical relocation of key factories to concealed sites in the vast forests of central Germany, or even in deep underground caverns.

The entire German Sixth Panzer Army, which would spearhead Hitler's Ardennes assault, could be entirely refitted with new tanks and transferred in total secrecy hundreds of miles from the Russian Front to the Belgian borderlands in less than three weeks. Hardly the sign of a moribund system.

The intricate railroad network would deliver troops, equipment, vehicles, and draft horses to staging bases about twenty or thirty miles behind the combat zone, well beyond enemy artillery range, from which point the troops could march to the front within a day or two.

Hitler's world, in the fall of 1944, was alive and well as he saw it from his heavily guarded sanctum, the labyrinthian command complex in East Prussia known as "The Wolf's Lair." From there the ailing Führer directed the receding fortunes of his hard-pressed legions on all the battlefields of Europe, and it was here that he hatched his plans for the great winter counter-offensive to be launched against the faltering Allied armies on the Western Front.

For the German military, the most direct break-out route to Paris had always been through Belgium, leading out from the Schnee Eifel region through the Belgian Ardennes. The Eifel was an extension of the Ardennes on the German side of the border between the two countries. Here in this sparsely populated belt of rolling hills, picturesque river valleys, and villages known among European *cognoscenti* for their somnolence and idyllic vacation locales, the Germans had always found the going easy in their periodic break-outs to the west. Hitler had only to review the military history of Belgium in the twentieth-century wars of Western

Europe to feel superbly confident that a break-out through Belgium was the way to go.

The military momenta which had repeatedly surged across this varied terrain have almost always been from east to west, Germany attacking France through Belgium. One notable exception had been Napoleon Bonaparte, who, in the early 1800's, had discovered that the shortest road for him from Paris to Berlin and points eastward, likewise ran through Belgium and the Ardennes. And history shows that it was finally in Belgium in the spring of 1815 that a coalition led by the English and Prussians had dealt the French emperor his final defeat on the fields of Waterloo.

From his "Wolf's Lair" in East Prussia, Hitler could plan and ruminate in splendid isolation, and could see it all clearly. He had built this stone-and-steel temple of war overlooking a rocky and mist-shrouded Baltic coastline shortly after the launch of his ill-starred invasion of Soviet Russia in June 1941, at a time when he was riding the crest of his spectacular early successes. Soon, however, he would abandon this imperial headquarters, the very site where that traitorous military cabal had made that infamous attempt against his life, and would soon be moving his staff and entourage across the entire breadth of Germany to Castle Ziegenberg behind the Western Front. East Prussia and the great Eastern headquarters complex would fall to the Russians several weeks later.

But on this particular day—on a gusty, windswept Sunday afternoon in mid-October 1944, some two months before his Panzer hordes were to lumber like primordial monsters out of the snow-shrouded forests of the Ardennes, the Führer's thoughts were taken up exclusively with the exciting new prospects for reversing the trend of the war in the West.

The Americans had just snuffed out the last S.S. resistance in the city of Aachen, that ancient capital of Charlemagne's Holy Roman Empire. This was the first German city to fall to the American Army; symbolically, it was a painful loss, but strategically not all that important. The Americans had paid dearly. It had cost them six agonizing weeks and a heavy toll in lives and equipment to subdue the German garrison and the hard-core S.S. regiment which had tenaciously held the main downtown district. Several prime American divisions had been badly mangled in the bloody, close-quarter fighting. But most importantly, the Americans had lost crucial time and the momentum that they had built up as they had come storming out of northern France in pursuit of a thoroughly defeated and demoralized German Army in the closing weeks of summer.

Now the Führer was preparing to pay the Americans back for Aachen, and for Antwerp, and for the series of humiliating defeats of the last four months—since Eisenhower's audacious landing on the supposedly impregnable French beaches on D-Day, the 6th of June, 1944.

Precisely at 2:00 P.M. on this Sabbath day, a tall, hulking S.S. colonel, nattily attired in an impeccably tailored black leather tunic and riding breeches, was escorted swiftly and respectfully through the maze of security to the inner sanctum of Hitler's private study and map room.

Despite that the Führer had never fully recovered from the trauma of the July 20 assassination attempt, and was further plagued at this time by a lingering throat infection that had severely weakened him and affected his vocal cords, he had explicitly directed that there were not to be any extraneous intrusions during his confidential conference with his close friend and fellow Austrian, S.S. Lieutenant-Colonel Otto Skorzeny.

The Führer did his daily "homework," the plotting and tracking of all significant strategic and tactical developments on all the war fronts, in this cavernous concrete bunker some forty feet underground. The only others present in the vaulted room were three helmeted S.S. captains standing discreetly at the alert a few paces behind Hitler's chair. Armed with submachine guns, they never shifted their gaze from Skorzeny, who had been required to undergo a complete body search after depositing his own side-arm and ceremonial S.S. dagger at the sentry post when he was driven into the fortress.

During his entire session with Hitler, Skorzeny would have the feeling that he was under constant surveillance by many pairs of invisible eyes scrutinizing him from behind curtains and screening partitions and even from an overhead loft. The extra-tight security was understandable in the aftermath of the abortive bombing attempt on the Führer's life some three months earlier.

Notwithstanding the wide disparity in age and station between the two men, Skorzeny, a relative youngster at thirty-six and Hitler's junior by some twenty years, enjoyed his Führer's highest confidence and trust in all matters large and small. There was a rare natural affinity between them, stemming perhaps from the fact of Skorzeny's Austrian roots and the manifestation early on of such qualities as steadfastness, discretion, and imperturbability in the Nazi cause, going back more than ten years to the very first days of the National Socialists' early struggle to subvert the independence of Austria.

As an early card-carrying member of the Austro-Bavarian Nazi network, Skorzeny had always been available and ready to step in at the most crucial moment to pull Nazi chestnuts out of the fire, no matter where, or whatever the difficulty or risk. Skorzeny had risen to become the most distinguished and, indeed, the most effective by far of all the "special situation" operatives in the Central Security Office of the *Schutz Staffel*.

Upon entering the Führer's presence, the impressive, scar-faced colonel snapped smartly to attention, drawing himself up to his full height of six feet four inches, and clicked his heels with arm raised high in the Nazi salute.

"Heil Hitler!"

The Führer, showing some fatigue but obviously pleased to receive Skorzeny, rose to greet him and motioned to a chair in front of a massive marble conference table awash in charts and maps.

Aware of Hitler's legendary impatience with small talk and

banalities, Skorzeny took the initiative in steering the conversation toward current business.

"*Mein Führer,* I wish to respectfully report on the satisfactory conclusion of my mission in Budapest."

"*Ja,* Otto, I know about it . . . it was masterfully done. And where is the worthless young traitor now?"

"He is in one of our 'sanitariums' under appropriate security. He will not be coddled, I assure you, my *Führer.* The facility is in Vienna. And we were able to do this without harming a precious hair on his head!"

"Good . . . and what about the father?"

"Admiral Horthy is likewise in protective custody, as your 'personal guest' at the Schloss Hirschberg, as you ordered, *Führer.*"

"Well done, Skorzeny. The one in Austria, the other in the Bavarian Alps." Hitler chuckled appreciatively. Skorzeny was a true professional. Everything always went so right with him.

Then suddenly in a coldly malevolent mood, "That Horthy has been a thorn in my side for too long. It is good to be rid of him—the darling of the Jewish bankers of Budapest. He and his son are lucky to be alive, thanks to your solicitude. We'll decide their cases later. There will certainly be heavy penalties. In the meantime, you have saved Hungary, my dear fellow, although I understand it was not entirely an onerous chore."

"Budapest has its advantages, Sir."

"You're a devil, Skorzeny. You're the only one I know who has been able to distill any joy out of this war."

A sly twinkle shone momentarily in Skorzeny's one good eye. "It is an honor and a privilege to discharge my duties to my *Führer* and the Fatherland."

"I must tell you, Skorzeny, I never cease to be amazed by the workings of your engineer's mind. I wish I had at least ten more like you. You make it all look so simple and straightforward."

"You honor me, my *Führer.*"

"You know, I am surrounded by such incompetents. My

generals and my doctors, they are all such clumsy fools! Everything is impossible for them!"

The Führer's allusion to his doctors threw a cloud over the previously upbeat tone of the conversation.

Skorzeny had been in Hitler's presence on numerous previous occasions in the later years of the war. Shrewd appraiser that he was, he was now taken aback by Hitler's debilitated physical appearance.

He fleetingly recalled the meeting about a year earlier when an ebullient Führer, in high fettle, had personally given him the assignment of rescuing Benito Mussolini, the deposed Italian dictator, from the traitorous Italian politicians who were preparing to put him on trial for war crimes. That mission had been the high point of his career, and the one for which the Führer had graciously awarded him the Knight's Cross to the Iron Cross.

It now pained the younger man to observe the ravages of the intervening year's trials and traumas upon his revered chieftain.

Hitler had aged twenty years; he was stooped over, unsteady, frail, and hoarse-voiced. His left arm hung limply at his side, and his facial features were disfigured by scaly red blotches. Only the eyes retained any of the old fire and excitement.

Hitler rang for his adjutant, who appeared instantly. "Attend us here, Klinge. I want the maps of the Ardennes front. Also refreshments for the Colonel."

Two stewards entered, one with a tray for Hitler, from which he tendered some medications and a cup of lemon-water. The other turned to offer a tray holding a choice of liqueurs to the colonel, who, at the Führer's insistence, in a rare concession to *Gemütlichkeit,* self-consciously accepted a cognac which he barely touched.

Klinge then proceeded to display a set of relief maps of the three eastern Belgian provinces of Malmedy, St. Vith, and Eupen, showing in three-dimensional detail the topography and the various features and waterways coursing through the region. The adjutant and an assistant stood ready with pointers and report binders to clarify and amplify the forthcoming discussion.

Skorzeny had to enjoy a special and unique status to be accorded this open-handed confidentiality and flattering attention. But the towering Austrian had earned the Führer's highest regard, having proved his unique value over and over again.

And now there was again a critical need for his special talents.

He was, after all, the indisputable Number One among that handful of covert operatives from whom the Führer received such facile dedication and who understood the Führer's every instinct and innermost motives. Those dedicated men were the true "specialists" of modern warfare. They didn't require massive military formations to achieve their assigned objectives. They were immune to enemy counter-strategies. They were the true-blue, self-effacing, "low-overhead" operators who never failed, never complained, and who waited unobtrusively in the wings for their special orders. They were not inhibited by the decadent and hypocritical constraints of "honor, morality, decency, or Christian ethics." They understood, moreover, the patriotic commandment of "silence." They could be drawn only from the rosters of such loyalty-tested organizations as the *Sicherheitdienst*, the security service of the S.S.

While the regular German Army supplied the masses of manpower needed on all the front lines, from the very beginning of his early preparations for war Hitler had known that the truly decisive factor in his final victory would be the dazzling assortment of select groups and individuals to be found in the special bureaus of the *Schutz Staffel*, the S.S.

Hitler opened the strategy discussion by taking a few minutes to review for his guest the underlying precepts of the science of Blitzkrieg. Despite that those two foremost Panzer tacticians, General Heinz Guderian, the pioneer of Blitzkrieg, and Field Marshal Erwin Rommel, its most gifted practitioner, had both recently fallen into official disfavor—Rommel having just days earlier been the victim of a coerced suicide under orders of the highest security authorities—the Führer drew generously from their theories and writings in discussing his proposed tactics.

"As you are well aware, Skorzeny, the basic theorems of war are universal, never changing. Only fools refuse to recognize this. We have today on the Belgian Front a classic opportunity to strike a mortal blow at an unsuspecting enemy. It is Poland and Holland all over again." The Führer was reliving the glories of the past when his armies, in close tandem with his invincible air forces, had moved with lightning speed, and when Poland had been taken in less than two weeks, and Holland fell to his Panzers in a matter of days. That was in 1939 and 1940, respectively.

Skorzeny sat in attentive silence, concentrating on the large hanging map and allowing Hitler to develop the subject.

"In the Ardennes, right there, is a ragged eighty-mile front where the Americans have settled into some portions of the West Wall. They are acting as if it is rightfully theirs, and like they don't have a care in the world!"

Hitler's voice was scratchy. He paused for a few seconds, taking a sip of the lemon-water, then he continued as Klinge pointed to the segmented hill country where the borderlands of Germany, Belgium, and tiny Luxembourg converge.

"Right there is a low-priority American corps manned by several understrength divisions that are stretched out to the limit. The Americans rotate their depleted units into this line for rest and refitting. They have decided for some reason that the terrain is unsuitable for any major action. They cling to their myopic strategies, oblivious of history. And right there is the glaring weak spot in the entire front, just begging for a massive Panzer strike. And, Skorzeny, realize, only 200 kilometers beyond that weak link lies Antwerp with its indispensable harbor. If we retake Antwerp, the Anglo-Americans are finally *Kaput;* they are cut asunder and will strangle in their own evil juices!"

It was glaringly simple. Skorzeny realized that Hitler had indeed laid open a once-in-a-lifetime opportunity to reverse the tide of battle in the West. The Führer, somewhat spent by this outpouring of unbridled enthusiasm, would soon let Klinge take over the exposition.

"Right there, Skorzeny, in the hills of the Eifel and in the forest of the Ardennes is where we will make our most decisive play! Now, Klinge, would you take over. Outline the operation for the Colonel."

The Führer fell into a fit of coughing, then took a few more sips from his lemon-water.

The adjutant continued, returning repeatedly to the maps to show conspicuous gaps in the American positions as well as other tactical features that would bear on the early phases of a surprise attack.

The Führer rested his eyes and leaned back in his chair as Klinge held forth.

"The initial breakthrough, Colonel, will be achieved by fast-moving Panzers striking with overwhelming force at these enemy weak spots. Continued success is dependent on two vital conditions. First and most critical, the shoulders of the breakthrough must be protected at all costs from enemy counter-attack. This, of course, is to assure the integrity of our lines of reinforcement and supply."

Skorzeny could go along with that. Basic Blitzkieg tactics.

The adjutant was pointing first at the Malmedy sector on the northern end of the attack front, and then at the mountainous terrain of tiny Luxembourg at the southern terminus.

Klinge went on. "Secondly, there must be a powerful mobile force in reserve which can be pumped through the breach in strong subsequent waves. Thus the point of the dagger is driven deeper into the enemy with fresh forces. If successful, the opening wedge will ultimately shatter and trap the enemy in a cauldron from which there is no escape."

Skorzeny nodded in approval. This again was basic Blitzkrieg theory.

Skorzeny was next favored with a rather curious "insider's" tidbit. Incredibly, as of this time, Field Marshal Gerd von

Rundstedt, the proud old commander-in-chief of the Western
Front, and all of the senior generals under him who would be
responsible for pulling off this spectacular upset victory, had not
yet been given any advance inkling of this grandiose new attack
plan. They were not to receive a briefing until the planning had
reached a more definitive stage, when it could be transmitted in
final form. And furthermore, there was reason to believe that the
military professionals, the prima donnas, would be decidedly cool
to the whole idea, particularly since the concept had been hatched
and nurtured by such a non-professional as the Führer. The
Führer's faith in the regular Army generals relative to competence
and commitment, never very high, was now at an all-time low.

"They dream only of retirement to their big estates. They are
farmers. They have no stomach for war. They are useless. They live
in the past. One cannot work with them. They do not understand
the new Germany!" On this Sunday afternoon Hitler unburdened
himself fully to his friend Skorzeny, from whom he was seeking
some measure of encouragement that his daring plan was both
feasible and keenly conceived.

Because of the implicit faith that Hitler had in Skorzeny, in
preference to the regular military leadership, the Colonel had, at
an earlier time of shattering crisis—in the aftermath of the
abortive bomb plot of July 20, some three months earlier—been
one of the first to be called in to help stabilize the ship of state and
ward off any follow-up coup attempts by the cabal of traitors. He
had indeed, at that delicate moment, been highly instrumental in
swiftly putting the Nazi house back in order.

Despite that he was the acknowledged master of the swift
surgical strike, Skorzeny had also seen his share of blood and guts.
He had, early in the war, served with the Panzer forces in Holland
and then in Russia, where he was wounded in action. He indeed
had authentic Panzer credentials. He was just the right man to
serve as the sounding board for the Führer's daring and innovative
scheme, which would combine the heavy-footed Panzer with the
stealth of the masked infiltrator.

Klinge, himself a highly decorated Panzer veteran, then zeroed in on the two major prospective problem areas where Skorzeny's unique talents could fit perfectly into the equation.

First . . . a swift surreptitious surgical strike deep behind the Allied lines for the purpose of seizing the most vital Meuse River bridges some sixty miles inside Belgium to forestall their destruction by Allied sappers. This bold and brilliant tactic would both prevent the withdrawal of trapped Allied troops, or their rescue or reinforcement by fresh Allied troops, as well as insure the unimpeded deeper penetration by victorious German Panzer forces in the later stages of the battle.

And secondly . . . some even more exotic measures to help seal off the Panzers' exposed northern flanks from the flood of American reinforcements which would be streaming towards the battlefield after the first alarms were set off.

While the two situations posed dissimilar tactical problems, a common simplistic solution for both dilemmas was now floated. This would involve the daring and imaginative use of a special force of English-speaking troops—organized in two separate brigades—and outfitted in American uniforms authentic to the minutest detail—driving American jeeps, trucks, and even tanks. German units to be disguised as Americans!

Klinge presented the proposition to Skorzeny: "Colonel, the Führer is offering you this historic opportunity to strike a telling blow against the enemies of the Fatherland. He wants you, Colonel, to command both phases of this special operation."

Skorzeny, the daredevil and gambler, was now in his element.

Klinge ventured on into the details. "The first brigade, which we shall call the '*Kommandos*,' will break up into approximately a hundred squads of four or five men each. They will be driving American jeeps and shall appear to all the world as American M.P.s."

Skorzeny brightened visibly, "Inspired, Colonel."

Klinge went on. "Their function will be the systematic misdirecting of road traffic, the posting of bogus directional signs,

and otherwise to create confusion and chaos in the first hours of
the attack, when a high degree of such disorganization and panic
must be introduced into the American reaction. Any questions,
Colonel?"

"None, Colonel."

"Good. It is no secret that the Americans are forever plagued
by a shortage of local maps. Consequently they are subject to
confusion and paralysis in the critical early hours of an operation.
These 'M.P.' squads will be deployed along the northern shoulder
of the attack, principally in the Malmedy district, where the first
American reinforcements, both of armor and infantry, must be
diverted or delayed by any means possible."

Skorzeny nodded in appreciation of the carefully designed scenario. And what about the second group?

"Your second group, Colonel, shall be designated in the orders
as the 150th Panzer Brigade. It shall be similarly equipped with
appropriate American uniforms and armored vehicles. Its role shall
be to appear as an American armored column falling back in the
direction of the Meuse River. It shall keep moving rapidly without
interruption to the American rear until it reaches three specified
crossing points on the Meuse. When reaching those objectives they
will take up, shall we say, 'defensive positions' around the bridges,
to prevent their destruction by the Americans, until the arrival of
our own Panzer spearheads! You understand that our forward
spearheads must not be impeded from crossing the Meuse River in
the later phases of the operation. That is vital for attaining our
long-range objectives. The Meuse bridges are vital."

Skorzeny was really impressed. The plan had scope, imagina-
tion, and verve.

"Are we correct in assuming, Colonel, that you will have no
serious problem, on principle, with an operation in which enemy
uniforms and equipment are utilized to gain an otherwise
unavailable critical advantage?"

To Skorzeny and those of his tight fraternity of special
operatives, the use of enemy uniforms and equipment to

perpetrate a hoax of this kind was perfectly natural and acceptable. They understood only too well that war was a dirty business.

Had not an earlier Gestapo squad, composed of Polish-speaking agents and decked out in Polish Army uniforms, on the night of August 31, 1939, some five years earlier on the very eve of war, "attacked" the German radio station in the border town of Gleiwitz, "captured" the building and broadcast a wildly provocative "Polish Message To The World" laden with intolerable insults against the German Reich, and then escaped into the night leaving a number of "German troops" dead at the building entrance?

Those "dead" were drugged inmates of a nearby concentration camp, especially selected for their fair complexions and Aryan-like appearance. They were executed at the scene, and when found dead in bullet-torn German military garb would appear to unquestioning "friendly" newscameras to be the "German" victims of a murderous "Polish" incursion on German territory!

And an outraged Führer had dutifully addressed the German nation on the following day, issuing the call to arms and announcing that German armies were crossing the Polish frontiers at that very hour to "defend" the Reich from just this sort of Polish villainy. And so the Second World War was unleashed upon a fitful world.

In justice to Skorzeny, the Gleiwitz caper had not been his type of operation; it was definitely not his style. His keen engineer's mind preferred the "white glove" surgical challenge, to achieve immediate substantive results, preferably with a minimum of bloodshed, rather than merely the perpetration of a staged charade for propaganda effect. And Gleiwitz was certainly not the sort of accomplishment that one could gloat about in one's post-war memoirs and still retain the patina of the glamorous swashbuckler. The Colonel always left the really despicable chores to others in the Gestapo, those for whom nothing was excessive, unworthy, or unreasonable.

Responding to Klinge's genteel inquiry, Skorzeny declared with pride and obvious sincerity, "In war one must do whatever is necessary. My only guiding principle is to serve my *Führer* in any capacity that he may command."

Everyone was now on the same wavelength.

In a final examination of the maps of the prospective battlefield, it was obvious that the several rivers meandering through the area could represent a major inhibiting factor; but on the other hand the road network, such as it was, would definitely yield a major advantage to the attackers. Almost all the arterial roads ran in an east-west direction, thus facilitating the flow of attacking German armor and infantry from the point of penetration westward to the enemy's lightly defended rear areas.

The Americans, on the other hand, in seeking to seal the breach, would move their countervailing forces southward from Holland and the Aachen enclave, or in the case of Patton's Third Army, in a northerly direction, to reach the battlefield.

The north-south roads were fewer in number with only a few main roads, generally narrow and unpaved, intended only as local connections between various small towns and villages. Moreover, newly committed American forces, being unfamiliar with the area, would be susceptible to "Operation Confusion" and the attendant delays which Skorzeny's ersatz guides and M.P.s would visit upon them.

The Führer himself now offered a final summary of the excellent prospects. "I tell you, Skorzeny, the Anglo-Americans are in deep trouble. They have outrun their supplies and they are low on manpower. They foolishly squandered their last reserves and their only airborne divisions in that ill-advised airdrop at Arnhem. They are now shipping green, inexperienced troops from America to replace their losses and these people are not trained or hardened for static defensive warfare."

Skorzeny had to agree with the Führer's impressive reasoning. After all, Hitler had five years of constant and intimate immersion in the tactics and grand strategy of modern warfare. Skorzeny was further astonished to learn that the Führer, in order to better maintain tight personal control over the progress of the great assault, was preparing to quit the massive Rastenburg command complex in East Prussia and shift his personal headquarters to the Western Front.

By the time the lengthy meeting ended, Skorzeny knew exactly what was expected of him, and he fully endorsed the forthcoming enterprise.

Hitler bade his countryman farewell, assuring him that he would be provided with the men, weapons, and vehicles to complete his delicate assignment. He impressed on the Colonel that this mission was "the big one." Leaving the Führer's presence, Skorzeny began an honest assessment of the prospects for ultimate success. He was a professional. He had decidedly mixed feelings.

For the next seven weeks, through early December, hundreds of English-speaking officers and men would be recruited for Skorzeny while an intensive training program went forward. Rather than the traditional drills and field exercises, Skorzeny's volunteers were put through rigorous classes in English language and syntax, diction and elocution, as well as the latest street slang and idiom of the multifaceted American G.I. By the end of the program, Skorzeny's volunteers were supposed to look, act, and talk just like the genuine article, just like the myriad varieties of Okies, Arkies, Texans, Chicagoans, and Brooklynites, etc., who would be roaming the forests of the Ardennes on D-Day.

Since Skorzeny's own broad-ranging travels had never included a visit to America, he himself unfortunately could not certify the authenticity of the various acquired accents and characteristics. But several of his key staff officers had lived, worked, and studied in the U.S.A., including one aide who had been a faculty member for some years at a prestigious American university.

At the same time, mountains of captured American tanks, jeeps, personnel carriers, and vehicles of all sorts were being hastily repaired and refurbished at a secret repair depot. American uniforms, reclaimed from battlefield dead, were likewise being salvaged, cleaned, and altered to fit some hundreds of these prospective infiltrators. No details were overlooked. A ghoulish collection of personal effects, even letters and photographs garnered from the dead, were to be supplied to the bogus Yanks so they could converse convincingly about fictitious "girls back home," and the latest bits of Americana—movies, sports, the recent elections, and the like.

Back home in Brooklyn, New York, in Siloam Springs, Arkansas, in Pottstown, Pennsylvania, and everywhere else in the U.S.A., there were only eight shopping days left until Christmas, when suddenly, all along the eighty-mile American frontline in Belgium at precisely 0500 hours on Saturday morning, the 16th of December, the trees parted, the giant Panzers shoved their angry pig snouts forward and the Volks Grenadiers in their white parkas gripped their *Schmeissers* and started walking westward across the snowfields.

At the tips of the Panzer spearheads rode Skorzeny's rogue squads, meticulously coached and rehearsed in their duplicitous roles, wearing their counterfeit G.I. uniforms under white winter ponchos which they would discard as soon as they had crossed the American lines. Every man knew in precise detail what he was to do. They quickly fanned out in the lightly held rear zones disguised as American M.P.s, as helpful guides, as line repairmen and the like. Their disguise was perfect, totally convincing in the initial hours of the onslaught. They could joke and kibitz casually with the unsuspecting G.I.s who were in need of directions to get to an assigned position, or otherwise open to friendly conversation. They proceeded smoothly and effortlessly to cut telephone lines, to studiously misdirect road traffic, to play havoc with the road signs, and to generally inject a bizarre new set of complications into the American predicament. Their effect was insidious, pervasive, and immediate.

As the alarms registered on the American side, truck convoys, tank columns—indeed entire battalions soon found themselves inexplicably lost and misdirected away from assigned battle stations. The entire telephone system between the American rear headquarters and the front was compromised in the first crucial hours, including the main phone cables connecting American First Army headquarters in Belgium with Paris and General Omar Bradley's Army Group Headquarters in Luxembourg. Front-line commanders were effectively isolated from higher headquarters—information could not reach the rear echelons where speedy decisions had to be made.

In addition to the monumental failure of Allied Intelligence to furnish any warning of this massive attack by a quarter million men and three Panzer armies, the induced early confusion of the defending forces was to prove doubly calamitous, particularly since the Germans had chosen a Saturday morning to launch their attack. General Dwight Eisenhower, in Paris, was to receive the first word of the German breakout while attending the wedding of a favorite staff person, while many other senior officers had left town for the weekend.

An additional destabilizing operation, the air drop of almost a thousand German paratroops, many in similarly ambiguous costume, was carried out the following day in the pre-dawn darkness. The airborne effort, while a tactical failure, poorly planned and executed, and carried out on a shoestring basis, nevertheless compounded the confusion on the American side at a time when all energies needed to be focused on the main defensive challenges.

Although most of Skorzeny's saboteurs and double-dealers were finally apprehended and neutralized by D plus three, their overall impact on the course of the battle was considerable—succeeding as they did in injecting a debilitating panic and paranoia among the American troops and their officers. Hundreds of thousands of American and Allied troops along hundreds of miles of frontline were suddenly eyeing each other with suspicion. Whether on the roads, in the dense forests, or in deserted farmhouses, they were demanding secret passwords and all sorts of proof of legitimacy from anyone whom they didn't readily recognize as an old buddy. Wild rumors were spawned up and down the line, blurring the realities of the desperate crisis at a time when no one could be certain of the authenticity of any report.

For example, there were recurrent wild reports—baseless but nevertheless destabilizing—that saboteurs and hit squads had been parachuted in as far back as Paris, intent on the assassination or kidnapping of Ike and other top brass. As the wild rumors spread, many G.I.s on the frontlines heard that Paris itself was under German attack by airborne forces. Frantic and superfluous security measures were soon instituted at Allied Supreme Headquarters in Paris and at other sensitive locations.

The battle shaped up immediately along the entire Ardennes front as an unmitigated disaster for the defending Americans, whose commanders had only days earlier been looking forward with superb confidence to the final push to the Rhine and delivery of the final *coup de grâce* to Hitler's forces on the Western Front— but only after some well-deserved Christmas leaves in such beckoning locales as Brussels, Paris, and even London.

At this critical juncture Otto Skorzeny had again come through spectacularly for his Führer.

In early January of 1945, some three weeks after the launching of the Ardennes attack, U.S. Secretary of War Henry Stimson reported to the nation that the American Army had sustained unprecedented casualties on the Western Front during the 31 days of December 1944, numbering a total of 74,788 killed, wounded, and missing in action. While the month had started out very quiet and uneventful, the German offensive coming in the second half of the month had made December 1944 one of the worst months for total casualties in American military history. Against these figures, Stimson estimated the German casualties for the month at 130,000, including 50,000 taken prisoner.

Stimson also stated that one American division, the 106th Infantry Division, which had only recently arrived on the Western Front, had been particularly hard hit, sustaining total casualties of 8,663 men, effectively wiping out two of its three regiments and all of its supporting units. Many of the casualties represented missing in action, most of whom were presumed prisoners of war. The Secretary stated that at year's end the German tide had been stopped, and fresh American forces were retaking the offensive.

Kriegie Diary

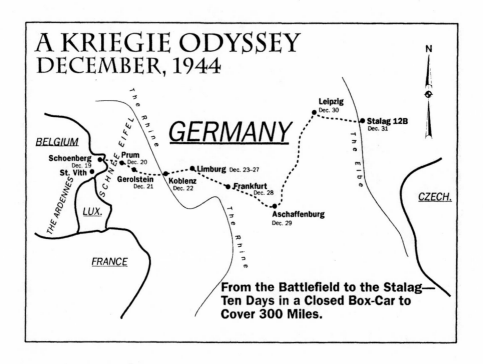

A KRIEGIE ODYSSEY
DECEMBER, 1944

N

BELGIUM

GERMANY

The Rhine

SCHNEE EIFEL

Leipzig
Dec. 30

Stalag 12B
Dec. 31

The Elbe

Schoenberg
Dec. 19
St. Vith

Prum
Dec. 20

Gerolstein
Dec. 21

Koblenz
Dec. 22

Limburg Dec. 23–27

Frankfurt
Dec. 28

Aschaffenburg
Dec. 29

CZECH.

THE ARDENNES

LUX.

The Rhine

FRANCE

**From the Battlefield to the Stalag—
Ten Days in a Closed Box-Car to
Cover 300 Miles.**

CHAPTER ONE

What A Difference
A Day Makes . . .

It was like being on the Titanic after she hit the iceberg. Total surprise, snafu, and pandemonium. The rear echelons—the cooks, the clerks, the artillery, and the medics—got hit first. Their bodies and wrecked vehicles, guns, and ambulances littered the road back to Schoenberg. A real shocker. How the hell could this happen? It was soon every man for himself—with no real way out. Screwed by the numbers.

—Tuesday, December 19, 1944.

PRIVATE FIRST CLASS Zeke Hyams was no stranger to trouble. But it had usually been more like just hard times rather than acute, life-and-limb-threatening trouble. Except lately.

Like anyone else at age twenty-two, Hyams had tasted from the cup of life. There were the good times and the not-so-good times. Born on the wrong side of the tracks to immigrant parents in Brooklyn, New York, Hyams had known his share of trouble like poverty, frustration, and disappointment. But he had also been blessed with the comfort and security of a close, loving family and the usual Brooklyn coterie of close buddies.

Most recently there had been the major unpleasantness of being caught up in the nitty-gritty of war—major war—infantry style. But that, too, was part of life. This war was a very serious matter, and everybody had to do their part. That's all there was to it. The Army was a fact of life—for everybody, even the civilians; even the civilians who never experienced war directly.

Hyams' outfit, the 116th Infantry Division, was newly arrived in what the newspapers liked to call "The European Theatre of Operations." They had been shoved into the old German Siegfried Line to take part, after New Year's, along with many other divisions, in the big push into the Fatherland. This was to be the final, inevitably bloody, assault on the Jerries' Rhine River defenses. Hyams was there along with many thousands of other guys who were just as inexperienced, and nervous, and scared. But they all figured that there must be some safety in numbers. That's what keeps raw young rookies going forward.

But this time apparently there was to be no safety in numbers. The other side had all the numbers on their side. And this was a totally new kind of trouble. Despite all the ups and downs in Hyams' life, until recently there had always in the past been some small prospect of adventure or a touch of frivolity around the next bend in the road. There had always been the prospect of daylight after every long night of darkness. But not this time. Now Hyams, born Haimovicz, was definitely the wrong man in the wrong place at the very worst of times.

For the first time in his life, Hyams was a real victim—defenseless, bewildered, in real trouble, and entirely bereft of any constructive ideas. What they would call back in Brooklyn "a real loser." He had been swept up in the eye of a swirling hurricane, at the very epicenter of Hitler's last desperate throw of the dice. Now everything was coming up roses for the Führer, while Hyams was way down in the pits. And there had been no safety in numbers. All the good guys were in the same pits.

That's where things stood now on this pitch-black and frigid December pre-dawn in the schoolyard in Schoenberg, this battered Belgian village in the midst of a major, all-out German offensive. The high-riding Jerries had converted the schoolyard into a collecting station for some of their thousands of newly taken American prisoners. This was the fifth day of the Führer's spectacularly successful surprise attack through the Belgian Forest of the Ardennes, and the border village of Schoenberg, formerly the site of an American regimental rear echelon, had suddenly become a bastion of German power, bristling with Jerry tanks and supply columns. The only Americans still alive were now prisoners of war, huddled in a schoolyard, defeated and disarmed.

It would be morning soon. Hyams stirred feebly, struggling to emerge from a fevered and tortured sleep. His brain was benumbed by the bitter cold, while hunger and fatigue had drained his last reserves of vitality. Frozen fingers groped in vain for the rifle, the omnipotent M-1 that he had lugged into combat and had pampered and caressed through slush and snow and rain and mud. Those nine pounds of machined steel were his passport to *Valhalla* and to some bright, shining city on the hill. But of course there was no rifle. There was nothing . . . he was weaponless. As a churning panic took hold, he clawed his way to wakefulness.

A chaotic violence hung in the night air like a suffocating blanket. The black sky throbbed with the rolling thunder of men and machines at war in the surrounding hills, massed artillery firing endless volleys, the deadly mortars belching forth their fiery malevolence. And periodically there was the sputtering drone of German rockets in flight—the new Jerry vengeance weapons, the "screaming meemies," the world's first ballistic missiles. While perhaps primitive, still they were very advanced for their time—in this winter of 1944—each delivering a ton of high explosive wherever they fell to earth, adding a new dimension of terror to the battlefield.

Eerie pinpoint flashes illuminated the dim western horizon where the last American hold-outs were still fighting and dying in St. Vith, some eight miles distant.

All about the schoolyard lay the shapeless mounds of G.I. forms, frozen and comatose, covering every inch of the snowy ground. Yesterday's warriors, now defeated and drained, they had been herded into this makeshift prison pen in straggling groups during a long and tragic night. Stripped of weapons and the last vestiges of a soldier's dignity, they lay in a death-like stupor, curled up like so many fetuses, nestled against each other for shelter against the icy wind, some cradling their heads atop steel helmets.

They were the foot-sloggers, the lowly but quintessential pawns of war. In every age and every war it is they who pay the bloody butcher's bill. It is they who slither in shallow trenches, who fight and bleed and often die in roadside ditches, in mudholes, in the deep forests, in shattered barns and abandoned houses where once normal people lived and loved and raised children.

The immediate German objective now would be St. Vith, that once- thriving crossroads town some dozen miles from the German frontier. It would pay an awesome price for sitting there astride two arterial roads. Hyams the infantryman had learned that cross-roads and rivers and bombed-out towns and abandoned farm-houses were, in the final analysis, what war was all about.

Division headquarters with its assorted brass would probably still be hunkered down in bombed-out St. Vith, by now outflanked, outfoxed, and in a state of desperate confusion. The Germans were certainly going to have St. Vith, even if it had to be blown asunder brick by brick. The Germans were on a very tight schedule.

Hyams now knew roughly where he was—and who he was—and what had happened to him and his unit last night in those ghost-ridden hills beneath this same convulsing sky. An American infantry regiment, surrounded, cut off, and abandoned by the world, had been cruelly eviscerated, and had died a slow and ago-nizing death. It occurred to Hyams that he, in contrast to the nondescript piles of collapsed humanity in the yard, was standing upright on water-logged and swollen feet, with his head con-torted back against the stone wall that encircled the open court-yard. Could he have slept for hours in this unnatural position? Asleep standing up—maybe for hours? Why not? Dumb animals do it.

Finding some open space, Hyams let himself slump wearily down into the frozen slush of the yard. Off of his feet, he would have a few quiet moments to reflect on the fate that had removed him from the roster of "active" participants in this war. He and all the multitude about him were now nothing more than sad statis-tics. They all would soon be cryptically listed by a beleaguered and regretful U.S. Army as casualties—"missing in action," along with all the dead and the wounded.

In this third week of December 1944 the immutable gods of war had suddenly and inexplicably turned thumbs down on Zeke Hyams and thousands of his comrades-in-arms in the American First Army in Europe. That mighty aggregation of men and machines had only days earlier been the centerpiece of General Dwight Eisenhower's Expeditionary Forces on the Western Front, poised to deliver the final blow against a reeling enemy. But suddenly that enemy, deemed moribund and awaiting the final *coup de grâce,* had struck with overwhelming vigor and cunning from behind a shroud of mist and snow. In four improbable days of lightning *Blitzkrieg,* an entire U.S. frontline corps of more than forty thousand men was unceremoniously chewed up and swept aside. And the Germans were just now getting their main Panzer forces into position!

The German Führer's men had meticulously prepared this monster surprise—even the Saturday morning kick-off—at a time when complacent American staffs were planning their weekend and Christmas getaways to such congenial nearby capitals as Paris, London, and newly liberated Brussels. Some horrified American rear-echelon commanders would soon be peering out the leaded windows of their turreted chateaus with their richly laden wine cellars only to see huge German Tiger tanks wheeling audaciously across the manicured terraces.

So swift and unexpected was the attack that it had taken two full days for the impact of the German assault to be fully assessed by Supreme Allied Headquarters back in Paris. When all the jolting weekend bulletins from the Belgian Ardennes were finally sorted out and digested, the orders to the encircled infantry divisions became an urgent "Attack to the rear!" or "Get the hell out, any way you can!" But that, of course, would prove to be much more easily said than done.

It was soon freely recognized at Supreme Allied Headquarters that there had been a monumental intelligence failure—costly, embarrassing, and potentially catastrophic. The Germans had attacked at shrewdly targeted hinge points in the American line with three beefed-up field armies—a quarter of a million men and two thousand tanks—all without tipping their hand and without arousing the slightest suspicions of Allied Intelligence. Stealth, concealment, and subterfuge in land warfare had been taken by the German Army to new heights of perfection.

On Monday, December 18, the third day of the German onslaught, the full dimensions of their hopeless situation had become transparently clear to the regimental officers of the nine thousand American troops entrapped in the German pocket in front of the Belgian border village of Schoenberg. Two decimated infantry regiments were completely encircled, cut off from each other and from any prospect of tank or artillery support. A promised air re-supply had accomplished only the misdirected delivery of most of the goods to the surrounding enemy. Yet orders from Division headquarters at St. Vith remained firm and unequivocal: "Schoenberg must be retaken at all costs!"

For Schoenberg was indeed the key to survival and escape. But the retaking of Schoenberg, now teeming with fresh German troops and armor, was patently an impossible dream. There was no way in hell for these battered and disorganized infantrymen, most of them new to combat, and out of food, medical supplies, and ammunition, to dislodge the German chokehold on the village.

Hyams was now fully alert. For him there was to be no escape in sleep. He had to marshal his thoughts and his resources at this juncture when his life had taken such a sudden, precipitous down-turn. But, despite the anguish and the foreboding prospects—the cold, the wrenching hunger pangs, the paralyzing fatigue and the assorted miseries—might he not consider himself damn lucky to be alive and in one piece? Had he not in these recent days seen close buddies shredded by bullet and shrapnel? People with whom he had so recently swapped stories, shared secret anxieties, and a few nostalgic moments looking at photos from home of girlfriends, wives, babies?

Killed or wounded. These were the norms in combat, the fore-
seeable finales, often seen and privately much contemplated. A
soldier cannot remain a stranger to death and suffering and pain.
But no matter what, the well-oiled machinery of the U.S. Army
was always there at hand, prepared to follow through and handle
the situation efficiently and smoothly. So long as one was alive the
medics were always there, capable and selfless, ready to take over
with their ambulances, hospitals, nurses smiling encouragement,
clean sheets, sun-drenched rooms, and—ah yes—plenty of good
wholesome food. And then, of course, there were the chaplains.
Hyams yearned mightily for the safety, warmth, and fresh clean
smell of a hospital bed.

But now? To wind up a prisoner of the Nazis? Who was there
to take charge of this crummy situation? This was never considered
by anyone. "Godamn, nobody ever said anything about this kind of
a mess!"

There was hardly anybody awake to talk to, and Hyams needed
to talk to someone, to vent his anxieties, and his confusion, and his
despair. All his life, whenever he was under pressure he found it
helped to set up some sort of dialogue with himself if there were
nobody else to talk to. It was like talking to yourself, but it helped.
Hyams used to think it was due to a lonely childhood, him being an
only child.

He whispered softly to himself, "Just be sure to give them only
your name, rank, and serial number. Absolutely nothing more.
They'll probably have interrogators. Tell them nothing!"

Then he countered, "But they don't seem the least bit interested in any of that crap. They act like they already know everything they need to know. What have I got? Some valuable secrets?"

Hyams' muddled brain sought refuge in the past—back a few
hours to the surrender scene—probing among the ruins for some
faint ray of light, for some encouraging tidbit upon which to pin
some hope, however meager, for the future which was now so decidedly bleak.

Yes, there was something positive, after all, and it was

important. Something solid to hang on to. The "Geneva Convention," that was it, the "Bill of Rights" of the military prisoner. Yes, that was it. The German officer in charge at the time, so crisp and businesslike, had made a solemn pledge that the rules of the Geneva Convention would be strictly obeyed. It was a condition of the surrender, or so it was understood. Not that it really would have made any difference; there were so few options.

This meant there should be food and water and some sort of decent treatment for these zombie-like survivors. All was not lost.

"'A solemn pledge,' you say?"

Well . . . who could say? Anyhow, some kind of a pledge. Any pledge was better than nothing. There might even be some sort of German breakfast in the offing, like as soon as the sun came up, and they could set up a field kitchen. Visions of juicy sausages and fresh-baked German biscuits began to dance in Hyams' fevered brain. And possibly even some hot coffee to take the edge off the cold? Or were those nothing more than the empty dreams of a sick man?

But Hyams soon brought himself back to reality. Hell, even just bread and water would make a big difference, or just bread . . . or just water!

Thirst and hunger had compounded the sense of despair prior to the surrender. It had been days since there had been any real food. Emergency rations had long since been exhausted.

And now, casting about in the gloom beyond the encircling stone wall, Hyams thought he recognized some of the features of this blacked-out village. The church and the schoolyard seemed vaguely familiar, as if seen in some dimly remembered dream. Then it came to him. His ill-fated battalion had truly passed through this very same village, on the same street, about a million years ago. He remembered an inn, shops, even a *Bierstube*. Actually, it had only been about a week earlier when they were fresh troops on their way to the front, bright-eyed and innocent, being carried effortlessly to war aboard an unending caravan of G.I. trucks and jeeps.

Hyams vaguely recalled the excitement and adventure that had then permeated the crisp, cold air. Every female form along the route would evoke a shrill chorus of rebel yells and piercing wolf-calls. Every wine shop, every *Bierstube,* every establishment that might offer some small diversion was carefully noted for future reference. War in a foreign land must have its rewards. Young studs can find their kicks anywhere. Ass, that is foreign ass, is after all, what war is all about. Or so these apple-cheeked youngsters thought at the time. It was the flip side. There was death, and there was ass. Take your choice. Either or both.

It was then considered an ideal posting—considering. Quiet and peaceful, picture postcard stuff. On the tourist maps the entire region is known as *Der Belgischer Naturpark.* A sort of idyllic regional park renowned for a proliferation of secluded health spas and some of the loveliest scenery in all of Europe—that is, in the summer. Sort of like a Belgian version of the Catskills.

In winter, however, the sparsely populated border region took on a ghostly solitude and the dead silence of hibernation.

It was in Schoenberg, in this very village, that Hyams and the men of Third Battalion had disembarked from the trucks and begun a trek into the hills to the old Siegfried Line bunkers and trenches which they would occupy. The front line which Hyams and his buddies would take over was almost ten miles inside the Fatherland. There was no hint of danger. It was strictly a routine operation, taking over a lightly held defensive line along a forested ridgeline. He recalled the crunching sound of thousands of footsteps in the virgin snow.

The march into the hills that moonless night had taken them quite uneventfully across the German frontier. On German maps the region is referred to as the *Schnee Eifel. Schnee* is the German word for snow. And there was plenty of it. On the Belgian side of the border, this expanse of pine-studded hills is part of the Forest of the Ardennes. There was nothing ominous or foreboding about stepping onto the soil of the Fatherland that night. The Germans were there of course; just about a mile across the no-man's land, but they were in a strictly defensive mode, licking their wounds—on their last legs. Or so the story went. They were *Kaput*. Their days were numbered. One good Allied offensive would finish them off. No cause for concern. Just light patrolling activity for the present.

The rough terrain, criss-crossed by numerous streams and rivers and lacking any sort of decent road network, precluded any meaningful tactical opportunities for either side. For being right up there on the front, things didn't seem that bad at all, that first night.

So the 116th Infantry Division, some fourteen thousand strong, newly arrived in the European Theater of Operations, yet untried and untested in combat, was assigned to cover almost twenty-five miles of this sleepy front. They were here to condition themselves for upcoming combat assignments of a much more serious nature, for they were earmarked to be among the lead divisions in the definitive final assault on the Fatherland itself, up to and across the River Rhine. The assault was scheduled for kick-off some few weeks hence, so this current assignment was meant to give officers and men a taste of front-line duty without much risk or exertion.

And now all these beaten and battered survivors of that earlier march into the hills of the *Schnee Eifel* were back in Belgian Schoenberg, having absorbed all the cruel lessons of war in just a few chaotic days. And now of course, Schoenberg was no longer an American base, but rather a bustling German stronghold.

While sitting there on the frozen ground trying to get some circulation back into his sorely twisted neck and back, Hyams painfully shifted his deadened legs. A popular stateside lyric tolled insistently in his brain.

What a difference a day made.
Twenty-four little hours!

How sad. How true.

And then, what about the officers? The company commander? And all the other brass—the lieutenants and the captains and all the rest of the authority figures? Where were they? What had been their fate in this ghastly comedy of errors?

Yes, that had been a sorry sight, indeed. As the big surrender was being played out, all the American officers had been unceremoniously culled out and marched off *en masse,* on the double, by a yelping Jerry field sergeant. The Jerry non-com had handled them as if they were a mob of snot-nosed recruits in basic training. There was a full colonel, a lieutenant colonel, and a passel of captains and lieutenants. It was a very painful sight to see. It was the last that Hyams was to see of any American commissioned officers for a very long time.

The lieutenant colonel, a spit-and-polish West Pointer, had personally negotiated the surrender with the Jerries. He had known that the concentrated mortar and artillery barrages were sure to be followed before nightfall by mop-up waves of Jerry infantry and tanks. Ammunition was exhausted. The wounded were lying where they fell—with no way to get them out.

He knew that there was no way out—and no way in. No hope of relief, and finally no purpose. The regiment and its battalions had been written off. They were no longer any deterrent to the enemy advance, which had by-passed them on all sides. The entire American front line had been out-flanked and perforated at will by the rampaging German tide. Entire regiments were caving in up and down the front. The front line was no longer relevant in the developing disaster.

The authority for the surrender must have come from the top, from a despairing division commander in St. Vith, or maybe even higher, like the corps commander. The decisive battle would have to be joined many miles to the rear by a hastily re-assembled Allied Army. The Germans would have to be stopped before they got to the Meuse, the next big river, or the consequences would indeed be irreversible. Once across the Meuse, the flatlands of Northern France would be wide open. This was the classic invasion route taken by the Germans in other successful efforts both in this and in earlier wars. The only difference was that in the past they had always pulled it off in the milder months of spring or summer. This time it was late December, in the season of rain and snow and muck and slush; and this was a particularly harsh winter shaping up. All the professionals know that tanks do much better in dry clement weather when visibility is good and the ground is firm. In warfare, the season and the weather are almost always the ultimate determinants of success or failure. By all the textbook rules, this thing could never have happened.

But of course Hyams was in no way privy to the larger questions of strategy. That was not his department. He was the man on the ground, now reduced to a cipher, a zero—less than zero. And moments after the surrender, his orders would suddenly be coming hot and heavy in guttural German from these self-inflated victors, who seemed perpetually driven by the tightest of schedules. Everything on the double! Buck-ass privates swaggered about imperiously in their white camouflage parkas, acting like they were go-damn field marshals.

The G.I.s had learned within minutes the meaning of such peremptory commands as *"Schnell!"*—*"Aufstehen!"*—*"Fünf!"*— and so on: "Hurry it up!"—"On your feet!"—"Ranks of five!" All armies have the same commands; they're universal, except the language and the accompanying expletives may be different.

"Hände hohe—Hands clamped behind the head. And keep them there, you fuckers!"

And another word was heard repeatedly. It had a heavy sounding, unmistakably Germanic rasping sound: *"Kriegsgefangene."* A typically German compound noun, with the rolling *r* and the heavy *g*, meaning, of course—"prisoners of war." This would be foreshortened in prisoner lingo to "Kriegies." That's what Hyams and the others had become. They were no longer G.I.s or combat soldiers or infantrymen. They were "Kriegies."

The surrender had been taken by a Jerry regiment newly transferred from the Russian Front. Seasoned troops—Grenadiers. They must have relished this, an easy victory over a green American division. Their flowing white parkas were perfect camouflage in the snowy terrain—one of the lessons learned in Russia, no doubt.

There was one of those godamn white-robed, *Schmeisser-*wielding troopers crouching behind every boulder and every tree. They knew that they had these inexperienced Yanks between a rock and a hard place, that it was mass surrender or mass death for them, and the decision had to come quickly. Like *Schnell!* Mopping up is another thing that war is all about.

Then, after all the early formalities had been completed—like the very important searches for contraband such as cigarettes and jewelry—a new set of German guards had taken over the halting procession from the battlefield back to Schoenberg. These were older guys, *Volksturm.* Rear-echelon types—overweight, stodgy—carrying World War I vintage muskets with fixed bayonets. Obviously not "combat-rated." More like citizen soldiers. But they didn't mind using their ancient weapons for enforcing their marching orders—for striking, shoving, or poking the stragglers. The old *Herrenvolk* flame was not dead. They had once been the Kaiser's soldiers; now they were Hitler's soldiers, aglow with pride in the superman exploits of their frontline brethren.

The younger ones, the shock troops, the Volks Grenadiers, the regulars and the dreaded S.S., were all still back there on the front, in the armored spearheads, probably taking St. Vith house by house, bashing in skulls, killing and being killed.

Inside the schoolyard the whole world was still asleep. It seemed like only Hyams was awake and conscious. The rambling soliloquy continued to course through his aching head. "Can this be for real? Those bastards were talking about wiping out the entire First Army and pushing all the way back to Paris!"

"They should live so long! Jerry *chutzpah!*"

But of course Hyams had learned that in war anything is possible. And then Hyams began to wonder how he could ever explain all this to the folks back home—if he ever got back home.

And what about the voluptuous Sylvia, his recently acquired dream girl and faithful pen-pal, who was waiting for him in East Flatbush—so patient and so full of love? How long would she wait? Why should she wait? "Missing in action" could be for a very long time! Especially to an eighteen-year-old *knish* with a shape like hers. It was all too painful to consider.

And how soon would the folks be getting one of those dreaded telegrams? That was another thing that was too painful to contemplate.

And how would the U.S. Army ever know who was dead or alive?

"Missing in action" has a very sickening ring to it. Something like cancer. Not necessarily fatal, but definitely not good news. It could be almost as distressing as "killed in action."

And of course there was the other nagging question that wouldn't go away. The really big question. How was this war really going? Like over-all, the big picture. How could the American army collapse like that in just a few short days? The Germans were supposed to be on their last legs, out of fuel and tanks and ammunition. The bombings had destroyed their cities and railroads and factories. Or had it?

Everybody had been saying that the war could be over by Christmas. Total victory was at hand. But of course the Germans would have to surrender unconditionally, with no *ifs* or *buts*. Unconditional surrender or nothing. Yet here were the godamn Germans . . . all over the place . . . fresh, tough, optimistic and full of beans. Tanks as far as the eye could see, and no apparent shortage of any of the essentials of war!

Hyams shook his head, "They don't seem at all like a defeated army. They look victorious as hell."

"Does this mean that this friggin' war will never end?"

"It sure as hell is not going to be over by Christmas, which is like next week if my memory serves me."

If only he could write to Sylvia and tell her how much he loved her and how much she meant to him. He would have to come across very strong and very upbeat.

But how could he ask her to wait? What could he really promise? He was really only a ghost now, invisible and voiceless to all the normal people of the world. As far as the rest of the world was concerned, he was "missing." And it was not like being missing in Canarsie. Fate had picked him up and cast him across a great divide from which there was no known way of return. He had gone from "alive and well, and missing you terribly!" to just "missing," period.

CHAPTER TWO

The Long March To Prum

*'On your godamn feet! Keep it moving!' . . . A long day's
shuffle. Will never forget this. Sore feet, no food, no water,
no rest. They've got to ease up. Maybe when we get to
Prum. It can't go on forever. Even the guard (Andreas) is
bitching. He's got sore feet. Very interesting guy.*
                    —Wednesday, December 20, 1944.

"A*UFSTEHEN! Aufstehen! Die Verfluchte Nachzugler! Schnell!"*
The angry orders rang out at the first crack of dawn as a
detachment of elderly citizen-soldiers enveloped the schoolyard
like a pack of snapping terriers. "On your feet, you godamn
stragglers! On the double!"

Kicking, clubbing and pummeling, they set upon the bewildered
and half-awake Kriegies with a vindictive fervor. These shiftless sad
sacks were the same Americans whose high-flying brethren had
been daily raining down fire and brimstone on innocent civilians in
peaceful German towns from the safety and comfort of their giant
B-17 bombers. These crumbs had come, uninvited and unprovoked,
to meddle in a European war that was none of their business. There
had never been any thought or intention to attack America. They
had no business making war against Germany. They should have
stayed back there in their New World, like in Chicago or Kentucky
or wherever the hell they belonged. They could blame their president, that Franklin Roosevelt, for their predicament.

And now it was time to move them out, to get these *"verfluchte
Kriegsgefangene"*—godamn sad sacks—on their feet and onto the
road, the road that would lead to the beckoning interior of the
Fatherland.

The muddled Yanks roused themselves in the midst of this sudden torrent of guttural jabber and painful blows.

"What the hell! What the fuck is going on?"

"Line up . . . quickly . . . everyone . . . *Schnell!* . . . ranks of five . . . quickly . . . move it. You there, on your godamn feet . . . *Schnell!*

"Food? Water? There will be plenty of food and water for everyone in Prum. *Schnell,* in line . . . quickly . . . ranks of five . . . let's go!"

"Prum? Where the fuck is Prum?"

"There will be good food and hot coffee in Prum. Everything you want. *Schnell!*"

So where is Prum?

"Only fifteen kilometers! The sooner we get there the sooner you will have your food and hot coffee! *Schnell!* On your godamn feet! *Fünf! Fünf!*"

"Fifteen kilometers? Godamn, that's ten friggin' miles. Practically a day's march. That's bull crap. How the hell are we going to drag our asses ten friggin' miles in the shape we're in? Feet frozen and blistered! And empty bellies, and no water!"

"Let's go . . . hurry it up . . . you there . . . on your godamn feet!"

"Yeah, but we were promised food last night. What about the Geneva Convention? There's got to be some food or nobody's going to make it to Prum, or anywhere else!"

"*Schnell . . . Schnell . . .* Everyone . . . *Fünf . . . Fünf . . . Ausmarschieren . . .* Forward march!"

Rifle butts and bayonets are irrefutable convincers. Despite the gripes and the protests the moribund column was soon formed up on the road and shuffling in lethargic cadence away from the schoolyard, in the direction of a paved two-lane highway. A procession of young men turned prematurely old and feeble, painfully dragging their swollen feet. Hardly the picture of fresh and eager young troops who only days earlier had been preparing for the final assault on Hitler's Fortress Germania.

Soon, as additional prisoners streamed in from other nearby holding pens, the marching ranks swelled to a couple of thousand men, or the equivalent of two full battalions. It was a very mixed bag of characters. Hyams was surprised to find himself marching shoulder to shoulder with hundreds of combat-wise G.I. veterans from some of the more fabled infantry divisions like the 28th, a Pennsylvania National Guard outfit which had a distinguished battle record going back to Normandy.

The 28th Infantry Division had been holding a stretch of the Ardennes front a dozen miles to the south of Hyams' outfit. They were much feared and respected in combat. The Germans called them *"Die Blutige Eimere"*—"The Bloody Buckets." When these guys spoke it was with the authority and pungent wisdom gained from weeks of intensive combat experience. Blood and guts talk— mostly about this earlier battle, a three-week experience that they had been through in the Hurtgen Forest, about thirty miles up the line; and about such things as satchel charges, flamethrowers, bengalore torpedoes, mine fields, pill boxes, and many hundreds of exploded or incinerated Germans. Glory talk. Hardly ever of fallen buddies and the down side of battle. Those memories were too bitter to reminisce about. Those were the memories that come in the silence and the solitude of the night.

The Ardennes had been a minor engagement, nothing to talk about compared to that battle. These guys were still living and fighting the Battle of the Hurtgen Forest and they couldn't let it go.

It seemed that after three bloody weeks in the Hurtgen inferno, where every thousand yards would cost both sides maybe ten thousand casualties in dead and wounded, these poor bastards had been posted to the tranquil Ardennes for some well-deserved peace and quiet, sort of like an all-expense-paid winter vacation. They were supposed to rest and recuperate and take in fresh replacements to make up for the fifty percent losses they had suffered in the Hurtgen *Wald*. The "three R's: "—rest, recuperation, and replacements. But they hadn't bargained for this kind of R&R.

They were great talkers. They griped, they cussed, they philosophized. They had stories; and Hyams was a rapt listener, for their gruff chatter distracted him from his own gripes and anxieties. They were excellent company on this trek to oblivion.

They would talk about their officers and even their commanding general, whom they affectionately but irreverently referred to on a first-name basis, calling him just "Norman." He was still their hero. It was downright refreshing, a positive reminder that some things were still as they were meant to be. Sharing the trauma of captivity with these colorful characters was a tonic to Hyams' spirits. Although they had seen such heavy action up and down the Western Front, still they ended up now in the same Jerry bag, and this assuaged an emerging sense of failure and guilt in Hyams about the collapse of his own inexperienced outfit.

One of the Buckets, a grizzled PFC of Pennsylvania Dutch parentage, knew the German word for it. He said it was just one of those things that are written in the stars. It was fate, destiny. In German it is *"Die Schicksals-Tragedie"*—also known in plain English as "Der Royal Screw-Up."

Hyams was reviving. He was still cold, hungry, and miserable, but he felt better mentally. He took a few deep draughts of the brisk morning air and began to look up and take some notice of the passing scene.

Surveying the assortment of middle-aged guards who now held sway over his tight little world, he began to notice a particularly disturbing feature common to almost every one of them. The plodding citizen-soldiers, almost without exception—the tall and the short, the robust and the scrawny—all of them were sporting that same clipped-style Hitlerian mustache that Charlie Chaplin had used in the movie *The Great Dictator* to tickle the movie-going world of his time.

It was incredible! A caricature, a touch of the burlesque, a scene out of an old Charlie Chaplin comedy! But Hyams wasn't laughing; he found this not funny, but strangely ominous. Of course Hyams had not read enough history to know that through the ages both the humble and the high-born of every society emulate their high muck-a-mucks in all manner of compulsive ways—not only as to morals but also in mores, dress, and style.

Frenchmen at the time no doubt slicked their hair à la *Napoleon,* while Italians probably affected the handle-bar whiskers of King Victor Emmanuel; and in the days of the old Austrian Emperor Franz-Joseph, all the young men in Vienna must have had their sideburns come around in a graceful arc to join their mustaches exactly like the popular Emperor. The urge to conform is what underlies the big sell throughout history. These middle-aged Germans were no different.

Since the surrender Hyams had not thought about what might be lurking behind the crisp and business-like Jerry façade. The enemy troops who had materialized out of the forest in the *Schnee Eifel* all appeared rather normal, ordinary guys without any particular animus or grudges. He had heard about the S.S. but had not seen them in combat. The guys he had seen were like ordinary G.I.s. Now the odious spectacle of all these middle-aged *Bürghers* affecting the same classic Hitlerian look gave rise to the troubling question, "Are they all godamn Nazis?"

He reviewed his limited options. By now he was ready to give up on the Geneva Convention. Nazis wouldn't be influenced by such cockamame considerations. Life among the Nazis was something he had never contemplated; now he was facing nightmare possibilities. Escape was the only answer. But how? These citizen-soldiers were old and clumsy, but they were in a lot better shape than their prisoners, and one of them might perchance be a crack shot with his musket. And then he'd be a hero, and get an Iron Cross, and Hyams would be lying dead in a ditch. And even if he could successfully elude the guards, where the hell would he go? No, it had to be onward to Prum, like it or not. He had to stick with his buddies for now, and hope for the best. He realized that he was now a helpless pawn. This was how the people on the Titanic must have felt after the horns started blowing. He had mentioned something about the Titanic in his diary notes the day before. It was the only example he could think of.

Bright spots? There had to be some bright spots. That is, relatively speaking. And then in desperation he remembered that he was indeed not totally without resources. He still held two minor trump cards . . . of dubious value but they were something. First and most important was the dry pair of woolen socks which he carried in the inside pocket of his light field jacket. This was crucial under the circumstances. Like many others, he had ditched his woolen G.I. overcoat as too burdensome and irrelevant in the heat of battle, an ill-considered action which he had since come to regret. But just knowing that he possessed a pair of dry socks helped to ease the gnawing concerns. This could be even more critical to survival than a cumbersome woolen overcoat.

Hyams' other secret asset was equally priceless: a stash of four uncrushed foil-packaged and sealed American cigarettes in mint condition—two Chesterfields and two Camels, which he had saved from a long-ago field ration. That foresighted action could yet prove to be a real life saver.

This was Hyams' bankroll, and like all bankrolls it helped to create a soft inner glow of security and peace in the owner.

After the surrender, the Jerries had, despite the earlier "guarantees," dexterously relieved their prisoners of most personal possessions, especially that most exotic of wartime commodities, American cigarettes. Miraculously, the young Volks Grenadier who had frisked Hyams had been momentarily distracted by a shiny 17-jewel Bulova on the elevated wrist of the G.I. next in line.

At the next piss break, Hyams withdrew discreetly off into a ditch by the side of the road. There he hastily removed his mud-caked boots and gingerly peeled off his wet socks. They were soaked, and they had the putrid stench of rotting flesh.

After airing out and massaging his bare feet for a minute or so, he pulled on the dry socks. It seemed like his whole life had been turned around in that instant. The dry socks changed everything. The Hitler faces receded. He was indeed braced.

He also forgot, in that moment, the gnawing hunger and all his other troubles. He was, for the moment, a king among men.

The wet socks he proceeded to drape about his body, beneath his shirt, one at each armpit. It was an old infantry survival trick, body heat would dry the socks within a few hours. And with dryness, the stench would dissipate. For the next hour or two, Hyams had a new lease on life. With dry feet, the kilometers and his predicament were less soul-searing.

The date was December 20, only five days to Christmas, but nothing on that march was remotely reminiscent of the holiday spirit. As the morning sun warmed the air, the hunger pangs and the concerns intensified.

Hyams would occasionally try out a few words of his high school German on one or another of the guards. "How much further to Prum?"

"Only twenty kilometers."

"But it was only fifteen kilometers early this morning when we left Schoenberg!"

"Twenty kilometers . . . and then plenty food and water." This was the final verdict.

Hyams was not unduly surprised that the Jerries were playing an insidious numbers game. What could one expect from a gang of Hitler-faces?

One guard finally admitted that the true distance from Schoenberg to Prum was about twenty-five kilometers, but there would certainly be food and water in Prum, as promised.

Everything they needed would be had in Prum. The glib bullshit poured forth.

The march continued. Sick prisoners, some in real distress, dropped by the side of the road. They were being brought down by either trenchfoot, or dysentery, or exhaustion, or dehydration, or "all of the above." Their fate would remain a mystery. The Jerries were not taking kindly to drop-outs. You had to be really, really sick to get to a Jerry aid-station. The main body of marchers never slowed up except for the mandatory piss breaks, although the volume of these excretions had diminished to an insignificant trickle from shrunken bladders.

As the morning dragged on, Hyams noticed that the march was also taking its toll on some of the elderly German guards, who began to visibly tire and wilt. They became noticeably concerned with their own sore feet and sundry pains and discomforts. There was audible grumbling among them at the unrelenting pace. Some of the Hitler-faces reflected anguish, pain, and resentment at a fate which had cast them into a military role this late in life.

A parity was thus developing between the prisoners and the captors. Both the victors and the vanquished were now moaning about swollen feet and the long hard march.

Someone next thought to inquire as to whether there might be some sort of lunch break coming up, now that the time for breakfast had long passed.

There were wry shrugs from the guards. No comment. The subject was off limits. However, they themselves were okay on this score. They had all been provided with generous sack lunches early that morning in Schoenberg. Again, it was tough shit for the Kriegies.

Prum, the place nobody had ever heard of before that morning, now became the shimmering Valhalla on the hill for thousands of desperate Kriegies.

But the guards were not totally unaffected by the prisoners' plight. Seeing young men brought down by fatigue, sore feet, hunger, and thirst is not a pretty sight. It was, in a sense, an affront to the captors' own manliness. There were eventually some fleeting evidences of genuine compassion.

During the piss breaks, when the guards would delve into their bulging rucksacks for bread and sausage and then light up a quick smoke, many of them would turn their attention elsewhere as some prisoners would venture out a few yards into adjacent fields to forage for whatever plant roots and gleanings could be gathered or dug up from the frozen ground.

At one point a cabbage patch was thus raided; later a turnip patch. The raw vegetable matter was life-sustaining when washed down with handfuls of snow.

In a last desperate search through his pockets, Hyams discovered a crumpled little cellophane packet containing a few grains of concentrated bouillon powder, a relic of a long-forgotten emergency field ration. It tasted so awful that it had to possess supernatural nutritive value. Why else would the U.S. Army spend its hard-earned money on a thing like that?

It was during these later breaks that the mellowing of the guards could be detected. Conversations would come around obliquely to the subject of *"Amerikanische Zigaretten."*

Did the prisoners have any?

Hyams kept his cool. He opened a cautious dialogue with one particular guard, one who had earlier let slip some decidedly un-Nazi-like opinions about the state of affairs inside Germany. There are chronic complainers in every army, and Hyams had found one here behind a sharply clipped Hitlerian mustache. It was the same one who earlier had levelled with Hyams about the true mileage to Prum.

Hyams learned, in carefully measured stages, that the man's name was Andreas, that he was not German but rather Austrian. And that Austria, once a separate country, was now just a province of Hitler's Greater Reich.

Andreas was well informed about the history of the Nazi movement in his country. "But it all started in Bavaria." According to him German Nazism had come of age in Munich, in fabled Bavaria just across the border from Austria. Bavaria and Austria were always very close and interrelated, something like New York and New Jersey.

Andreas noted apologetically that Hitler and some of his top lieutenants were of Austrian birth and further that he, Andreas, had always been anti-Nazi. But of course, Andreas explained, it was impossible to speak out or resist in any way and still survive in Hitler's Greater Reich. Hyams knew that.

While Hyams was enthralled by the man's candor, he had strong reservations about Andreas' readiness to unburden himself.

But the Austrian obviously needed to talk. Hyams also knew how that was. Now he listened as Andreas went on.

The man was forty-six years old, quite elderly by Hyams' standards. In civilian life he had been a cabinetmaker, a craftsman of fine furniture. A seventeen-year-old son was serving in the Jerry infantry on the Russian Front, and he was worried sick about the lad's survival chances, considering the Russian winters and the grinding conditions of the war in the East.

Despite his Hitlerian lip-hair, the man was literally bursting with anti-Nazi sentiment, which he freely confided to Hyams as though they were bosom buddies. Then, taking on something of a conspiratorial manner, Andreas blurted out a most outlandish confession to Hyams: his most fervent wish was to get himself captured by the Americans! Hyams' wistful response was "Amen to that!" If only he, Hyams, could somehow manage to get himself re-taken by the American Army! How wonderful that would be! But the American Army was nowhere in the immediate picture. Poor Andreas knew, in his simple wisdom, that the war was lost for Germany and that the only way out of the trap was to somehow wind up in American hands. Hyams thought that was a laudable ambition, one worth pursuing. The only problem for Hyams was that he was now being moved in the wrong direction to meet up with the American Army. But he hoped that Andreas might someday soon realize his dream.

But Andreas' candor really stopped Hyams in his tracks. He looked around furtively to make sure that there was no one within earshot. Luckily nobody was paying any attention. Was this guy a nut? What a defeatist way to talk when his Nazi cohorts were riding the crest of victory.

In the Greater Reich this kind of thinking could be treason at its worst. Hyams just knew that people had been shot in Germany for thinking less dangerous thoughts than what this friendly ex-carpenter was now giving vent to. Hyams didn't want any part of this. A Jew fraternizing with a defeatist? Bad politics—curtains for both of them!

Yet on the other hand, maybe Hyams had actually stumbled

onto a real human being behind the crummy façade of the Charlie
Chaplin mustache.

Hyams lapsed into a pensive silence. He should henceforth let
Andreas do all the talking. He was in no position to encourage the
poor man in his dangerous thoughts. Besides, what could be
gained from a lot of idle political chatter? This was not the time or
place for it. Hyams certainly did not want to draw attention to himself and to the fact that he spoke and understood German. Andreas
might not be a Nazi, but there were bound to be some Nazi
sympathizers in this group of elderly guards, and they could
certainly earn a merit badge for reporting any irregular or disloyal
communication between a prisoner and a guard.

However, despite his apprehensions, Hyams and Andreas, a
disparate twosome, did indeed become fast friends, incredibly ex-
panding their dialogue in the course of the next few hours as they
plodded eastward together. All the other guards were too tired and
too disinterested to take note of the budding friendship. They were
both really prisoners, both spiritlessly playing out their assigned
roles in this side-drama of war.

Major uncertainties and imponderables were now beginning to
mount up for poor Hyams, who was beginning to suspect that he
might indeed need a good friend from the German side, since the
matter of his Jewishness was beginning to explode in the innermost
recesses of his beleaguered psyche. It was a heavy secret to bear
when there were so many other problems.

He was acutely aware that the G.I. dogtags jangling around his
neck were engraved with a capital "*J*." His stomach cramped up as
he listened to Andreas' long list of grievances, and he began to recall the persistent reports of the crazed Nazi vendetta against the
Jews, collectively and individually, reports which he had somehow
discounted or had always been too busy to worry about. He had
previously managed to blank out this vexing situation. But now, he
wondered, might it not be downright suicidal to be marching into
Germany as a prisoner marked with a capital "*J*"? And if indeed it
was, as he strongly suspected in his bones, what was to be done at

this late stage to avert the very real possibility of falling into an irreversible state of "missing" at the hands of one of these real Nazi fanatics?

Andreas . . . could he perhaps be the divine messenger sent to counsel and protect Hyams in this hour of danger? Why not? Who else was there to turn to?

Hyams warily brought the conversation around touching on this delicate question . . . specifically, the Nazi thing about the Jews.

"Is it true about the Jews?" was the way it came out.

Andreas was suddenly guarded, as he looked cautiously about. He brought his left hand up to cover his mouth. *"Ach, Mein Himmel!"* he whispered softly, "And that's another thing. What they did to the Jews was just shameful, inexcusable! It was degrading just to see this!"

Hyams felt that he should not pursue the subject with this volatile Austrian. He knew that Andreas would only confirm his worst fears. His heart sank. He experienced abject panic down to the soles of his now-perspiring feet. All the news was bad. So bad that he was no longer hungry or thirsty. Now he would have real problems, the kind that bread and water couldn't cure.

Trying to mask his alarm, Hyams quickly changed the subject. He inquired casually how much further to the fabled town of Prum.

About ten kilometers to go, according to Andreas' best guess.

As the late afternoon shadows deepened on the road and the streams of busy traffic going in both directions, Hyams was a man beset with problems. He felt trapped and very alone. He knew that he was dragging himself along on a fool's treadmill—to oblivion. The worst part was this new feeling of being alone with no one to turn to. Andreas was of course a grand fellow, but really in no position to be of real help when the chips were down.

CHAPTER THREE

To Prum And Beyond

*Horses and slaves . . . and concubines, yet. It's the
Unholy Roman Empire revisited. Romans v. Christians,
Nazis v. Jews. My good friend Andreas fades out. Will
miss him. Really helped me brush up on my German.
Yiddish and German so much alike. Amazing. Andreas
worried about me. Poor guy, he's got worries. So do I.
This is a hell march.*
            —Later the same day, December 20, 1944.

HYAMS decided that he couldn't allow a paranoia to bring him
down. He was a military prisoner protected by the Geneva Convention and international law. A man's religion or lack of it was his
own private affair. Things were bad enough without dreaming up
new problems. This Andreas could be one of those perennial
"gloom and doom" guys. Hyams would have to think positive. The
real issue was physical survival without food or water. Once they
got fed in Prum he could take a fresh look at the whole situation.
Life must go on.

True, this Germany was a very weird place. Here, only some
ten miles behind the front, it was like being on a different planet.
For one thing, it was a land of horses, horses everywhere, the big
lumbering kind of horses that had long ago pulled the old coal and
ice wagons and had long since disappeared off the streets of
Brooklyn. There were untold hundreds of those horses that day
just on the stretch of highway between Schoenberg and Prum. It
was an eye-opener for Hyams, who thought that all modern-day
horses were lean and sleek and agile, and made their living as cow
ponies, rounding up cattle on the western ranges, like in the

movies, or by running for high stakes at such places as Jamaica and Belmont Park.

Here on this road on this day there were endless convoys of horse-drawn wagons and carts moving continuously in both directions. Towards the front these creaking and archaic vehicles were loaded to the gunwales with men and supplies and were towing all sorts of heavy weapons like howitzers and artillery pieces. Returning from the front, they were empty except for the inevitable backwash of war, the casualties: the wounded, the disabled, and the body bags.

Despite that the Germans had written the book on *Blitzkrieg,* "Lightning War," and were forever obsessed with speed, they appeared completely dependent on the common dray horse for their close-up transport needs. The vaunted German war machine, despite its highly sophisticated chariots of war like the invincible seventy-ton Tiger tanks, which could outshoot, outrun, and outperform anything that had yet been fielded by the Allies, was markedly deficient in the basic transport and support systems which were so taken for granted on the American side.

Having to be constantly sidestepping the steaming piles of horse dung on the road was yet another galling humiliation for the already totally deflated Kriegies. Anguished cries of "Aw, Shit!" or "Screwed by the numbers!" were a constant refrain as the marchers threaded their way through a maze of manure.

Yet there was a certain earthiness and serene nobility about these brawny draft animals, like the good feeling one might get in a well-stocked barnyard. Their presence in such great numbers was probably a good omen. It showed that the Third Reich had not completed its technological leap into the future.

To the passing Germans, afoot and in the wagons, the long, shuffling column of decrepit Americans must have been a comforting spectacle, confirming and re-enforcing all the glowing reports of Germany's military resurrection. They gawked at the Kriegies much as ancient Romans might have leered at newly taken Carthaginian slave-captives. Only the heavy chains and leg-irons were needed to complete the picture of abject despair and humiliation.

As for the presence of slave-captives, Hyams soon came to realize that the Third Reich had apparently written the book on this subject as well. The countryside was overflowing in every direction with labor gangs, both male and female, of every shape and description, all closely shepherded by armed guards. The laborers appeared bedraggled, emaciated, and thoroughly dispirited. The guards, again mostly the elderly citizen-soldiers, were alert and ready for any sign of slacking off by their charges. This was obviously some sort of compulsory punitive service assessed against masses of miscreants. But it was strange that there should be so many wrong-doers in such a monolithic and tightly controlled society as Germany had become after twelve years of Adolf Hitler.

Here Andreas explained that, since the war, all manner of foreign workers had been appearing spontaneously in these work gangs in the German midst. They were there, but they were invisible. No one spoke of them. There was the presumption of criminality. That was the most ready explanation. They were like a gift from Providence to be harnessed, like the draft horses, to the Nazi war effort.

There were Russians, Poles, French, and on and on . . . an endless variety of nondescript groups from every stratum and every ethnic group on the European continent. There was even a generous sprinkling of Italian prisoners, dragooned into forced labor from the demobilized ranks of a former ally.

There was a lot for the apprehensive Hyams to see and figure out on this, his first full day of prisonerhood. He observed such details as that the workers were all tagged with conspicuous colored patches of various shapes sewn onto their tattered garments. There were triangles, squares, and other geometric shapes, all apparently intended to differentiate between various groups and categories.

Andreas said only the S.S. knew exactly what all the shapes and colors meant, but the scuttlebutt had it that the greens were for "common criminals"—thieves, murderers, and the like—while the blues were for political enemies, suspected Communists, agitators and trouble-makers. Yellow was for racial undesirables, like Jews and Gypsies, for instance, and the bright pinks the sex offenders—homosexuals, deviates, and general "sickos." They all fell into the broad category of "Enemies of the State."

There was plenty of work for everyone. Here in Germany there was no unemployment problem; no strikes, no collective bargaining, no lay-offs, and very little complaining. And there was no shortage of workers so long as there were enemies of the state.

For much of the distance to Prum, the road ran alongside railroad tracks, and these gangs of slave labor were everywhere along the right of way. Road workers were filling bomb craters and clearing rubble. There were ditch-diggers . . . farm laborers . . . railroad gangs repairing damaged track . . . crews loading and unloading wagons and rail cars . . . civilian and military prisoners marching everywhere under guard, from one work station to another. A large billboard by the roadside reminded the passers-by that "Wheels must turn for Victory," and the Germans seemed to know how to keep the wheels turning.

Later, Hyams' column passed by a large cyclone-fenced railyard, empty except for about a dozen Pullman-type sleeper cars parked on a siding in the middle of the yard. The heavy steel-mesh fence was topped off by thick rolls of concertina barbed wire, giving the whole place a high security, prison-like setting, a "Do Not Enter Under Pain of Death" aura. As the Kriegie column moved along the perimeter of the yard, Hyams sensed something very different here; this was no ordinary "stockade." There was, within this preserve, an indefinable aura of domestic tranquility. Milling about the cars were scores of young females, what in British literature might be referred to as "bonnie lasses." They appeared busy, energetic, and unabashedly serene and vivacious—not at all downtrodden or disenfranchised like all the other captive groups.

This was very rare. Anything resembling such contentment or normalcy had not previously been observed in prisoners—or anybody else for that matter—so close to the front. This was, after all, a war zone. Yet there they were, larger than life—all of them somewhere in their late teens or early twenties, uniformly blonde, buxom, blue-eyed, and pink-cheeked. Most were happily busy with housewifely chores, while a few were cavorting about in shorts and halters despite the crisp cold.

Some of the creatures were vigorously wielding mops and brooms as they cleaned and swept out the sleeping cars, which appeared to contain regular living compartments complete with curtained windows, flower pots, and all the stereotypical amenities of a cozy honeymoon hotel on wheels. A number of sleek and pampered house pets, felines and poodles, were visible about the premises. The only thing missing to complete the idyllic setting were white trellises laden with perfumed roses.

Hyams at first thought this was some kind of mirage, a fevered delusion brought on by the combination of weird cicumstances, hunger, splitting headache, fatigue, worry, and a budding case of bronchial pneumonia. But there they were in their numbers, all these succulent babes lolling about, doing their laundry and housekeeping routines, and several even hanging black lace undies out to dry for all the world to drool over. Others just basked languidly in the last feeble rays of the afternoon sun, while still others tended assiduously to cascading golden tresses.

All the while, the pulsating rhythm of a popular German ballad wafted across the compound from a blaring phonograph inside one of the cars. Incredibly, these girls, caged behind barbed wire and within artillery range of the front line, were all doing exactly what girls do on a lazy day at home, like in Pittsburgh or Boise. And inside that peaceful sanctum there was a palpable absence of angst. There was no war, no killing, no slow and wrenching starvation in their snug little bellies, only a certain tender tranquility that was starkly inconsonant with what the hell was going on all about them.

To men caught in the bottomless pit of privation and despair, as were these foot-dragging Kriegies, a "tender morsel" would be something to stimulate the salivary glands, something nutritious and delectable to eat. Girls, female companionship, sex objects to excite the erotic passions would at that moment be way down in their priorities, unless the females in question also happened to be offering some solid food, like maybe beer and sandwiches!

Yet the sight of these Pullman hostels and their comely tenants couldn't fail to create a flutter of unease among the passing Kriegies. All the involuntary reflexes surfaced. Heads snapped, pulses quickened, pupils dilated, throats constricted, nostrils flared, pelvic muscles tingled and loins ached as all eyes fixed on this sudden abundance of bouncing pulchritude just a stone's throw off the line of march.

But there was a remarkable absence of the follow-through manifestations of male arousal. No ear-splitting chorus of banshee shrieks, no wolf calls or piercing whistles, as there surely would have been a few days earlier when sex was the driving hunger in their lives. Such chest-pounding exuberance was a thing of the past. The humiliation of defeat and capture had all but extinguished the fires of machismo.

Hoping it was all just a mirage that would soon fade out, Hyams caught the eye of the alerted Andreas. The dumpy little Austrian, his stomach full of black bread, margarine, and pig sausage, now showed his pewter-filled teeth in a wicked grin and undertook to explain with an abundance of gestures and sly winks.

What came out was not that much of a surprise. The girls, of course, were military prostitutes, a "special services brigade" conscripted from the "inferior" sub-races of Eastern Europe—usually of Slavic or Polish stock. To make his point, Andreas had to draw on one of the few Anglo colloquialisms in his vocabulary: "floozies," which lent itself easily to the German idiom.

Andreas warmed to the subject, on which he seemed well briefed. These carefully selected *Mädchen* had to be the fairest and the blondest to qualify as S.S. concubines. While non-Aryan, of course, they had to come as close as possible to that pan-Germanic paragon of unsullied Nordic racial purity. The Nazis had always allowed that there were some non-Aryans who were racially compatible, especially for certain purposes, and these girls were obviously racially compatible for those purposes. And they were indeed pampered and spoiled and, according to Andreas, plied with quantities of French champagne and Russian caviar, which he thought was shameful in these times of national shortages and belt-tightening.

According to Andreas, the Waffen S.S., the combat arm of the S.S.—to whom nothing was denied, whether in tanks, special weapons, or any other amenities, maintained a fleet of these rolling brothels for the sexual gratification of their front-line heroes. These were the same heroes who right now were driving the big tanks hell-bent for the River Meuse. They should soon be ready for a hefty dose of R-and-R, and this was one of the "special brigades" that would see to their needs. Ingenious.

These girls, Andreas surmised, were Polish—and the exclusive private preserve of the elite S.S. divisions which were operating in the area. They were definitely off limits to the Volks Grenadiers and regular Wehrmacht, who did not rate these delectable fringe benefits. Perhaps another underlying reason for Andreas' low opinion of the Nazi elitist dogma.

Andreas didn't know whether the girls were paid volunteers or forcibly recruited into the service, or both. As if that made a big difference to the enfeebled Hyams, to whom the fancy bordello on wheels was just another facet of this repugnant Jerry world of involuntary servitude. Nazi-sponsored white slavery coupled with racist male chauvinism. Though Hyams was more concerned with the absence of food than the absence of *amour* in his life, he had to admit that there was a certain expeditious logic to the *wagon-lit* concept, sinful and repugnant though it might be. Heroes can't live on medals and decorations alone; even if they are "elite" heroes.

The march continued, and soon the weary marchers entered the battered outskirts of Prum, the place that was supposed to be bursting with provisions, where the hungry would be satiated, where all the wrongs of the day would be righted. Relief was at hand. At this time of heightened expectation, Andreas, that gush-

ing fount of useful information, now called on Hyams for a few answers to pressing questions he had on his mind. He sidled over
alongside his newfound friend and discreetly tossed a most
thought-provoking question at him. It was the sort of inquiry that
indicated he must have somehow developed some real respect for
Zeke's insight and strategic savvy. The question, posed very
succinctly in the hushed, conspiratorial tone of which Andreas was
a master, was: how much longer did Hyams, from his current van-
tage point, think the war could last? The Austrian, aware that there
might soon be an abrupt parting of their respective ways, was hoping to extract some last-minute words of wisdom from this amiable
Yank with whom he had come to feel a sort of kinship. After all,
Zeke was in the unique position of having now seen both sides on
their home turfs. So why wouldn't his judgment be sought on this
portentous question? And it showed that Andreas was capable of
projecting ahead beyond the confines of a depressing present
towards a brighter future, when the war would be only history.

Hyams didn't shrug off the query, despite that this seemed to
be neither the time, nor the place for such a weighty question. He
was flattered by it. It gave him some weighty matters to ponder
and assess objectively, and to escape in his mind for a few brief
moments from the morass of strictly mundane bullshit into which
he had sunk. He took time out to savor the deeper aspects of Andreas' question.

Based on what he had seen that day, he was less impressed
with Germany's long-term prospects. The flotillas of horse-drawn
transport, the *ersatz* feel about all of the German rolling stock, including the wood-burning trucks and other improvised vehicles,
which chugged painfully and noisily about, all these indicated that
the Germans were really way behind in such essential things as
transport and fuel. The world's finest battle equipment needs to be
backed up by modern logistical support. Hyams, who had once
been college-trained as accountant and auditor, sensed that there
was a glaring gap between the first-class military hardware available to the Germans at the front and the rather primitive equip-

ment and dependence on forced labor to be seen only some dozen miles behind the front.

Even though American power had been catastrophically absent on the Ardennes front in the past week, Zeke knew that ultimately American resources and staying power in this contest were on an unremitting upward curve, and the Germans were not going to be parading in Paris on New Year's Day, as some Jerry windbags had been taunting their prisoners.

Hyams could sense the premonition of impending defeat even among the German guards. Andreas was not alone in his deeply pessimistic outlook. The dead hand of human misery touched every aspect of German life here behind the front, even as the Nazis played up this spectacular upset victory over the Western Allies.

Hyams put his brain in gear. Andreas' question bore directly on his own as well as Andreas' future prospects. In very short order Hyams did come up with an answer. "Six months!" he proclaimed, and then added the thoughtful postscript, "More or less."

Andreas accepted the verdict in silence, but he was sad. He was probably hoping it would not take that long to bring down his Führer; six months could be an eternity both for him and for his teen-age son on the Russian Front.

Hyams fell silent after the pronouncement. He himself was shocked by his answer. How would he, a Jew from Brooklyn, adorned with a set of Jewish dogtags, survive six long months in German captivity, when it seemed a certainty that each sunrise would bring renewed perils. He knew he was on a sure fatal collision course. The only question was "when."

It was time to bite the bullet, to take the kindly Austrian fully into his confidence. He tested the waters by asking how the Germans treated prisoners of war who happened to be Jewish. Andreas didn't need time to reflect on that one.

"They shoot them!" he snapped in vehement disapproval.

In a mood that was still deflating like a punctured balloon,

Hyams then let out the deadly secret. He haltingly informed the middle-aged guard that he was Jewish.

That stopped Andreas cold, but only for a second. Darting a pained look at his American prisoner, Andreas inquired if Hyams was carrying any letters or papers that would betray him.

"Well, no, not really, except for my dogtags; they have my religion."

Shaking his head sadly, Andreas earnestly advised his new friend, "Throw them away. Get rid of them. They will cost you your life!"

This urgent directive posed a real dilemma. Hyams had some real decisions to make. Dogtags are not issued to be blithely discarded when one imagines oneself in trouble.

It was dusk as the column of prisoners entered the town limits of Prum. They were now about twenty miles inside the Fatherland, deep in the province of Rheinland-Pfalz, which is famous mainly for its great wines and its contribution to good living. Prum, at the hub of several important roads and rail lines, was another of those strategically situated towns that had become staging bases for the German offensive.

The town seemed relatively intact and functioning despite much evidence of recent air bombings. Rubble-clearing crews were hard at work as Jerry tank and troop convoys moved through the narrow cobble-stone streets.

Hyams felt like he was walking in his own funeral procession. How could he just throw away his dogtags, that obligatory link to the U.S. Army?

The column followed the railroad track into a large marshalling yard. There would certainly be a soup kitchen here, and supply wagons loaded with loaves of black German bread and cool, clear drinking water. Hyams needed strength to think and to act, without food there could be no strength, only panic leading to despair.

There was a halt for a short break. This would be the break during which the food would finally appear. But that was not to be. It was during this hiatus that Andreas and the rest of the guard detachment seemed to vanish into thin air! Within minutes the prisoners were surrounded by a fresh group of *Volksturm* guards. New orders came loud and clear.

"Aufstehen!" "On your feet!" *"Fünf!"* *"Schnell!"* The column was immediately reformed and started out again heading due east out of town!

A few hardy souls complained loudly, "Hey there, what about the food rations? Water? It was all supposed to be in Prum. That's what they kept saying."

"Only twenty more kilometers to go."

The next stop was to be the town of Gerolstein, deeper inside the Reich! Still no food, no water, no rest!

All those promises of food and water to be had in Prum! Just bait to keep these poor wretches on their feet and marching eastward. There was a big fat zero—just a lot of bullshit rhetoric—and there were no chaplains to complain to, like in a normal world. Where were those people when they were really needed?

More of the Kriegies now began to collapse. The new guards used their rifle butts on those who fell by the roadside. Most responded by rejoining the march, but a few just lay there, impervious to threats and blows.

Death marches are nothing new in the annals of warfare. The Japanese had pulled off a famous one in the Phillipines early in this war. It had been widely reported that they marched masses of G.I. prisoners on a 100-mile death hike. Hyams figured the Nazis were surely capable of such expediency.

The Germans were brisk and eager, unlike Andreas' old worn-down crew, from whom there had been at least some semblance of empathy. The column moved inexorably on.

Hyams knew that he would soon have to make a decision about the dogtags, which now hung like heavy stones around his neck. But the U.S. Army had always stressed the importance of hanging on to one's dogtags, come what may.

How could he now just chuck his tags away?

Who knows, these friggin' Jerries could take a very dim view of a military prisoner who showed up without dogtags. It could get very sticky. "Sticky wicket, old chap!" Yes, it could be a real sticky wicket.

But on the other hand, if Andreas was right those cockamame dogtags could bring instant death.

At about ten o'clock that night, on the road between Prum and Gerolstein, Hyams removed his dogtags and buried them deep in a roadside ditch. So much for the question of positive identification. If he was to die in Germany, let the friggin' Jerries figure out who he was. At least those jangling dogtags would not be the cause of his undoing.

He had placed his trust in the word of a decent old man, one whom he would have been sworn to shoot on sight little more than a day earlier.

CHAPTER FOUR

The Panzer Captain's Quest

A coiled cobra on the road to Gerolstein . . . Just kept thinking, "Brace yourself, Zeke," . . . and praying. Andreas had called it right. Also my first case of fear-induced diarrhea. No fun. Or maybe it was just a case of the G.I. shits, in place. But I'm definitely no hero. Hassan took the hit. Poor guy. I owe him.

—Early morning (1:00 A.M.) Thursday, December 21, 1944.

ON THE second night of their captivity, Hyams and his mates were swallowed up on the road by the steady stream of enemy traffic moving toward the front. The Germans were moving their heavy stuff under cover of darkness on this overcast moonless night to elude the prying eyes of Allied daytime air reconnaissance.

At the front, the Panzer tides were still pouring headlong through the ever-widening gaps in the American line. The enemy was throwing his last reserves into this campaign, determined to maximize the initial breakthroughs, and to strike the deep decisive blows that would change the course of the war on the Western Front.

Interspersed with the straining horse teams there were impressive columns of heavy armoured vehicles of all kinds, including generous numbers of the feared Tiger tanks manned by fresh and exuberant S.S. crews.

In the midst of all this frenzied activity, the long straggling column of American Kriegies, wending its sad way mostly in the roadside ditches, presented a truly humiliating image of defeat. In the thirty-six hours since these Yanks had laid down their arms in the

Snow Eifel they had been force-marched more than thirty agonizing miles, and despite the glib promises, there had been no food or
water, nor much consideration shown to the lame and the sick.

This was not a wilderness trek through some uncharted desert
where such neglect and privation could be understood and accepted by the victims as an inevitable hardship of war. They were
passing through relatively unscarred countryside well inside the
German homeland, abounding with farms and villages with well-
fed civilian populations and neat houses with scrubbed sidewalks.
Thus far the area had not been subjected to the ravagement of
land warfare. It was still snug and secure behind the formidable
defense belts of the Siegfried Line. In this safe, abundantly supplied region there had to be wells, storage tanks, or pipelines from
which drinking water could be drawn to slake the parched throats
of these pathetic trekkers.

And there also had to be food depots where rations, however
meager, could be drawn to allay the hunger of these prisoners. The
guys from the "Bloody Bucket" division knew a lot about the
Geneva Convention and its provisions for the treatment of POWs.
They had captured hundreds of Jerry prisoners in days gone by—
when the roles had been reversed—in Normandy, at Aachen, in
the *Hurtgen Wald*. The Jerry prisoners had always known and
vociferously demanded their rights under the Geneva Convention,
which said that prisoners were supposed to receive equal rations as
the captor nation's own troops. Of course, that might seem like a
bit much to expect. But that was, in fact, exactly what the Jerry
prisoners got from the American Army! The guys from the 28th
Division had seen this with their own eyes. There had been none
of this starvation bullcrap of no food or water.

Hyams was sure by now that the whole scenario of glib
promises and total deprivation was purposeful. The Kriegies could
thus be reduced to zombies, their last reserves of physical and
mental vitality drained out of them. No one on the receiving end of
this debilitating regimen could muster the will for any sort of escape effort or any other form of resistance. Nothing in their Army

training or in the so-called "survival conditioning" had prepared the Americans for this sort of contingency.

Eventually sheer fatigue sets in and resignation takes over. One tires of one's own bitching and griping. One shrivels up and withdraws inward to conserve that last ounce of energy.

Around one o'clock that morning, as the column of prisoners moved trancelike in the direction of Gerolstein, yet another powerful German Panzer convoy suddenly loomed squarely ahead in the darkness. The deafening roar of the engines and the clank of the heavy steel treads jarred the Kriegies awake. There were perhaps twenty of the behemoth Tigers tearing at a good clip toward the front, splattering cold sloshy mud in all directions, their blacked-out headlamps emitting ghostly slits of spectral light in the gloom.

As the prisoners scattered off the road to avoid being run down, some just collapsed into the drainage ditches, others continued their groping and stumbling along on their feet. The hushed talk among the guards was that these monster tanks were elements of the legendary S.S. Führer Panzer Squadron, possibly the most elite armoured unit in the German Army! Supermen driving super-tanks on their way to put the finishing touches to the faltering American First Army. The Tigers were part of the mighty follow-up wave which would swamp the last beleaguered defenders of St. Vith and then strike out for Bastogne.

Aboard the lead tank, a hysterical S.S. captain was taking an in-ordinate interest in the thin files of cowering Kriegies. Despite the darkness, he was intent on checking out each individual prisoner as his tank clanked by. Then the reason became apparent.

He was calling out frantically, in both German and Oxonian English, "Sind Juden hier?"—"Are there any Jews here?"

The Hauptsturmführer was persistent. Ignoring the strict blackout condition maintained by the column, he kept sporadically flashing on his tank's floodlight to better discern the faces and possible tell-tale racial characteristics of the slinking prisoners. Despite the urgent need for him to keep moving forward, he would not be deterred from his special quest.

In their debilitated and squalid condition, the prisoners must all have looked very Jewish to him high up there in his conning tower. They were all equally bleary-eyed, grim-faced, bearded, stoop-shouldered, dirty, and unkempt—the very same stereotype portrayed so graphically in all the Hitler Youth handbooks.

His steel hard gaze suddenly came to rest. The hawk had found his sparrow!

Hyams was sure that he was the one that the bastard had zeroed in on. He was not aware of any other possible candidates in the immediate vicinity. The Nazi's gaze swept all about him, and Hyams felt the icy glare of the searchlight and the piercing steel of the x-ray eyes.

Hyams, the marked man, broke out in a cold, clammy sweat. His heart raced wildly as he realized that death would come within minutes or even seconds. Mesmerized as if by a coiled cobra, he did not turn away, keeping his eyes glued on the Nazi.

Andreas' words of the previous day rang repeatedly like a tolling bell.

"They shoot them! They shoot them! They shoot them!"

Good old Andreas . . . probably sound asleep somewhere in some warm hay-filled barn, out of the cold and out of danger. For him, maybe, the war might last all of six months; but not for the Jew Hyams, for whom the war would probably be ending within a matter of minutes.

The old geezer would really be crushed if he were to know of his friend's untimely denouement.

The S.S. man ordered his driver to slow down and then to stop as he leapt, cat-like, from the hood of the tank onto the road.

He strode briskly towards the ditch where Hyams and some others had halted, transfixed by the developing drama. Hyams felt his knees buckle and an ominous moisture ooze down his legs, as black terror engulfed him.

This was it. This was the end. That which Andreas had predicted with such uncanny accuracy just a few short hours earlier. Hyams had never thought of himself as any kind of hero. Being short and slightly built, he was more the accountant type. He had never sought out the bullies. Not that he would consider himself a coward. But this was something different.

Here he was the specially pre-selected victim, at the whim and mercy of a weirdly twisted bastard! With no chance at all to defend himself, to strike back, or to offer any meaningful resistance.

This would be just another cold-blooded premeditated murder in a roadside ditch. It would never make the headlines. His "missing" status would just become permanent. Hell, he was already missing! But this was no way to go. No way to go.

In the last hours of combat Hyams had been resigned to death. Death had been a viable option then. But that would have been the death of a soldier. Here death would come completely without dignity or reason. A waste; a futile, meaningless death by execution at the hands of a creep who would walk away congratulating himself on his keen predatory instincts. Might even be a topic of fun back at the plush bordello in the railyards outside of Prum when all the heroes got together.

As the black-clad messenger of death approached within arm's length, Hyams shut his eyes in a split-second final prayer and farewell. When he opened them, the Nazi had passed him by, and had taken a short step beyond where Hyams stood . . . it wasn't Hyams at all!

The intended quarry, it turned out, was an inattentive little guy adorned with a 28th Division shoulder patch, who was standing directly behind Hyams in the ditch. He was just standing there looking down at his mud-caked boots, his thoughts maybe a thousand miles away.

The Nazi grabbed savagely for the man's jacket collar with his left hand, while his right hand went for the pistol holster at his belt. Hyams' shoulder was grazed by the assailant's elbow as he reached convulsively for the weapon.

He literally spat at his prey, "Dogtag, swine!"

As the terrified G.I. turned to face his tormentor, Hyams realized in a moment that the little man who had been pin-pointed by

the Angel Of Death was indeed the most Semitic-looking speci-
men he had ever laid eyes on. He was short, swarthy, with sad eyes
and an enormous hooked nose set off by a week's growth of dark,
stubbly beard. He just didn't have any chance at all. The poor guy
was a total sad sack, just like everyone else in the column, and a
walking invitation to the Nazi executioner.

Being taken totally unawares by this unprovoked attack, the little guy was rendered momentarily speechless. But he was plucky.
Struggling to regain his composure, he quickly stepped up out of
the ditch, pulled himself up to his full height of five-foot-four and
squared his shoulders back with cool dignity.

He next saluted smartly and stammered in a hoarse whisper,
"Sir . . . I'm not Jewish, Sir."

"The godamn dogtags, you swine!"

The German impatiently grabbed for the chainlet around the
man's neck, seizing the man's dogtags in one swift move. Trying to
read them in the dark, he almost pulled his victim's head off in the
process.

"Godamn, I can't make this out! What is your damned name?"

"Hassan, Sir, Elias Michael Hassan."

"Aha! Out of line, dog, right now! Here, back off the road!"

The tall, muscular tanker, towering above his prey and now
exhilarated by the scent of the kill, shoved Hassan back into the
ditch, never letting loose of him, as he prepared to drag him off
into the snow-covered field beyond.

"But, Sir . . . there's some mistake, Sir. I'm Roman Catholic.
Look at my dogtags. There's the 'C,' Sir. That's for Catholic."

"Catholic? Elias What? Hassan? What do you take me for, you
Jew bastard?"

"I'm Syrian, Sir. On both sides. God is my witness! My father
was born in Aleppo. My mother was born in Pottstown, Pennsylvania. That's where I'm from. We are Christians. I was baptized a
Christian, Sir. I have my Saint Christopher medal here, Sir. We
attend St. Stephan's Cathedral, Sir."

The Nazi was momentarily confused by Hassan's desperate torrent of professions and supplications. He paused . . . then looked about him, realizing that he might have perhaps erred in his hasty choice of a victim.

In a burst of bitter frustration, the S.S. man suddenly lashed out with his clenched fist in a ferocious roundhouse blow to Hassan's head. The valiant little guy reeled for about ten seconds, but stayed on his feet.

"You lie, you scum! I want you out of this line!"

"Yes, Sir, but I am not Jewish, Sir. My dogtags give my name and religion. Here it is, Sir. That's 'C' for Catholic, Sir."

At this point there was an angry shout from one of the follow-up vehicles. The *Hauptsturmführer's* idling tank was holding up the parade, and there wasn't room in the road to pull around it.

The *Hauptsturmführer* was stymied. This little character might possibly be Syrian and Catholic after all, or he might be a Turkish Jew masquerading as a Christian, the sonofabitch.

But the *Hauptsturmführer* couldn't go around shooting Catholic prisoners, not in front of all these witnesses. He'd best throw this fish back, and find himself one named Goldstein or Bloom.

He snapped the leather flap down on his pistol holster and swiveled around smartly.

He strode stiffly back to his tank, glaring poisonously up and down the prisoner lines. His eyes met Hyams'. Zeke, sensing again the paralyzing chill of the man's demonic hatred, turned away. The Nazi hesitated for a split second . . . then he clambered back into his war chariot.

The *Hauptsturmführer* was, after all, in somewhat of a hurry; he had a war to catch. On this night of December 20-21, his Panzer column was already long overdue at the front. While it would be nice to have a bit of deadly sport with some Jewish Kriegie, there really was not all that time to waste on this sort of game.

But he knew there were Jew-dogs in that wretched column . . . swine that should be culled out and liquidated.

And the *Hauptsturmführer* kept trying . . . Hyams could hear him calling out to the prisoner column as his Tigers moved on westward into the night.

The prisoners kept doggedly on their way. No one looked up, no one spoke. Most were too exhausted to fully comprehend the dynamics of this weird exhibition.

Zeke now knew for sure how valid Andreas' warning had been. "They shoot them." Andreas had probably witnessed a few of those executions. This Hassan guy had had a very close call. The poor unsuspecting sonofabitch. He was badly shaken, and just stood there in the ditch moaning and cursing and holding his head. Hyams felt for him, and could only hope that he hadn't been seriously injured by the savage blow to the head that he had taken, although it did not look good. Hassan was in pain. Hyams made a cold compress of snow for the man, and he prayed for Hassan. Hyams was keenly aware that Hassan, by being there with his hundred-percent Semitic appearance, had probably saved his, Hyams', life. Hyams, if challenged, could not, of course, have produced a lifesaving "C" dogtag—or any kind of dogtag.

CHAPTER FIVE

Gerolstein and
The Orient Express

*A never ending night of the miseries. Finally a new day .
. . a new town . . . a turn for the better. A feast of cheese
and crackers. Riding the Orient Express with Hassan,
Hornstein, still the guardhouse lawyer . . . and a packed
carload. Life goes on.*
　　　　　　　　—P.M., Thursday, December, 21, 1944.

GEROLSTEIN, some thirty miles behind the German front lines, was another of those idyllic Eifel villages, nestled among gently rolling snow-laden hills at the benign elevation of about 1,200 feet. Life there could be beautiful, just as it had once been in Belgian Schoenberg and St. Vith.

Rising from the banks of the swift-flowing Kyll River, the town is surrounded by great stands of virgin pine forest. Nearby spas and natural hot springs have been appreciated since antiquity for their curative powers. Local folklore has it that some two thousand years ago Gerolstein had been a favorite rest area for officers of the occupying Roman legions. In more recent times the lure of the waters had, in the summers, drawn a classy clientele from throughout Germany and neighboring Holland and Belgium.

In December of 1944 the Germans found the dense pine forests ideal for concealing concentrations of troops and armor, and with a generous rail network radiating out from town in all directions, they had turned Gerolstein, like its sister city Prum, into a major supply and staging base for the massive Ardennes offensive.

Normally the place could boast a static population of perhaps three thousand souls. But six days into the Ardennes campaign it was a beehive of German traffic and congestion. In addition to the civilian population, and the considerable numbers of German troops, and the ubiquitous work gangs and convoys moving endlessly through town, there were upwards of five thousand newly captured American war prisoners. These latter were packed into a number of holding pens around town, where strolling *Bürghers* could see for themselves and draw reassurance about the vincibility of American fighting men. It was a sight which the German populace could ogle and remember, and which could confirm the ecstatic war news headlined in the *Volkischer Beobachter,* the Nazi newspaper.

The Yanks and the pitiable condition they were in were thus a considerable propaganda asset to their captors. Most were down with fever, trenchfoot, dysentery, or any one or more of the other common afflictions of the frontline foot soldier in dire circumstances.

For Hyams, Gerolstein was just another place on a road to nowhere. After Schoenberg and Prum, he knew that the benevolent façades of these German villages and hamlets did not presage any relief for the prisoners. And the nagging question of the dogtags which he had so blithely discarded was another worry that kept coming back to haunt him.

He knew what Hassan's fate would have been if he couldn't have readily produced his dogtags. Those dogtags had saved his life. That had been the first challenge from the Nazi executioner. Without dogtags Hassan wouldn't have had a ghost of a chance. In the first pale light of day, a powerful new paranoia took hold of Hyams and drove him to frantic scheming. How could he come up with some plausible cover story if he were similarly challenged? Okay: he had lost his dogtags. It could happen to anyone. And then why couldn't he also claim to be Syrian? He would just say that he was Syrian and Catholic, just like Hassan. It might pass. Especially if he was prepared with this story and didn't stammer and stumble around. He would have to keep rehearsing the story. Mother born in Pottstown, PA., father in Aleppo, Syria. Why not? Of course there was no Saint Christopher Medal, but what the hell!

Hyams prayed to his Jewish God. He was scared, and he was everlastingly thankful to Hassan, who had taken a heavy hit both physically and in spirit and had been forced to practically grovel for his life. It was the kind of humiliation that takes a long time to get over. And physically, he was hurting. The left side of his face was swollen like a grapefruit, the eye swollen shut. He kept applying snow to the bruised area and spitting blood—and teeth. Hyams felt a strong kinship with the man. They had some important things in common. Hyams was a new convert to Syrianism. And of course they both now knew what the S.S. was all about.

The column arrived at the outskirts of Gerolstein just as the first rays of the dawning sun began to light up the snow fields. It had been a night of pain, terror, and despair.

On this bitter morning, Hyams and many others were giving up hope of surviving Nazi captivity, convinced that the Germans were intent on marching their prisoners into the ground, their only interest being to move them as far back from the front as possible, as quickly as possible, regardless of the cost in exhaustion and in lives.

The column came to rest in yet another barbed wire corral just outside the village. It was Schoenberg all over again except that it was a day later, still without food or water. Everyone collapsed to the ground. Sleep was the only escape.

But of course there was to be no such escape. Soon they were again rousted out and ordered to form up in ranks for marching. *"Fünf! Fünf! Schneil!* On your godamn feet! Columns of Five! Let's go!"

The Kriegies, too weak to resist or complain, dragged themselves into formation and began to shuffle forward on command. They were on the road again. Only this time they soon seemed to be heading rather purposefully into a busy rail-yard.

Then the column was halted again and the men kept standing in place, on the verge of collapse, for a seeming eternity. A herd of cattle, stolidly awaiting the prods of the drovers, while on a nearby track stood a long line of empty cattle-cars with doors ajar.

Hyams and the others had turned into feeble old men in the last few days. Every step along the way had become a test of endurance and grit. If they could now gain access to those rail cars, rather than continue to be force-marched on the open roads, then at least they would be off their feet and sheltered from the raw elements.

Finally, at some mysteriously appointed moment, the word came down. The column was started up. *"Schnell! Marschieren! Fünf! Fünf!* Columns of Five! *Schnell!"* Lined up in rows five abreast, the Kriegies were steered briskly towards the train of empty freight cars. Could there now at last be some relief? Could it really be? Or was this another cruel charade?

As the column of fives moved along the length of the train, the orders came at last to prepare to board.

No pampered passenger who ever boarded the most luxurious salon car of the fabled Orient Express was more appreciative of those plush accommodations than were the delirious Kriegies who now marched alongside those weather-beaten cattle cars. This was the Orient Express without compartments or bunks, without toilets, without dining car, and just without. But it could have been the Orient Express. And, as an added bon-voyage bonus like a rope thrown to a drowning man, as the column of fives moved forward, the end man in each row was handed a small parcel containing a package of hard rye crackers and a pint-sized can of processed cheese. The accompanying message was that each parcel was to be shared among five prisoners, and that this would be the total food ration for the next three days.

To complete this festive scenario, there was moving slowly along the track, a horse-drawn tank-wagon from which the revitalized Kriegies could at long last refill their empty canteens. Food and water, the staples of life. The world was beautiful.

Hardly believing this sudden change in their fortunes, the Kriegie ranks picked up the step as they were counted off and assigned to their cars. They clambered joyfully aboard, never losing sight of that every fifth Kriegie who had been entrusted with the magic packet and was now suddenly elevated to an exalted position of enormous power and prestige.

The rickety cars, known as "forty-and-eighters," were widely used across Europe since the turn of the century to haul live-stock—forty sheep or eight horses being their standard capacity. However, in Hitler's Third Reich, the Transport Ministry had found these wagons perfect for shuttling all sorts of low-priority human cargoes around the Nazi domain.

Untold millions of lost souls had ridden these carriages, often to their final destinations, often as many as a hundred men, women, and children packed in a car. These journeys were delib-erately designed to kill off the weak, while those who survived would be in a totally malleable condition upon delivery to their destinations.

But after each trip the wagons were always cleansed and sanitized, so the cars waiting in the yard at Gerolstein to receive the Americans were hygienically pure and as good as new, with little evidence to suggest the travel conditions of prior journeys and earlier passengers nor the numbers of dead-on-arrivals.

The Kriegies were packed in sixty to a car, but nobody was complaining. This was opulent luxury after the long, tortured march. As soon as the cars were filled up the heavy wooden sliding doors were slammed shut and padlocked by the guards.

Hyams had the feeling that not everyone in that unhappy column had been lucky enough to get aboard the train. There weren't that many cars. Ever the accountant, he had counted roughly fourteen cars in all. Well, the others would probably catch a later train. There didn't seem to be any train shortage in Hitler's Reich, judging from the heavy traffic.

Inside the sealed and darkened cars, narrow slits of daylight filtered in through a single tiny porthole at each corner. These were heavily overlaid with redundant strands of rusted barbed-wire, which would preclude any thought of escape or even of pass-ing the tiniest object in or out of the car, even a pencilled message. Very appropriate for hauling prisoners. As for ventilation, the cars were "self ventilating"; the thin, slatted walls provided no barrier to the outside weather. Protection from the cold and wind-driven rain or snow would come only from the shared body heat of the closely packed riders.

Sanitation facilities were provided in the form of two lidded wooden buckets, one at each end of the car. The buckets would be in constant demand.

There being no seats or benches, the men sank wearily to the floor in constricted squatting positions. There was no room for sitting with legs outstretched, and none for lying down, unless they took turns. But comfort was not a priority, the subject of primary urgency being the contents of the Jerry food parcels.

Groups of five hastily organized themselves around those king-pins who were clutching the food packets and who would usually take a strong proprietary interest in the entire proceedings. Having been handed that parcel by the Germans automatically endowed the recipient with all the power and prerogatives of a federal magistrate. That man, be he buckass private or Top Sergeant, would serve as the absolute arbiter of all disputes as to the division of the food or any other questions, including the timing and the rate of consumption.

Most of the Kriegies quite naturally opted for the immediate division and consumption of the entire contents of the packets, which in normal times would hardly qualify as a snack. But, as in all matters, there were some disagreements. Incredibly, there were some individuals who counseled frugality and even abstinence in the light of the Jerry caveat of lean times ahead, but these ultra-conservative viewpoints were usually overruled as the biscuits were carefully counted out.

There would be three or four crackers per Kriegie, depending on the count and who was counting. The cheese was likewise meticulously and painstakingly divided, in the absence of any sort of knives or utensils.

The starving Kriegies savored at long last their first bit of Jerry-issued sustenance, and washed it all down with generous draughts of cool, clear water from their canteens. Even as to water, the more prudent rationed themselves, knowing it might be a long time between refills.

And soon there was nothing again. But color returned to pallid faces, and eyes, dulled by hunger and fatigue, sparkled as empty stomachs knew food again. The German sour note of caution, of future hard times, had been blithely dismissed by most as gloom-and-doom talk. The Germans had made their point that they were law-abiding and human and that they knew about the Geneva Convention.

And then, hardly noticed by the momentarily besotted Kriegies, the train started to move ever so slightly. It began to crawl out of the yard and then onto the main tracks leading eastward.

It was now about mid-day on Thursday, December 21, not quite a week since the Germans had shattered the stalemate in the Snow Eifel, and this wheezing relic of a train was carrying the equivalent of an American combat battalion into the German interior, out of action, destined to sit out the war under guard, with personal plans and hopes on hold—indefinite hold.

As the prisoners started to get their bearings and to take charge of their newly emerging destiny, there was a thawing out, a relaxation at last, a mellowing, and finally even a few feeble attempts at good-natured humor and self-ridicule. There had to be some element of humor inherent in their situation. What else could they do now but try to make light of their predicament?

Hyams, now bouncing back from rock-bottom, felt somewhat revived. There might be some hope for the future after all. He felt strength coming back into his arms and legs. His mind and spirit were somewhat restored.

Casting about for familiar faces, he realized that Eli Hassan was aboard. Hyams was glad to see him. They exchanged knowing glances across the tangle of bodies. Despite a badly bruised and swollen eye, Hassen now seemed somewhat recovered from last night's jarring confrontation, when his life had hung by a slender thread. But Hyams sensed an unshakable melancholy about the man, a loss of buoyancy, a wound that would not soon heal.

Hyams next recognized another bearded face in the crowd, and then another. They were two old buddies from Third Platoon, K Company, a mismatched pair whose fortuitous appearance in the car now provided a solid link to the past. One, Marvin Purdy, was a tall, gangling backwoodsman from some place back in the Ozarks. His job had been to lug the 32-pound Browning Automatic Rifle around—a fearsome weapon, but a mite heavy to be carrying around cross-country all day. They always entrusted the B.A.R. to the tall, lanky, country guys. In civilian life Purdy had been a deputy constable in this little burg in Arkansas, a place called Siloam Springs. In many ways, Purdy had never left Siloam Springs.

That was why Hyams could never fathom the father-son affinity between Purdy and this other guy, Maury Hornstein. It must have been the attraction of opposites. Purdy was reticent, shy, soft-spoken, self-effacing, and a teetotaller—no smoking or drinking. Hornstein was loud, self-assured, opinionated, and strictly New York, and a self-proclaimed connoisseur of food and drink. He was about half a generation older than Purdy and came from a totally different world. Heavyset and jowl-faced, he looked like he belonged behind a mahogany desk somewhere, smoking a big Havana cigar like a big-time lawyer or maybe even a big-time bookie. He had obviously been miscast as a common foot soldier. He was too old and too bulky and too much given to flights of bombast and hyperbole. But there they both were, squatting on the floor. Hornstein was the man from Manhattan, but this was not the Eighth Avenue Subway he was riding.

The three old buddies from K Company began to exchange a few tidbits about last sightings of mutual friends. There were some confirmed losses. Hornstein had all the scuttlebutt on about half the roster of guys in Third Platoon.

"Hey, Hyams, this is the worst godamn experience of my life. Pure horseshit! These Jerries never heard of the Geneva

Convention. What can you expect?" This was definitely not Maury Hornstein's cup of tea. He was used to better things. Somehow the incident with the S.S. tank captain had escaped Hornstein's notice. Hyams wondered what the outcome might have been if Hornstein had been the intended mark.

And then Purdy weighed in. Around Hornstein he would sometimes venture into conversation. "Maury's taking it hard. He's right, ya know, he's too old for this sort of foolishness. By rights he should have been assigned to some headquarters job. He's got the experience to handle any headquarters job, ya know." Maury could always count on Purdy's full support and solicitude. As long as Purdy was around, Hornstein was Number One. And should a strong arm be, perchance, needed to enforce Maury's viewpoint, Purdy would always be ready to lend a hand.

There was, of course, so much to talk about, but there wasn't that kind of surplus of energy for too much talking or reminiscing. Everyone was just too tired and too relieved to be finally riding the rails and sitting or squatting rather than dragging themselves along on swollen feet through roadside ditches.

And the four tiny portholes, securely screened as they were, offered at least some openings to the outside world. Those who were curious enough could negotiate their way over dozens of bodies to get a glimpse of the German landscape as the train chugged along. But hardly anyone did.

The rickety train labored on, belching acrid black clouds of smoke and soot as it moved haltingly into the foreboding interior of Hitler's Fatherland.

CHAPTER SIX

The Train Yard At Limburg

Stop and go . . . stop and go. No fun. Shithouse blues.
V-e-r-y slow train, to Koblenz and Limburg.
—Friday, December 22, 1944.

A food ration. Thankful for anything. Then Xmas
carolling. Joy to the world. Then the RAF. All hell broke
loose. Death under a rose-lit sky. So much for Xmas.
—Saturday, December 23, 1944.

ON THAT FIRST DAY OUT OF GEROLSTEIN the train was in
motion only a small fraction of the time. It was understandably accorded the lowest priority in routing, and was constantly subject to
maddening stops and starts. Endless hours dragged on while it sat
parked unattended on remote spurs, while the main tracks were
cleared for the more important traffic moving troops and supplies
toward the front.

The hours of close confinement locked inside a standing cattle-
car going nowhere soon began to generate a whole new assortment
of unforeseen miseries among the hapless passengers. By nightfall
the packets of crackers and cheese were but a faint and irrelevant
memory of a momentary delight in a distant past. Hunger and tensions returned to the breaking point. The oppressive congestion of
so many unwashed and foul-smelling bodies within a cramped
space, and the impossibility of any sort of restful sleep led to fraz-
zled nerves and frequent outbursts of temper over the slightest
irritations, like "whose godamn feet belonged where!" or "get your
godamn elbow out of my godamn ribs!"

The two slop buckets took on a central importance as more

Kriegies came down with the inevitable cases of diarrhea and dysentery. Excretory politics involving such issues as prior rights and the equitable time-sharing of the facilities now took on paramount importance. Toilet paper, or any kind of paper, became a highly prized commodity . . . much more valuable than cigarettes had ever been. Someone in Zeke's car had found and preserved an old tattered edition of *Der Volkischer Beobachter*. This was immediately torn into appropriately sized little squares. It was a life-saver, for a while. Paper would soon become as critical as food and water.

Eli Hassan was not doing well. He was complaining of a splitting headache. Nobody could come up with an aspirin. Hyams and Purdy and most of the others maintained a lethargic silence at a time when Maury Hornstein was stepping up the volume of his complaints.

"I never thought I'd spend my final hours in a fuckin' floating shit-house. Godamn! We were better off on the fuckin' roads. At least we could move around . . . and breathe! This is the absolute shits! They're just gonna kill us all off by degrees! The fuckin' Heinies!"

The station names, when visible at the various stops, gave no hint of an ultimate destination. The places were all very German, very unfamiliar, and conveyed zero enlightenment to the prisoners. There was no contact with any guard or anybody else outside the confines of the car. They were being hauled around like dumb animals in a cage. The train ride, which earlier had seemed such a great boon, was by that nightfall not working out that way at all. The new imperative and the speculation was now about how soon they might be getting out of these accursed hell-cars, which, in contrast to the likes of the Orient Express, were nothing more or less than rolling, lurching, snake-pits on wheels.

The first overnight in the Stygian darkness of the boxcar was a physical and spiritual back-breaker. During those long periods when the train was stopped there was the feeling that the night would never end. But the night passed, and in the morning the meandering cortège, with its cargo of desperate passengers, pulled into a city with a vast marshalling complex with trains and tracks radiating out in all directions. This was the first German city that the Kriegies had seen. It was the major rail hub of Koblenz, on the left bank of the Rhine. The train had covered less than fifty miles since its departure the previous day from Gerolstein, an average speed of less than three miles per hour.

Koblenz, a sizeable city and historic bastion of German power in the west, looked very much alive and well to the bleary-eyed Kriegies who now scrambled to the port-holes for a glimpse of the sky and the outside world. The main rail lines, Berlin to Metz and Cologne to Mainz, ran through the Koblenz junction, and although the famous old railway station now lay in ruins, the hustle and activity in the yards, as perceived and heard by the Kriegies through their scrimpy port-holes, brought them back to life after the miserable night.

It would be three months before the armored columns of a revitalized American army would shoot their way into Koblenz, strategically located as it was at the confluence of the Rhine and Moselle rivers. But for the moment Koblenz was solidly German and pumping men and arms towards the Western Front.

The prisoners would endure several more sedentary hours in the yard at Koblenz. The cars were mercifully opened to allow the dumping and replacement of the slop buckets. Those few guards who appeared remained non-committal about the questions which concerned the prisoners most: food, water and how much longer in the cars? The railroad guards didn't know and couldn't care less. They had during this war, after all, seen untold numbers of such cars stuffed full of begging and pleading non-persons.

There would be a water ration in Koblenz, but no food. A water wagon appeared, allowing everyone to refill their canteens. A rumor sprang up that the train would be heading for a POW camp at the town of Limburg, just a few hours' ride from Koblenz. At least it was something to look forward to; it would mean liberation from the cars, if even only into a prison camp, where one could stretch the legs and get a breath of fresh air. And there would certainly be a food ration at the prison camp.

Hornstein had an opinion on this; he was confident that things had to be better in the prison camp. "Anything has got to be better than this miserable shit-wagon. We're dying in here. Another twenty-four hours and they'll be carrying us out in body-bags."

Hyams had no opinions. But he was concerned about Hassan, who seemed ill and dizzy and was plagued by a persistent headache. He just lay in a corner of the car with his eyes closed most of the time. Hyams thought he was getting worse. The black-suited bastard might have given him a concussion the other night when he hauled off at him in that blind rage. It would be much better to get to a prison camp where there might be some medical help available.

It was Friday, December 22; three days before Christmas. By mid-afternoon the train began to drag itself slowly back on the tracks heading out of Koblenz. Despite much protest and pleading, there had been no food issued to the Kriegies before the sliding doors were slammed shut and padlocked. They could now look forward to another endless night of hunger, frustration, and the shits. The train moved eastward with its intermittent stopping and lunging forward.

Before nightfall the brakes squealed once again, and as Hyams peered out of a porthole he could make out a station sign, Limburg. Finally a prison camp, a roof, a floor, a bunk, some food, however lousy. Whatever they could dish out in that prison camp was better than what they were getting—or rather—not getting on this so-called train.

As darkness fell the train remained motionless in the station yard without any word or sign from the Germans, although there was a general feeling in the cars that the train had arrived at its final destination. The Kriegies were to spend that night locked up in the cars, without food or fresh water.

Mercifully, they did not know that the train was to remain at rest and that they would remain inside those cars in the Limburg yards for the next five days and nights. In the entire week of debilitating stagnation inside the railroad cars they would have been hauled a total distance of less than seventy miles from their original entraining point at Gerolstein. The war that was raging less than a hundred miles to the west, on land and in the air, would reach out to them in the rail yard at Limburg, bringing death and injuries to many. But the future is most often mercifully shrouded in high hopes and fervent optimism. The events at Limburg could not have been known before they unfolded.

On that first morning in the Limburg yard, when the guards showed up with a work party for the daily ritual of emptying out the slop buckets there was a frenzied outburst of cursing and fist-shaking by the prisoners. Hornstein led the chorus, bellowing at the guards in a combination of pidgin German and English. Though not easily intimidated, he managed not to cross any thresholds that might sour relations totally.

"This is not fit treatment for human beings! This is not the way we Americans treat our *Kriegsgefangene!* Besides, we've got an injured man here who needs medical attention!" He acted like he was back in Louie's Deli on Seventh Avenue in Manhattan, where he might be reading the riot act to an inattentive waiter.

The man from Manhattan insisted on his rights. He hadn't gotten the message that a Jewish Kriegie was on very thin ice in this Nazi-dominated universe. Nor had he witnessed the S.S. captain's murderous assault on poor Hassan, as he had been situated more to the rear of the column at the time. Nor could he fully credit the story when it was relayed to him. But he was struck by Hassan's sick condition. All he could do was to keep repeating "asshole!" to himself in disgust whenever he visualized the attack by the Nazi upon a defenseless POW. He was a product of the tough sidewalks of New York, and he thought he had seen everything there, and that there was nothing more dangerous roaming about the Fatherland than some of the hoods he had handled on the Lower Eastside.

The word eventually seeped back that there was indeed a POW

camp nearby and that the Kriegies were shortly to be de-trained and taken to the camp, where they would be received and fed. And medical help would be available for those who needed it. This news allayed the protesters' anger, and everyone settled back to wait some more.

Hours passed with nothing happening, but by late afternoon a food truck pulled up to the train. The car doors were slid partially open to pass the rations in. There were chunks of rough black bread smeared with margarine and a kind of molasses. There was also fresh water. They were told that they would de-train "tomorrow."

This was the first food ration since Gerolstein two days earlier. While it took the edge off their hunger and was a boost to morale, the basic situation remained the same.

It was now Saturday, December 23, exactly a week since Hitler had launched his Ardennes attack. Unbeknownst to the Kriegies, St. Vith had fallen on December 21 after holding out for five days. It had been a costly and heroic resistance. Hitler's edict that pivotal St. Vith must be his by D Plus One had been thwarted. His grand push to the Meuse River had been irreversibly stalled by the gallant American resistance at St. Vith.

As the weather opened up on this Saturday, Allied bombers and fighter squadrons began to range in force over the battlefield and the enemy lines of communication. In addition to the loss of momentum, the Führer had now lost the most essential ingredient for his victory—that being continued heavy clouds and overcast necessary for keeping Allied air power grounded.

The German attack had also been stonewalled at Bastogne and other key Belgian towns as fresh American reinforcements reached the battlefronts. The tide of battle was turning. Two days before Christmas, there was now a return of optimism at Supreme Allied Headquarters, where the worst was seen to be over. But all this was beyond the pale of the Kriegies' knowledge or immediate interests and concerns. The men in the boxcars could not focus on anything beyond their own immediate predicament. Their world had been reduced to a cubicle encompassed by the eight-foot by thirty-foot dimensions of the inside of a sealed boxcar. But, on this evening, after receiving the ration of bread and molasses, the Kriegies took note of the approach of Christmas, and the remembrances of past Christmases and loved ones at home, and every deep joy and happiness that Christmas could evoke in happier times. And sure enough, as though on cue, the rickety cars standing in the railyard began to resound with the heartening strains of Christmas carolling.

Spirits soared. Voices rang out loud and strong, and eyes sparkled with hope and animation. With the early dusk, a sharp evening chill was felt among the huddled carollers, but the solace of this new spiritual experience lifted them out of their squalor. Everyone joined in, even the irascible Hornstein.

And then suddenly, without any warning, the skies overhead were lit up by showers of luminescent flares. And before anyone in the cars could realize what was happening, the air was filled with the ear-shattering drone of low-flying aircraft on the attack, the chatter of scores of heavy machine guns spitting hot lead, and the all-too-familiar thud of bombs landing all about. Wave upon wave of "friendly" bombers were zooming in, turning night into day with their parachute flares, blowing up buildings, tracks, and rolling stock, and raking the yard with their cannon and 50-caliber machine guns. Peace and calm gave way to wild pandemonium inside the locked cars.

As the panicked Kriegies hurled themselves against the bolted car doors, the sheer weight of their numbers would burst the doors open. Unfettered, they came tumbling out of the cars and running wildly for cover. In the ensuing panic, Hyams thought of Hassan, and last saw the injured man on the floor of the car, motioning feebly that he would remain where he was and take his chances. Hyams was drawn to remain in the car, but at the urging of others he leapt from the car and ran for cover. As it turned out, the car was virtually undamaged, but unfortunately Hassan did actually leave the car under his own power at the height of the attack, which turned out to be a fatal mistake for him.

The guard detachment had earlier abandoned the train and

fled to nearby shelters. As the prisoners dispersed in all directions, some throwing themselves into shallow ditches and trenches, others fanning out madly across the open yard, the attacking planes wheeled about and swooped down upon them again and again with machine guns blazing. The British pilots were now certain that they had chanced upon an enemy troop train jam-packed with fresh replacements for the front. The Kriegies, caught out in the open on this unfamiliar landscape, prayed silently and out loud. The train, standing there as a perfect target in the eerie pink light of the flares, together with the running figures dispersing helter skelter in all directions, all added up to a perceived rich plum for the fly-boys. After about ten minutes of persistent passes over the yard, the Royal Air Force Mosquitoes flew off into the night sky to return to their British bases. On the ground they left death and devastation.

As survivors slowly regained their footing, some tried to comfort wounded buddies, others stood numbly over their dead. Most of the rail cars had been damaged or demolished. Scattered about the yard in trenches and in the open were the dead and wounded. Squads of German troops were cordoning off the area to prevent escapes, as the dazed Kriegies were rounded up and coralled back into the cars that remained relatively intact.

Hyams and Hornstein returned to their car which had escaped serious damage. Everyone had evacuated the car, including Hassan, unfortunately. A headcount by the Germans showed that about a quarter of the original occupants of the car did not return. New men from the damaged cars were crammed in in their stead. Among the missing were Hassan and Purdy. Word came later that Hassan was dead. Purdy was alive but badly wounded, and being evacuated to a Jerry hospital.

Labor gangs appeared as if by magic and worked through the night, collecting the dead and wounded, clearing rubble, repairing tracks, removing the damaged cars, and recoupling the train. The Germans went from car to car, meticulously counting heads and tallying up dead and wounded to make sure there were no prisoners unaccounted for. The next day the Kriegies learned that their captors were satisfied that there had been no escapes. No live Kriegie had taken advantage of the confusion and momentary absence of guards to disappear permanently into the night. Why? Hyams wondered about this, but was too tired and disgusted to give it much thought. The two, Hassan and Purdy, would be missed. At least Purdy was alive.

Hyams thought hard about Hassan's fate. He had been hit by machine gun fire, by "friendly" strafing, after going through such testing ordeals as the Hurtgen Forest and, of course, the Ardennes. He had really been killed by the Panzer captain with an assist from cruel fate and the British Royal Air Force.

Sunday, December 24 was spent sealed up in the newly reconstituted train. The situation was growing more desperate. There were more cases of illness and diarrhea. The men were weaker, listless, and depressed. They now heard that the local Stalag was filled up and could not accept more prisoners. It seemed like you needed reservations! They would be departing soon for another prison camp somewhere further to the east, but there was nothing definite.

CHAPTER SEVEN

To The Elbe And Beyond

*Xmas . . . still here in the car . . . and still stuck in
Limburg. This is where that stinky cheese must come
from. Figures. Not good. Thinking of the guys who
caught it in the raid. Very sad. But Xmas is Xmas. And
welcome greetings from the Indian Red Cross. ??? A
strange but nice touch on this Oriental Express.*
                                    —Monday, December 25, 1944.

*Pulled out of the Limburg yard last night. Thank God.
Five days, and five nights of unmitigated hell. It's still
terrible but at least we're moving, and we're out of there
. . . maybe there's hope.*
                                    —Thursday, December 28, 1944.

IT WAS CHRISTMAS EVE,—*"Der Heilige Weinachtabend,"* as
the guards spoke of it. For the Americans in the cattle wagons
stranded in the Limburg rail yard, it was just another fitful and
depressing night. No food, no lights, no singing, no joy. The
Germans had not moved the train now for two full days and everyone knew that it and its human cargo were sitting ducks out there,
a conspicuous and inviting bulls-eye, a bit of unfinished business
for the roving British Mosquito bombers who specialized in these
close-in targets of opportunity. Why wouldn't the Brits come back?
The sounds of overflying aircraft had been heard all day. The Allied
bombers were out in force on this day before Christmas.

Hopefully the R.A.F. would take the night off. In addition to
the normal stresses, the Kriegies now lived in fear of a repeat

performance of the Allied bombing as they listened for the sound of incoming planes or the whine of the air-raid sirens. The rail junction at Limburg would certainly be an easy and juicy target.

But the night passed without incident.

At mid-morning on Christmas Day the car doors slid open to allow the passing in of Christmas food parcels—a glorious and memorable surprise for people who had just about run out of hope. These were authentic Christmas parcels, each containing about two pounds of assorted foodstuffs, and again "five" was the magic number. There was one parcel for every five Kriegies. The welcome parcels bore the imprimatur of the Indian Red Cross, and had originated in that sub-continent half a world away. The food items combined both British and Indian traditional tastes. There was canned fish, curry and rice, and then there were biscuits and jam and even a miniature plum pudding in each parcel.

Christmas was now Christmas, even in the middle of a bombed-out German railyard. After partaking of his share, Hyams ruminated about the strange workings of war at Christmas-time that would deliver a life-saving packet from faraway India to a bunch of unknown American G.I.s at the end of their rope in the heart of bomb-battered Germany. He guessed that these packets had been diverted by some Jerry supply sergeant from the intended beneficiaries, namely British Indian prisoners being held in one of Germany's many stalags. Hyams thought it was a magnanimous Christian gesture. Such is life. Nobody in Limburg was complaining.

The usual caveat of lean times ahead accompanied the hand-out; the parcels represented the total rations to be expected for the next three days. That seemed to be the standard Jerry message. Any distribution of food was accompanied by that message of three lean days to follow. The Jerries were not giving anything away. Again, groups of five speedily organized themselves around a head-man who would be vested with the usual magisterial powers. Some groups opted for one glorious Christmas bash, while others took a more penurious approach designed to make the parcels stretch.

Hyams took mental note of the entire proceedings for the book that he was going to write some day.

It all helped to pass the time.

During the lighter moments which followed the meager repast, Hornstein told a few "after-dinner" stories . . . all about foods he had experienced in happier times, like Borscht Belt stuff. He regaled the suffering Kriegies with mouth-watering descriptions of how they put together a "hot corned beef on rye" back at Louie's delicatessen on Seventh Avenue, with the kosher pickles and all, and the ice cream parlor that produced spectacular ice cream sundaes with hot fudge and sprinkled nuts at only fifteen cents for a triple scoop!

Finally, on Wednesday night, December 27, two days after the Indian parcels, shortly after nightfall as the Kriegies were re-arranging themselves for the night, the train slowly started to move under them. True to their word, the Jerries had not made any food distribution since Christmas Day. It had now been five full days, 120 hours, since the train had first pulled into Limburg station. They had been unwashed and unshaven for almost two weeks, and all now bore the unmistakeable pallor, the vacant eyes, and the sunken cheeks of the long-term prisoner. They had seen death strike at them from the skies, they had all been brushed by that gratuitous tragedy, but now the train was finally on the move. Any movement, any change, could only be an improvement. Anywhere had to be better than fuckin' Limburg!

The train started and shunted through the night and the following day. While there was some movement, the progress was still excruciatingly slow. Late the following afternoon, which would be Thursday, December 28, the train pulled into Frankfurt and ground to a halt in the railyard near the heart of the city—or what had once been the city. The distance covered from Limburg was about thirty-five miles; the time elapsed almost twenty-four hours. From the portholes of the prison cars the Kriegies could survey the flattened landscape, an unending vista of rubble and debris stretching clear to the horizon in every direction.

There was hardly a building left standing for miles around. This city of half a million pre-war population, which since the middle ages had been renowned as a world center of trade and commerce and the most important transportation hub in all of Germany, had been laid waste by an unremitting, 'round-the-clock bombing campaign—the Americans coming by day, the British by night. Now, at year's end in 1944, Frankfurt had been effectively taken out of the war.

Only the railway lines weaving their way through the shattered landscape seemed to be yet alive and functioning. This was the first time that the American prisoners had seen graphic proof on such a monstrous scale of what airpower could do to a large city. They knew that what they were seeing in Frankfurt had been duplicated many times over in all of Germany's major cities, and they had to marvel at the enemy's survival and grim determination after the punishment he had taken.

Surveying the ashes of Frankfurt, Hyams recalled his earlier prediction to the Austrian guard Andreas that the war would be over in six months, and he felt confirmed in that rather offhand and uninformed guess. Now if he could only survive those six months himself.

Remarkably, despite the bombings, the bridges across the Main River were largely intact, connecting Frankfurt with all the major German termini in every direction. Three road bridges and two railway bridges were still carrying a heavy load of traffic.

There was a ration of bread and tea, and then the Kriegie train rolled across one of these bridges and headed deeper into the Reich. The journey continued. This was Thursday, December 28th. For the next two days they travelled a seemingly aimless and meandering route, picking up some speed, through such parochial places as Aschaffenburg—Wurzburg—Eisenach—and then to another great historic city, Leipzig, where they were again side-tracked for a day and a night. The Kriegie train had now penetrated well over two hundred miles deeper into Germany and was approaching the end of its painful odyssey. Leipzig bore heavy scars of the aerial bombings, but nothing like Frankfurt.

After Leipzig, it was but a few hours' ride to an obscure, lonely little depot in a small town bearing the name of Grunau. The train had moved across an Elbe River bridge just minutes earlier, as it came finally to rest at Grunau station in the early evening.

The Elbe, Germany's most important river after the Rhine, threads its way through the country's heartland as it winds some seven hundred meandering miles from the forested mountains of Czechoslovakia to the great shipping port of Hamburg, where it empties into the North Sea.

The Kriegies had been hauled due east from the Belgian border some 350 miles to be deposited deep in the heartland of the European continent. The Czech border was only 60 miles away. It didn't occur to anyone that they were now situated much closer to the Russian Front than to the Western Front. The entire region for hundreds of miles around, including Berlin itself and the entire Elbe basin, was destined to be overrun by the Soviet Army, a fact which would have shocked and dismayed the disoriented Kriegies had they known it as they prepared to debark from the rickety old train.

The final destination was Stalag 12B, a prisoner-of-war camp located about two miles outside of Grunau in flat open countryside in the heart of the East German province of Saxony. This was to be "home" for this contingent of Kriegies for the next four months. They had spent ten or eleven days and nights inside those cattle cars; Hyams had lost count.

The Kriegies had been taken across Germany's two great rivers, the Rhine and the Elbe. Their chances of being liberated by the American Army were now somewhere between remote and nil.

And again it was *"Raus! Schnell! Fünf!"* as they dragged themselves out of the boxcars and lined up limply on a dirt road. They were stooped over like feeble old men. Standing up was an effort; walking, an even greater effort.

CHAPTER EIGHT

New Year's Eve

We've had the Cook's tour of Germany, and it all but did
us in. Finally we're back on terra firma. The ground felt
so good after that horrific train ride. Now we're old men
. . . shrunken, weak, beat; can hardly stand up. I think
some of the guys were ready to crack, mentally. The New
Year—it can't be much worse than the old one.

—December 31, 1944.

BACK in Times Square and all across America it was New Year's Eve. And so it was in London and Paris and all the other places in the Western world where people were free to enjoy and to act a little crazy if they felt like it. But in Grunau and in the Stalag there was neither gaiety nor laughter nor celebration.

Likewise, in the situation room of the U.S. War Department there was no cause for rejoicing this New Year's Eve. In the thirty-one days of December, the American casualties on the Western Front had come to a monstrous 75,000 killed, wounded, and missing. It had been a disastrous month, which could eclipse Ike's historic victories of the previous summer. The Führer, in one of the last convulsive actions of his ill-starred career, had certainly delivered a grievous thrashing to the American military.

As the Kriegie column of fives approached the Stalag, it was obvious that this was a high-security establishment, very structured. Nobody was playing games here. There were electrified barbed wire fences all about, and floodlights that turned the night into day. The guard towers, set at frequent intervals around the perimeter, were all manned by Schmeisser-wielding sentries, other guards patrolled with attack dogs at their sides. About what one might expect of a Jerry Stalag, or any other kind of Stalag, for that matter.

New Year's Eve began in the shower and delousing chambers. This was a most welcome and much-needed break for the filthy and foul-smelling Kriegies, who had given up hope of ever washing again. The shower room was of very generous proportions, equipped with fifty or sixty showerheads so that a whole company of troops could be showered and rinsed in a matter of minutes. The water was cold, but, incredibly, there was soap. The Kriegies showered while their clothing and even their boots were being disinfected. Hyams thought he had died and gone to heaven. Next, in rapid succession, came a perfunctory physical exam and a series of inoculations. All very standard and sensible hygienic routines. Someone at last was showing some concern for their health and welfare.

Then came the registration ritual, the issuance of a prisoner I.D. number and the picture-taking for the conventional mug shot. Orderlies would record a few vital statistics. The Kriegies were required to state their name, rank, Army serial number . . . and religion.

Hyams was now face to face with the question that had tormented him since that early conversation with Andreas on the road to Prum. However, it seemed under these circumstances to be an entirely innocent and routine question. The German PFC clerk seemed quite benign. He was nothing like the black-clad Angel of Death atop the Tiger tank before Gerolstein. But still Hyams had to hesitate for a moment on the religion question. Soon a searching glance was being directed at him. Then the answer came loud and clear, "Baptist!" Why not adopt the faith of Marvin Purdy, one of the finest men who ever put on a pair of shoes? Purdy, if he were there, would have been pleased. Hyams' answer was noted in the records by the German clerk without comment. That was it. There was no need to produce dogtags. The moment that Zeke had dreaded for so long now passed without incident.

It was like taking on a new identity. It felt good. He began to feel safe. He squared his shoulders. Andreas also would have approved of this.

Later, when Hyams remarked on the absence of chickenshit in the proceedings, Hornstein had an opinion. In a hoarse whisper that could be heard in the next building he confided, "Well, this is a *Wehrmacht* camp, ya know, run by the regular Army. There's no chickenshit here. This is legit! They play by the rules."

Hornstein was convinced. He was as proud of the place as if he were checking into a well-recommended hotel in the Catskills. He appreciated the efficiency and smooth operation of the place, and everyone was thrilled with the showers and the all-encompassing cleanliness of the place. It was almost worth the arduous boxcar trip to be received in such a well-run establishment.

There were no S.S. around. They were not involved in this operation. The prisoners who came through this camp were not intended for extermination. Their safety and survival was deemed to be in the Reich's general interest, so the S.S. left it to the Wehrmacht to look after. That was a break and a half.

On the question of religion, Hornstein had come up with a brilliant evasive answer. Despite his confidence that the Stalag was "legit," he was not going to tell the Germans that his grandfather had been a rabbi in Czarist Russia. He sidestepped, stating his religion as simply "American." The German clerk, only momentarily flustered, dutifully entered this in the record. He must have known that in pluralistic America there were countless variations in religions.

After the registration process it was feeding time. Nothing fancy, but it was sincerely appreciated. To the Kriegies it was sumptuous. A cup of watery turnip soup, a chunk of black bread and some Jerry "tea," which wasn't really tea. It looked like tea, however, and everybody called it tea. This was to be the standard Kriegie fare, issued once a day over the next few months. It also happened to be the first "hot" meal in over two weeks. How better to mark New Year's Eve?

Then it was off to the *"Quarantine Lager,"* a temporary holding compound where new arrivals spent about a week in isolation from the regular camp. The Jerries really understood how to run a prison camp. Typhoid epidemics they didn't need.

This Stalag had once been a training camp for about eight thousand Jerry troops. Now there were three times that number, over twenty-five thousand, of military prisoners of various nationalities confined in several separate compounds within the camp. It was not drastically unlike the average army camp in the U.S., except for the high-security prison setting and, of course, the lack of modern plumbing and electrical amenities. And the presence of the delousing facilities, something which Hyams could not recall seeing at any of the American bases where he had been posted.

It was like Hornstein said. "You're not really a prisoner of war until you arrive in the Stalag. Until then you're just a bum, a homeless, nameless nobody. You might as well be dead. Even the Red Cross can't help you. If you die, like those guys in Limburg, you wind up nameless in some mass grave. Nobody gives a hoot. You're just dirt!"

But now, within the ordered confines of Stalag 12B, the Kriegies had at last been registered on somebody's books. They had an official identity. They were part of a whole new—and organized—world. Like a brotherhood. They had status. Here, everyone—that is except the enemy, the guards—were all prisoners of war. Here, being a POW was normal and respectable. It was like joining the union. They were no longer the beggars of the road, the objects of pity or scorn, or sideshow freaks to be gawked at by enemy civilians.

CHAPTER NINE

Getting To Know The Brits

"Lager" is not necessarily "beer." It's also the Jerry word for "camp." Hence Quarantine Lager, and Stalag (Stammlager), etc. This is survivable . . . maybe. There's a British aura about the place. Lots of long-term Brit Kriegies. Interesting bunch.
—*Monday, January 8, 1945.*

THE week spent in the *Quarantine Lager* was a time for initiation into the Stalag way of life without being suddenly thrown into the tangled polyglot population of the main camp.

Here, as it would be every day in the camp, the 5:30 A.M. reveille was the opening and major scheduled event of the day. This was the morning head-count, or *"Zehl-Appel"* as the Jerries called it, conducted in the freezing yard, with all ranks standing at attention for the duration of the proceedings. It could go on for hours until every single prisoner was accounted for, including the sick and others absent for whatever reason. In the main camp, this involved a population of tens of thousands; in the *Quarantine Lager* a much smaller number, but it involved more absentees due to illness and general debility of the new arrivals. The Jerry Sergeant of the Guard knew that any slip-ups in the count could mean the Russian Front for him. So repetitive recounts were not unusual, despite the freezing temperatures of the early morning hours. So long as a Kriegie was alive and breathing on his own, he'd better be there where he could be counted.

Then it would be some hours before the once-daily food ration was brought into the barracks later in the day. This event would generally take place at around noon. The ration was always the same; soup (usually turnip), a slice of black bread, and Jerry tea. Sometimes, for variety, it might be rutabaga soup. Either turnip or rutabaga. The Kriegies would have to come up somehow with their own cups and utensils. The Germans had learned over the years that this one, rather scrimpy, daily meal was enough to keep the prisoners alive and ambulatory, unless and until they were to be brought down by illness, in which case they would let nature take its course. There was a clinic, but a severe shortage of medicinals. The average weight loss per man among the American Kriegies was fifteen to twenty pounds in the first three weeks of captivity.

Although the newly arrived Kriegies were meant to be temporarily isolated from the general camp population, every morning would see scores of camp denizens milling around outside the quarantine fence attempting to make contact with the bewildered new inmates. At first Hyams wondered what there might be about the newcomers to attract all this attention and why these visitors at the fence were mostly Russian POWs. This was the first time any of these Kriegies had seen any Russian military prisoners up close.

They were referred to as "Russkies" in the camp jargon. Many of them seemed just barely alive. While they must have been young men, of military age, and some of them might even have come out of elite Russian fighting units, they now appeared withered and emaciated; and moved about with great effort, like old men. They shuffled about in tattered rags, usually scrounging for food scraps or discarded cigarette butts. They constituted a pitiful underclass inside the main camp, where they survived by scavenging around the cook-house garbage dumps. Despite their general lowly status, there were a few stand-out exceptions, namely some more enterprising types who lived by their wits, usually by barter, at which they were quite adept. These individuals offered for sale all sorts of the most menial goods, such as old, toothless combs, battered spoons, worn-down toothbrushes, and fragments of mirror! All, no doubt, reclaimed from the personal effects of departed comrades, who were dying in the camp at the rate of ten to twenty per day.

To these more enterprising Russkies, what better trading partners now than the newly arrived rich Americans, who were surely laden down with U.S. currency, jewelry, and American cigarettes. This was the first contingent of G.I. Kriegies to be seen in this Stalag, and all the wheeler-dealers were there bright and early. But of course the white-caped Volks Grenadiers back in the Ardennes Forest had long ago relieved the Yanks of any significant tradeables such as watches, rings, and cigs, and especially money. The "wealthy Americans" were really not much better off than the shuffling Russkies. Hyams' stash of four cigarettes, which had earlier played such an important role in his long-term security plans, was now crushed and crumpled and thoroughly deloused. It might buy only a second-hand comb and toothbrush. But the Russkies were not interested in accepting damaged goods. They drove a very hard bargain. They knew this was a tough market, and they were the only game in town.

Not all the Russians, however, were operating at the same primitive level. There were, incredibly, some more affluent and higher-stakes operators who also showed up at the fence, as well as a few British prisoner-traders, who were interested strictly in currency and jewelry. No penny-ante stuff for these.

There was one Russkie in particular who stood apart from the rest, mainly because of the unlikely class of goods he was offering, but also because he presented a more dignified and substantial appearance than his compatriots. He could be loosely described as a sort of importer of fine merchandise. He had for sale, incredibly, an assortment of classy chocolates and bonbons, all fancy-wrapped individually, just as they must have come from some factory, presumably untouched by human hands—that is in the Stalag. The factory in question was in no less exotic a place than Vienna, Austria, according to the vendor's response to an inquiry. One could buy a single bonbon or a handful. One would have to pay in Anglo currency—dollars, British pounds, or American cigarettes. This was the last sort of commodity the Kriegies expected to be available here in Starvation Acres, and it added a brand new and heretofore unimagined mystique to the Stalag. The man became known to the Kriegies as the "Candy Man."

There was something very different about the Candy Man, aside from his exotic line of merchandise. For one thing, he was in good physical shape, had good color, and he was stocky—a very unusual condition in the Stalag. He was short and stocky with flaming red hair and whiskers, and his eyes were clear and friendly. There was a comic-opera look to him as he stood there wearing an oversized olive-drab greatcoat that came down to his ankles and was at least three sizes too large. The coat, of excellent quality, had obviously been owned at one time by a much taller and larger man; obviously acquired through a trade. He never said very much, but was always pleasant and alert as he stood there patiently holding his large cardboard box filled with these delectable edibles . . . like caramels, marzipans, and nougats and such. He didn't seem to ever make any sales, but he was never discouraged, showing up every morning and leaving after about half an hour.

Hyams would find out later that the Candy Man had a sort of permanent stand at the camp market square, the main trading bazaar, where he went after his morning stint at the quarantine fence. Nobody knew how he came by his very unique inventory, nor whom he would be selling these goodies to. Hyams would guess that only the Stalag commandant, or other top brass, could afford the fancy goods that the Candy Man was offering. It was the kind of stuff one would take home for the wife, or a mistress. But the ways of commerce are sometimes very mysterious, especially in a Stalag.

But most of the big dealers were interested in acquiring American wristwatches, usually offering about two hundred American cigarettes, a veritable king's ransom, for a seventeen-jewel Bulova or Longines or Witnauer Swiss-movement piece. Only jewelry-grade time-pieces were in demand; the cheaper off-brands could not be given away! It seemed there was no market for them at all, despite the fact that the Timex five- or seven-jewel watches were very sturdy, reliable, and even waterproof and shock-proof; and if a

Kriegie should happen miraculously to have a watch on him, it would likely be one of the popularly priced Timex variety.

There were other traders who hawked food items like whole loaves of German bread, or slices of bread, in exchange for cigarettes. The going rate was twenty cigarettes for a full two-kilo loaf. But there was nobody in Hyams' group who was in any position to entertain these tempting offers. And besides, if one were to pass a hypothetical packet of cigarettes through the steel mesh of the fence, what was the guarantee of delivery of the bread? This was strictly a "buyer beware" situation. There were no guarantees, express or implied. A Kriegie would have to maintain a healthy skepticism in these transactions. The American reputation for gullibility must have preceded the Kriegies in the *Quarantine Lager.*

But at least there was here some semblance of normal human activity: the interplay of ambition, scheming, chicanery, the lure of the marketplace, the promise of aggrandizement, of improving one's lot through crafty wheeling and dealing. Here the Kriegies would begin to sense the live beat of the Stalag, and there was a certain revival and exhilaration in all of this.

In sharp contrast to the Russkies, the British prisoners who approached the quarantine fences were as a group surprisingly fit and alert. They also seemed to possess up-to-the-minute detailed information from all the battle fronts. When they heard that the newly arrived Kriegies were captured in the St. Vith sector in Belgium, they briskly reported that St.Vith had indeed fallen to the Germans after a bloody siege, but that the enemy had been finally contained on the Western Front, the tide had turned and the Allies were pushing "him" back to his "original line of departure." The crisp military jargon bespoke an authoritative, up-to-the-minute, and professional, prisoner grapevine. Many of the Brits were indeed professional career soldiers. It was as if they were getting daily military briefings, or getting the *London Times* delivered every morning to their doorstep.

The British were really something else. Almost without exception, they had taken their imprisonment with great dignity and aplomb. For one thing, they never appeared in public out of uniform—a remarkable phenomenon in the eyes of the randomly attired G.I. Kriegies, who had long since abandoned any concept of a prescribed uniform. While the British uniforms might be threadbare and worn, they were invariably neat and clean, trouser creases always razor-sharp, boots polished, all buttons and unit insignia meticulously in place. The trouser creases were maintained through the hard years of confinement by folding them carefuly underneath the sleeping pads at night. This really worked for the Brits. The reputation of the British of dressing for dinner in the African bush or in the remotest corner of the Empire was not just a myth after all, if even here they could manage that crisp sartorial correctness.

The British Kriegies numbered about a third of the total prisoner population, perhaps eight thousand out of the total of twenty-five thousand in the camp; but for Hyams and many of his pals they would essentially provide the color and vibrancy of the entire Stalag experience.

Outnumbering the Brits and confined to a separate compound (although they seemed to have the freedom to roam about the entire camp) were the Russian prisoners, who numbered perhaps ten thousand. As was immediately evident to the Yank Kriegies, they were, for the most part, in deplorable condition. They were the resident beggars of the camp, generally ignored by the Brits and the others, except, of course, in the trading situations.

The American contingent, including all the December and January arrivals from the Western Front, would eventually come to about two thousand. The rest of the camp population came from almost every nationality under the sun, including some three thousand French, and hundreds of Dutch, Danes, Belgians, Poles, Italians, Czechs, and including even a score of Dutch Indonesian merchant seamen who had been picked up by a German U-boat after their ship was torpedoed on the high seas.

When the quarantine period expired, the Yanks were transferred into the main Anglo section. Here each barracks held a total of about five hundred men, of which three-quarters would be British and the rest American. Though their two nations were the closest of allies, for most of the Brits this was their first close contact with the American G.I. It was soon apparent that there would have to be a period of adjustment before the two groups could get to understand and accept each other as good neighbors.

There was at first a palpable frostiness and ill-concealed disdain towards the Yanks. This was the result of, among other things, the rankling G.I. "invasion" of the British homeland, which was used for years as a staging ground for millions of American servicemen assigned to the European war. The Brits were painfully aware of the Yanks' reputation for the inevitable and well-publicized "making out with the birds" back home. Many of those "birds" were the wives and sweethearts of the British Tommies who were away in various remote theaters of combat getting killed, wounded, or captured. These newly arrived sad sacks were the same Yanks who while stationed in Britain with their fat paychecks and nylon hose and all sorts of nifty inducements—up to and including promises of marriage—had been scoring so heavily back in Blighty with the British womenfolk. At the same time the Brits, particularly the long-termers, had been on the receiving end of the dreaded "Dear John" letters. All of them were worried sick about losing wives and sweethearts to the free-spending and free-wheeling Yanks who had found a cozy home in merry old England; nor did they want their sisters, nieces, or cousins getting involved with these over-paid and over-sexed saviours from overseas.

Furthermore, the generally unkempt and pathetic condition of the Yanks who now trouped into their scrubbed and orderly prison barracks was jarring to the tidy housekeeping ways of the British "hosts." Rightly or wrongly, the Yanks were tagged as overbearing, dissolute, poorly disciplined, irresponsible, and slovenly. Much of the resentment was exacerbated by the stark contrast between the reality of the Yanks' current circumstances and the exaggerated glamour and swashbuckling images that had been projected through rumour and rampant suspicion.

It would be weeks and months before the barriers of suspicion and prejudice came down, before the younger and more liberal-minded Brits would be forthcoming with signs of genuine friend-ship and advice to make the transition go easier for the newcom-ers. Some of the stiff-backed old-timers never did open up to the Americans.

And many of these Brits in Hyams' barracks were indeed larger than life. Some of these guys were the most illustrious military specimens of the British Army, genuine heroes, like the guys who had held the beaches in the final days at Dunkirk in June of 1940, to cover the withdrawal of the battered remnants of the British forces—the same remnants around which the British would ulti-mately re-build their entire ground forces. That was in June 1940, and now it was January 1945! For those "blokes" this was the fifth year of captivity; yet they sauntered about in the exercise yards, erect, shoulders squared, heads held high, brass buttons gleaming, moustaches meticulously trimmed. They were like something out of Central Casting on a Hollywood movie lot!

Then there were the "Desert Rats," the intrepid tankers of the British Eighth Army who, years earlier under the command of their revered Field Marshal Montgomery ("Monty" to his men) had outfought and out-foxed the Desert Fox himself, Field Mar-shal Ervin Rommel, and his Afrika Korps in the North African deserts. They had re-written history at such places as El Alamein, Tobruk, Sidi Baroni, and El Agheila—obscure, windswept, tse-tse fly infested desert outposts, for which valiant men laid down their lives so that A. Hitler and Company would never make it to the Suez Canal, that strategic jugular of the Middle East.

And then there were the "Red Devils," the brash young para-troopers of the ill-fated British First Airborne Division, who had carried that same Field Marshal Montgomery's colors into the Dutch town of Arnhem only four months earlier, in September 1944, in a historic surprise airdrop that was supposed to short cir-cuit the entire war, only to be trapped and slaughtered on the ground. This time Monty's magic hadn't worked. It had been a tragic and very costly blunder. Some of those survivors were now in Hyams' barracks, sulking in early retirement.

It was truly a Hollywood cast of characters. There were the somber six-footers of the King's Household Guard regiments, the Coldstream Guards, the Irish, Scots, and Welsh Guards, the men of all the legendary British regiments that had fought and bled in this war, as well as the blokes of the Indian Army and of the ANZAC (Australia and New Zealand Army Corps). Hyams was particularly grateful to the Brits of the Indian Army, whose misdirected Christmas goodies had been such a life-saving bonanza a few weeks earlier in the blood-drenched railway yard at Limburg.

And then there were the daring Canadian commandos who had tested the German coastal defenses at Dieppe on the French channel coast at a cost of 50 percent casualties in August 1942. That was two years before the combined Allied invasion of Normandy. These Canadians had shown, at great cost, that the landings had to be massive and overpowering, and that Dieppe was the wrong place to try it. The people in Hyams' barracks had paid their dues on every field of battle in the European Theater of Operations.

But it was the "old men" of the camp, the several hundred British troopers who had been at Dunkirk, who held the greatest fascination for Hyams, as he sought to glean something of their story. Back then in June of 1940 they had seen the battered remnants of a British Expeditionary Force evacuated in small boats under a curtain of fire, from their rapidly shrinking last toe-hold on Hitler's continent. They had paid very dearly in blood to buy those few precious days from the vindictive German Panzers.

And when their guns fell silent, when the battle was over, they had been the first Anglo troops to know the sick vengeance of the *Waffen S.S.* Over ninety men of the Second Battalion, Royal Norfolk Regiment, were marched by their German captors into a patch of woods at a spot called Le Paradis, near Dunkirk, France, and summarily executed by machine-gun fire. The *Waffen S.S.* had not changed or mellowed appreciably in later years, as they proved in the snows of Belgium four and a half years later. In December

1944, in the early days of the Ardennes campaign, when S.S. Panz-
ermen were flushed with their initial successes, some three hundred American prisoners, in separate incidents, were summarily
executed at their hands. So Hyams felt a common thread of experience and a great personal sense of gratitude toward these silent
and stalwart men.

Now all these "blokes" were here in this closed world, sealed
off and "preserved in formaldehyde" in this German prison camp
in the heart of Europe. They spoke with cockney accents, with
Scottish, Irish, and Welsh brogues; they came from every county in
the British Isles and from every corner of the Empire. And if one
had a discerning ear, one would quickly learn to pinpoint a
Northumberland man or one from Gloucestershire, or a bloke
from Surrey.

They were reticent, reserved, self-effacing men, each of whom
could write a fascinating chronicle about his war experiences.
Some would swap a story now and then with his fellows, but always
observant of the rigid protocol and the rules of seniority with
which the British military operates. A sergeant-major did not
buddy around with a lance-corporal, no more than a lance-corporal
would chum with a lowly private. There was an ingrained snobbery
between the non-commissioned grades in the British Army. It was
built into their system to a degree that was unknown in the American Army. And there was a fierce pride and discipline that had not
been diminished one iota by the years of their captivity.

The Germans had early on allowed the Brits a semblance of
self-rule, recognizing this internal hierarchy of the prisoner population. The Americans were to be integrated into this British system of "self-government" in the barracks and within the prison
compound. There was thus restored some semblance of military
order among the American prisoners, who, up to that point, had
been in a totally amorphous state without any real lines of internal
authority.

And now there was an entire lexicon of new terms which the
Americans would pick up from the British. "Blighty" of course was

Britain, the beloved homeland. "Fags" were cigarettes, preferably American. "Bloody" and "ruddy" were adjectives applied to any other words—most often, however, to the "Jerries." "Parade" was a drill or formation, and "Parade-Ground" was the prison yard. "Skilly" was Jerry soup; "Bakshis" was "seconds." "Mate" was buddy, and "blokes" were guys. "Revier" or "Lazarett" was the sick bay or clinic.

"Dixie" was a tin cup or any other container into which skilly or tea might be poured. "Griff" was the news report. "Lorry" was a truck. "Honey-bucket" was the horse-drawn pump wagon which came to syphon out the latrines. "Klim" was canned dried milk powder sometimes included in Red Cross parcels; it also was "Milk" spelled backwards. "Bully" was "awful good," or it could be the canned corned beef sometimes found in parcels from home. "Civvy street" was the civilian life, past or future, which everyone dreamed of returning to.

The variations and permutations were endless. "Gorblimey" meant "bless my soul," or something like that, and "muck up" was exactly the same as the corresponding four-letter word combination in Yankee talk. And, yes indeed, the British did have a sense of humor—only it was different. Hornstein didn't think they were funny at all, however—probably because they didn't talk or act like New Yorkers and didn't understand Catskill humor the first time around.

CHAPTER TEN

A Bit Of Blighty

Learning the ropes. A tiered society inside the barbed-wire fences. Journalism is alive and well. It's a break; tea and crumpets with the bloomin' editor . . . with a splash of Klim. Not too hard to take.

Tuesday, January 23, 1945.

THERE was something about the British military charisma that challenged and bedevilled the Germans. The British had long ago written the book on empire-building, where the Nazis were but stumbling novices. The British had achieved, through the centuries, with relative ease, that pinnacle of international power and prestige that the German Nazis now coveted for themselves. There was that lingering envy of the British aristocratic order, the legend-encrusted elite regiments, and the romantic battle histories immortalized in both fact and fiction. The British were perhaps the hoped-for junior partners in the Nazi millenium, the cousins with whom an eventual rapprochement and accommodation might be arranged after that proud island kingdom was conquered and Nazified.

Of all his long list of enemies, it was only the British whom Hitler privately acknowledged as having some style and "class" to impart to his Germans. Possibly the British attribute that most bedevilled the Nazis was the unshakeable British conviction that they were, if not always the best, then certainly unique in this world of men.

The British POWs in the camp were accorded a special status in relation to the other prisoner groups at this late stage of the war. They were left in relative peace and allowed all the military courtesies and the minimum amenities prescribed by international law, including a flow of supplementary food parcels from the International Red Cross, as well as a continuous supply of tea—real tea—from the home-folks. Tea had always sustained the British through good times and bad. In this relatively stabilized environment, the G.I. Kriegies would fall heir to some of the niceties and advantages which had been allowed their British counterparts.

Despite hardship conditions, the Brits had indeed managed to turn the few dismal acres of their compound into an enclave of British values and lifestyle, however reduced. This would be their own tight little island in a sea of misery and deprivation. To this end they would seek to exclude, or ignore, all external influences which they found inimitable to their culture and way of life. This meant that, for them, the Germans might as well not have been there. The Jerries were relegated to an insignificant role, to be tolerated and out-maneuvered at every turn. They also felt similarly about the Russians, who were nominal allies; the Russkies did not merit any efforts to reach out to them or establish any linkages. The Russians were the great enigma. One rarely spoke of them or thought about them. But they were always about in great numbers. They were the silent masses, the derelicts, the untouchables, the "unwashed beggars" of the Stalag.

To the British, who had been weaned in an imperial society, many of whom having served in the more congested and populous colonial territories of Asia and Africa where human life was cheap, the presence of these shadowy hordes must have been reminiscent of those indigenous native populations which were forever impoverished, subservient, and underfoot. The Russkies here were hardly seen as allies, but rather as the victims of a particularly harsh war only tenuously related to the main effort. Their presence was accepted with indifference and equanimity, serving to reinforce the sense of class and caste that was so deeply ingrained in the British imperial career soldier, which so many of these Brits were. There was the crown, the royal family, the aristocracy, and, way down the scale of humanity, the bloody native masses.

Hyams, being from Brooklyn where the divergent ethnics all considered themselves at the very least co-equal, was shocked to find a major segment of the Stalag population in such abysmal circumstances. He remembered the Russian section near his home in Brooklyn, with its quaint onion-domed church. These Russkies were somewhat reminiscent of the Slavic kids he went to high school with. Only here in the Stalag, except for the few entreprenurial types who mingled and dealt, they were all prematurely old and shriveled, and there was no way to really communicate with them.

And these were the "lucky" ones. They were among the last remnants of over six million Russian prisoners taken by the Germans since June 1941, when European Russia had become a free-fire zone for the Nazis. They had escaped the programmed annihilation by starvation, privation, and the mass executions by S.S. death squads. Yet even here, in the relatively benign environment of this "model" Stalag, there were daily funeral processions in which wagon-loads of dead Russians were carted out to a nearby cemetery for burial. There must have been a thousand or more buried out there in a special section of this village graveyard. There also were the graves of other Allied prisoners who had died in the Stalag.

For the Anglo prisoners, however, there was the International Red Cross with its bulging warehouses in Switzerland, only a few hundred rail miles away. From there came those little things intended to make life in confinement bearable—like playing cards and chess sets to while away the empty hours, books and magazines for the camp library, musical instruments, barber implements, and soap and shaving kits. Beyond that, there were the occasional food packets—three or four pounds of packaged foods, enough to give half a dozen Kriegies a taste of the good life. And, most appreciated of all, there was a mysteriously fluctuating ration of priceless American cigarettes. For it was the cigarettes which could, if collected and husbanded, turn a pauper into a prince inside the Stalag.

To survive in a German Stalag without the occasional largesse of the Red Cross would be virtually impossible. The Russkies were not included on the gift list of the International Red Cross, for whatever reason, having to do with international politics no doubt.

So, with the tea packets from home, and the occasional food parcels from the Red Cross, the Brits made the best of their prolonged confinement. Further, to engage the mind and the senses during these long months and years they created and carried on a rich and varied agenda of "cultural" activities. To the British, theater and the world of the Music Hall was what major-league baseball is to an American. Theater had always been their special art form, be it tragedy or comedy. Consequently there were, not one but two competing British theater groups, the "Empire" and the "Lyceum." Both were styled after the two authentic circuits back home that had, over the years, brought such rich diversion to the London boroughs and out to the farthest provinces. Each group had a wide repertoire of variety shows and dramatic, comic, and musical plays. The troupes would periodically visit the various barracks and perform such old favorites as *The Women, The Barretts of Wimpole Street,* . . . musicals like *College Rhythm.* There was even a Shakespearean troupe for more high-brow tastes.

Using the most basic materials to create the required illusions, costumes, and lighting effects, the productions were masterfully put together. As in Shakespeare's time, the women's roles were quite convincingly played by Kriegie-actors decked out in plumes and feathers, speaking their lines in high falsetto tones as they swished about the makeshift stages, to a good-natured chorus of whistles and cat-calls.

In addition there were serious concerts organized and performed by Kriegie musicians. There were groups that played modern music and jazz. There were variety routines featuring clowns, comedians, tap dancers, and jugglers. It all added up to the Kriegie version of the USO and NAFI shows that entertained the troops in the outside world, only without the glamorous movie queens and the big-name entertainers. The Kriegies themselves were the "stars" and had to create their own glitz and "glamour."

For Hyams and the G.I. Kriegies it was all a great new educational experience. They were spellbound by the animation and high spirits of the performers and the enthusiasm of the audiences, who invariably brought down the house. They were back in Blighty at some rollicking music hall, rather than sitting half frozen amidst a crowd of ragged POWs in a dismal and drafty prison barracks.

One could take in a concert, musical, or variety show at least once a week. In addition to these performances, there were lectures on a variety of subjects. Hyams attended one given by a sergeant who had been a police official in civvy street. He spoke on "The Experiences of a London Police Sergeant." Others lectured on "The Elements of Horsemanship" and "How to Win at Cricket." Whatever the subject, the lectures, just like other events, always drew good crowds.

As the days grew into weeks, the interaction between the G.I.s and their British "hosts" developed and blossomed into some real friendships. Hyams found one and then another Brit in his barracks with whom he could really communicate. Friends were important to Hyams. He had always been a "people person," as old Andreas had come to appreciate on that earlier occasion.

One of his new British buddies was a twenty-three-year-old Cockney paratrooper, Jock Witherspoon, who, despite his diminutive physique, was a sort of swaggering young bantam cock, fiercely proud of his service with the crack Red Devils, and of the British Army and all that it stood for. Because of their similarity in age and big-city outlook and orientation, the two were destined to become fast friends. Jock could just as easily have come from the Red Hook section of Brooklyn. In a twenty-three-year-old, cockiness is both normal and laudable—especially if the bloke is a genuine war hero—with guts and savvy—and the battle citations to prove it.

The other bloke . . . well you couldn't say that there was much similarity between Hyams and this one. But still there was something. It's not always obvious what there is about people that will draw them into friendship. This fellow was older, probably in his mid-thirties, but could easily pass for fifty. Percy Taggart was one of those long-termers. By now you could say a "professional" Kriegie. He had the military history and the deep emotional scars. He had been taken at Dunkirk. He was dour and bitter and pretty much turned off on the world. He didn't like Russians, he didn't much like Americans, and there was enough Irish in him that he didn't much care about the English. Life had not dealt kindly with Taggart.

While he was missing in the war, his wife and baby daughter had gone missing on him back in Blighty. Taggart never even got a "Dear John" letter out of it, just an excruciating silence for five years. Even the Red Cross couldn't help Taggart. He was just the opposite of Witherspoon. Of course he was more than ten years older than Witherspoon and had suffered much more pain in his life. All the cockiness had long ago been knocked out of him. But he was nobody's fool.

It was Taggart who, in a mellow moment one day, came up with a super idea for Hyams. He casually passed along a tip that the camp "newspaper" was looking for an American "reporter" to join its staff, now that there was such a substantial Yank representation in the Stalag. He thought that Hyams might be a suitable candidate for that "cushy" position. He mentioned the name of the "editor" and suggested that Hyams call on him. Hyams jumped at the idea. This sounded like it could be a real chance to turn this whole Stalag experience into something educational and constructive. And Hyams was, after all, no stranger to writing and journalism. He had been the current-events editor of his high school newspaper. He knew how to write a story lead . . . the who, what, when, and where of it.

Already feeling like a newspaperman on a hot story, Hyams presented himself the following morning at the "offices" of *New Times*. There actually was such an office adjoining the camp headquarters building, and there were a number of editorial people—British Kriegies—busily engaged in the same activity one would expect to find in any city room the world over. They were typing, gabbing, arguing—and occasionally sipping tea; a not entirely disagreeable way to be marking time inside a prison-camp in Eastern Europe in the dead of winter. It was all there except the frantic chain-smoking and butt-laden ashtrays. And, sure enough, there was an editor overseeing the entire operation. The editor was a British gunnery sergeant who long ago, in civvy street, had been a reporter for a city newspaper. He considered himself a professional, and he was. Like all editors, he was very busy and harassed. But he did agree to talk to Hyams and, yes, there had been some interest in taking on an American cub reporter to broaden the editorial horizons.

Since Hyams had some high school journalistic experience and was, in any case, the only applicant for the position, it was a foregone conclusion that he was their man. He was accepted on the spot. Since it was a non-paying, strictly volunteer enterprise, there was no need to check his references. Sergeant Hensley was impressed with the applicant's authentic Brooklyn idiom, and besides, any American who could pass muster with Corporal Taggart had to have a way with people, a quality essential for any good reporter.

And so Hyams embarked on yet another new phase of his prisonerhood, as a working and tea-sipping member of the Fourth Estate.

The newspaper, of course, was not really a newspaper as the Western world knows newspapers. It was a wall newspaper as seen in the old newsreels about village life in China. It was put together on large sheets of paper and posted on a wall in a conspicuous location within the camp. It was all there, column by column, and complete with screaming hand-lettered headlines. And of course, the news was not real news. Inside Hitler's Germany, in or out of the Stalag, there was no way anyone could get by with printing real news. The content was more like that of a weekly magazine filled with innocuous and non-controversial stories of an entertaining or lightly informative nature. And of course it enjoyed a "captive" readership.

As in all mass publications, crime stories, authentic or fictional, were great copy. There was a popular weekly series of famous murder cases handled by Scotland Yard over the years. There were sports articles on rugby and cricket and the like, and all manner of human interest stories, animal stories, and some science stuff.

Hyams was first assigned to assist the science editor, who was involved in a series of articles on the advances of medical science since the nineteenth century. He was to write 300 words on the discovery of Penicillin. The camp library, with its several hundred volumes acquired through the kind auspices of the International Red Cross and the YMCA, was invaluable for research. Hyams found that the new wonder drug—which had truly revolutionized the practice of medicine in this war, not to mention its peace-time applications such as the curing of clap—had been discovered by a British scientist, where else but at the University of London.

Next came a story assignment on hypnotism and its applications in para-psychology and so on.

Seeing his work product in print and his name on the masthead as "junior staff reporter" catapulted Hyams onto a new plateau, both in self-esteem and in the general pecking order of the camp. He was no longer just one of the faceless masses. He was feeling good about himself, and being invited to take tea with the best of them. Taggart was impressed, as was Witherspoon. Hornstein never said much about it, but he must have been somewhat impressed.

As a member of the working press, Hyams got to circulate among some of the truly "exotic" characters who were floating about the camp. He got to interview the old Candy Man. The dialogue was conducted at first in pidgin German, and finally in Yiddish. The guy was Czech—and Jewish, of course. His name was Tibor. Tibor Weisskopf. He had a great story, but it was all strictly off the record. He could write a book. He had seen the insides of more ghettoes, labor camps, prison camps, and Stalags, both Russian and German, than anyone. He had been caught up in combat on various Eastern European warfronts, serving one side and then the other!

It began when Tibor was dragooned, early in the war, into the Nazi labor battalions in his native Slovakia when that country had been transformed into a Nazi-occupied satellite. While digging trenches and ditches for the German Army, Tibor was captured by the Russians, who were too busy at that time to concern themselves with his true identity and his true sympathies and loyalty. So he was incarcerated as a POW in a Russian camp. That, he said, was very rough, even for him. That led him to volunteer to serve in the Russian forces as the only way to get out alive from the Russian internment camp. Then, most recently, Tibor had been captured by the Jerries while serving in combat with a Soviet paratroop brigade. As far as his German captors knew he was just another Soviet paratrooper. He told his story to Hyams, but it was all extremely confidential. Hyams was impressed with Weisskopf's ability to establish himself so comfortably in the camp. He was the quintessential survivor. To Weisskopf, Stalag 12B was nothing less than an Anglo country club. He knew that it was the Anglo presence that did it. And more than anything, he wanted someday to see America. But first he would have to go back to Nazi-occupied Slovakia to search for his wife and babies. He was very pessimistic about that; he had few illusions about that.

Hyams and Weisskopf became good friends. Despite disparities of age, culture, background, and experience, they really had much in common, and they understood each other.

The life of a newspaperman was fascinating, and educational as hell. Hyams would look forward to mid-morning tea at the "office," and the challenge of the varied daily assignments. Days passed into weeks, and weeks into months. Life took on a normalcy of sorts, but it was not boring. He was no longer just the kid from Brooklyn, but was becoming a seasoned cub reporter and observer of the human condition under conditions of extreme stress.

CHAPTER ELEVEN

"We Bring You The Griff"

Just realized that it's spring. It's been a cold, hard winter.
Lots of funerals. At least the Jerries give the deceased
(even the Russians) a decent burial. And now winter has
given way to spring. With spring comes new hope. The
news from all the fronts is very encouraging. The Jerries
are being rolled back on the Western Front . . . and on
the Russian Front. Good news everywhere. Flash . . .
Limburg, bloody Limburg, was taken by our troops the
other day. They reported that the Stalag, the one that
was too full to accept us, was a hell hole . . . G.I. Kriegies
were walking skeletons, many sick and many dead. I
wonder what ever happened to Purdy.

Tuesday, March 27, 1945.

PROBABLY the most meaningful special benefit the Brits enjoyed was the privilege of free movement within the entire camp—not that anyone would want to venture too far afield, as, for example, into the Russkie compound. But this freedom included the right to move between barracks and made possible the free flow of news and information. Every prison environment is rife with rumor and submerged grapevine networks. But here, incredibly, the news came daily, in great depth, authoritatively, at an appointed hour, and it was straight from the BBC in London.

New Times was not the only, and hardly the most significant, journalistic enterprise at the camp. There was this remarkably smooth functioning news reporting operation that was going full tilt and being studiously ignored by the Jerries, and this one was reporting "hard" news at a very professional journalistic level. An inside group of British prisoners maintained a powerful secret radio receiver, which got all the BBC broadcasts from Britain. It was a clandestine operation protected by a tight Kriegie security screen. Its code name was "Operation Griff." There were the signal operators, writers, and ad hoc analysts who transcribed and organized the reports together with commentary for full dissemination to all the Anglo barracks. These were visited faithfully every morning by one of the sizeable crew of roving "newscasters." After posting look-outs to warn of the approach of any stray German guards, the readers, usually middle-grade British noncoms, would mount a makeshift podium and proceed to read off, in business-like but unhurried fashion, amazingly detailed summaries of up-to-the-minute griff, as received within the hour via the BBC.

The underlying rationale of the entire operation was that every Anglo Kriegie had a god-given right to be informed daily of all the straight news of the war. This was the world-wide news, including the Far East and the Japanese war in the Pacific. All the war news available to the newspaper-reading and radio-listening public in Britain and the U.S. was instantly known and disseminated inside the Anglo barracks in Stalag 12B. Of course the Kriegies were mainly concerned with the war that was swirling about them in Central Europe. These daily griff reports described all the relevant military events of the prior day, the good news and the bad, the advances and the setbacks of all the Allied forces on both the Western and the Eastern Fronts. Precise locations of all major actions were given so that the Kriegies could plot the progress on every front, on the ground, at sea, and in the air, day by day.

And so it came to pass that the new American Kriegies had learned in mid-January, within days after they were integrated into the main camp, that the U.S. First and Third Armies, after having absorbed the full impact of the Hitler strike in the Ardennes, had now shifted gears, retaken the offensive, and were beginning to reclaim lost ground. Late in January came reports that German-held St. Vith was under strong American attack. However it was not until February 4 that the Germans were finally driven from St. Vith, several days after Schoenberg had been retaken by the Yanks. Hyams and Hornstein remembered well that once-quaint village nestled in those dark, brooding, and blood-soaked hills. Memories were still fresh as they heard in mid-February that Prum, that once shining city on the hill where there was supposed to have been rest, food, and water for a column of bone-weary prisoners, had finally got its comeuppance. It had fallen to Patton's Third Army. And on March 1 there was the mention of Gerolstein, another way station on the Kriegies' rocky road into Germany, now taken by the Americans.

Then in March came word of the stupendous break at the Ludendorff Bridge at Remagen, Germany. A Jerry screw-up let this most strategic bridge across the Rhine River fall intact into American hands. Hitler's last line of defense in the West had been irreversibly compromised. Hyams remembered from way back that rivers and bridges were what war was all about. Even little rivers and flimsy pontoon bridges. But a major bridge across the Rhine! That was the beginning of the end for Jerry. The news report said that Hitler was holding the elderly Field Marshal Gerd von Rundstedt personally responsible for this fiasco. Poor Rundstedt, the last of the old lions, who had been repeatedly called back out of retirement whenever Hitler experienced a new panic attack. Now Hitler didn't trust him anymore, and he was to be permanently replaced as Commander-In-Chief of the crumbling Western Front.

And then, in the days following, there was fierce fighting at Koblenz, another well-remembered way station on that endless trainride. That city fell to the advancing Yanks on March 17. Later in the month it would be Frankfurt falling to the Yanks, and then the other sadly remembered places like Limburg, which was indelibly etched in every American Kriegie's soul, and then Aschaffenburg. Hyams was reliving his life. It all had a bittersweet taste. Victory was sweet; the memories were bitter.

All this time the BBC was also reporting on the surging Soviet advances across Eastern Europe, but those places, of course, somehow didn't evoke the same poignancy or immediacy in the Yanks, although a look at the map would show the Red Army tentacles groping inexorably closer to Grunau and Stalag 12B. And all during this time the air war on both fronts was being brought home to Germany with a vengeance. In mid-February the reports told about the destruction of Dresden in forty-eight hours of horrific bombing. Dresden was less than forty miles from the Stalag. The bombers had streamed overhead in great flotillas. Later, casualty estimates in the stricken city ran to an incredible 70,000 dead and untold thousands of wounded. Storybook Dresden, the focal point of East European culture and history, would never be the same.

In early April the big news was about the Ruhr, Germany's last great industrial trump card. Essen and the mighty Krupp armaments works were knocked out of the war. The synthetic oil works outside of Essen were destroyed, and with them the German secret of producing motor fuels out of cheap brown coal. Field Marshal Walter Model, the Führer's favorite and the man entrusted the previous December with command of the German armies in the Ardennes breakout, would now choose suicide over surrender. Arnhem, the Dutch city that was the northern gateway to the Ruhr, and where Jock Witherspoon's airborne comrades had paid such a heavy price some seven months earlier, fell to the Allies on April 15.

On the 19th of April, the U.S. First Army took Leipzig, which had been the last stop on the Kriegies' extended rail trip before the Elbe and Grunau. And on April 21, Russian tank columns entered the flattened suburbs of Berlin, where the Führer was hiding some 40 feet underground in an impregnable bunker, and where he still maintained that the final victory would be his.

While *New Times* continued to produce the human interest and non-controversial stuff on its wall editions, "Operation Griff," with its roving newscasters, was delivering the hard news. Curiously, the Germans themselves also went through the motions of furnishing the Anglo prisoners "access to current war information." Perhaps to compete with the illicit news network, the Germans would distribute in each barracks, three or four times weekly, the latest issues of the national Nazi newspaper, *Volkischer Beobachter* (National Observer). Since the publication was in the German language and used the German *Fraktur* typeface, it was essentially indecipherable to most of its in-camp "readership." The entire gesture seemed pointless, probably the brainchild of some Nazi bureaucrat in the Ministry of Propaganda, but it was another element in the special status accorded the British prisoners in the eyes of their Jerry captors. It did, however, keep the Kriegies supplied with quantities of newsprint, which they put to various utilitarian uses—paper being one of those commodities which modern man has become desperately dependent upon in his daily life. This was, after all, their only source of toilet paper.

Hyams, with his rudimentary knowledge of German, would attempt to decipher the major front-page stories in the *Beobachter*. He found it to be, just as everyone knew it to be, the perfect prototype of a propaganda sheet, produced for the sole purpose of glorifying the Nazi apparatus and the German military. Incredibly, there was no hint anywhere of the obvious deterioration of the entire German position. Everything was always upbeat, and final victory was just around the corner. At a time when their armies were in desperate retreat on all fronts, the German homefront reader was told, for example, that their "valiant forces had that day delivered a shattering blow" to the invading Allies at point A, throwing the "aggressors" back with horrendous casualties; two days later the front would have receded some miles to point B, deeper inside German territory, where the "forces of the Fatherland were stepping up their heroic and successful assaults against the reeling enemy forces!"

"To drive the enemy back" really meant that the Germans themselves had been compelled to withdraw. "To inflict massive losses on the invaders" meant that they themselves had taken heavy casualties. "To advance" meant to fall back. "To prevail" meant to suffer defeat. This was the deliberate gross obfuscation and falsification perpetrated by the editors of the *Volkischer Beobachter* against their faithful and believing readers.

While all news in wartime is necessarily managed and politicized, the stark contrast between the British style of reporting the news both good and bad versus the Nazi method of glaring reverse double-talk underscored for Hyams the horror of the Nazi mentality and its mission in this war. This was not only a war waged for land and populations, but for the total imposition of thought control on their own people and all of the conquered peoples of Europe. The rulers of Germany had established a Kingdom of Darkness in their own land and everywhere else in Europe where their influence was dominant.

It was remarkable proof of the power of a controlled media that the overwhelming majority of the German people continued to believe the wildly optimistic news reports of the *Volkischer Beobachter* and the German radio right up to the moment when American or Russian tanks would appear on their streets—even after their cities and towns had been laid waste, their armies decimated, and profligate sacrifice had been made of millions of their young men on far-flung battlefields.

By contrast, the British passion for "full coverage" inside the prison-camp was not satiated merely by the excellent reporting of the itinerant morning news crews. Every Anglo barracks was favored periodically, usually about weekly, with a lecture in depth on all the major strategic factors involved in the approaching denouement of the war. There was one commentator in particular, a thirty-year-old British corporal who was brilliantly articulate and a keen analyst and strategic thinker, who had become an authentic camp celebrity and would make regular weekly rounds for unhurried hour-long discussions of the latest worldwide developments. His expositions included a rigorous question-and-answer follow-up segment.

The Anglo-American Kriegies, isolated here in the heart of Hitler's Reich in the late winter and early spring of 1945, were being currently and minutely informed on the progress of the war and having animated discussions about every important development, to a degree unknown and unimaginable to any citizen of the Führer's brave new world.

CHAPTER TWELVE

The Passing Of A President

*A bolt of tragic news, the death of President Roosevelt.
The fickle finger of fate. A stunning counter-point . . .
ironic, fateful, tragic . . . affecting everyone. Even the
Jerries are stunned.*

Friday, April 13th, 1945.

THE time that Hyams and his fellow Kriegies from the Schnee
Eifel had spent at Stalag 12B would see the European war reach a
wild crescendo with Hitler's Reich crumbling in ruins, as competing Anglo-American and Soviet armies slugged their separate ways
across the entire breadth of the Fatherland.

The Kriegies were sheltered and insulated from the desperate
struggle being waged in scores of cities and hundreds of towns and
villages, and on the roads and open spaces all across Germany, in
ever-closer proximity to their sealed-off Stalag. It was akin to
having free seats down front on the 50-yard line at a hard-fought
professional football match; only, of course, this was a deadly game
involving world history, vast armies, and countless human lives.

To catch a small glimpse of the real war on those clear mornings during February and March, the Kriegies would only have to
gaze upward into the German skies and follow the vapor trails of
massed flights of American B-17 bombers cruising majestically towards targets deep in the German hinterland. The air fleets were
virtually unchallenged by the *Luftwaffe* at this stage of the war.
Some mornings they would count as many as 300 or 400 of the
four-engine bombers crossing overhead at altitudes of five or six

miles, seemingly impervious to the occasional white puffs of anti-aircraft fire reaching out to them.

The news kept getting better day by day. The daily briefings by the British newscasters during early April were truly exhilarating. Everything was finally coming together both literally and figuratively. Four powerful American armies, the First, the Third, the Seventh, and the Ninth, were closing in on central Germany. The British and Canadians were likewise making a clean sweep through Holland and Northern Germany, destroying the German naval bases on the North Sea coast and taking out the last remaining capital ships of the doomed German Fleet. On the Eastern Front, the Russians were equally successful everywhere. Daily the Anglo-Americans and the Russians were uncovering new cess-pits of depravity and horror as the concentration camps were overrun, and the hideous toll of the Nazi vendetta against humanity was exposed to the world.

But overriding the stench of death was the sweet smell of victory. To the Anglo-American Kriegies, every day in early April 1945 was a veritable holiday, full of hopeful tidings—a bright new dawn dispelling the night of fitful bad dreams.

Nevertheless, despite this steady flow of military successes, there was a gnawing concern among the more seasoned Allied prisoners. The Jerries had been known to undertake the last-minute evacuation of Stalags and concentration camps to thwart their liberation by advancing Allied armies. The move would be to some enclaves of last-ditch Nazi resistance deep inside Czechoslovakia, in a safe mountainous bastion where the last fanatics would make their last stand. This evacuation routine had earlier befallen several other Kriegie camps in Eastern Germany and Poland which were directly in the path of liberating forces. The results were always disastrous for the prisoners. Every Kriegie knew what it meant to be in enemy hands and herded like cattle on the open roads, without adequate food, shelter, clothing, or footgear, especially during the hard winter months. And then there was that other most-dreaded of all prospects, an S.S. takeover of the camp, which could raise hideous new facts of life. It would not be out of character for the S.S. to take all the Anglo prisoners as hostages to bolster their bargaining position before the final curtain came down on them.

Despite these forebodings, the Kriegies would look forward eagerly every morning to the uplifting visit of the news couriers. But on the morning of Friday, April 13, the British "reporters" were uncharacteristically subdued and solemn as they made their morning rounds. On this morning the news was dominated by a dramatic and momentous human loss that would reverberate across all national boundaries and among all civilized peoples.

In Hyams' barracks, the reader, visibly unnerved and choked with emotion, announced that the American President, Franklin Delano Roosevelt, had died suddenly and unexpectedly of a cerebral stroke at his vacation cottage in Warm Springs, Georgia. The sixty-three-year-old leader, revered by all the peoples of the free world, had been elected five months earlier to an unprecedented fourth consecutive term in the White House. He had served a total of almost twelve and a half years in the presidency, and had guided his nation successfuly through a series of shocks and trials, both in war and in peace, only to be struck down at the very hour of greatest triumph.

As a hush descended on the assembled Kriegies, the reporter went on to express the condolences of the British prisoners to their American comrades whose great leader had truly fallen a victim of the war, a military casualty as much as the men who had laid down their lives in frontline combat.

The Yanks were stunned and confused by this lightning bolt of tragic news at a time when everything was going so well. The British prisoners took it equally hard, as if it had been someone out of their own pantheon of national heroes. They remembered only too well that it had been the staunch and unswerving commitment of the American President to their cause that had seen their nation through the critical early years in 1940 and 1941 when they had stood alone against a seemingly invincible Nazi tide. They, even more than the young American G.I.s, realized how close the Western world had come to total disaster, and how much the fallen American President had contributed to the now-impending defeat of Hitler and his satanic new order. The Brits understood the significance of the partnership that had been forged between Britain and America during the war years by the two charismatic leaders, Roosevelt and their Prime Minister, Winston Churchill. On that day in Parliament, Churchill took the unprecedented step of moving for adjournment in tribute to the fallen President—a heretofore unheard-of honor for a foreign head of state. Churchill and the British had, for all intents and purposes, achieved their victory in battle; but they had lost a dependable partner, benefactor, and good friend, whose absence would be sorely felt.

The Brits at Stalag 12B could not let this momentous loss fade into history without some tangible show of their deep feelings. With their flawless instinct for parade and pageantry, a full-dress memorial parade was held in the Stalag yard at 1000 hours on Saturday morning, April 14, to honor the memory of the fallen President.

To the wide-eyed wonderment of the thousands of G.I. Kriegies watching on the sidelines, the Brits turned out *en masse,* in seemingly perfect dress uniform, ranks impeccably aligned, the sharp commands ringing out crisp and clear as some eight thousand strong, including Guardsmen, Desert Rats, Red Devils, and a full complement representing almost every regiment in the roster of the British Empire, formed up and for the next hour put on an unforgettable display of precision marching and trooping of the colors in their final salute to a fallen leader.

In addition to the Americans, scores of German guards and thousands of Russians and others stood by in reverent awe as the Brits went through their paces to the dirges of bag-pipes and drums under the baton of a fiercely mustachioed Sergeant-Major out of His Majesty's Coldstream Guards. The Sergeant-Major, tall and ram-rod straight, exercised the same taut control of his troops there in the Stalag courtyard as if they were passing in review for His Majesty, the King, at Buckingham Palace.

This was a picture of unblemished military *esprit* that would be imprinted forever on all those present. Hornstein stood aghast. He was impressed. He wished for a camera. He wanted to record this once-in-a-lifetime spectacular. He felt a personal tie to F.D.R., who had been governor of New York State when he, Hornstein, always a faithful Democrat, had been a junior-grade state employee in Albany, the state capital.

The British made their point. They paid this deeply felt tribute to an American leader to whom they owed a great deal. Without Roosevelt, the fate of Britain might have been entirely different than it was on that day, April 14, 1945. The Brits did nothing more than show their appreciation—in a very classy way.

Later in the day Hyams learned, in a bull session with some Brit staffers at the *New Times* office, that exactly eighty years earlier, almost to the very day, another American President had met death, also at the very moment of victory in a tragic and all-consuming war. Abraham Lincoln was shot at Ford's Theater in Washington on the night of April 14, 1865. Now precisely, four score years after that day of tragedy, the world was sadly marking the passing of Franklin Delano Roosevelt, at a time, just as at Lincoln's death, when a special wisdom and understanding were desperately needed in the aftermath of war.

Hyams thought it ironic that he should learn of this weird historical coincidence in American history from a British Kriegie.

There was another incident related to the passing of the President, which again involved an expression of grief and concern and a gesture of condolence from a rather unexpected source. Meeting up with his old friend, the Candy Man, at the market square shortly after the memorial parade, Hyams was surprised to find the man genuinely stricken by the tragic news, as if he had lost a close relative. He was actually in tears.

"Your President was the great hope of the world, Mr. Zeke. It is a very cruel blow at this time. What will happen now? I am afraid it will set things back. The Nazis will take new heart. What do you think, Mr. Zeke?"

Hyams could offer Weisskopf scant encouragement. As he turned away in silence, the Candy Man pressed a small package of goodies upon him. "Please accept this small token of appreciation, Mr. Zeke, for your friendship which has meant so much to me. We all need strength to survive. Friendship gives one that strength."

The Candy Man had class. The exquisite almondy richness of the marzipan confections did indeed help to momentarily lift Hyams' spirits. Weisskopf seemed to have an endless supply of these outrageously delicious goods.

The BBC kept the Kriegies informed of the continuing world-wide bereavement over the untimely loss of this beloved leader who had been perceived, not only in the free world but universally among the subjugated and oppressed in Hitler's world, as a beacon of hope and redemption. Everywhere around the globe, in cities and in remote villages, on every continent, men and women were in shock. The refrain was always the same: "We have lost a good friend!"

Even among many of the Jerry guards there was a noticeable feeling of shock and compassion. Within their secret hearts, many seemed to share in this loss of a world leader to whom all persons of goodwill could look with respect and admiration in this time of world-wide turmoil and uncertainty.

The BBC went on to report the curious fact that the American government had even received a message of "profound sympathy" from the Imperial Japanese government, with whom American forces were locked in a desperate and bloody conflict across the great expanse of Asia and the Pacific. And in Moscow and else-where in the Soviet Union, all flags were at half-mast and many Russian citizens were seen weeping in the streets.

And in America, all across the country there was a hushed in-terlude as the seventeen-car Presidential train, filled with domestic and foreign dignitaries escorting the President's coffin, slowly wended its way from the capital to Roosevelt's ancestral estate at Hyde Park in New York State, where he had been born and where he was interred on Sunday, April 15.

In what was to be one of its final issues, *New Times* put out a memorial edition to the President on the Tuesday following his death. Hyams was a contributor to this edition, having been able to find considerable material in the Stalag library dealing with the early political career of the President and the "New Deal." Roosevelt had been a charismatic leader and innovator from the first days of his presidency. He was a "class act." Hyams had never voted in a presidential election, having been under-age in 1940, and too busy with the war in November, 1944 to have thought about presidential politics; but he came from a solidly Democratic family, and Roosevelt was his man.

CHAPTER THIRTEEN

A Night To Remember

The Russkie "Nutcracker Suite" with Jerry caught in the
middle. They didn't stick around for the final curtain.
This is very heavy. Words fail to describe the exquisite
joy of freedom. It's a rebirth, a new lease on life.
Sunday, April 22, 1945.

IN THE week following the death of the President, the sadness and sense of loss was gradually allayed by the continuing flood of good news from the various battlefronts as many of the last holdout German cities fell to the Allied steamrollers. Forward elements of both the American First and Third Armies were racing headlong toward the Elbe, retracing the very route taken by that rickety old Kriegie train that had carried Hyams and his buddies on that long slow ride from the West into Central Germany.

U.S. First Army, however, after taking Leipzig, less than fifty miles from the Stalag, seemed to be taking a breather, and their patrols penetrated no further than the Mulde River, still about forty miles to the west of the Stalag. The news reports made no mention of them moving closer to the Elbe River line. This was puzzling, particularly since they had a virtually clear field. So there was U.S. First Army, Hyams' old outfit, slowing down only a couple of days' march from the Stalag. Probably waiting for orders.

But the Russians, on the other hand, just kept coming from the East. Their armored spearheads were fighting in the suburbs of Berlin, while in the center of the Russian Front, in close proximity to Stalag 12B, the legions of Marshal Ivan Konev were surging steadily forward. In mid-April there remained only about eighty miles of relatively flat, open country between Konev's troops and Stalag 12B, with no major waterways or other natural barriers to impede them east of the Elbe. They were moving forward on this front at a rate of about fifteen miles per day, encircling and capturing thousands of German troops.

Russian reconnaissance and tactical aircraft were overflying the camp with increasing regularity. By the 21st of April, one week after the death of President Roosevelt, the griff had it that the Soviets were within ten miles of Stalag 12B. The Kriegies realized that their own situation would soon be resolved one way or another. It was now a realistic probability that the camp would indeed be taken by the Soviets rather than by the American forces. With each passing day the fear of being evacuated and taken out on the road again by the Germans to some unknown "safe" destination began to recede, for the enemy was rapidly running out of options and maneuver space.

On Sunday morning, April 22, there was a new electricity in the air. The tension of waiting and wondering would soon be over. Liberation, that shining and elusive dream, was now finally to become a reality. Sweet visions of what life had once been like, long ago . . . home . . . the longed-for reunions with wives . . . babies . . . sweethearts . . . kinfolk . . . white bread . . . apple pie . . . that favorite deli in Brooklyn . . . Sunday concerts in Prospect Park . . . the music of Kay Kyser and Glenn Miller . . . the Grand Ole Opry in downtown Nashville . . . the all-but-forgotten and delicious tidbits of normal life . . . everything that had been put on hold. All now re-emerged in suddenly re-awakened psyches.

The rumors that morning were that Russian patrols were now only a few miles from the camp, and at the rate they were coming, it should only be a matter of hours before they'd be poking through the East Gate.

Still, there were the skeptics. They pointed to the German guards who seemed very calm and unperturbed, going about their normal duties including the hours-long *Zehl-Appel* that morning. Was this because the Jerries got all their news from controlled media like the *Volkischer Beobachter?* Or was it because they knew something the Kriegies didn't? Something didn't seem to add up. The Jerries were apparently not preparing to mount any sort of defense of the camp, to offer any serious resistance to the on-rushing Soviets; nor were there any signs of preparation for evacuation. So what would happen? Would the camp be subjected to a Russian attack against the Jerry guard troops? This, of course, would not be so good for the prisoners. Or was all this BBC griff just so much over-inflated hyperbole based on wishful thinking? The Kriegies spent hours in agitated discussion and analysis of various theories of what the coming hours might bring.

The real optimists advanced the sweet possibility that the Americans might still get there first, should the Russians be stalled or slowed up for any reason. This was much preferable, but it became less likely with every passing hour.

The "news analysts" had reported that the Elbe-Mulde dividing line had been formally agreed upon by the top Allied commanders as the common limit for both the American and Soviet advances. Only a few days earlier the Soviet High Command had notified General Eisenhower that, in keeping with this understanding, the Russians would clear the entire east bank of the Elbe River from Prague in the south to Berlin in the north. And Stalag 12B was definitely on the east bank of the Elbe. So it was up to the Russians to take the camp. Indeed, by April 23 the Russians had completed the encirclement of Berlin, and everywhere else along their broad front the German resistance was melting away. It was apparent that the Russians would not be stopped before reaching the Elbe.

So strong and steady was the Russian momentum that the Anglo-American forces advancing from the west now became concerned with a possible full-speed head-on collision between these hard-driving friendly juggernauts, both engaged in highly fluid pursuits of a vanishing enemy on an ever-shrinking battleground. It was definitely a new and uncharted maneuver, this massive joinder of Allied forces, armies that were in language, custom, and style totally disparate, with rather few open channels of field liaison to prevent mistakes or mishaps. The common-sensible advice that went out to the Anglo-American forward commanders was "For God's sake, treat them very nicely!" This was no time for any untoward incidents.

In sharp contrast to the Anglo-American levels of excitement, the Russian prisoners, like the Jerry guards, appeared totally passive and unimpressed by anything that might be happening beyond their immediate horizons. If the Russians were indeed stirred by the prospects of imminent liberation, there was precious little outward evidence of it. The Russkies had no doubt been so dulled by their experience in captivity that few were capable of registering enthusiasm for anything. But there must have been some who were biding their time, anticipating the impending role reversals with the new opportunities for vengeance and reprisals. There were doubtless many scores to be settled with their erstwhile captors.

In the Russo-German War there had been an intense buildup of high emotion akin to religious fervor on both sides. The German objectives in the invasion of the Soviet Union had not been limited to military and political considerations. They had sought quite openly to maximize the human toll on the enemy, to eliminate huge numbers of indigenous populations and to alter dramatically and permanently the demographic and economic status quo in Russia.

In the massive surprise attack against Russia in June 1941, all the consuming ethnic hatreds and passions of a Nazi-galvanized Germany had burst forth in an orgy of destruction against an historic adversary who was at the time thought of as genetically inferior, backward, and irretrievably corrupted by Bolshevism. Those broad Russian steppes, in German hands, could furnish limitless quantities of grain and oil; and ensure Germany's world supremacy for a thousand years or more.

Was it envy? Greed? Frustration? Paranoia? All of these and more combined to power the German lunge through the heart of Russia and up to the gates of Moscow, Leningrad, and Stalingrad.

And indeed the human toll was maximized in Russia. Historians would agree on over twenty million people killed in the less than four years of that titanic struggle. Some estimates would run as high as thirty million combined military and civilian deaths.

Correspondingly, the treatment of captured enemy personnel by both sides reflected the ruthless nature of the war on the Eastern Front. Masses of Russian POWs were systematically liquidated, particularly in the early stages of the conflict. Prisoners were denied access to any international relief sources. Even in the later stages, little effort was made to ensure or encourage survival of captured enemy personnel.

The Nazi Manifesto had ordained a "holy war" against an entire spectrum of "inferior races and groups" of Eastern Europe. So these Russkie prisoners in Stalag 12B were not really supposed to be there. There were theories that these Russkies might have been selected as the "token" prisoners, as window-dressing to demonstrate that the Jerries did in fact keep Russian prisoners alive. Nobody knew for sure. But the Russkies knew.

As this Sunday wore on, there was the continuous thunder of heavy fire from the east, and the Jerry guards were at last visibly activated as they began to scamper about on urgent last-minute chores like scrounging up civilian clothes and stocking up survival supplies. Soon the German field uniform would become a severe liability, almost as dangerous for its owners as a Jewish dogtag had once been for the Kriegies. They were obviously preparing for a hurried departure while trying to maintain a brave façade.

Hyams was again reminded of that familiar ditty, "What a difference a day makes." He knew well what a difference a day could make in one's fortune and in one's life.

The universal Jerry preference was to somehow reach the American lines and to surrender there. Old Andreas had had that same dream some four months earlier. But the Americans were still a good distance away to the west, and on the far side of the Elbe. Getting across the Elbe would be a problem. And the Russians, like avenging angels, were closing in fast.

At curfew time the camp streets were deserted as all inmates returned to the shelter of their barracks for this night of high drama and wild anticipation. The artillery fire was now laced with the staccato cough of small arms and drawing ever closer to the camp. With any luck at all this would be the Kriegies' last night as prisoners.

Orders had been in effect for some time among the Anglo-American Kriegies to remain in place and not to make waves if and when the Russians should enter the camp. Similarly in the event that the Germans should withdraw and leave the Stalag open and unguarded, normal routines were to be maintained. The Kriegies were to remain inside the camp. There was to be no thought of free-lancing about in the no-man's land, which would surely be a free-fire zone.

In Hyams' barracks, the Brits were poring over hand-drawn maps of the local countryside. They were remarkably knowledge-able about the surrounding towns and villages, the terrain features, and the local road network. Hyams marveled at the British intelli-gence-gathering capability while cooped up in a hermetically sealed Stalag. Witherspoon was drawing and re-drawing the ap-proaching battle lines. He could have been a bloody Field Marshal; just like Monty, his hero. But it was all very simple, really. The Germans were trapped between the river and the approaching Russian tide, and all the fight had gone out of them. All they could realistically do was run—run and hide.

The newsflash that everyone had been awaiting with bated breath hit the Stalag at precisely 10:26 p.m. The Jerries had aban-doned the camp lock, stock, and barrel, and were on the run, head-ing toward the Elbe. The camp was open. There were no guards, nobody manning the guard towers, no guard dogs, and both the west and east gates were symbolically swung wide open. Twenty-five thousand inmates were suddenly free. They were free men— free at last!

The news took a few minutes to sink in. There was only a hushed, prayerful silence during those first minutes. Some Kriegies never moved, or said anything for a half hour or more. This was a time to be alone with one's thoughts, and prayers of relief and thanksgiving. And there were tears. Strong men sobbed or wept in silence. They wept for the war, for fallen comrades, for the lost years of their lives. They wept from the pent-up pain. They wept with happiness and relief. And even later there were no sudden outbreaks of wild cheering. The jubilation, when it came, was muted and turned inward.

Hyams looked about him. He had to capture the reactions of these men for that book that he was going to write. This was the climax, the magic moment that changed everything for everyone inside that Stalag. He looked at Taggart, the five-year man who had spent a big chunk of his life in foreign captivity, cut off from everything that meant life and love to him. Taggart just sat there, dry-eyed and numb. It would not be easy to pick up the threads of his shattered life. He probably wouldn't know where to begin. But now he could at least make a try at it. Somewhere out there was a little girl, almost five years old, who was the daughter he had never seen or held in his arms. What would she look like? Could she accept him as a father? How would he find her?

Everyone was immersed in their own private thoughts. There were fleeting remembrances of those who hadn't made it to this magic moment. This was not a time for talking.

To fully appreciate the blessedness of freedom, to savor its true joys, one must be denied freedom for some interval of time, and then to have that precious gift restored. So was it with the men of Stalag 12B on that night of April 22, 1945. The exquisite pleasure of freedom regained was almost worth the entire cost of months or years of imprisonment.

When Taggart finally spoke, it was in an uncharacteristically superficial vein. He addressed himself to Hyams and Hornstein. "Well you two, it won't be long before you see your beloved old New York again. Say, is Brooklyn a part of New York? I never could get that straight."

Taggart didn't pursue it. He wasn't good at small talk, and that was enough small talk to last him for a while. He lapsed back into silence as Witherspoon was reporting on the Russkie prisoners. It seemed that those lifeless zombies had come back to life. In the short interval since the Jerries had absconded, the Russkies had somehow armed themselves with guns and knives and had taken off after them. The war was not quite over for them.

The lights burned late in the Stalag barracks that night. Everyone was on a high. It was a night to remember . . . like New Year's Eve, but without the champagne, or beer, or music, or singing, or anything else for that matter. And nobody was singing "Auld Lang Syne." But it was one hell of a milestone, and life had definitely taken a major turn for the better.

CHAPTER FOURTEEN

The Cossack Ponies

What a day! What a glorious day! The first day of freedom!
Wow! The Russians put in their appearance. That was
something to see. Everyone is on cloud nine. And we got
our first ration of Russian skilly . . . quite an improvement
. . . topped off with fistfuls of strong Jerry stogies. That
really got to Hornstein. These are exciting times.
                                    Monday, April 23, 1945.

THE first morning of freedom. It was very early morning. Everything felt different. The world was different, the air fresher and
sharper, the skies clearer. The barracks looked different. They
weren't all that shabby and depressing. They were like, well . . .
they were still the same old barracks, but you might say they suddenly looked more like regular army barracks than prison barracks.

Everyone had slept the sleep of free men, and now they were
refreshed and exhilarated. Free men—in an open Stalag—and not
a Jerry in sight! The world was beautiful once again.

At the usual appointed time for the morning headcount, at precisely 0530 hours, the prison yards were filled with milling crowds
of Kriegies, despite that there would be no *Zehl-Appel* that morning. But it was the place to be, to be together with one's buddies, to
exchange bits of the latest griff, and to savour the moment. The
Jerry sergeant and his platoon of headcounters had passed into history. It was as if they had never been. Free men don't have to do
things like line up at 0530 hours on cold winter mornings for a two-
hour headcount. But old habits die slowly.

The senior British non-coms stepped into the power vacuum. Order and military discipline were to be preserved. The Kriegies were not all that free. They were still in the military, and now once again, technically on active duty. Germans or no Germans, command and control was still a part of life. Anarchy would not be tolerated. The approaching Russians must see a disciplined body of troops, lean and mean. And somebody would have to feed the 25,000 lean and mean inhabitants of this former Stalag, now that the Germans had abdicated that responsibility. And of course free men expect more food than prisoners do. No starvation rations for them!

Hornstein echoed everyone's sentiments: "Freedom; it's wonderful. Now all we need is a decent breakfast to go with it!" That word "breakfast" had a beautiful, nostalgic ring to it. The Kriegies could hardly remember ever having a good, hearty breakfast—or any breakfast for that matter. That was another one of those things that were not thought about, or spoken of, like sex; all the old familiar pleasures of life had been put on hold for the duration.

The British non-coms stepped naturally and easily into the shoes of authority, as the rich baritone voice of the British Sergeant-Major carried across the compound, and the Kriegies formed up in ranks.

"Stand easy, men!—This is a very special time for all of us. As you know, Jerry has departed for parts unknown. Good riddance, I would say. But you must bear in mind that this camp and the surrounding area are still enemy territory. Anything can still happen. We are not home free! I'm sure you all understand. We have reason to believe that the camp will be occupied by Soviet forces at any moment. In that event, we will be relying on the Soviet Army for security and logistic support."

He cleared his throat and paused for a full minute or two. This was a new situation for him, but his poise and control never failed him.

"Needless to say, these people will be accorded full military courtesy and our full cooperation. This must be clearly understood.

We greet them as the valiant allies that they are. That is really all for now, except that it may be some time before things get properly sorted out. Your barracks commanders will keep you posted of all developments. And, oh yes, there will be a reveille parade at 0530 hours tomorrow morning as usual, and every morning thereafter! You will all be there! Thank you all, and good luck! . . . Batta-a-al-lions dis-s-missed!"

Hyams noted that the formation was crisply concluded in about ten minutes, a far cry from the interminable morning routines conducted by the Jerry oligarchs.

The ranks had hardly broken when a tremendous chorus of yelling and wild applause erupted from the direction of the camp's main street. That could only mean that the Soviets had indeed arrived in the camp.

Kriegies converged toward the narrow dirt street in a mad rush from all directions. This was the pay-off, a historic, never-to-be-forgotten high point in life. This would be a sight to remember and cherish. These were the same blokes who had fought the Nazis to a standstill in their own country and had then turned around and rolled them all the way back to where they were now, deep in the heart of the Fatherland. There would surely be a display of military might and firepower to strike terror in the heart of any Jerry who might still be inclined to resist.

However it was nothing like that at all. There were just four solitary Russkie horsemen riding casually in a strung-out single file, in a slow and steady canter, along the entire length of the Stalag street. The riders and their mounts showed deep fatigue. They were dust-covered, bedraggled, and almost spiritless. And that was all there was. Not a jeep or any other kind of motorized vehicle in this understated cavalcade. This was no victory march. There were no greetings to the assembled throng, no waving, no flags, no conquering hero stuff. Unsmiling and unperturbed, they studiously ignored the wildly cheering Kriegies, never slowing down or acknowledging in any way the tempestuous ovation and adulation that was being showered on them by the thousands of ex-prisoners who lined their route. They seemed bored and embarrassed by the whole thing.

Evoking the story-book imagery of the Russian Cossacks of old, the horsemen were clothed in the traditional fur-lined, ear-flapped military headgear and heavily padded cold-weather garb. Rifles, machine pistols and ammo bandoliers hung across their backs. Their mounts were small Mongolian ponies, not very impressive in appearance, but renowned through history for endurance and toughness—probably ridden by the cavalry of Genghis Khan. The entire picture was more like something out of an earlier century in the frigid wastelands of Czarist Siberia than an advancing military unit in the heart of Central Europe in the spring of 1945.

These were forward scouts, proceeding some distance in front of the main units. Spurring their ponies along, they just kept going, and within a few short minutes they had disappeared through the West Gate. This was probably not the first German prison camp they had opened up; and probably when you've seen one you've seen them all. For them the war was not yet over. There were pockets of Jerry resistance yet to be scouted and liquidated this side of the River Elbe.

As usual, Hornstein was the first to articulate his reaction. For him it was a real let-down. "Is that it? Four broken-down Cossacks riding pathetic little ponies? Not even a jeep or a motorbike? This is a modern army? These guys are like back in the middle ages! How the hell are they supposed to be winning this war?"

And then Hornstein had another gripe. "Godamn, you never have a camera when you really need one. Nobody is going to believe this back home. It's really true, one picture is worth a thousand words. How the hell could anyone describe what we just seen?"

Witherspoon was surprisingly well informed about these diminutive Siberian horses. "Those buggers are perfect for the Russkie winters. They don't freeze up like a tank in forty below zero. They're not so dumb, them bloody Russkies."

Hyams was taking it all in, jotting down notes and impressions in his little notebook. He was also trying to find some deeper meaning to all of it. What was the message? Then he had a flash-back . . . to that night on the road from Prum to Gerolstein, that road that was clogged with German Tiger tanks, where poor Hassan had been compelled to plead for his life. There had to be some message. Was it that super-tanks and super-jocks don't always win in the end? That was probably the message; but he would have to ponder that sometime.

In the crowd stood Taggart. He had seen the four horsemen. He had nothing to say, or practically nothing. He just kept mumbling under his breath, "Bloody Russkies!"

The morning passed and the excitement subsided. Soon there were no Russian liberators. No Jerries. No breakfast. And finally, no mid-day soup. It was a small price to pay for freedom, but a painful one.

Then in late afternoon a sizeable convoy of Russian vehicles finally rolled into the camp. These were administrative troops, including medical personnel, cooks, and other people who could take over the management of the camp. They were strictly business. They moved into the headquarters compound and began immediately to get things organized, for which the newly liberated Kriegies were duly thankful.

Official notices, printed in English and several other languages, were posted about the Stalag. They bore **"GREETINGS"** from the Russian Army, roughly as follows:

To Our Valiant Comrades In This Historic Struggle!
YOU ARE NOW FREE!

THE SOVIET ARMY IS HONORED TO HAVE JOINED IN YOUR LIBERATION FROM THE FASCIST WARMONGERS, AND WILL CONTINUE ITS TIRELESS EFFORTS TO CRUSH THE REMAINING ENEMY WHEREVER HE IS TO BE FOUND. YOU ARE FREE TO REMAIN IN THE CAMP UNDER THE JURISDICTION AND CONTROL OF YOUR SENIOR OFFICERS. SHOULD YOU LEAVE THE CAMP FOR ANY REASON, BEAR IN MIND THAT ACTIVE HOSTILITIES CONTINUE EVERYWHERE IN THE REGION AND THAT NO ONE CAN THEREFORE GUARANTEE YOUR SAFETY OUTSIDE CAMP.

TAKE NOTICE THAT ANY PERSONNEL TEMPORARILY
OUTSIDE THE CAMP REMAIN SUBJECT TO THE LAWS AND
AUTHORITY OF THE SOVIET OCCUPATION KOMMANDATUR.
SIGNED: COL. IVAN KOGASHENKO, COMMANDER,
"G" CAVALRY BRIGADE
ARMY OF THE USSR

The Russians were settling in. They were obviously pleased to have effected the liberation of some ten thousand Anglo-Americans as well as thousands of others, including their own people. This Stalag was a major prize. The administrative troops were bright and cordial, many of them capable of conversing in broken English. There was a goodly number of female personnel among them, including military police and medical people, even doctors. They did not encourage any congeniality with individual Kriegies, but preferred to handle all communications through channels with the senior British non-coms.

Later in the day the Russians indulged in a real touch of class. They distributed from one of their "Studebaker" lorries (all American-made vehicles delivered under the lend-lease program were, for some unknown reason, universally referred to as "Studebakers" by the Russians) fistfuls of German cigars to mobs of appreciative Kriegies. Come one, come all! Starving Kriegies were soon running around with pockets full of big black cigars! A few were brave enough to light up. This was undeniably a once-in-a-lifetime auspicious occasion, even on an empty stomach. There was an endless supply of the stogies, "liberated" from a local German military storehouse.

All this made a great impression on everyone, especially Hornstein, who in former times was never seen without a cigar clenched firmly in his teeth. That was of course long before the Battle of the Ardennes. Hornstein proclaimed himself an aficionado and judge of fine tobacco, and he said that these were damn good cigars, but, like all cigars, they were not meant to be smoked on an empty stomach.

The Russians must have had the same thought. Supply wagons

started rolling in as they reopened the soup kitchens. They considerably enriched the Jerry recipes, even including some heretofore unheard-of quantities of fresh meat. The Kriegies were duly appreciative. In the short space of twenty-four hours, life had taken on a totally new aspect in the Stalag. "What a difference a day can make!"

That night was a time to kick back, relax and take stock. In Hyams' barracks there was a non-stop bull session going on beneath dense clouds of acrid cigar smoke. Ignoring the coughing and cursing by the non-smokers, Hyams and others were enjoying the distinctive aroma and charisma of these freebie stogies. Cigars bespeak substance, achievement, contentment . . . feeling good about oneself. There is just something about a good cigar. Hornstein, squelching the complainers, quoted that famous caveat, "Never trust a man who turns down a good cigar!" He credited Mark Twain with that one.

Witherspoon, while steadfastly declining to light up a cigar, was nevertheless in great spirits. Mark Twain didn't mean anything to him. "I'm learning to tolerate these Russkies. You know there was a goodly amount of meat and potatoes in that skilly tonight."

"My dear Jock, I want to thank you, before I forget, for your generous donation of cigars to the Hornstein reserve. And just to make one other point, Jock: that was not just common, ordinary meat in the skilly tonite. That was, my dear chap, genuine filet of Siberian Pony, a truly rare delicacy, I'll have you know."

"Whatever you say, Maury. And you're more than welcome to those bloody cigars, mate."

Hornstein was in his glory as he puffed away on a big cigar and expounded to a captive audience on the finer points of gastronomy. He soon led into a description of his favorite restaurant in New York. "Last night—my first night, you might say, of freedom—I dreamed about one of those two-inch-thick filet mignons smothered in mushrooms, with a side of potatoes au gratin, like they bring you at Schulman's Roumanian on Delancey Street."

"Please spare us the details, Maury. But, you know, if I ever get to New York I think I would like to try that place!"

"Jock, if you ever get to New York, it's a promise. I will throw a party at Schulman's—with booze, broads, the works . . . the likes of which you'll never forget! And that goes for old Taggart, too."

Hyams perked up. "How about me, Maury? Does that go for me too?"

"Sure, kid. I'll show you how the other half lives. You know I wasn't always a foot-slogger in the crummy infantry. I was quite the man about Manhattan, you know. Plenty of money and broads, them Broadway dolls. I've got a few stories to tell."

"And I love listening to you tell 'em, Maury. But what about now? When do you think we're gonna get the hell out of here?" queried Witherspoon.

"Ah, there you got me, kid. We are now sailing on, what you call, uncharted seas. When we get the hell out of here is anybody's guess. But real soon, I hope!"

"Damn right." Taggart now bestirred himself as he took a few drags on his newly lit cigar. "I don't trust these Russians. No bloody way! I don't trust them at all. We're not free until we're back with our own forces. No sir! This bloody war can still take some unpredictable turns. Mark my words."

As if on cue, a short stocky figure in Russian garb, appearing from nowhere, was seen hesitantly making his way toward the group. He was looking for Hyams, who immediately recognized the Candy Man and jumped up to greet him. "Hi Tibor, old buddy, how are you? I was hoping I'd get to see you. Isn't this a great day?" And then sensing the man's unease, "What's wrong?"

"Dear friend, Mr. Zeke, I have come to bid you farewell. This is a very sad day for me. I could not leave tonight without paying my respects to you, and wishing you a safe return to your family and loved ones."

Hyams was perplexed. "You're leaving? When?"

"Tonight. In a few minutes. All the Soviet prisoners are being evacuated tonight. Who knows where? Maybe to fight, I don't know. Many of course are too weak and need medical care. I myself am fine, but we all must go."

"But maybe now you will get home soon," Hyams offered.

"Home? Where is home for me? Dear friend, I have no home. There is no home for me. This was my home. This miserable Stalag, where at least I could escape from the truth, from my losses, from my pain."

Witherspoon was annoyed by the man's intrusion and his dampening effect on what had been an upbeat conversation. Russkies had never been welcome in the Anglo barracks. It was just understood. "Cheer up, mate. The war's over for you. You'll be home soon with your fellow Russkies and all this will fade away like a bloody nightmare."

Tibor looked at Witherspoon, shook his head in silence and smiled weakly as if to ask how one like Witherspoon could fathom his grief. He then turned back to Hyams, and Hyams saw the tears in his eyes.

"Three innocent babies—my oldest boy was five when I last saw him—my beautiful young wife, my parents, and brothers and sisters; my wife's parents and her sisters. . . . They are all gone. I know exactly what happened in the Polish camps—to the women and children and the old people. I have no hopes, no illusions."

"But Tibor, you are assuming the worst. You can't believe everything you hear. There are all sorts of stories, I know, but people survive. You will see. You will find your family alive and well."

Tibor Weisskopf swallowed hard. He knew the truth. "Thank you my friend. I will always remember you. You are a fine man." He shook hands with Hyams and then offered his hand in turn to Witherspoon, Hornstein, and Taggart, all of whom after a split second's hesitation took his hand. He then turned sadly away and walked stiffly out of the barracks.

"Cripes, isn't he the Jew-boy who stood in the market square every morning, rain or shine, hawking his ruddy chocolates and bon-bons?" Witherspoon inquired.

"Yup, he's the one."

"Is he a Russkie? What is he anyhow, Russian or what?" Witherspoon wanted to know.

The explanation of course was somewhat complicated — too complicated. And Witherspoon didn't really care. But Hyams tried to capsulize Tibor's story, the little bit he knew of it, even though Tibor had never wanted any "publicity." But that wouldn't matter now.

"Is he Russian? Well, yes and no. He was captured by the Jerries while serving in the Russian Army. I guess that made him Russian. But he was actually a Slovakian Jew who had volunteered in the Russian Army after escaping from a Nazi labor camp on the Russian Front. If you can follow that. And that's not the whole story, but that's roughly the way it was, if I remember correctly."

"And oh yes, Jock, old bean, he was a paratrooper, believe it or not. Maybe short on glamour, but long on moxie. A sergeant in an airborne brigade with the Czech Legion. It was a volunteer outfit that the Russians put together of Czechoslovak guys who wanted to fight the Germans. Tibor got captured by the Jerries on a jump into his native Slovakia. That's how he wound up here in a Russian uniform. I thought it was a hell of a story. Of course he didn't want any of it spread about. He said that I was the only one he had confided the story to."

There was a period of silence as they considered the elements of Tibor's tortuous odyssey. The man's visit had introduced a sour note in the otherwise rosy tone of the evening. And nobody was willing to give the man credit for the ability to survive against the odds. Hornstein was put out. "How the hell does he know he won't find his wife and kids? That's an awful assumption to make." He took a long, pensive draw on his cigar. "Hyams, you sure know some weird people."

Hyams rose to defend his "Russian" friend. "Well, I don't know, Maury. He didn't ever impress me as a lunatic or a big dummy. A pretty shrewd guy, I would say. But let's hope he is crazy, and his wife and kids are waiting at home for him. I sure hope so."

It was time to douse the cigars. It had been a big day. The Kriegies would soon be ready for bed. Tomorrow would be another big day.

CHAPTER FIFTEEN

Life Among The Russians

Excursions in the countryside . . . chicken dinners . . .
civilians, some not so friendly . . . all you can eat . . . my
kingdom for a bromo. A whole new wide-open world . . .
I hitched a ride in a "Studebaker." Crazy drivers.

Tuesday, April 24, 1945.

AFTER THE RUSSIAN TAKEOVER and the removal of their own people, there remained in the Stalag upwards of ten thousand Anglo-American and Allied Kriegies who had been too long confined under sub-minimal conditions. Now feeling free and unrestrained, they were ready to check out the wide world on the other side of the fences.

Just beyond the double fences and the watchtowers there were broad expanses of greening countryside, seemingly untouched by war, with lush vistas of quiet abundance stretching in every direction—a delight to the senses and a tonic to the spirits. A scant quarter mile from the Stalag there were peaceful farmyards overflowing with cackling hens and crowing roosters, fat long-necked geese, waddling quacking ducks, and everywhere fresh eggs and incredible bounties of fresh dairy products of every description. The barns were filled with prize cattle, hog pens replete with sows and suckling pigs, and in the cellars were bins loaded with every imaginable variety of pickled and preserved meats, fruits, jams, sauces, and vegetables, plus flour and all the ingredients for baking bread, biscuits, puddings, and whatever gastronomical delights one might have conjured up during those long lean months of semi-starvation.

The valley of the Elbe in this spring of 1945 was literally overflowing with all the blessings of the good life. There was no evidence in this rich and abundant farm country of wartime privation or a reduced standard of living, despite the shattering military defeat that was being visited at that moment upon the armies and the government of the Third Reich. Inside the farm houses there was also ample evidence to confirm that until recently Germany had in fact been the undisputed master of all of Europe. There were to be found generous stashes of such fancy goods as French perfumes and French wines, Polish vodka, Danish hams and cheeses, and a wide variety of other delicacies from every corner of the European continent. There were also displayed on the cupboards and mantlepieces of every home numerous photographs of husbands and sons in uniform in happier days. Some were posing in front of the Eifel Tower in Paris or on a boulevard in Warsaw, or cavorting with buddies at sidewalk cafes in any number of European capitals overrun by the German war machine, or others waving proudly from in front of fortified bunkers on the French channel coast. Quite a few wore the uniform of the S.S. Many photographs were enshrined as mementoes of fallen heroes.

A goodly number of these homesteads now stood empty and abandoned, their owners having fled from the feared reign of terror that the Russians would presumably impose on the occupied German territories. In many cases the absences appeared permanent, the prospect of Bolshevik retribution being just too much to accept. Some families, on the other hand, opted to remain at home and take their chances, hoping that sons and husbands returning from the war could more easily rejoin them if they stayed put.

The Russian occupiers naturally had the first call on the best accommodations. The more substantial houses were taken over, as a matter of course, for various Russian headquarters and as housing for their officers. Other vacant homes, those by-passed by the Russians, were soon occupied by roving Kriegie bands who would take up temporary residence. The Kriegies, professional survivors all, might stay for a day, or a few days, and then move on to greener pastures. While in their diminished physical state they were not quite up to such serious infractions as forcing themselves upon defenseless *Hausfraus,* they were nonetheless interested in scouting out all the lesser possibilities, starting out with perhaps the appropriation of a few succulent head of poultry and all the appurtenent trimmings for a decent home-cooked dinner. They all understood that the good life must begin with an ample supply of good wholesome food.

The farms and homes nearest the Stalag were the first to be denuded of livestock and provisions. After a few days of freedom, one might have to go several miles to find a henhouse or a barn still undiscovered by the roving Kriegies.

The Russians tolerated this low-grade anarchy during the early days, until such time as their regular occupation troops replaced the combat units and instituted a formal set of rules and regulations which safeguarded to some extent the rights of the civilian population against the depredations of the newly-liberated hordes.

Kriegies who had survived for so long on a semi-starvation diet were now virtually killing themselves with orgies of gluttony followed by the inevitable aftermath of illness and miseries. Shrunken stomachs were not able to cope with unlimited quantities of rich food. But many of the Kriegies felt that this was not a bad way to go, to die with a full stomach. The quest for more food began anew each morning. Hyams himself had always been a moderate eater. How many chicken dinners should one eat in a day?

The Russian occupiers generally took a very benevolent view toward all these Kriegie shenanigans, particularly where the Yanks were involved. Most often they would just look the other way. They understood living off the countryside. They themselves were past masters at it. It seemed that nothing was too good for an *Amerikanetz,* who could do no wrong in their eyes. They never interfered with moderate looting of foodstuffs, so long as no intemperate physical force was perpetrated by a Kriegie against the owner's person or property.

However, on more than one occasion Hyams saw one or more burly Russian troopers kick in a bolted door or steel shutters while a group of G.I. Kriegies stood by impatiently waiting to enter the premises in their never-ending quest for food. The Russians would then step back and turn their attention elsewhere.

The Russian appetites ran to other things, such as their insatiable thirst for hard liquor, always blamed on their forty-below winters. Their capacity was monumental. Anything went—Vodka, Kümmel, Brandy, Cognac, Schnapps, Slivovitz—and the higher the proof the better. Every German household could be counted on to contain some domestic reserve stock, and whenever a liquor cache was uncovered it belonged to the Russians without question or dissent. Their "water" canteens were for carrying distilled spirits or nothing at all. The idea that canteens might be intended for carrying water was inconceivable to them.

And they were constantly offering grandiose toasts . . . to the final defeat of Fascism . . . to peace . . . to the newly created United Nations (that organization was being convened for the first time that very week in San Francisco) . . . to the memory of the departed American President . . . to the United States of America . . . and so on—and on. The pattern was thus set for a natural and amicable division of the spoils, for to the starry-eyed Kriegies, the two all-consuming passions were the freedom to come and go and the freedom to feed. Alcohol of any kind, in any quantity, was not one of their priorities at a time when their minds and bodies craved food and nothing else.

And then, of course, women.

While women per se held little interest for the Kriegies so recently delivered from starvation and its attendant lassitude, the Russians, on the other hand, found the German women of all ages irresistible. The Russians had never imposed upon themselves any sort of bans against "fraternizing" with civilian populations in newly occupied territories. The buxom *Fraus* and *Fräuleins,* so blonde and blue-eyed and so defenseless and frightened, were just so much "red meat" for the lusty Russkies.

Much of this "fraternizing" was carried out under duress, sometimes even at the point of a gun, as must happen in all wars when a victorious army finds itself on the loose inside the enemy's home turf. To the victor belong the spoils. That's what war is all about. As Hyams had once so aptly put it, when he was a young PFC being carried to the front, "Ass is what war is all about." The Russians strongly concurred in this old axiom of war.

While there were plenty of Russian women serving in the Red Army and even in the same combat units with the men, those women soldiers didn't look like they were there for "messing around." They were strictly business and they weren't defenseless and frightened, two conditions which can excite the basest instincts in a man who is under the corrupting influence of vodka, slivovitz, or schnapps, or all of the above.

Hyams, the news-hawk, was out there in the lush springtime countryside taking all this down in his little notebook. He knew that he was in the middle of a big and fast-breaking story. This was a new breed of Russians, totally unlike the lethargic and uncommunicative Russkie prisoners he had observed in the camp. Hyams had picked up a few words of basic Russian during the Stalag months and so could engage in a few stinted dialogues with some individuals among the occupying troops, many of whom were likewise picking up scraps of English. He marveled at their aptitude for new languages, and their almost universal fluency in German, which facilitated full communication with the locals.

All the Russians, almost to a man, reflected respect and admiration tantamount almost to a child-like affection for the Americans. Down to the lowliest private, the Russians showed unstinting gratitude and appreciation for the mountains of American supplies and equipment that had been pumped through perilous Arctic sealanes to keep their armies going during the worst years of the war. And mention of the word "Studebaker" never failed to produce a rush of back-slapping and hand-pumping. The Russians really appreciated all those "Studebakers" which America had provided.

Great numbers of Russian women soldiers were seen in all the frontline combat units, as well as in the various support roles traditionally assigned to women troops, such as chauffeurs, clerks, nurses, and even military police directing traffic. They were tough and they were strictly business, receiving no special consideration. They pulled their weight and then some. The horse-drawn supply carts, which brought up the rear of the marching columns of infantry, would usually carry one or more disabled individuals suffering from blistered feet, hangovers, or other transitory conditions; what might be referred to as the "walking wounded" in G.I. parlance. But these were always of the male gender; Hyams never saw a woman-soldier getting this kind of a free ride.

The Russian women were sturdy peasant types for the most part, of rather square configuration, broad of beam and shoulder. They handled their weapons with ease and confidence, and were obviously well experienced in their use. Their one concession to feminity was that they wore skirts instead of breeches. Judging from their stern demeanor, Hyams doubted that they were concerned with any such female gimcracks as make-up kits, fragrances, colognes, or any other such bourgeois contrivances. Not that quite a few were not attractive by Western standards, but they had all put in hard time in a very tough and demanding war, and it showed.

As in all wars, and in all armies, the women of the Soviet Army played an indispensable role in the medical services—as nurses, medical technicians, and even as frontline doctors. Hyams had early on observed a young woman doctor serving with the Stalag administrative unit. She was young and pretty and very business-like, and she had caught the eye of Corporal Jock Witherspoon quite seriously. But she was strictly business, and Jock needed a few weeks of rest and recuperation before he could get serious about a woman. And besides, how could they even talk to each other?

The war was not yet over. Final victory in Europe in the form of the unconditional surrender of the Third Reich would not yet come for a couple of weeks. There was still some scattered fighting and dying. The Russians were pressing forward on all fronts from Berlin in the north to Czechoslovakia and Austria in the south. The Kriegies of Stalag 12B were still stuck on the fifty-yard line with nothing to do but wait. But at least they were no longer prisoners and they were no longer starving, and they were surrounded by friendly allies who were constantly drinking to their health.

CHAPTER SIXTEEN

Link-Up At The Elbe

Another once-in-a-lifetime historical happening . . . and I was there. The world's greatest cub reporter. I was there when East and West met, for the first time, on the bonnie, bonnie shore of the Elbe River. This has got to be my crowning journalistic achievement! And hooray for the seven G.I.s whose names will be inscribed in the history-books. And hooray for Texas.

Wednesday, April 25, 1945.

H ISTORY WAS BEING MADE IN QUANTUM LEAPS right there along the course of the Elbe River, as every day—indeed every hour—would produce spectacular new developments. Hyams, now the inveterate journalist, responded like an old fire horse to every clanging bell that smacked of a story. Seeing the Russian Army in operation and the richly varied types that made up that army was a story in itself and a lesson in history for those who would only look about them.

In the early afternoon of the 25th of April, on the very same day that the BBC was reporting the opening ceremonies of the United Nations in San Francisco, with all that that event portended for the future, Hyams decided to go exploring toward the Elbe on the chance that there would be some sign or hint of a converging American presence. It was not only the chance of a story that drove him, but nostalgic hopes and yearnings to see some G.I. faces that looked healthy and triumphant for a change, the faces of men, probably flushed with victory, who had never seen the inside of a

Stalag except perhaps as liberators. He knew that somewhere along that big river was where the link-up of the Americans and the Russians would occur. And why wouldn't he, as a free-lance reporter, so to speak, and right there in the immediate neighborhood, have a crack at the story, if, and when it happened? Even though it was obviously a long shot that he, on foot, could place himself at the precise spot where such an historic chance meeting should occur.

It was a balmy spring day with not a cloud in the sky, and all the baby birds were fluttering and twittering about as if to herald yet another portentous event. It was a great day to be free and out on a big story, even if the hunch should lead nowhere.

Hyams had only the vaguest idea of how to get to the river. He inquired of a German peasant, then of a Russian female M.P., who was not too sure herself. But he knew he would have to go generally westward. He pressed on for about an hour across a peaceful landscape, past the usual assortment of farms and fields and crossroads hamlets. Everything appeared very normal. The Russians were going about their regular business; they were relaxed and beginning to behave like garrison troops.

Then, as he came over the crest of a knoll approaching the village of Strehla on the east bank of the river, Hyams hit pay dirt. Beside the narrow unpaved road some hundred yards up ahead in an open field stood a small gathering of Russian military, possibly twenty or more officers and enlisted men, clustered around two G.I. jeeps loaded with half a dozen carbine-toting Yanks. A crackling electricity animated the entire scene as everybody, Yanks and Russians alike, all grinning from ear to ear, were talking, gesturing, and laughing all at once.

Hyams thought it had to be a mirage, a trick played on his over-stimulated brain by the hectic pace of events of the last few days. But there was really no mistaking what he was seeing. Those were unmistakeably American G.I.s in their Stars and Stripes-emblazoned jeeps, the red-white-and-blue, the little flags snapping in the breeze, and the exhilaration and euphoria on all the faces. It was the real thing. And Hyams was there, or almost there.

By one of those fortuitous chance occurrences, or perhaps by some inexplicable pre-destination, Hyams had been drawn to this hallowed spot where he would find this first American patrol to establish contact with the Russians at the Elbe, a military happening which was to be recorded in all the official books of military history. Hyams broke into a mad sprint and within seconds was standing at the edge of what could only be described as a scene of high emotion and jubilation. This was bigger than any wedding or bar-mitzvah Hyams had ever been to. This was a different magnitude of joyous happiness, almost delirious. A meeting of brothers who had come together across an ocean of blood and pain and death. Brothers who only moments before had been strangers. Now they stood there together in victory, a victory so dearly bought.

The Yanks spoke English, of course. The Russians spoke mainly Russian, some German, and a few fractured words of English. But there was hardly a need for words. Laughter and broad smiles transcended words. Everyone understood. These were indeed happy and triumphant faces, flushed with victory, just as Hyams had set out to find in his quixotic quest. The warm embraces, the back-slapping, the ardent hand-pumping, and the eyes said it all. Then after some eye-wiping and throat-clearing, American cigarettes and candy bars were produced and passed around. And then Hyams found himself standing beside the lead jeep and bending over unabashedly to plant a long, slow, slobbery kiss on the cold, grimy, steel hood. Old Glory never looked better to him than at that delirious moment.

And then out came Hyams' little notebook to record the names and hometowns of the patrol members and the outlines of their poignant story. Taking Hyams to be a reporter from the official Army newspaper *Stars And Stripes* who had mysteriously materialized out of nowhere, several G.I.s turned their attention to Hyams and began to recount some background of their fascinating story. Hyams dutifully took it all down.

The patrol leader was, fittingly enough, a Texan. A wise choice. Texans were typically affable, gracious, smooth, and could be expected to get along well with strangers. Lieutenant Albert L. Kotzebue was all of that. He was a tall, easygoing, likable First Lieutenant out of the 69th Infantry Division, which had recently fought its way into the city of Leipzig. On the previous day he and his platoon had been selected by his regimental commander to carry out a jeep-mounted patrol of some thirty-five men through the no-man's land of the Mulde-Elbe buffer zone, to find and establish contact with the Russians. To be chosen for this delicate and sensitive mission was a signal honor for the platoon.

On its first morning out, proceeding cautiously eastward, the patrol was overwhelmed by vast numbers of dispirited German soldiers seeking desperately to surrender to the Americans. That was a problem. Their orders had said nothing about taking prisoners, especially in the thousands. There were also some newly liberated American and Allied POWs and bands of former slave laborers, many close to death, all of whom sought to place themselves in the care and custody of this heaven-sent Yank platoon. At every step of the way, the patrol thus found itself "liberating" vast hordes of assorted humanity, when its assignment had been simply to find and connect with the forward elements of the Russian Army. One Yank pointed out the obvious, that a 35-man patrol can do just so much "liberating." Hyams recalled the four dour Russkie horsemen who had similarly appeared as symbols of liberation that first morning of freedom in the open Stalag. They had "liberated" over twenty thousand prisoners, but they couldn't do much more than "declare them officially liberated."

Hyams pressed on for more background. The G.I.s were proud of their mission, and they were proud of their lieutenant. Earlier that day, after having covered some thirty miles from their base camp, the patrol entered the farming village of Leckwitz, less than two miles from the Elbe on the opposite shore from Strehla. From a distance they spotted a lone Russian cavalryman in the village, who, when approached, grudgingly directed them towards the river in the direction of Strehla. Unknown to them at the time, that Russian horseman was the very first Russian soldier encountered by any Allied unit in the several probes to the Elbe undertaken on that day. The time was 1130 hours on the morning of April 25. Zeke wondered half seriously whether that horseman might have been one of those grim-faced scouts who had passed through his Stalag three days earlier. The reported lack of any response or acknowledgment certainly matched the style of those earlier riders.

Shortly thereafter, the lieutenant had made visual contact with Russian troops on the east bank, and leaving the bulk of his party behind on the opposite shore, he took six enlisted men and moved the two specially marked jeeps across the river aboard a cable ferry. The Russians accorded the Yanks a tumultuous welcome as they landed. At the time Hyams arrived on the happy scene there were several field grade Russian officers present, colonels and the like, plus a Russian photographer and two motion picture cameramen. The Russians, unlike the Americans, had come well prepared to document this historic event for posterity.

Hyams realized that this would be a major scoop for the Stalag newspaper. This was real news. This would call for a special edition. If only there were a way to get pictures. As a matter of fact, the G.I.s expressed wonderment that he hadn't brought along a photographer. They still thought he was from the *Stars and Stripes.* He took copious notes of everything, dutifully recording the names and hometowns of the several enlisted men who had accompanied Lieutenant Kotzebue across the river. Their hometowns ranged all the way from Texas to Chicago to Brooklyn and to South Dakota and Pennsylvania. One of the G.I.s was a Polish-American from Chicago specially assigned to the patrol for his knowledge of conversational Polish, which was the closest they could come to Russian.

After a protracted exchange of mutual congratulations,

compliments, and the inevitable toasts in vodka and schnapps, the American patrol members, now more than somewhat de-sensitized, were invited to the Russian area headquarters in the nearby village of Bauxdorf, where a Russian-style banquet was to be tendered in honor of the occasion.

The lieutenant was thus placed in a sensitive diplomatic role, being wined and dined as an official representative of his forces. This was something else that had not been covered in Officers' Training School. Protocol in a situation like this no doubt called for returning toast for toast—or at the very least, not declining any toasts. Especially when one's hosts were offering such free-flowing, down-home hospitality. The lieutenant never forgot that standing orders on the American side were "Be nice to the Russians."

Hyams, after about half an hour in the midst of the festivities, began to have second thoughts about remaining at the party. After a few cautious sips from a canteen cup full of vodka, he started looking for a way out. This was only his third day of freedom. He was not yet ready for this sort of heavy action. He knew that in order to get back to the Stalag under his own power before night-fall he'd better withdraw from this celebration, especially since the Yanks would be too busy and too distracted to offer him a jeep ride back home to the Stalag.

While the patrol's mission had been one of reconnaissance and fact-finding and reporting back, the effusive welcome that the Americans received was so overwhelming that the celebration took on a life of its own. Hyams thought this could become another "lost patrol." The lieutenant also seemed to be aware of the potential problem. He had found the Russians; what would he do now? Hyams took his leave. He could only hope that the patrol would find its way back to the American lines.

Redundancy is standard operating procedure in all well-run military operations. Indeed on that same never-to-be forgotten day several other patrols from the American 69th Infantry Division had set out on parallel missions to seek contacts with the Russians along the Elbe. So it would turn out to be something of a race, a fact possibly not explained to the lieutenant. One patrol commanded by a Major Craig and another commanded by a Lieutenant Robertson both reached Russian lines on the Elbe. Major Craig's patrol later joined Lieutenant Kotzebue's group on the east bank. With the arrival of the American major, some of the higher Russian brass, up to a Major-General, decided to take a hand in the welcoming festivities.

When word of the Russian predilection for grandiose toasting and partying spread on the other side to the upper echelons of the American command, some higher ranking officers began to head for the Elbe. On the 26th, the general commanding the 69th Infantry Division arrived on the east bank at the town of Torgau to a joyous Russian reception. On the next day, April 27, his superior, the commander of the American Fifth Corps, General Huebner, arrived at the Elbe for a welcoming ceremony and banquet tendered by his Russian counterpart, the commander of the Russian 34th Corps.

The American, British, and Soviet governments jointly announced to the world on April 27 that East and West had met on the Elbe at Torgau, about eleven miles downstream from the obscure and now forgotten little village of Strehla. Due to a foulup in PR communications and orders, the contact that had been achieved by Lieutenant Kotzebue, actually the true "first," would not be accorded the signal honor of first official link-up.

Other than Hyams, who had only the most dubious journalistic credentials, there had not been any American media representatives with the Kotzebue party, nor any high-ranking American officers, nor official "proof positive" of the event. The patrol led by Lieutenant Robertson, though effecting a slightly later contact, managed to return to the American lines before the Kotzebue patrol, bringing with them a couple of exuberant Russian officers who furnished live corroboration of that link-up.

Lieutenant Robertson would be photographed with the Supreme Commander, General Dwight Eisenhower, and would become the official hero of the day, although the Army historians would acknowledge the actual achievement of the Kotzebue patrol.

On April 30, General Courtney Hodges, commanding the U.S. First Army, came to Torgau for a meeting with Marshal Ivan Konev, the Russian commander of the First Ukrainian Army Group. The military link-up between East and West was now solid all the way up to the top echelons of command.

Lieutenant Kotzebue's history-making first at the village of Strehla would soon be completely overshadowed by the mad swirl of events. The day after their rendezvous with destiny, he and his men found themselves on the east bank of the Elbe in Russian territory, still being wined and dined by the Russians but strangely ignored by their own division commander, with no clear instructions as to how to proceed or when to return to base.

From the 26th through the 28th of April several of Lieutenant Kotzebue's men visited the Stalag for a leisurely look around. They graciously accepted letters and post-cards from the American prisoners to be mailed home through the G.I. postal system, and also furnished the Kriegies a quantity of recent issues of *Stars and Stripes*. These thoughtful gestures made the American ex-prisoners feel that they were once again part of the U.S. Army.

A melancholy descended when the brightly painted red, white and blue jeeps pulled out of the Stalag after the last visit on April 28, and headed out the West Gate in the direction of Strehla and the Elbe. The Yank Kriegies were once again cut off from their American umbilical cord. The spotlight of the world had shone briefly on their little corner of Germany. For a few brief days, Hyams and the Kriegies had been front and center on the stage of history, and now all the brass had returned to their respective headquarters, and the focus of world attention quickly shifted away. The eyes of the world were now on bombed-out Berlin, where the Führer and his entourage were holed up in an underground bunker with the Russians closing in, and the final act of *Götterdämmerung*, The Twilight of the Gods, was being played out there.

CHAPTER SEVENTEEN

Farewell To 12B—
Then A Look At The
Dark Side Of The Moon

*Time out for fun and games on May Day. The Soviets on
parade, and at play. It's their Fourth of July. Time out
from the war. They earned it.*
                                    Tuesday, May 1, 1945.

*Move to Krondorf. A touch of first-class luxury in
military accommodations. Guess my days as a Kriegie
are over at last. The next move should be out of Germany
and home! Mixed memories. Won't miss the Stalag, but
will miss some of the guys who came through here.*
                                    Wednesday, May 2, 1945.

*A look at the dark side of the moon. Behind the genteel
façade of Krondorf.*
                                    Thursday, May 3, 1945.

AND THEN CAME MAY DAY, the Soviet high holiday. It was
their day to celebrate the Russian Revolution of 1917, to salute the
achievements of the proletariat, the heroic Russian people, and the
invincible Red Army. On May 1, 1945, the Russians indeed had
much to celebrate and rejoice over. After four grueling years of the
bloodiest war in history, a war that had raged relentlessly back and

175

forth across their homeland with an horrendous toll in lives and property, their armies now stood proud and victorious over the vanquished aggressor after linking up across the broad waist of Germany with their Allies from the West.

After initially absorbing a series of crushing defeats that had left Germany in control of vast tracts of the Russian heartland, the Red Army had rallied at the very gates of Moscow, Leningrad, and Stalingrad, denying these cities to the invaders, and had then driven the Germans back a thousand miles to where they now stood deployed across the entire length and breadth of Germany.

The once-fearsome Wehrmacht together with all the vaunted S.S. legions, had all been ground into the dust, even as the tattered remnants of the Nazi hierarchy were being hunted down as criminals. Only the day before, Adolf Hitler had taken his own life rather than be taken alive by Soviet troops in Berlin.

It was indeed a time for exalting the triumph of the Russian spirit, the indomitable will and strength of the Soviet people and their armed forces. The Soviet Union now stood, as one of the "Big Three" of the world, an equal partner with America and Britain at the birth of a new era in world affairs.

And now the Kriegies of Stalag 12B would see yet another facet of their Soviet hosts. The Russians, whom they had first observed in captivity as listless and totally dispirited and whom they had only recently come to see as fierce and highly effective fighters, would now appear anew as spit-and-polish parade-ground soldiers.

This would be not only a celebration of May Day, but also a well-deserved victory bash, albeit a few days premature in a technical sense. As the day began this Tuesday morning, every Soviet individual, man and woman, appeared in full regalia. Their boots gleamed sharply; their uniforms sparkling clean and crisp. The men were clean-shaven, the women freshly coiffed, with radiant school-girl complexions. Unit insignias, citations, and generous rows of medals and ribbons were proudly strung across broad chests and ample bosoms. These people had a "parade presence" reminiscent of what the Brits had demonstrated some two weeks earlier at the Roosevelt memorial parade. Any army that could accomplish what the Soviet army had accomplished had to have those essential qualities exemplified by an iron discipline and a hefty measure of *esprit de corps.*

The Russian dress uniform was khaki or dark olive with red trim, and consisted of a tunic bloused at the waist by a wide leather belt, with cavalry-type breeches for the men, and knee-length skirts for the women. Officers and enlisted ranks wore relatively similar uniforms, except for fabric quality and texture. Commissioned ranks were also marked by distinctive shoulder boards and collar insignia.

All armies have their own elite corps; the Russians had their Red Guards, or the "Guardia." The Guards wore special Red Banner emblems on their collar tabs and on their headgear and tunics. They were young, highly motivated and indoctrinated, and they had all seen extensive front-line duty. Row upon row of medals and ribbons attested to their gallantry in combat. Most of the Russian units that had taken up front-line positions on the Elbe were of the 58th Guards Infantry Division under the command of Major General Vladimir Rusakov, whose troops had first met Lieutenant Kotzebue's patrol on April 25th.

Much of this day was given to formal reviewing, marching and parading, to be followed soon thereafter by some free-spirited rejoicing and high jinks. Sumptuous quantities of meat, caviar, vodka, and schnapps were provided, and for the Kriegie guests in the Stalag a special holiday meal was prepared consisting of a rich stew of meat, potatoes, and rutabagas, to be washed down with gallons of strong Russian tea.

Exactly one week after the entry into the camp of that first Russian patrol of four dust-caked cavalrymen, the Russian Army was entertaining its Kriegie-guests in lavish style on the occasion of this holiday. Hyams was beginning to feel more like a pampered guest than an ex-Kriegie. Only the physical fact of the Stalag remained as a reminder of his former status. In every other respect, Hyams and the other former Kriegies were now free men, although they were not free to go home as yet. Going home, back to the U.S. Army, was bound to happen in very short order, in a matter of days, or one or two weeks at the most. So why not make the most of this Russian party? This was another one of those once-in-a-lifetime events. The vodka flowed freely, it was a balmy afternoon, and the rollicking good-fellowship and gaiety was in stark relief to the prevailing gray and wintry mood of recent months.

Among the displays of holiday abandon was an impromptu low-altitude flying show put on by a vodka-fueled Russian pilot in a vintage 1918 single-engine bi-plane. After a seemingly interminable stint of aerobatics, looping, and friendly buzzing of the camp area, the barnstorming character finally flew off, to everyone's great relief.

For the aviator, and for most of the Soviets, this was a brief reprieve from front-line duty, and a chance to get "gussied up" (as they say in Brooklyn) for a holiday celebration in the midst of war. This was probably their first carefree day off in a long time, and they revelled in it. The festive mood infected everyone, the joyous atmosphere being constantly re-inforced by the incredible torrent of good news from all the war fronts as the day wore on.

By nightfall everybody was satiated with food and drink. The Kriegies had gorged themselves, and would have appreciated a supply of Bromos. But it had been very exhilarating to be part of this experience. Everybody was feeling good. The starvation days were over; the prospects for the future were dazzling.

On the next day, Wednesday, May 2, it was back to business for the Soviets. The party was over. Columns of troops took up the march to various still-sputtering war fronts, but nobody expected anything more serious than occasional mop-up action against a fading enemy. Any Jerries still in the war were looking for opportunities to surrender, although their preference was usually to surrender to the Americans. Unfortunately for them, the Americans were not going to show up east of the Elbe.

Reflecting the good fellowship and congeniality of the May Day partying, the Russians, in a gesture of true friendship and concern, decided that the Anglo-American Kriegies deserved better than to be left any longer in the squalor of the Stalag. They should be relocated to a more appropriate setting, one befitting honored guests and gallant allies.

Since the repatriation of thousands of Kriegies across the unsettled Mulde-Elbe buffer zone to their own forces was not yet logistically feasible, the Russians came up with a better idea. On the morning of May 2, they notified the Anglo-American Kriegies of their intention to relocate them to more suitable living quarters in nearby Krondorf, and that they should be prepared to abandon the Stalag. This notion won the immediate and enthusiastic endorsement of the Kriegies. Even Taggart, chronically suspicious of Russian motives, allowed that this could be a gracious and compassionate gesture. Soon the first contingents were on the road on a twelve-mile march to the nearby city of Krondorf. A convoy of "Studebakers" accompanied the march for those unable to proceed under their own power. The destination was a vacant German military complex that had served in former years as a very prestigious officers' college.

After the Russians had settled the Kriegies into their new dormitories and fed them in the spacious mess-halls, they sent them all to the clinic for complete physicals. This clinic, staffed by Russian medics and some local German doctors, was a very busy place. Medical teams, both civilian and military, were processing great numbers of refugees and liberated slave-workers, many of whom were suffering from advanced malnutrition and other more ominous afflictions. The Kriegies, however, got top priority and were run through the various stations swiftly and efficiently, being checked for the usual Stalag-related problems such as personal hygiene, malnutrition, dysentery, chest and bronchial conditions, and for any evidence of venereal or other infectious diseases.

Unlike previous routine exams experienced in the U.S. or British military, these procedures were conducted mainly by young

Russian female practitioners. This was another surprise for the hushed and self-conscious Kriegies. But a doctor is a doctor . . . except for one, who was definitely special at least to Jock Witherspoon. He was smitten senseless by this petite, blue-eyed brunette "Leftenant" who was cute and winsome in any language; she had first caught his eye as she had wheeled her bicycle through the Stalag some days earlier.

Witherspoon had to be dragged bodily out of the clinic, but not before he managed to learn the name of this extraordinary physician. She was First Lieutenant Irina Svobodin, and she was not amused by the cocky little paratrooper's attentions.

This was to be the first "post-confinement" infatuation of any Kriegie known to Hyams. After an extended starvation regimen, it normally takes about two weeks of a meat-and-potatoes diet to start the sex hormones flowing again. Witherspoon had apparently recovered his sexual libido after only about ten days of Russian rations. And of course it was only natural to then fall for a Russian girl.

All this rekindled a few tender memories in Hyams. What about Sylvia? Lovely, luscious, sweet, patient Sylvia. What was her situation? Had she waited? Was she still his girl? What would it be like to be back in her arms? Would she be the same? Fantasy images began to swim in his brain. But he was unsure of himself. He was still a mere shadow of his former self. He wouldn't want her to see him now. It would be some time before he'd be back on his feet, physically or emotionally. He'd been gone a long time. But it was good thinking of her, and he was pretty sure she'd be there waiting for him. He felt better.

On the second morning in Krondorf, Witherspoon was determined to re-visit the clinic for a glimpse of his beloved Irina. Hyams accompanied him in the interests of maintaining some dignity and decorum. They located Irina at work in a section of the clinic that had been set aside for a special group of patients. She was part of a medical team treating about two hundred Dutch-Jewish litter cases that had been evacuated from some nearby death camp in eastern Saxony. The name of the place, constantly repeated by the victims, was *Grossrosen*. About half the patients were children between the ages of five and twelve. It struck Hyams that these were practically the only children he had seen among the masses of refugees crowding the roads and highways in the area. What had happened to all the children? According to the medical workers, these children could only have survived if the Nazis had had a special reason for keeping them alive. All the evidence pointed to medical experimentation as the most likely reason. Many bore a variety of surgical scars, and all were severely affected mentally and emotionally in addition to their physical debilitation. It would take a miracle for any of them to survive to normal development.

The adults were dying at the rate of five or six per day from a condition described as "spontaneous gangrene," despite the best efforts of the Russian doctors and the several German doctors who had been recruited from the town. Spontaneous gangrene, called *Noma* in the camps, was a type of infection that arises from no apparent external cause other than severe and prolonged malnutrition, and eventually becomes irreversible.

After a few minutes of wandering among the adult patients, Hyams realized that they were all of one gender, girls and young women, many with close-cropped hair, as if their heads had recently been shaved. Some were branded with tattooed serial numbers on their forearms. But there was not one man among them. This was another enigma. And then he realized that perhaps ninety percent of the refugees seen on the roads were women. There were puzzles, but no answers.

Even though the average Kriegie in the Stalag had lost between 15 and 20 percent of his normal body weight, the skeletal condition of these survivors came as a sobering shock. Some had shrunk to half their normal weight. Many adults appeared child-like in size and physique. Most of them hovered in a state of emotional disorientation and depression which could only have resulted from a prolonged period of the most severe mental and physical stress. Quite a few were delirious and raving. They had literally been driven to madness. Others, pitifully weak and seemingly at death's door, remained rational and lucid.

When they learned that Hyams was an American, these survivors became tremendously agitated, pleading for him to carry messages for them, to locate relatives in America, to find someone who could rescue them, to help them recover, to help them find loved ones.

In stunned and bitter silence, Hyams recorded in his little notebook the foreign-sounding names of these victims and their relatives dredged from confused and blurred minds. Just for them to talk to someone from the outside world and demonstrate that they could remember something from before the nightmare was for them a stimulant and tonic in itself.

Hyams walked out of that ward of death and despair with a grating new awareness. The war and the Stalag experience and the link-up of East and West had been momentous stories, but now he realized that there was another story. It was the story of programmed depredation and murder of entire peoples, effectively concealed from the world by the perpetrators. And he began to sense the incredible dimensions of this hidden story.

He would now pay more attention to the steady flow of faceless ex-prisoners and slave workers traveling through Krondorf in all directions. Ever the inquisitive reporter, Hyams would also meet and converse with a number of German civilians in various walks of life, most of whom were in despair at the sudden turnabout in their lives—from victor to vanquished. This was understandably very difficult to accept. They were unable to understand the sudden collapse of their military forces when all the propaganda mills, right up to the very end, had been confidently promising a glorious German victory.

He would inquire of some of these German civilians what they might know of the plight of the Jews, recalling the early words of the Austrian guard, Andreas, during his first day of captivity, on the road from Schoenberg. He had said then, much to Hyams' shock and dismay, "*Ach, mein Himmel,* what they did to the Jews was just shameful—inexcusable! It was degrading just to see this!" Most of the townspeople questioned there in Krondorf would just turn away in silence. Some would protest that they had never themselves been Nazis. Others, apparently sincere and deeply troubled like good old Andreas, would profess horror at the unfolding tragedy. But it was difficult for Hyams to accept the protestations of ignorance from people whose family members were high-ranking career military officers or whose teenage sons, those too young for military service, still defiantly wore the *leder-hosen* of the rabid Hitler Youth movement as they strolled or rode their bikes along the tree-lined avenues of Krondorf.

After the months spent in Germany and the attendant emotional roller-coaster he had experienced, and despite the recent highs when military victory was at last assured, Hyams was now very deeply anguished by what he had seen in the clinic relative to the pitiful condition of the Jewish patients. Though torn by these new sightings, he was uplifted by the fact that he and his comrades were no longer prisoners, no longer Kriegies. That felt very good. Here he was just a "guest" of the Soviet Army, and free to observe and study the conditions around him. It would all go into that book that he would write someday, someday. But he was still a long way from Bushwick Avenue in Brooklyn, where he really wanted to be. He had seen enough of Europe for now.

Still, the war was not quite over, and the way home was still foreclosed by the military dynamics of the moment. Krondorf would still be home for Hyams and his ex-Kriegie buddies for the time being, perhaps for another week or two. And the people in the Russian clinic would not go away, and were a heavy reminder of another story that needed to be faced up to. That was the dark side of the moon.

In the
General's House

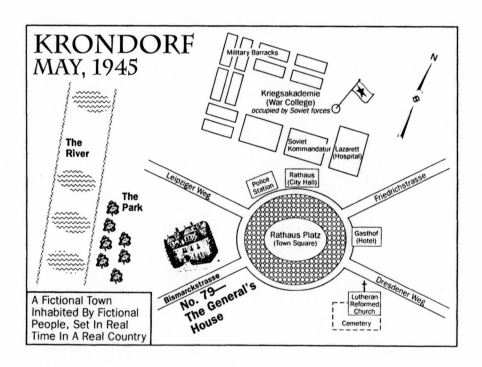

KRONDORF
MAY, 1945

The River

The Park

Military Barracks

Kriegsakademie
(War College)
occupied by Soviet forces

N

Soviet
Kommandatur

Lazarett
(Hospital)

Leipziger Weg

Police
Station

Rathaus
(City Hall)

Friedrichstrasse

Rathaus Platz
(Town Square)

Gasthof
(Hotel)

Bismarckstrasse

No. 79—
The General's
House

Dresdener Weg

Lutheran
Reformed
Church

Cemetery

A Fictional Town
Inhabited By Fictional
People, Set In Real
Time In A Real Country

CHAPTER ONE

Sonya's Nightmare

IT WAS A TENSE AND EVEN GHASTLY NIGHT. They heard that poor woman stirring about all night; she would wander through the upstairs from room to room. Sometimes she'd scream like a banshee. Sometimes she'd just whimper like a whipped puppy. Sometimes she'd be softly humming a lullabye to an imaginary child she was cradling in her arms. Poor Sonya. The other women took turns trying to calm her down, but she was up all night. A very bad situation; particularly in the delicate circumstances prevailing.

No one hardly slept that night in General von Hesselmann's grand house. It was as if a restless ghost, maybe even the ghost of the General himself, kept moving through the house. Of course there was always the possibility that the General himself could reappear and come stomping through the massive oaken front door into the grand vestibule. The General in the flesh, that is, which would be even worse than the General's ghost. A neighbor had reported however that the General was definitely missing in action somewhere in the frozen wilds of Russia, and hadn't been heard from in many months.

But mostly it was just Sonya who kept most everybody awake.

The problem, it seemed, was that poor Sonya was mentally afflicted, and as such was often given to such things as weird nightmares and hallucinations and nocturnal wanderings. It seemed that she had never recovered from a terrible happening that took place a long time ago in her native village in Poland. It was a long time ago, on a quiet Sabbath morning, way back in the hot summer of

1942. That was almost three years before she was now to find herself crying and moaning in the dark in the General's fine house in Krondorf.

The summer of 1942. It was in the third year of the reign of Dr. Hans Frank, Adolf Hitler's friend and legal adviser extraordinare, who had been entrusted by the Third Reich with the stewardship of newly conquered Poland. Neither Sonya nor anybody else in her tiny village had ever heard of Dr. Hans Frank, nor did they even know what a legal adviser was. Nor did they need to know. But they knew that the Germans had imposed a hellish regime upon Poland with the coming of the tanks and the shrieking dive-bombers and the jack-booted men sporting the swastika. A regime that reached into every village and hamlet and touched every individual's life, particularly if they were Jewish. It was a regime that smelled of tyranny, deliberate cruelty, and wholesale death . . . death on a scale that had never before been imagined in any of the dark superstitions or ghost stories that haunted village life.

The rabbi and the talmudists in Sonya's village would search back in the voluminous chronicles of their long history for a modicum of comfort and guidance. Those ancient villains of antiquity had been very evil and very powerful and had inflicted much suffering on their ancestors. But these were modern times, when man had emerged from the dark ages. These were times when men could fly like birds, and race across the land in horseless vehicles, and even talk to each other and be heard across vast oceans and entire continents. How could it happen in this age that men's souls should be so mean and hardened and corrupt?

But their people had survived over the centuries, and even the millennia, of evil and persecutions. In this century there had been pogroms and massacres here and there, almost everywhere. So what could be done? Only prayer and faith and good deeds could avert and deflect the evil decrees. God in his own time would smite down the evil men and lift up the righteous.

This was a Sabbath morning in the middle of August. Despite the early hour it was very hot. Sonya was dripping with perspiration as she dressed her little daughter for the Sabbath. Little Miriam was only two-and-a-half years old. She had never known a life when men were free of fear and wrenching anxieties. But this day was the Sabbath, and the child was bursting with joy and anticipation. She insisted on brushing her own blond curls. She was a big girl.

Sonya's young husband had long ago been taken away to a labor camp. She had never heard from him after that. He had never seen his angelic curly-haired child. All the young men were gone. She lived with her widowed father, one of the elders of the village. Life was a daily struggle against hunger and despair. But the Sabbath was beautiful, a day of renewal that brought hope and dignity and a few hours of peace for reflection and prayer. Sonya wiped the perspiration from her brow as she readied herself for the walk with her child to the synagogue.

Then suddenly, without warning, they descended on the dusty, sleepy village like a swarm of angry locusts.

A convoy of military trucks roared into the village, shattering the Sabbath calm. They screeched to a halt around the synagogue, encircling the ancient structure as though it were a military objective to be taken by storm. Armed German soldiers sprang out of the trucks and rushed about in every direction, entering the synagogue and breaking down the doors to every house in the "Jew" street.

Within minutes they had collected everyone. The young and the old, the sick and the lame—everybody was lined up in the village square while the soldiers continued to search the houses. They said they were looking for money and jewelry, but whatever money or jewelry there might once have been had long ago been extorted from these hapless village folk. They had long ago been pauperized by the relentlessly efficient special police. But the search went on. Every door was battered down. Every hidden nook thoroughly explored, including cellars and even drainage pits.

By this time the sun was almost directly overhead. The heat was suffocating. Then they started up the truck engines. Everybody was ordered into the trucks. Everyone knew what that meant. There were no free rides for Jews in Hitler's world. Pandemonium erupted as clubs and truncheons and whips were brought out against the panicked villagers. There was no escape. The trucks were filled up with screaming mothers, babies, tots, old men, young boys, old women, and young girls. Those who jumped off were beaten mercilessly and then driven like cattle behind the trucks as the behemoths lumbered off with their miserable human cargo. S.S. troops on motorcycles brought up the rear of the convoy, herding those who had jumped off the trucks. There would be no escape.

The destination was a clearing deep in the forest some two miles from the village. It was high noon as the first truck entered the clearing. And there everyone was ordered out onto the ground. The word, endlessly repeated, was *"Schnell!"* Things could never go fast enough for these expediters of death.

In the middle of the clearing was a long trench, six feet deep and perhaps a hundred yards long. It had been freshly dug that morning. The earth-moving equipment and the operators stood by.

Everybody from the village was ordered to line up along both sides of the trench, facing each other. The old men prayed, the women wept, the older children wailed, the tots kicked and fussed. They were hot and tired and thirsty.

Then came the order to undress! *"Schnell, Schnell,* you Jew dogs!" The final indignity!

The soldiers walked up and down the lines, kicking, beating and cursing. Rifle butts came smashing down, whips snapped, fists flew. "Everyone must undress! *Schnell! Schweinhunde!"*

Miriam, in her mother's arms, turned to Sonya and whispered quite calmly, "They are going to shoot us, Mother." And after a moment, as the bedlam heightened, "Let us run, Mother!"

Sonya was petrified. There was nowhere to run. There was no way to run. And then Miriam asked her mother why she had put on her best Sabbath dress that morning! There were no answers to the child's questions.

Sonya's father, a tall bearded man in his sixties, refused to disrobe despite the whipping and the gun proddings. He stood firm. He would not undress. He would not stand naked. So they shot him first. He fell forward into the ditch.

The soldiers opened fire. Sonya was resigned to death for herself and the child. She prayed for it to be over with. Then a tall, blond young trooper stepped up to her and grabbed the child from her arms. Miriam cried out in fright and the young man calmly threw the child to the ground like a rag doll, then drew his pistol and shot her several times.

Then the blond young man raised his pistol to fire at Sonya. She fainted and fell into the ditch as the man continued to fire.

Machine gunners blazed away at the ranks of naked victims, and then they continued to pour fire into the writhing and screaming piles of dead and near-dead. Then the bulldozers moved in to cover the graves.

And then silence descended on the clearing in the forest, and the executioners were gone. And Sonya, driven mad by what she had seen and endured, crawled out of that shallow grave, covered with excrement and blood. She dug for the body of her child, she threw herself back into the pile of corpses, she clawed down deeper in a blind rage to find someone, anyone, alive. She would not leave that scene of carnage for many days, returning always to search the steaming trench.

Months later she would find herself again in a living hell. That living hell was Auschwitz. But nothing mattered. She was already dead.

And now it was almost three years after the murder of Sonya's villagers. And now Hitler was dead. And the Third Reich was practically dead. Europe was awakening from a nightmare, but Sonya was reliving her nightmare this night in, of all places, the sumptuous home of a missing German general whose mean-tempered son would deny this group of refugees the overnight sanctuary of the home even though he and his mother were living elsewhere. In her desperate confusion poor Sonya was convinced that this was the very same blond young man who had torn Miriam from her arms on that long-ago Sabbath noon in the clearing in the Goraj Forest.

This was certainly not the way Private First Class Zeke Hyams, once of L Company of the 334th Infantry, more recently of Stalag 12B, had foreseen this self-assigned mission of mercy. It had all seemed so simple. They had come upon this group of distressed young women caught up here in Krondorf in the ebb-tide of a winding-down war; it seemed like there were scores of them all across the landscape. Frightened, desperate, "walking wounded," so recently out of the concentration camps. They were hungry, harassed by the Russians, with no safe place to stay; slinking about in the shadows, in desperate need of a few staples of life, like some minimum nutrition, and some safe refuge to marshall their wits and their strength to continue their faltering odyssey back to their homelands. It was fate that Hyams and his friends chanced upon this particular group. Just fate. And these people couldn't just be ignored, swept under the rug. Then there was this grand house standing empty on a gracious tree-lined avenue in this charming German town. What could be more natural than to commandeer the house as a temporary haven, even if only for one night where the women could spend a safe, warm, restful, and restorative overnight?

Yes, but Hyams, Hornstein, and the Brit, Witherspoon, were themselves "guests" of the Soviet Army at this particular juncture during the final week of World War II in Europe. Well, sort of guests. Fate had placed them here behind the Russian lines when their Stalag had been overrun by Soviet forces. And as guests of the Soviet Army, or of any army for that matter, one just doesn't do things like taking over the house of a local general—even an enemy general—without permission. That is, not if one wishes to stay out of the local guard-house and continue on his own way home to Brooklyn or Manhattan or London as the case might be.

And now the loud wailing punctuated by piercing shrieks emanating from the house during the night-time hours would certainly attract the attention of the Russian military police. Especially since

Frau von Hesselmann, the owner, must have already filed a trespass complaint with the authorities. Probably she would feel free to add burglary, malicious vandalism, and who knows what else to the complaint. It could be difficult to explain this unauthorized intrusion and takeover of a family residence by five women and three men in such wanton disregard of an owner's property rights. The Russians were very tolerant of the more benign shenanigans of the recently liberated Anglo-American Kriegies. But this would be stretching hospitality beyond all reasonable limits. The Russians ran a tight ship. They would not allow anarchy. This could unleash an imbroglio of official charges and red tape that could have very unpleasant ramifications—even as to the American authorities, to whom, of course, Hyams and Hornstein would soon have to answer. Not to mention Corporal Jock Witherspoon, who would also soon be answering to His Brittanic Majesty's Royal Army people. So recently out of Stalag confinement, Hyams was now sweating out a possible court martial. Maybe it wasn't meant for Hyams ever to be a free man again.

Where had they made the fatal error? Probably they should have called it quits after they delivered the wounded girl, Kati, and the two sick girls to the Russian hospital and then got the rest of the girls generously provisioned up with bread and cheese from the Russian commissary. That Russian hospital was full of sad cases. Women and children who were skin and bones; people driven out of their minds, ranting and raving; others waiting to die from the irreversible effects of long-term malnutrition and all sorts of complications brought about by torture and privation. The Stalag was bad, but Hyams had never seen or imagined anything like that, especially since these people were all non-combatants.

But they probably shouldn't have gone that extra mile to actually provide a house for these five girls to spend the night. That was too much. That had been the fatal error. That was the Pandora's box. But it had seemed so right. Doggone, it's only human nature that a distress call will beget a rescuer. Hyams had read that somewhere. But human nature doesn't count in a place like this. And definitely not in a situation like this. In a Russian-occupied Jerry town—when the only real purpose in life was to get the hell out of Germany and get home as quickly and uneventfully as possible.

But of course, Maury Hornstein had known that it was a bad idea from the beginning. What was it that he had said? "Hyams, you godamn fool! Don't you know that no good deed ever goes unpunished? Just count me out on this one." Hyams had to admit that it was probably a stupid idea. But of course Hornstein had finally gone along with the plan, however grudgingly.

CHAPTER TWO

The Eight Of Krondorf

HORNSTEIN WAS ABSOLUTELY RIGHT, OF COURSE. There was the language barrier to consider, not to mention the cultural barrier. And the newly liberated Kriegies themselves were not on totally solid ground as far as their own physical state was concerned; they themselves were in need of physical and psychological rehabilitation. This was neither the time nor the place to get involved with the local inhabitants, especially people who were in such dire straits and would need long-term help.

In Hornstein's tough New York street-wise world, good deeds might be okay for Boy Scout medals, but they were definitely not recommended as a practical matter. Hyams had to agree, under the circumstances. Live and learn. In Hornstein's world, people learn to mind their own business and not to stick their noses into other people's problems. Of course Hornstein was a much older man. He was thirty-three. Eleven years older than either Hyams or Witherspoon. Even Witherspoon had been reluctant to get involved in this caper. He had also learned about life the hard way— on the streets of London and then as a brash young paratrooper in His Majesty's First Airborne Division, the elite Red Berets, not to mention such things as the ill-fated Battle of Arnhem in Holland, and eight tough months in the Stalag.

The night was shot, and they would have to vacate the premises at the first crack of dawn. They had promised the lady of the house, Frau von Hesselmann, that the three ex-POWs and their five female wards would be gone in the morning. So there was nothing for Hyams to do as he lay awake, except to reflect on the strange turn of events of the last twenty-four hours. On the previous morning life had seemed so simple, straightforward, and satisfying. There were so many dazzling prospects for the future. He had written in his diary, for Thursday, May 4, 1945:

> *Living the life of a gentleman . . . my own bed, hot*
> *showers, soap, pleasant cafeteria dining, no more*
> *scavenging off the countryside . . . who could ask for*
> *anything more? Of course, it would be nice to have a*
> *little 'walking around' pocket money. The shops are open,*
> *even the beer joints. I might like to treat myself to a beer,*
> *or a souvenir of some sort, or maybe even a little gift for*
> *Sylvia. But I'm not complaining.*

That would have been Morning Three in the lovely town of Krondorf, nestled picturesquely on the east bank of the Elbe, safely inside the Soviet zone of occupation. Life had taken on a new and unaccustomed normalcy for all the "Kriegies." That, of course, was Stalag jargon for prisoners of war. The Russians had provided a truly luxurious facility for the British and American Kriegies so recently liberated from the miserable confines of Stalag 12B. Some dozen miles from the Stalag there was this unused German military complex, which had until recently served as a Jerry officers' training college. Something perhaps like West Point or Annapolis.

There were modern four-story brick dormitories with all-modern plumbing and amenities. There were airy, well-lighted living and sleeping accommodations with enough beds for every Kriegie to sleep in splendor in his very own bed, in contrast to the "three-to-a-bunk" condition which was standard in the Stalag. No more Kriegie bunk-mates; no more sleeping on hard wooden slats. After the nights on the rickety cattle car that had earlier brought the Kriegies across Germany, and compared to the crude conditions of the Stalag, this was heaven. And then, after a brisk morning shower and a shave at a marble-topped wash basin with mirrors and all the modern accoutrements, they went downstairs to the dining hall for breakfast, with seconds and refills just for the asking.

There was a modern well-equipped hospital, a clinic, a gymnasium, generous-sized athletic fields and parade grounds, all set amidst lush park-like surroundings. The Kriegies could hardly believe their good fortune. Life in this place was certainly a turnabout from anything they had experienced since they had left their native shores. It was akin to being transferred from Alcatraz to a posh hotel in the Catskills.

Krondorf itself was an ancient and picturesque town situated about midway on the course of the Elbe River, not too far from the major metropolis of Dresden, that once-glittering capital of the ancient kingdom of Saxony. The town bespoke a solid and long-established European elegance and prosperity, due perhaps to its fortuitous location relative to river, rail, and highway transport facilities linking the rich provinces of Saxony and Bavaria. The pre-war population had been about thirty thousand busy and contented *Bürghers*, including the military complement of instructors and staff at the Officers' College and numbers of retired military career people who might have at one time or another been assigned at the military school.

Now, in early May 1945, including large numbers of Russian troops, the thousands of newly arrived Kriegies being temporarily quartered at the Officers' School, and the myriad refugees and war victims drifting through in all directions, there must have been upwards of seventy thousand highly diverse souls crowded into Krondorf and its environs, more than double the normal population.

The central district of the town, including the Officers' School, had miraculously escaped serious damage from both the intense aerial bombings that had recently been visited upon nearby Dresden and the heavy artillery fire that would ordinarily precede the Russian ground advance. The total result was that physically Krondorf was almost totally intact and looked like something out of a tourist travel brochure.

In the ten days or so since the Germans had obligingly decamped from the Stalag and thus spared the camp and its occupants the hazards and unpleasantness of a Russian assault, the Kriegies of Stalag 12B had seen a remarkable turnabout in their fortunes. By now most had shed some of the old prison pallor, were an average of eight to ten pounds heavier, and had regained a sparkle in their eyes and a spring in their step. Most importantly, they knew that, for all practical purposes, the war in Europe had been brought close to that final victory which would enable them and their buddies to go home at last. It was now just a matter of days; as soon as the logistics could be worked out between the Russians and the Americans. The Allied and Russian forces had established a full link-up along the Elbe River; the initial historic contact between the forces had taken place just a few miles downstream from Krondorf.

They also knew that somewhere behind those approaching Anglo-American lines there was a bundle of accumulated back-pay waiting for them . . . in real money. Not in cigarettes or "Stalag currency," but in pounds sterling or genuine U.S. dollars that could be spent anywhere in the civilized world—like in Paris, London, New York, or anyplace in between. That magical stuff could buy some of those almost-forgotten refinements of life, such as a drink at a sidewalk cafe in Paris, a good steak dinner, an evening on the town with old friends . . . or with new friends. And of course, girls—that is, the Western brand, like the pin-up types . . . something along the lines of a Betty Grable type: blond, blue-eyed, long-legged, and contoured. The dazzling Pepso-dent smile type! Or, of course, whatever type might be available.

The Kriegies had been suddenly transformed and reincarnated back into a world where all the prospects had turned rosy and bright. And where hunger per se was no longer the only driving force in life.

After lunch on this fateful day, instead of just hanging around the fancy barracks killing time until the next meal, the trio of constant companions—Hyams, Witherspoon, and Hornstein—had drifted out to explore the town and take in the local sights. They thought they'd check out the town square and then head for the riverfront, just like tourists with some time on their hands. Dinner was going to be sausage and red cabbage and fried potatoes. And they didn't want to be late for that.

It was a perfect spring day; a gentle warm breeze was driving billowy white clouds overhead. The rain, if any, would come at night, leaving the day crystal clear. Perfect tourist weather. Hyams was reminded of another scene, many months earlier, before the Battle of the Bulge and the death marches and the four months in the Stalag, when his entire division of some fourteen thousand men had been crammed aboard the once-elegant liner, the *Queen Elizabeth I,* and carried speedily across the North Atlantic to join the Battle of Europe. There had also been a strange, incongruous sort of vacation feeling about that crossing. He remembered his pal Hornstein strolling the crowded decks, looking to all the world like a retired millionaire on an ocean cruise as he puffed away on his big Havana cigars. Hornstein now seemed in that same well-fed, expansive frame of mind. He had apparently not been excessively scarred by all the intervening events. His big complaint now was that he had run out of stogies. There had not been any subsequent distributions by the Russians after that first one. Hornstein, who never lowered his expectations, was expecting all the comforts of Manhattan, where there was a handy cigar store on every corner.

The three Kriegies had sauntered casually across the spacious town square with its Gothic city hall and ancient hotel and shops and houses, taking it all in like any peacetime tourists might do. They were learning the layout of the town and the various side streets. There was a flow of vehicles and pedestrians of all descriptions moving freely about. German civilians were beginning to venture out to the local shops; there were Russian soldiers, some afoot and others pedalling bikes; here and there an American or British Kriegie enjoying the day and his new freedom; and occasionally they glimpsed those groups of pale and emaciated women scampering about in the shadows, looking as if they had just escaped from some horror movie.

The trio was soon heading in the direction of the park at the riverfront. They could stretch out on the grass and maybe catch a snooze. Just like in the old days at home. It was a lazy, uneventful afternoon.

Hyams had just commented, "Isn't it nice to see civilians again?" when his eye was drawn to a pair of those faceless and frightened young women up ahead. They seemed almost bird-like in their nervous, halting gait. The women were coming toward them, and their paths would cross. What particularly caught Hyams' attention were the brightly hued ribbon rosettes that each girl had pinned to her tattered outer garment. It was obvious that these were some sort of colors intended to identify their nationality. But red, white, and blue? These weren't Russian or German colors.

American colors? Could these be American girls here in this very unlikely location in the heart of Germany? Hardly!

"But!" Hyams was by now always prepared for the unexpected, "these gals could be French. The colors are French . . . the tricolor, you know. Those rosettes are similar to what the French Kriegies wore in the Stalag! But they seem very, I don't know, very skittish, very nervous."

The next best thing to meeting American girls in Krondorf, of course, would be to meet French girls. And of course there would be an obligation to assist and defend French girls from the Russian peril, just as there would be if they were American or British. Chivalry would demand that.

Hornstein was dubious. These girls didn't have that French look. He shook his head, "Not a chance. They're not French; I wouldn't bother, but you can try out your French on them and see what happens."

As they approached within nodding distance, Hyams tossed a polite *"Bonjour"* at them in fractured French, just to be polite, nothing more. These girls were not exactly what the Kriegies had lately begun to see in their reveries. There was just too much reminiscent of war and sadness in their eyes. After a brief hesitation, one of them shyly acknowledged the greeting, likewise in French. This could, perhaps, be interesting. After all, the French were allies, and these gals could be in distress, floating around here, friendless, in Russian-occupied territory. But upon closer examination, things just didn't add up. These young women had no suggestion of the perky vivacity that the Kriegies had found so charming in their respective earlier sojourns in France. These two women were more reminiscent of the Russkie prisoners of the old Stalag days than of the French *mademoiselles* so immortalized in fact and fiction.

The women, sensing disapproval, hurried along on their way. For that matter, the Kriegies themselves didn't project an image of total respectability in their nondescript Stalag attire. Yet there was something about the two women, something like the riveting appeal of a wounded bird, that struck the Kriegies as their eyes followed the two figures who now seemed intent on getting away. Their heads were covered with kerchiefs drawn tightly around pale and pinched faces from which eyes squinted and blinked nervously. Their clothing was ill-fitting, threadbare, and ragged. On their feet they wore wood-soled clogs, which were obviously uncomfortable and difficult to walk in. They were hunched over and very tense and ill at ease, and they whispered among themselves in some strange tongue, definitely not French. They somehow reminded Hyams of the concentration camp survivors he had observed that morning at the Russian clinic, except that these people were walking and talking, and able to navigate under their own power.

"Godamn, they're just more victims of the friggin' war!" declared Hornstein in conclusion. "There's millions of them. Nothing we can do."

"Hold on, mates, why can't we take them back to the Russkie clinic and get them some food, at the very least? They sure look like they could use it." Witherspoon would use any excuse to get back to the clinic. He was in love with a perky young Russian medical lieutenant. Her name was Irina, and that was all he knew about her. But he had been smitten, and hope springs eternal; and a paratrooper never gives up.

Witherspoon's enthusiasm carried the moment. There was

something about these women that tugged at the heart. That special sadness coupled with defiance. Hyams suddenly knew they were Jewish, they were his people, and he was going to help them. He ran after and caught up with them.

"*Pardon, mademoiselles, comment allez-vous? Est-ce que vous avez besoin d'assistance?*" It was high school French, but it got the message across.

There was a moment of nervous consultation between the women, and then one turned and responded to Hyams. She was the spokesperson. He judged her to be in her thirties, but she might have been younger. Probably was. There was a sudden urgency in her voice. "*Oui, Monsieur, nous avons besoin de secours médical, s'il vous plaît!*"

Then the other, a younger girl in her teens, joined in beseechingly, "*Et de nourriture, s'il vous plaît, Monsieur!*" They needed medical assistance and food. And now it was more like panic.

Witherspoon and Hornstein joined the group. The women searched the faces of the men in an unspoken appeal. "We could take them to the Russkie clinic, like I said." Witherspoon was energized.

"I think they're Jewish," said Hornstein.

At this the older woman, who must have been multi-lingual, betrayed a new fear. "No, no . . . we are not Jewish, not Jewish," she protested in both French and in German for emphasis.

There was an awkward silence until Hyams spoke up, "I am Jewish," pointing at himself as if to reassure her. Then they looked about at the other two Kriegies. Hornstein gave one of his cutesy smiles and nodded sheepishly, "Sure, what else?" And Witherspoon just blanched and averted his gaze. He was not ready to undertake any new commitments, even to comfort two confused refugees.

The women suddenly erupted in a cascade of tears, even as they rushed forward to embrace Hyams.

There was instant bonding. They gushed out their story, both speaking at once in German, in French, in Yiddish, and even some English. But the clear outlines of their story emerged in a remarkably logical sequence.

First they explained the tricolor rosettes. They were Czechoslovak Jews, and the French tricolor had been adopted as the Czech national colors back when that republic had been carved out of the old Austro-Hungarian Empire after the first World War in 1920. So much for the tricolor rosettes. Not French, although there were strong cultural ties with France, and French was the second language taught in most Czech high schools.

These two were only the scouts sent out to reconnoiter for food and medical help by a larger group of Jewish women now immobilized and in hiding nearby. There was a total of eight girls in their group. They had escaped two weeks earlier from an S.S. death march after months on the road from one of the horror camps in Poland. They had been driven like cattle through the Polish winter. Few had survived. These eight survivors had reached the outskirts of Krondorf, and they were holed up in an old abandoned schoolhouse outside of town, hiding first from the Germans, then from the night-marauding Russians. They were trying to get back to their homeland to look for surviving kin or anyone from their past. The Czech border was only some sixty miles in a generally southeasterly direction. The road home would lead through the old Czechoslovak Republic, but there were still considerable German forces holding out inside Czechoslovakia and around Dresden and further south along the Elbe. Confused and demoralized, the girls were now stranded here in Russian-occupied territory, in the backwash of the ebbing war, friendless and helpless.

"So what else is new?" muttered good old Hornstein. He had exhausted his supply of cigars the other day, and he was in a foul mood. There wasn't a single cigar store in Krondorf.

But there was more to the girls' story. This was just the background story. On the previous day, while moving along a deserted back road leading into Krondorf, as if they didn't have enough trouble, one of their group had stepped on a German anti-personnel mine buried in the road. The resulting blast had shattered the girl's leg and inflicted grievous facial and head wounds. The girl had received no medical attention, other than what little her comrades could do for her without any medical supplies. She was now in very grave condition in the old schoolhouse where they had spent the night. They were desperately in need of professional medical help for the stricken girl, as well as some sort of safe haven and food for the rest of them.

Now Witherspoon felt vindicated. These people must be brought immediately to the Russkie clinic.

The group of women could not remain where they were for fear of marauding Russian troops who, on their nocturnal drunken rampages, had made life hellish for them. Yet they could not travel further with the wounded girl.

The younger girl kept repeating, "She will die unless we can get her to a hospital. We can take you to where she is. Please!"

The entire scenario was one of abject despair. The Kriegies, for whom the violence and trauma of war had once been so real, were now stunned by this tale of unmitigated misfortune. The younger girl, who was referred to by her companion as Marta, kept pleading for help for the group.

Witherspoon was possessed of an irresistible desire to get back to the Russian hospital for no matter what reason. This was a perfect cause, and he enlisted without hesitation, taking up the cry, "Let's get going, mates. What are we waiting for?"

Hornstein wanted to know how far it was to the "hiding place." Eva, the spokeswoman, was ready. "It is only about two kilometers, sir."

"Fine. How are we going to carry this wounded girl two kilometers or more, or whatever the distance is, to the hospital?"

Eva had the answer for that one too. It seemed that the girls had in their travels acquired a two-wheeled farm cart, upon which they had brought the wounded girl to the shelter of the schoolhouse and which could now be used to transport her to the hospital.

The appeal could not be ignored. It wasn't as if the Kriegies had any other pressing commitments at the moment, and Witherspoon saw this entire thing as a heaven-sent opportunity. So despite Hornstein's numerous reservations and doubts, they set out on this mission of mercy as Eva and little Marta led the way. What had started out as a casual "good day" between strangers on the sidewalks of Krondorf was "taking a turn into some uncharted waters," to borrow another of Hornstein's favorite expressions.

Within a half-hour the rescue party arrived at a dilapidated structure set back some distance off a deserted back road. It was almost completely hidden by brush and tall weeds. It looked as if it might indeed once have been a country schoolhouse. There were no signs of life from within as they approached. Eva and Marta went on ahead to inform the occupants of the good news that help was coming. When the Kriegies entered they found a total of eight women in the place, including the two scouts Eva and Marta and the wounded girl who lay deathlike on the cart. Of the others, two were apparently down with some fever or illness, lying immobile on straw pallets on the floor. One sat apart on her haunches in a corner, mumbling to herself. Two were alert and moving among the sick and the wounded in a valiant effort to minister to their needs, although they themselves were in a state of utter exhaustion.

The sight of the bloodied girl—ashen-faced, emaciated, in terrible pain and agony from her wounds, one of her legs mangled and swathed in bloody rags, and a gaping jagged hole in her cheek—brought back all the ugly memories of battle and death and suffering. The Kriegies were struck by the tragic irony of these grievous wounds, inflicted on the very eve of liberation by a silent, concealed engine of destruction, upon one who had survived the Nazi hell. It was yet another testimony of the blind and unrelenting vindictiveness of war.

The die was now cast. The Kriegies, no strangers to tragedy and pain, had responded to a desperate cry for help. Even Hornstein had to agree that although these were indeed uncharted waters, there could be no turning their backs on these unfortunate people.

There was one girl who was sort of the Mother Superior. Her name was Norma, and she seemed to make all the final decisions for the group. She was not trustful of strangers, and it took several minutes for Eva and Marta to convince her of the identities and the credentials of the would-be rescuers. Hyams tried to explain, but she averted her eyes. However, she soon started to issue instructions for the move. She said that they would have to move the two sick girls as well as the wounded Kati to the hospital. They would all be leaving the schoolhouse.

The cavalcade set out on the return to Krondorf. There were the three Kriegies and the eight women, including the one they called Kati, who was was being wheeled on the cart, two who were too sick to walk on their own and had to be helped, one who was physically okay but distracted and definitely out of it mentally, and four whom one might consider able-bodied but who were at the edge of physical collapse from hunger and exhaustion.

It was mid-afternoon when the group entered the Officers' Training Complex and headed for the clinic where Irina worked.

CHAPTER THREE

Bismarckstrasse No. 79

THREE OF THE WOMEN were received immediately into the care of the clinic. The two ambulatory cases were diagnosed as suffering from paratyphus, an illness common among the survivors and treatable with antibiotics. However, Kati, the wounded girl, would require immediate surgery. Her life hung in the balance.

Witherspoon was thrilled that his Irina was on the case. He could not contain his profound admiration, tantamount to worship, for the Russian girl-doctor whom he had first observed one day riding her bicycle in the Stalag soon after the Russian take-over. She had then been with the first Soviet medical contingent assigned to check the physical condition of the Kriegie population in the camp. That had been about ten days earlier, and he had been smitten. He now kept asking, "Did you see how calmly she took charge? And how she got those medical orderlies hoppin'? Blimey, they had Kati prepped for surgery within seconds! What a woman!"

He was really hooked. But if Irina was ever aware of him, she certainly gave no indication of it. She was all business. She had to be. She was a doctor, with a heavy patient load.

After being satisfied that their sick and wounded would be properly treated and looked after, the group of five remaining women, under the direction of Norma, agreed to accompany the Kriegies to the commissary. They were famished, and here they were offered a feast of cabbage soup with meat and potatoes. They thought they were in heaven. After some urgent negotiation with the mess sergeant, Hyams saw to it that they were each given half a loaf of bread and a block of cheese to carry away with them. The women were incredulous at this turn of events. It was as if some heavenly gate had opened up for them and they had suddenly been welcomed back into the world of the living.

It had been a hectic afternoon for the three Kriegies who had started out for an innocent stroll in the town only a few hours earlier. They had now somehow involved themselves in the lives of these eight stranded orphans of the storm, and had assumed some sort of ephemeral responsibilty for their short-term welfare while in Krondorf. Moreover it now became apparent that the women might become somewhat of a long-term fixture in the town, because they would not leave until there was some medical disposition of Kati's case as well as of the other two patients.

By this time Hornstein was again reciting his mantra to the effect that "no good deed ever goes unpunished," while Witherspoon was disgruntled by Irina's continued failure to acknowledge his existence. They were all now standing awkwardly about on the front steps of the commissary. The girls had their precious food packets, and all but Norma were effusively grateful for this sudden upturn in their fortunes, yet they remained deeply concerned about Kati's condition. Norma was thinking ahead to their next moves as they discussed among themselves the advisability of returning to the old schoolhouse for the night. This was not a happy prospect, but where else could they go?

Norma, the "Mother Superior," as Hornstein came to call her, would have the final say. She opted for returning, in spite of the known dangers from nighttime harassment. She was tough. The others reluctantly agreed that there was no alternative. Where else could they go, indeed?

But Hyams didn't think that was right. It was now late afternoon. After what these girls had been through, they deserved a better break. Some decent lodging for the night certainly could be found for them in this town so brimfull of stately old houses, many of which appeared empty and deserted.

Hornstein and Witherspoon were predictably horrified at this suggestion. This could open a veritable Pandora's box of unforeseen problems and complications. Hornstein tried to reason gently with

Hyams. "Look, kid, we've helped these gals out in a big way. The medics said that Kati couldn't have lasted an hour without that plasma. And now they're going to save her life. Of course, she might lose the leg, but that is something out of anybody's control. The same with the other two . . . that Olga and Sari, I can't even keep their names straight! Now that they're on sulfa, their fever will be coming down. They'll be okay in a few days. We've done a great thing for these people. Now it's time to turn them loose. They will manage fine. What did they do before they found us? They survived. So let's just mosey on back to the barracks before we get our asses in a real sling. If we mess around here in town and get picked up in the curfew we will only end up in the Russkie stockade! And you might never get home to your beloved Sylvia! Remember big-bosomed Sylvia who's waiting for you back in Brooklyn?"

Witherspoon agreed. "We can't adopt five women, mate. It's just not in the cards!"

Hyams was not going to wash his hands of this situation. For some unfathomable reason, a major humanitarian chord had been struck in his breast. "Look you guys, you can go back to the barracks. I've got to find these gals some decent place to stay. They're stuck here 'cause they won't leave town until there is some word on Kati and the two sick ones. I know there's plenty of vacant houses, and I'm going to find one and move them in. Give me a half-hour. If I can't find anything, then they can go back to the schoolhouse!"

With these words Hyams took off, after first telling Eva and Marta of his plan. These two were the most sympathetic and the most communicative of the group. They understood, and concurred with a grateful smile and a nod. They got Norma to hold off her final decision to return to the schoolhouse.

At Hyams' departure, Witherspoon decided that he, too, would leave. He wanted to return to the clinic to find out when Irina got off duty. "Maury, I've got to get back there and see the Leftenant. Isn't she terrific? The way she's in charge? She really inspires confidence. And her English is not all that bad. We can really understand each other. Did you notice how our eyes always meet?"

Witherspoon reset his red paratrooper beret at a jaunty angle. Short and slightly built, he was the consummate military dandy. High-spirited, feisty, and cocky . . . a perfect Jimmy Cagney prototype. And like all paratroopers the world over, he was most proud of his magnificent jump boots, which, despite the long months in the mud of the Stalag, were still in "mint" condition, the leather still retaining its original lustrous shine—no small phenomenon considering the many miles of hard usage that they had seen. Witherspoon was mission-oriented, and right now his mission was to reconnoiter the clinic for the purpose of making contact with the cute "Leftenant."

But Hornstein was not about to encourage the little guy. Between Hyams and Witherspoon he was really losing control of events. He didn't like not being in control.

"Godamn, forget the 'Leftenant.' What the hell is wrong with you? We've got a problem here! What are we going to do about that crazy Hyams and this bunch of women that he's got us tied into?"

"Got 'us' tied into? Not 'us,' mate. All I did was help out in a bloomin' little errand of mercy. Like a good scout. Okay. Mission accomplished as far as I'm concerned, mate. Now you can tell Hyams that I've got other fish to fry. Cheerio, old chum!"

Eva, standing by and overhearing the exchange between Hornstein and Witherspoon, was pained and embarrassed. "You have already done so much for us. You have saved Kati's life. That is what the young Russian doctor said. She is very nice. She is assisting in the surgery. She said you deserve all the credit, and we will never forget you. But now we do not wish to burden you further."

At this favorable mention of Irina and her reported comment about the Kriegies' role in saving Kati's life, Witherspoon beamed ecstatically and his former diffidence melted away.

Marta added her own benediction, "God will repay you for what you have done."

Witherspoon cleared his throat. And then there was a heavy silence all around. Nobody knew how to make the next move, how to disengage from this awkward situation. After an interval of shuffling and shifting about, just as Norma was taking command of the situation and reiterating her determination to return to the schoolhouse, Hyams reappeared. He had been running. He was waving and shouting. "I've got a place! It's perfect! You won't believe it! Let's go, all of you!"

Norma would have none of it. "You have already done enough for us. Now we must take charge of our own problems. We are strong; we will manage. The most important thing was to get the help for Kati and the other two."

Hyams spoke to Hornstein and Witherspoon. "It will be dark soon. We've got to get them through this night, and in the morning they can go out and find a place for themselves. But floating around town after dark would be definitely bad. I wouldn't want that on my conscience. I've found this house just off the main square. It is not occupied. They can shut themselves in and get a good night's sleep. Then they're on their own."

Despite the strong reservations expressed by Norma, the girls were strongly tempted by Hyams' suggestion. They were ready to investigate the house.

"But whose house is this?" Norma demanded to know. "We are not beggars or vandals! We cannot move into someone's house without permission, even if we might like to."

Hyams was losing patience. "It is not occupied. The owners are away. They might never come back. This is war! There is no one to ask. Who knows? Who cares? This is only for a day or two."

Norma was holding out, irritated by Hyams' logic. She was the mother hen, old beyond her twenty-one years . . . three of which had been spent in Auschwitz. She just wasn't swayed by the daring and innovative ideas which Hyams seemed constantly to be coming up with. She didn't trust strangers. And these three Kriegies were, after all, strangers, even if they had brought a new positive dimension into her life and the lives of her companions. But she was not about to give up control to this brash young American who seemed to think that all problems had easy solutions.

"There is still some daylight. We will find a place, even if it is a chicken coop!"

Hyams gave up. "This is a safe, clean place. If you want to sleep in a chicken coop, then by all means, be my guest!" He turned away in anger and frustration. And then the girls united against Norma's obstinacy. After a few minutes of excited jabber with some muted giggling, the verdict was returned. Norma was overridden.

The entire group now set out for the house. The three Kriegies went first, with Hyams in the lead; the five women brought up the rear, with Marta, the youngest pulling the farm cart, and Sonya tagging along behind, seeming oblivious to what was going on.

In a few minutes they were back in the town square, and then Hyams led them off into a tree-shaded street that radiated off from the square, behind the city hall. It was one of the prestigious old residential streets of the town. The sign read BISMARCKSTR. The house that Hyams had zeroed in on was Number 79. It was an imposing three-story Georgian structure, which had obviously once, not so long ago, housed some people of considerable means and status. The place was in excellent condition, judging from the carefully maintained exterior. Every window was tightly shuttered against the uncertainties of the approaching night and the general disorder of the times. It was certainly not a house to be taken lightly.

Hyams stood there beaming proudly as the hushed Kriegies and their female wards gazed in awe upon this mansion. Hornstein was the first to explode. "You're crazy, Zeke. You are absolutely bananas! And now it's practically nighttime and we've got to get these ladies back to their schoolhouse in the godamn dark. This is a real screw-up, Hyams!"

Witherspoon just stood there shaking his head. This day was not turning out to his liking at all. As for the girls, they didn't know whether to laugh or cry. This was all so ridiculous. But Hyams remained adamant and undaunted.

"This here is the place. I've checked it out. I've even talked to a neighbor kid. It's deserted. It's empty. There's no one living in this house. It's ours for the asking!"

"You're daft, man. This is a bloody mansion." Witherspoon just kept shaking his head as he spoke. "Just because it might look bloody deserted doesn't mean that it is. There could even be some real live Nazis holed up in there. There's plenty of die-hards around. One bloke with a Luger can do us all in, you know! This is definitely the wrong place, mate!"

"I tell you I've been inside. I got in through a back door that was unlocked. There's no one living in this house, and there hasn't been for some time. I could tell. All the furniture is covered up, and there hasn't been a fire in the hearth for ages. I even checked the cellar. It's full of wine and booze and enough food to feed a regiment. If these girls get themselves one night's sleep in there and a couple of square meals, they can look the world in the face again. What's wrong with that?"

While everybody was standing around in a quandary, Hyams walked decisively through the unlocked garden gate. He seemed completely familiar with the layout of the place. Within seconds he was heard turning the heavy lock on the front door and then he swung the oaken portal wide open. He stood there in the doorway, looking to all the world like the rightful owner of this very impressive house, beckoning his guests to enter.

And so it came to pass that the three Kriegies and their five female wards found themselves standing in the high-domed, gilded, and mirrored drawing room of Number 79 Bismarckstrasse.

The richly panelled chamber was bathed by the light of an overhead crystal chandelier as Hornstein found the switches and turned on all the lights in the house. The Kriegies didn't want any surprises springing out at them from any dark corners. The place was truly palatial, and someone apparently had been paying the light bills.

The ripening prospect of actually moving into this fabulous house was yet another dramatic turn for the Kriegies, as well as for the women, who in the recent past had known only the shelter of water-logged ditches or cattle cars or Stalags or concentration camps or open snow-drifts, or, most lately, an abandoned ruin of a schoolhouse.

But the big shock of the day for the women came when they saw themselves reflected in the magnificent Venetian mirrors. It was probably the first time since the beginning of their ordeal in the Nazi camps that they had seen themselves reflected in a mirror. They had all put in their hard time in Auschwitz and had then endured the entire miserable winter on the road, poorly shod and clothed, being driven like cattle by the S.S. across Poland and East Germany. Ninety percent of the people who had left Auschwitz in January before the Russian advance had succumbed to hunger, cold, exhaustion, and disease. These people were definitely survivors. They stood there aghast at the toll taken by the long months of starvation and terror and degradation. They were looking at strangers. They could not recognize themselves. They looked away. Several broke down sobbing and in tears, covering their faces with their hands. They could not bear to see themselves. It was too much. Only Norma and the distracted Sonya had refrained from looking into the mirrors.

Magda, a woman possibly in her mid-thirties, who showed traces of one-time beauty and poise, tugged at her face and her hair. "My God! I am an old woman! I look like an old hag! What they have done to me!"

She had spent two years in the Nazi hell camps. She had seen a ten-year-old son led off to the gas chamber. She had once been beautiful and glamorous, the wife of a physician. Marta came to her side, placed an arm about her shoulder and tried to say something comforting. The teenage Marta looked to Magda as an older sister. She consoled her, trying to be lighthearted. "Now why should you, dear Magda, look better than the rest of us?"

This broke the tension, and some smiles returned to tear-streaked faces. They were all in this together. They had plenty of company in their misery. What now to do but laugh about it and at themselves? It hurt too much to cry.

Norma had seen enough. She would have no part of this opulence and luxury. She was adamant. "We do not belong here. There can only be trouble here, either with the German owners or with the Russian police. We do not belong in this magnificent mausoleum, with its paintings and statues and silks and satins."

But it was Magda who made the argument for remaining. She talked of getting a night's sleep in a real bed, of soap, of a bath, of a touch of comfort, even of luxury. In her past she had not been a stranger to luxury. Leave this sumptuous house only to be terrorized in some hovel by drunken soldiers and vagabonds of the road? How could they turn their backs on this place, which stood vacant and unused by its owners? What harm could there be in it?

Eva joined in, "Why on Earth should we deny ourselves a night's sleep and perhaps even a decent bath?"

"Which God knows we so desperately need!" This was Marta, blushing fiercely, but determined to help make the point.

Sensing Norma's unspoken concern about the "seemliness" of the arrangement, Hyams pointed out that the women would have the privacy of the house to themselves. "There is a gardener's cottage in the rear yard where my friends and I can spend the night. You will have this whole place to yourselves. And at the first crack of dawn we'll all get out before anyone will know we were here!"

Norma was again out-argued and out-voted. She finally had no choice but to agree that with darkness there was no way that the women could forsake the safety of this house.

This left Hornstein and Witherspoon as reluctant and uneasy partners in this strange enterprise that Hyams had so blithely concocted. Hornstein voiced new misgivings. "This place has been lived in fairly recently. In no way is this an abandoned house, no matter what Hyams says!"

"Abandoned? Hell, the cellar is filled to the rafters with tons of food supplies, cognac, vodka, French wines, you name it! And upstairs there are crates of French soaps and cosmetics and bloody perfumes. This place belongs to some high bloody muckamuck, and sooner or later somebody is going to show up, and I just hope we're not here when they do. And the Russians. It's bloody incredible that they haven't yet discovered this place." Thus spoke Witherspoon, and he was not happy.

But within minutes the women dispersed through the house, intent on turning the place into a home, if only for one night. And the Kriegies decided to make the best of it—the stately surroundings, and the comfortable lounge furniture. As things settled down, Hyams was all smiles. "The gals are in the kitchen, fixing dinner. Cheer up, you two. Pretty soon dinner will be served in the main dining room, and I think these gals can really cook up a storm. Why doesn't somebody bring up a couple of bottles of wine to go with dinner, while I build a fire. It's getting a bit nippy in here."

The ancient grandfather clock in the front hall was just chiming eight bells, the perfect time for a leisurely continental dinner. Witherspoon rose from his easy chair to head for the stairway leading down to the wine cellar. And at that very moment the Kriegies were suddenly frozen by the soft clicking of the lock tumblers in the front door. Within seconds there were two unfamiliar figures standing in the entry foyer. They were certainly unfamiliar, and larger than life. But they looked like they belonged there. They were the owners of the house, breathing fire, come to reclaim possession of their property.

And these were not the sort of people one could just ignore, or tell them to "Get lost!" or "Take a hike, mates!"

CHAPTER FOUR

The General's Wife

THEY were mother and teenage son. They were very blond, very erect, very Aryan, very arrogant, and very miffed.

The woman, tall and stately, was the picture of mature Nordic womanhood as she stood imperiously in the entry foyer. Strikingly attired in a calf-length black leather coat, her ash-blond hair was drawn tightly back in a severe bun, exposing a classic high forehead and blazing green eyes that relentlessly scanned every visible square inch of the interior of the house. She was none other than Frau General von Hesselmann, the legal owner of all that she now surveyed in horror and disbelief.

She stood there in haughty silence for a full minute or longer, letting her unspoken message of profound disdain slowly register. By her side, exuding defiance and contempt for the by now thoroughly cowed Kriegies, was a tall, handsome, golden-haired youth, blue-eyed and cherub-faced, in his mid-teens. He wore the leather breeches and white knee-high knitted stockings favored by the Hitler Youth. This was her son, her only son, and his name was Kurt; and he considered himself the man of the house since his father, the General, was away on extended war business somewhere on the now-defunct Eastern Front.

The two of them strode purposefully into the drawing room. In the bright glare of the lamps and the huge chandelier, Frau von Hesselmann betrayed some puzzlement at the audacity of this takeover of her palatial home. There was certainly nothing covert or timorous about this bald-faced intrusion and occupation of her house by this band of motley miscreants.

Squarely facing this threat to the sanctity of her home and its priceless contents, she spoke out in a firm voice with remarkable aplomb and self-control. At this point she was addressing herself to the Kriegies. The women were not present, all being occupied elsewhere in the house; their presence in the house, however, was not unknown to her. The sounds of female conversation and some laughter and the clinking of utensils were clearly audible from the direction of the kitchen.

The lady spoke with clipped Teutonic authority. She didn't intend to have to repeat herself. "This is a private residence and you have absolutely no right here. There are many witnesses. You were seen by the neighbors as you entered, and this has been reported to the military police. You must leave immediately! And I must warn you there are severe penalties for looting!"

Hyams, the author and chief architect of the housing plan that was now about to collapse on his head, was the first to recover his power of speech. He stood alone and defenseless before the lady. He had ignored all the warnings and all the doubts and reservations expressed by Hornstein and Witherspoon, and . . . oh yes, Norma!

Fending off panic and marshalling his wits, Hyams thought he detected a hairline chink in the lady's armor plate. It occurred to him that, after all is said and done, nobody who was so firmly on the losing side in a war to the bitter end, like this one had been, could now be so high and mighty. The lady and her son were putting on a righteous but falsely aggressive front.

Her use of the term "looting" gave Hyams his opening. She was indulging in reckless slander. It was demeaning and insulting. There was no basis for this scurrilous remark. Nothing had been removed from the house; nothing was out of place.

"Madam, with all due respect, there is no question here of looting! We are not here to steal or loot anything!" Frau von Hesselmann had overstepped the bounds of civility, and Hyams was not going to let her get away with it. This was no way to talk to "guests," albeit uninvited guests!

Speaking of looting, how the hell had these respectable citizens come by all those fancy French perfumes and all that wine and champagne and the rare brandies from every corner of Europe, and the Danish hams and all the rest of those exotic foreign goodies ad infinitum? Not to speak of the invaluable collection of *objets d'art* that were everywhere in evidence beneath the dust covers. They sure as hell hadn't paid retail for all that stuff. Germany and her generals had been successful in all their early farflung campaigns, like in Poland, in France, in Norway, in the Balkans, and even in Russia. German homes were now full of mementoes of all those conquered territories. Nope, Hyams suddenly realized that she was really in no position to raise that issue. Not that anyone intended to go into such matters at this time. But he would have to topple her off of her high horse.

"We understood that this house was not occupied, that is, it was not being lived in at this time. It appeared to be boarded up. You must admit that. And our intention was only to get a night's shelter. There are many abandoned homes, while there are people, you know, who are homeless and hungry and desperate. We could see no harm in it!" Hyams was beginning to think he had a case. And he was beginning to suspect that she was bluffing about notifying the Russian military police. She would certainly not want to draw attention to this lavishly stocked house.

By this time a couple of the girls had filtered in from the kitchen. Hyams didn't know whether that was going to help or hurt his case. Frau von Hesselmann would not appreciate a bunch of females messing around in her kitchen.

"I am the owner of this house. It is not abandoned, and it was not boarded up. And whether it is occupied or not is certainly no concern of yours! I demand that you leave, all of you! And immediately!"

Finally Hornstein emerged from the shadows and was ready to lend a hand. He addressed the lady in his most affable manner. His one-time involvement in New York City politics had definitely done something for his debating eloquence.

"Dear lady, we're not here to steal or to damage anything. This is a grand house, and we respect that. It would certainly be a crime to disturb the house or the contents. We're only trying to help some unfortunate people who are in desperate straits. It is really an emergency situation. And we were planning to leave in the morning." Hornstein and Hyams made their pleas in English, and the lady was responding likewise in perfect English. She was obviously a person of education and refinement who could possibly be reasoned with.

But she stood her ground. Generals' ladies don't capitulate. "I am not interested in your reasons or motives. You would be wise to leave before the police arrive. Breaking and entering is a very serious offense that will be dealt with harshly!"

Then Kurt, the handsome, self-righteous one, felt compelled to reinforce his mother's stance. But his rancorous attacks only raised the debate to a new level of acrimony. He was vindictive and insolent. He equated the Kriegies and their companions with "street criminals . . . bent on plunder." His position, reiterated repeatedly and forcefully, was that the intruders must vanish as if by magic, instantly, into the night.

This was hard to take from one so young and haughty. The results were entirely predictable. Witherspoon took an intense dislike to the young man and had to be restrained from slapping him down, while the Kriegies became ever more confirmed in their decision to stay put for the night.

It was in the midst of this impasse that a new development heightened the intensity of emotion between the contending sides. It was Sonya, the girl who never spoke and who was not quite right in her mind. She had drifted into the drawing room behind the others, all of whom kept discreetly in the background.

As Kurt came to assume the leading prosecutorial role in the confrontation, Sonya appeared riveted by the antics of the animated youngster. She fixed her gaze upon him, intently studying his eyes and features. Then suddenly her own face contorted in anguish, and she began to flail her arms frantically as she struggled in vain to produce some coherent words. Marta moved to her side and enfolded her in an embrace to calm her as Sonya broke down sobbing, all the while continuing to shake an accusing finger menacingly at Kurt. She would not release him from her hate-filled glare.

Both the Frau and her son were momentarily thrown off balance by Sonya's irrational and hysterical performance. There were now new cross-currents at work. The Frau seemed to be somewhat less self-assured.

Hyams thought it best to ignore Sonya's outburst. He returned to a rational pleading of his case. "Will you tell us that you actually live here in this house at the present time?"

Frau Hesselmann would not lie, even to gain an advantage. So she sidestepped the question. "The house is locked up and it shall stay that way!"

Hyams again appealed to her sense of compassion. And then she replied in an icy tone, "There are special camps for the displaced. Where they are fed and given medical aid if they require it. That is where your people belong if they are indeed in such dire straits! This is not a camp for the displaced." She obviously thought that some psychiatric care was indicated for Sonya, at the very least.

Now the Frau had again stepped onto thin ice. Summoning Norma to come forward, Hyams grabbed the girl's arm and ripped open a sleeve to the elbow, exposing a serial number tattooed on her forearm.

"These 'people,' my dear Madam, have all been to your camps. They have all been branded like cattle in your camps. If you want to listen, they can tell you more than you would like to hear about the death camps in Poland."

The Frau was not prepared for this impassioned counter-attack. She shrank back instinctively, softening slightly. "It is very unfortunate. But we are at war. We did not start this war. It is a great tragedy for everyone. We also have paid dearly."

It was now Hornstein's turn at bat. In a sweeping gesture, taking in the grandeur of the room, he asked, "Have you really paid so dearly? There is not the slightest evidence here of hardship or the kind of losses that many people have suffered in this war. You can see for yourself that these women are in desperate need, and also that we are not vandals. The issue here is only about a night's lodging, nothing more!"

"I cannot surrender my house to anyone. The Russians have an obligation to protect the civilian population. They will know how to deal with you." With this the Frau, with the boy at her side, strode from the room to launch an energetic inspection tour of the rest of the house, obviously to assess the damage for her report to the authorities.

After a few minutes, they returned to the drawing room. They had checked the locks on such things as cabinets, wardrobes, closets, wine racks, and the several pantries. They had apparently not found anything very serious to complain about; nothing of real value had been disturbed. They decided that they had no choice but to permit the Kriegies and their "guests" to remain the night. They would have to postpone their major eviction effort until the morning, if the intruders were to still be there.

Kurt's parting shot as he and his mother prepared to take their leave was an angry warning that the house had better be cleared of its uninvited guests by first light in the morning. He then, almost reflexively, completed a motion with upraised arm that may have been meant as a gesture of hostility and defiance. At that moment Sonya let out a piercing wail. Some ancient and excruciating wound had been torn open. And this time the words and the accusations came in a cascading torrent of emotion.

"He's the one! That's him! I know that man. He killed my baby! Dear God, he is a murderer! He is the one!"

Things were getting sticky. The women huddled around the screaming Sonya, trying to calm her. "He is only a boy, Sonya. Please try to calm yourself. You are safe . . . nothing can happen to you. And he is leaving. He is only a boy, Sonya."

"No, no . . . he is the one. He shot my baby! Not once but again and again . . . and my father . . . and all the villagers! He is the one; I tell you. We must kill him before he can kill anyone else!"

Frau von Hesselmann and her son left the house in rapid lock-step. They didn't want to hear any more of Sonya's rantings. She was obviously very sick, and they were now convinced that these people would have to be evicted from the house by whatever means possible. But nothing could be undertaken until the morning.

The girls finally got Sonya put to bed. They would later report that she lay awake for hours in the darkness, then alternating between wild-eyed wakefulness, quiet moaning, muffled lullabies to a long-gone child, and occasional wild hysterics through the night.

The girls had all withdrawn to their upstairs sleeping quarters when the Kriegies re-assembled in the comfortable surroundings of the drawing room with its overstuffed easy chairs and footrests. The mad pace of the day's activities was beginning to tell on them. Now there was some quiet time to take stock of the situation. It certainly didn't look like the Hesselmanns were going to accept their presence in the house without making some kind of big stink over it.

Hornstein, the oldest in years and experience, "smelled big trouble a-brewing." They had best be gone by early morning before those Hesselmanns returned.

Witherspoon concurred whole-heartedly. "I would definitely not like to run afoul of those bloody Russkie M.P.s. That's one trouble I damn well don't need."

But Hyams remained strangely upbeat. "Not to panic, gentlemen. I don't see how the lady can turn us in. The Russkies would only take the place over for themselves, and then she'd be shit out of luck, for sure! No, those two are just bluffing!"

"Unless, mate, they've got some special drag with the Russkies, which is not impossible, you know! The owner of this house is, after all, a bloody general!" Witherspoon understood the universal military psyche. A general is a general in anybody's country.

Less than eight hours had passed since the Kriegies had left the quiet security and comfort of the cadet barracks. They had set out for a walk in the town, minding their own business and expecting to be back in time for dinner. How had they been swept up in this outlandish caper?

They all wondered about it, even Hyams, whose enthusiasm and possibly naive optimism had carried them along on what had started out as a minor mission of mercy, to help get a wounded girl to the hospital. Now they were in this strange house, whose influential owners were rightfully put out and determined to regain possession of their property. They had set themselves up, on their own initiative, as the guardian angels of a group of confused and beaten women who were practically helpless to cope with a host of emotional and physical problems. Had they unwittingly injected themselves into the middle of the European snakepit of unforgiving and unrelenting tensions, where people get killed and worse just for being of the wrong ethnic mix? Did they need this, just at the time when everything was going so well for them, and when the prospects of a peaceful and uneventful return to home and hearth and all the good things of life were so bright and shining?

Hyams finally summed it up. "We're getting the hell out of here first thing in the morning. These gals will have at least a decent night's rest and some decent food, and then they'll just have to manage on their own."

Hornstein and Witherspoon couldn't agree more. They were bone tired; the day had not turned out well for them. They didn't need these new complications in their lives.

Later Witherspoon came back in the house from inspecting the gardener's cottage in the back yard. "Godamn, there's a broken-down cot back there, but there's not a single godamn blanket or pillow, or anything. This is going to be a rough night. Do you suppose we can find some bloomin' blankets in the house without disturbing these little ladies?"

"We'll manage, Jock. Why can't we just bunk down in here on these sofas and chairs?" Hyams was about ready to collapse. "The hell with the gardener's cottage—I just said that to calm down that skittish Norma; she acted like we were going to rape them. We'd freeze to death out there in that shack!"

"Damn, I wish we were back in the cadet barracks!" Hornstein could kick himself for allowing Hyams to finagle him into this mess.

CHAPTER FIVE

Return Of The Candy Man

THE NIGHT passed slowly and torturously. With the dawn came some return of sanity. Sonya had finally been quieted after raising hell all night.

This Saturday, the fifth of May on the calendar, promised to be another brilliant spring day. For the eight people, the Kriegies and their wards, who spent that troubled night under the General's roof, it was the first time in many months that any of them had slept in an actual house, a home that was meant to accommodate a family and to afford comfort and convenience, and even luxury, for its occupants.

The house at Number 79 *Bismarckstrasse* seemed even more elegant and imposing by daylight than it had appeared during the previous night.

The women—all, including Sonya who was now subdued and strangely pensive—had risen at dawn. They bathed; there were all kinds of soaps and fragrances. Then they rummaged through the wardrobes that held the fine lingerie and clothing of the lady of the house. They debated whether they had any right to appropriate any of the lady's finery. Some said she would never miss it if they did. Others disdainfully dismissed the notion. Eventually they all succumbed to the inevitable. They took what they needed. They had re-entered the world of the living, and there were minimum necessities.

Was this the "looting" that the Frau had predicted? Not really. In Auschwitz, such "borrowing" was a way of life, except that in the camps, the taking was from the dead, or the nearly dead. It was called "organizing." It happens in all wars. At all levels of society.

The Germans were great for "organizing." Their victims could also "organize." This was definitely not looting.

The Frau would understand. Even the General would understand.

They prepared to leave. Their time was up. They got Sonya ready. She was still occasionally hallucinating, but she was manageable. Only time could help poor Sonya. They didn't want to leave without paying their respects to the Kriegies, so they decided that they would fix a fine breakfast with whatever ingredients were at hand as a parting gesture of appreciation. They remembered well the way to a man's heart.

Norma and young Marta headed downstairs to the kitchen and soon there were the tantalizing sounds and aromas of food preparation wafting through the house. And soon the Kriegies were showered, dressed, and eagerly ready for breakfast, which would consist of canned Norwegian sardines, cheese, biscuits, marmalade, and piping hot tea—real tea. Even a General wouldn't turn that down.

Norma, moving through the kitchen and the several pantries, couldn't believe the supplies of cocoa, real tea, real coffee, herbs and spices, and the sugar and flour. It was as if there never had been a war. There were no shortages of anything in this house.

And for Marta, all this was a revelation as well. In her seventeen years she had now come full circle—from the long months of despair and terror and starvation to this elegant house, brimming with all the good things of life that one could dream of. And now, fixing breakfast for a group of hungry men took her back to a time not so long ago, to a happy and all but forgotten time, to her own home and her own family, when she had helped to prepare meals for her father and two brothers.

As Marta puttered dreamily, Norma admonished her to make haste. "Right after we serve the breakfast, we must tidy up and get ready to leave. We have to get back to the hospital to check on Kati and Olga and Sari."

But Marta was not of the same stern stuff as Norma. "I do like it here. I wish we could stay for a while. These *Kriegsgefangene* . . . I will miss them. They're so nice."

And, as if on cue, the three Kriegies appeared in the kitchen, where they were beckoned to the table as Norma and Marta served the breakfast. There were mixed feelings all around. This blessed domesticity was beginning to register hard with them, especially Hyams, and to a lesser degree with Hornstein. Witherspoon could take it or leave it. His thoughts were with the elusive Irina.

The time of departure had been tacitly set for a prudently early hour, like about 0700 hours. By that time the Kriegies figured to have the house vacated, and to be on their way back to the cadet barracks. But the breakfast was proceeding at a rather leisurely pace when, at about 0730 hours, the street out front suddenly came alive with the sounds of motor vehicles coming to a screeching halt and the arrival of a number of Russian military vehicles. Within seconds, a squad of business-like Russian troopers was moving toward the General's front door.

Thus the innocent failure to effect a timely departure had resulted in some potentially troublesome complications. For some reason, Hyams felt that he was to blame for the impending disaster, that he had been dragging his feet, subconsciously delaying the departure and the separation. In heaven's name, why? He steeled himself.

Hornstein was ready with the appropriate comment. "We are fucked, kid!" Trouble with the police was the last thing in the world a Kriegie might wish for. At best it could mean a slight delay in getting back to American Army control. At worst it could mean possibly some sort of criminal charges, a trial, and a whole range of thoroughly unpleasant consequences too horrible to contemplate.

Hyams had never before been in any kind of trouble with the law. He saw himself as a nice law-abiding kid from Brooklyn. And now not only had he gotten himself screwed up, but he had involved poor innocent Witherspoon and Hornstein in this no-win situation. And with the Russians, yet. Why had he thought that the

Frau was bluffing? Real people don't bluff. Only Brooklyn people bluff.

The first one to come marching through the front door was the Frau herself. She was wearing the same black leather coat, which in the light of day only strengthened her image of unforgiving righteousness. She now held all the trump cards. And right behind her was the victorious, smirking Kurt, wearing the same leather breeches. They hadn't been bluffing. They would now exact their pound of flesh.

Closely following the mother and son was an official-looking civilian, who, it soon turned out, was none other than the town mayor, a Herr Klausner. He was new in the job, and looked harmless enough. He had a politician's round face, friendly eyes, and a big beer belly. He was not your typical Nazi; he was probably not a Nazi at all. He was probably hand-picked by the Russians. He was only there because the Frau was too important a person to be lightly put off, and it was his job to handle special situations. And this was obviously a special situation. But the Bürghermeister was not really a threatening type; he was more of a negotiator.

However, the Frau was backed up this time by some real muscle. She hadn't come to negotiate. She wanted her pound of flesh. Coming through the front door in single file behind the mayor were three Russian military types, real enforcers, and there were several more waiting just outside and in the vehicles.

The situation had very serious overtones. Back in Brooklyn, in a situation like this, Hyams and his friends would be calling in a lawyer. Here Hornstein seemed like the closest thing to a lawyer. He had worked for the government back when he was a civilian— the New York State Board of Revenue and Taxation. Hyams felt that Hornstein, a figure of some maturity, obvious respectability, and worldly know-how, should step forward and straighten things out. He could explain that they were all just on their way out and that the house was at that very moment being surrendered back to its rightful owner. This whole thing was nothing more than a minor misunderstanding that would be resolved momentarily.

All Hornstein could do was grit his teeth and swallow hard. "You sonofabitch," he rasped at Hyams, "you've really done it. We've got our ass in a real sling, you bastard! And for what?"

"And for what?" That was a good question, the kind there was no easy answer to. The kind that Hornstein was good at asking. Hornstein was apparently not going to take the lead. It would be up to Hyams to handle the situation. He had indeed gotten them into this. He had found the house, he had pushed the idea. It was all his doing. But after all, the Russians were supposed to be allies. No major crimes had been committed. Nobody had been murdered, or raped . . . or anything. What was stolen? What was damaged?

The lead Russian was a sergeant. He had an aura of authority. He was obviously a no-nonsense problem-solver. The green collar tabs identified him as being with the occupation authorities. He was short, stocky, and ruddy-faced, with tufts of flaming red hair showing from beneath his khaki cap. As he stepped forward to admonish the Kriegies his eyes lit upon the flustered Hyams. He froze for a split-second in disbelief. Hyams was not prepared for what followed as the Russian sergeant lunged forward, grabbing Hyams in a crushing bear hug. "Mister Zeke! My dear friend Mister Zeke! What an unexpected pleasure! How are you, my dear fellow? And your friends? I remember them! What a surprise!"

"Blimey, it's the bloomin' Candy Man!" Witherspoon looked like he was seeing a ghost.

Hyams could not believe this. "Tibor . . . ?" Life had recently become a succession of rapid and unpredictable convolutions. Nothing followed logically or predictably anymore. Was he dreaming all this? Was this Tibor? Tibor Weisskopf from the Stalag, the same Tibor who served in more different armies and had seen the insides of more concentration camps and Stalags than any living man, who only days earlier had taken that tearful farewell on the day the Russians had taken over the camp? Tibor, that fellow Jew, who had sort of adopted him, Hyams, early on in the Stalag as a long-lost cousin and close buddy? Tibor, who was never without an inventory of fine Viennese bonbons, the purveyor of fine delicacies, the shadowy well-heeled entrepreneur, when everyone else in the Stalag around him was existing on the edge of starvation? The same Tibor? How could it be? And how could it be that he would now appear at the very moment of crisis in such a position of obvious authority?

But it was Tibor, all right. The very same Tibor. "Yes, my friend, it is I, Tibor! And what kind of problem have you here created in the home of this fine lady? She is very upset, and rightfully so! We must find a solution to this problem. No?"

Tibor was the consummate bureaucrat, as well as the consummate survivor! His face was wreathed in a broad, loving smile even as he spoke.

As astonished as the Kriegies were at this new turn of events, it was Frau von Hesselmann and her overbearing son, the plaintiffs in this proceeding, who were taken totally by surprise, as they saw their cause crumbling. For them, too, the events of the recent past had been a succession of unfathomable twists and turns. And now to find the Russian squad leader on such good terms with the intruders was a most bitter pill for them.

But there was to be yet another shock in store for everyone, another piece of human drama which would eclipse even the Weisskopf-Hyams reunion.

As Weisskopf exchanged greetings with the much-relieved Hornstein and Witherspoon, several of the girls appeared timidly in the background. They were apprehensive and fearful, not wanting to be included in a Russian dragnet and not knowing whether it might not be wisest to make a run for it while there was yet time. However the events that were now to follow would preclude all that. There was suddenly a piercing shriek of recognition and indescribable elation from one of them. It was Marta. And it was the sight of Weisskopf that precipitated this wild reaction. She rushed toward him and threw her arms about him in a desperate embrace. She hung on for dear life, now alternating between bursts of joy and relief and tearful sobbing. "Tibi . . . oh Tibi . . . "

Weisskopf was not prepared for this. "Dear God . . . little Marta . . . is this really you?"

"Tibi, Tibi . . . Tibi . . . yes it is me, Marta! Oh, Tibi, I didn't think I would ever find anyone alive anywhere!"

It was the sudden eruption of a dormant volcano, as wave upon wave of pent-up emotions poured forth from the hysterical girl. She clung desperately to Weisskopf, who was himself overcome by the intensity of this event, which obviously had plumbed the deepest emotions and memories both for him and the young Marta.

A hush descended on the dozen or more people assembled in the Hesselmann foyer and drawing room as this drama was playing itself out. Marta's explosive recognition of Weisskopf, coming within seconds of Hyams' similarly dramatic and fortuitous reunion with his old Stalag buddy, really amounted to a one-two punch to the Hesselmanns and their entourage of Russian troopers, not to mention the *Bürghermeister.* The mission of eviction was now totally derailed. And everyone, except of course Weisskopf and little Marta, was now in a state of total confusion.

When Weisskopf recovered some degree of composure, he turned to Hyams, but he was still too choked up to talk. Finally some words came forth. "Dear friend, Mister Zeke, can you believe this? My wife's baby sister, a sweet child who is like my own sister. And to find her here! And it is really through you that I have found her. I don't know what to say. I owe you so much." As Weisskopf spoke his eyes scanned the faces of Marta's companions, as if trying to recognize one or another of the women. He was obviously looking for his wife. And then, "Marta, child, do you have anything to tell me?"

Marta's lips moved but she was unable to speak. And then she collapsed on the floor as if to find a hole to crawl into. She hid her face in a torrent of sobbing, she could not face her brother-in-law. She moaned and whimpered and still no words came forth. Weisskopf understood only too well, but he had to ask, "Marta, dear, what do you know of Gita and the children? Please."

Marta, still kneeling on the floor, buried her face in her hands.

Weisskopf knelt down beside her and whispered hoarsely from a parched throat, "Is anyone alive?"

Crying softly, Marta finally let the words slip from her lips, "Oh Tibor, how can I tell you? There is no one. They are all gone. Gita, the children, my parents . . . everyone, Tibor. Forgive me, Tibor, for being the one to tell you. I saw everything with my own eyes."

Tibor embraced the shuddering Marta. They were both kneeling on the General's fine Persian carpet. They were both awash in tears. Their lament was the only sound in the room.

Hyams had never seen Weisskopf in the Stalag when he was not strong, defiant, resourceful, and with that conniving twinkle in his eye. Except for that last night in the Stalag barracks when he had come to say goodbye. He had dreaded the liberation—the repatriation. He had said that the Stalag was his last refuge from the truth he did not want to face. That had been a turning point in the tortuous road which he had travelled for so long. He had known then that the tragic confirmation would not be long delayed. He had no doubts about the bitter truth that he would have to face up to.

But now the man had been run through by the rapier wielded by his beloved little Marta. He stayed down on his knees for a long time. And then he arose and helped Marta to her feet.

CHAPTER SIX

Weisskopf In Charge

TIBOR led the sobbing Marta from the room. They withdrew to a small pantry off the kitchen for a few minutes of quiet conversation. He soon returned to the drawing room. He was calm. He was again the squad leader, ready to carry out his singular mission. He glanced fleetingly at the stately Frau von Hesselmann, who averted her eyes.

He then walked over to Hyams. Hornstein and Witherspoon hovered close by, as if to lend some moral support to the bereaved man. But he addressed only Hyams.

"It is no surprise to me, Zeke. I knew it. I've known it for a long time. I have lived with this. I told you in the Stalag. And you could not understand, dear Zeke, why I should want to remain a prisoner in the stinking Stalag. This is why I dreaded the liberation. There I was shielded from reality, from the truth. Even though I knew everything, it is still a shock. The poor girl . . . it was hard for her. She is alone. She has lost everyone. She came from a beautiful family, very beautiful people. So have the others lost everybody. They are all like Marta—alone. Like me. I am alone. All alone. It is a terrible shock."

Hyams couldn't think of anything to say. There were no words. Weisskopf had to continue. "I met a Pole months ago who escaped from Auschwitz. One of the few who ever managed to escape. This man told me everything. I have lived with this sorrow, but I always hoped for some miracle. And now they are all in heaven, where they don't need any more miracles. Now we who are left need a miracle to survive this sorrow."

After a short period of respectful silence, when everyone was left with their own thoughts on the series of events that had been played out, the Bürghermeister was the first to speak. Clearing his throat, he addressed himself apologetically to Weisskopf. He hesitated to intrude, but he wanted to get on with the business that had brought them all to the General's house that morning.

"With all due respect, *Herr Sergeant,* could we take up the question of Frau von Hesselmann's grievance, or would it perhaps be better to defer the matter for perhaps later in the day? Another time that might be more convenient for you?"

Weisskopf betrayed a momentary lapse of attention, some confusion. "Grievance? What is her grievance?"

"It is the house, *Herr Sergeant.* The lady is entirely within her legal and moral rights to recover possession of her house. *Nicht wahr, Herr Sergeant?* Is that not so? That is her only request. She is entirely within her rights."

Weisskopf could now zero in on the question. He was back on top of things. "'Possession of her house?' Nobody is going to steal her house! What would you have me do? Should I place these people under arrest for criminal trespass? For taking shelter so they can have a night's rest in a secure place? So they can survive? Has anything in the house been damaged or destroyed? Can you tell me that?"

The mission of the Bürghermeister had been fatally undermined by what had transpired in the last few minutes. It had become irrelevant and ridiculous. He was beating a dead horse and he knew it. And Frau von Hesselmann knew it. Only Kurt remained fiercely defiant.

The Bürghermeister continued lamely to press his case. "*Herr Sergeant,* as you know the civilian population has been guaranteed the protection of their homes and personal property. We do not dispute the unfortunate circumstances, but Frau von Hesselmann has the full right to be secure in her home. You must agree with that, I am certain."

Weisskopf was, if nothing else, a superb negotiator and advocate. His command of the German language was complete, as was his fluency in Russian and several other tongues indigenous to Central Europe, like Czech and Hungarian and Polish, and, of course, Yiddish. It was this facility with languages that had earned him the highly desirable post as a sort of ombudsman in the local Soviet headquarters. He was the local trouble-shooter for the town commandant, and his discretionary power in such matters as he was now involved in, was, from a practical standpoint, absolute. But he could not risk being seen as totally arbitrary. He would have to continue some sort of charade of official impartiality, but there was no way that he would be a party to the summary eviction of these people, his people, who had taken refuge in the General's house.

He brought forth his most Solomonesque manner as he prepared to hand down his judgment. "*Comrade Bürghermeister,* I am a simple soldier. I know only what I see. I have seen no crime committed here. No stealing—no looting—no vandalism—no one assaulted or abused, or even so much as physically touched." Weisskopf let his eyes roam about the room for an instant or two, inviting the inspection of the room and its contents by the Bürghermeister.

He went on, "You can see, *Comrade Bürghermeister,* that there is not the slightest damage to either the house . . . or any of the truly fine furnishings. And further, I understand, Comrade, that the house is not presently occupied by its owners, that the gracious *Frau* and her young son are living elsewhere, quite comfortably with relatives, at another nearby location. So that they are not actually being dispossessed or put to any direct disadvantage by these people. Is this not so?"

The Frau and her strong-willed young son were becoming noticeably more restive with each succeeding new thought that Weisskopf was so eloquently driving home. And Weisskopf went on.

"I am sure you will agree, *Comrade Bürghermeister,* that a fine home like this one, left unoccupied and unattended in these times, will attract a host of tenants who might be infinitely more problematic and threatening to the welfare of the property than these people who obviously mean no harm and are temperate and considerate of the owner's best interests. I suggest that you think about those very realistic possibilities."

The sweet progression of Weisskopf's argument now proved too much for the stiff-necked Kurt. His face had turned deathly pale, his eyes narrow slits of icy anger. He burst forth with demonic fury at Weisskopf, throwing all caution and restraint to the winds. "You are a liar! We live here! This is our home! All our belongings are here. Your friends shall not remain in this house, no matter what! They promised to be out by early this morning, and we intend to have them out! No amount of talking will change that!"

Frau von Hesselmann tried to deflect the young man's vitriolic outburst. Nothing was to be gained by needlessly alienating this smooth-talking Jewish sergeant. This was a delicate situation that should not be exacerbated by reckless passions running amok. Frau von Hesselmann was no fool. Despite her wish to be rid of the intruders, she could not disagree with the specifics of the sergeant's case. She and Kurt were, in fact, living temporarily on the estate of an elderly aunt nearby. There was a very spacious house with generous grounds and live-in servants who offered some protection and security during the difficult early phases of the Russian occupation. Both the aunt and a loyal manservant had a calming effect upon the boy during these troubled times, when he felt deeply the absence of his father.

She was relieved that Weisskopf chose to ignore Kurt's outburst, but she was becoming acutely concerned at the explosiveness of the current situation. Her life was very difficult with Kurt going through this identity crisis. He had been raised to believe implicitly in the everlasting invincibility of the German nation and the infallibility of its leaders. Life had recently inflicted a series of shattering disillusionments upon the young man. It was almost too much. The unconfirmed disappearance in action of his father, with the attendant uncertainties, the devastating and humiliating military defeat at the hands of an enemy who for years had been certified as inferior and uncouth . . . and much more . . . had all combined to embitter the young man. And now to be challenged in his father's home, at a time when he saw himself as perhaps the last of the Hesselmanns, was clearly placing an extreme tension upon him. She thought that Weisskopf was clever enough and decent enough to understand.

Weisskopf continued to address his remarks to the Bürghermeister. He spoke quite calmly and reasonably. "Really, Comrade, I can see no undue hardship to the lady and her young son if these people are allowed to remain for a few days until they can resume their travel homeward. I am sure none of them would wish to remain here in Krondorf a single day longer than necessary. You can imagine that they are all anxious to get home as soon as possible."

The witch's brew bubbling hotly within Kurt now boiled over again. "These are very tricky games you are playing, Mister Jew-Sergeant, but they won't work. This is a German house. It is the home of a German General. We do not play games. These friends of yours are all foreigners, uninvited in our midst. They must leave this house—and immediately, just as it was agreed. We don't want any of these people sleeping in our beds! Or making this their home even for a few hours. We know their ways. We are not naive. You must get them to leave—and now. There is no reason for delay!" The Frau's worst fears had come to pass. She knew that Weisskopf would not meekly accept these venomous sentiments and taunts from a brash teenager. She turned on her son, white with anger. "Silence, Kurt! This is unforgivable!" The young man had betrayed her, had recklessly undercut her legitimate quest to regain possession of her home. She was embarrassed and ashamed. And now because of Kurt, she was beholden to the Jewish sergeant. She owed him something, even if only an apology. It was most distressing.

Weisskopf turned slowly and deliberately to face Kurt. He silently stared the boy down for a long minute that seemed like an eternity. And he then turned to the mother.

"Your young man, Madame, is not just disrespectful, insolent, and, I must say, mean-spirited, but he also suffers unfortunately from an illness which is very common in your Third Reich. It is the same illness that has caused the death of untold numbers of innocent people, the death of all those that were near and dear to me. His mind and his tongue are infected with this poison. And this could be very dangerous for him, Madame, if I were to report this incident. Racial slander is a very serious offense. Frankly, it is by far the most serious offense that has been committed under this roof today!" Weisskopf spoke slowly, letting every measured word sink in. He knew the case was now closed. Kurt had foreclosed it.

The Frau was visibly shaken. This was the first outward evidence that she had the normal range of feelings . . . fear . . . humility . . . shame . . . perhaps compassion. But she maintained a regal dignity, even as she pleaded for understanding. "Sergeant, please, I must apologize for my son's inexcusable outburst. He is little more than a child trying to carry a man's burden. Perhaps the world he grew up in was truly a sick world. I can assure you that neither I nor my husband ever were Nazis, or held the views that my son, in his desperation to regain what he considers to be my property, has so thoughtlessly and crudely expressed."

Weisskopf responded slowly and thoughtfully and with respect. "I understand, Frau von Hesselmann, that your husband was a high ranking career military officer." He realized that he had used the past tense. He had been told that the general was missing, not necessarily dead. It was awkward.

The Frau set things straight. "My husband is Major-General Erich von Hesselmann, a man of honor, I assure you, *Herr Sergeant.*" She brought the tense back to the present.

"So we have heard, Madame. Unfortunately we are dealing here with your son's behavior." Weisskopf would not soon forget nor forgive the young firebrand's temper tantrum.

And now the Bürghermeister came to the aid of the Frau. "You must understand, *Herr Sergeant,* many young people are confused, perhaps even bewildered, one could even say poisoned, by the war and its politics. It is not a good situation, especially for the young who were raised in the war, and taught only to war and to despise entire nations and, yes, entire races of people."

Weisskopf knew all about it. The war and its politics, as the Bürghermeister put it, had done much more than just confuse the young people. Those whom the smug Bürghermeister called "confused" had killed his wife and three small children, and had inflicted unspeakable losses on every one of the young ladies whom the impatient young "gentleman" was now seeking to evict from his home. And the guilty ones, the confused ones, still remained wildly confused and troubled.

Frau von Hesselmann now saw the situation clearly. "Sergeant, perhaps there is some way that we can permit these people to rest in the house for a few days . . . with the proper assurances, of course. We do not wish to appear totally unfeeling in this regard."

The confrontation was dissolved. Weisskopf looked around at the Kriegies. Everyone, even Witherspoon, was in favor of accepting the Frau's invitation to remain. It was a gracious gesture. She was really a gracious lady, caught in a difficult and awkward situation.

Weisskopf responded for everyone, "That would be only fair and right, Madame. These ladies are themselves recovering from severe physical trauma and hardship. They desire, I assure you, nothing more than to return to their own country as soon as feasible. And likewise the men are former military prisoners whose only wish is to return to their own lines as soon as the way is clear."

"Amen to that!" was Hornstein's contribution, while Hyams came up with a suggestion to ease any remaining qualms on the part of the Frau. It was fair and reasonable. "The lady could visit the house as often as she likes to assure herself that everything is in order. We would welcome that. It is only fair. Everything will be kept in good order. She can come every day. Twice a day if she likes. She'd be more than welcome!"

Frau von Hesselmann nodded approval. Hyams' suggestion of the open door was convincing proof of sincerity and honest intentions. She felt better about the whole thing. These people were decent.

"But she better not send that young fire-eater!" was Wither-spoon's prescient comment. He said that loud and clear. The Frau heard and understood well.

And Witherspoon had one other aside for Hyams, "You'd better not make too many rash promises concerning the wine cellar, mate!"

The Frau and her unhappy son left within a few minutes, but not before carrying out another methodical check of cabinets and closets. The General's study and the family's master suite were securely locked up. And then after this, the Bürghermeister took his leave. Everything was now legal and amicable in the General's house. The girls were much relieved. They now had the prospect of living in this fine home with the owner's permission—however grudging—even if only for a few days. It was something like being Queen for a day—or two or three. They felt legitimated.

The three Kriegies crowded in on Weisskopf. He was all smiles. Despite the shattering confirmation of the loss of his loved ones, he was standing tall. He was the hero of the day, a small triumph to ease the anguish of Marta's tidings. Witherspoon suggested that they all drink a toast to the man who had dispensed such Solomonic justice. Weisskopf begged off.

He promised to return that night to have a schnapps with them. He then led his squad out of the house. As he made his exit, his head was bowed and his shoulders sagged. It was, yet it wasn't, the same old Weisskopf.

It was not quite ten o'clock on the morning of Saturday, May 5, 1945. It was just three days before the final unconditional surrender of Nazi Germany to the Western Allies, and to the Soviet Union on the following day. That would end this war in Europe, a war like no other war before it, which had raged for almost six years, destroying nations and peoples, killing combatants and innocents alike, and poisoning the minds of entire generations.

CHAPTER SEVEN

A Real Friday Night Dinner —
One Day Late

THE JEWISH SABBATH begins at dusk on Friday night. Orthodox Jews traditionally greet the Sabbath as one would greet a bride at her wedding, with song and rejoicing, with wine and good food, and with prayerful appreciation that their God had ordained the Sabbath as the time for reflection and learning and respite from all worldly cares.

The General's house would be the scene of such a Sabbath celebration; but, due to circumstances beyond anybody's control, the Sabbath celebration, the welcoming of the Sabbath bride, would be observed a day late—that is, on Saturday night. The previous night, when there might have been a proper Sabbath observance, had seen that sudden tense confrontation with the Frau and her son, which pre-empted any thoughts of Sabbath and peace and thanksgiving. So on this Saturday night there would be a Sabbath feast. It was most appropriate under the circumstances . . . and the girls did themselves proud. They had all been raised in the faith, and all of them were familiar from their early upbringing with the customs and traditions of the Sabbath celebration, which in traditional Jewish homes is the high point of the week. They remembered the favorite dishes that would grace the Sabbath tables at home—the appetizers, the entrees, the side dishes. They decided that this Saturday night was the time to celebrate their first Sabbath of freedom from fear and hunger and oppression.

The Kriegies—the three of them, Hyams, Hornstein, and Witherspoon—had early in the afternoon undertaken a "shopping expedition" in the surrounding countryside, using the girls' farm cart to haul fresh provisions back to the house. They brought back meat and poultry, milk and eggs and butter and cheese, and fruits and vegetables. The girls baked the traditional Sabbath white bread and cakes and pastries and even strudels. The menu would include two styles of poultry entrees, chicken soup, a side dish of stewed carrots with raisins and potatoes—and there were puddings and fruit-filled crepes, and all sorts of other fancy desserts. There would even be an invited guest to share the dinner, Corporal Dennis Taggart of His Majesty's Royal Norfolk Regiment, an ex-Kriegie and barracks mate, and good friend from the old Stalag days. Of course, Tibor Weisskopf was expected. He had made it all possible. But he didn't show up until late in the evening. He had official duties to attend to.

Other than the procurement of the necessary provisions from various farms and dairies in the area, the Kriegies didn't have to lift a finger. In that part of the world, men didn't participate in any of the kitchen chores—neither the cooking, nor the dish-washing, nor the cleaning of pots and pans. The kitchen was exclusively the domain of the females.

After dinner, when the women undertook the considerable clean-up, there was nothing at all for the men to do but retire to the drawing room with its comfortable easy chairs and sofas. It was a time to relax, engage in a wide-ranging bull session, and avail themselves of a wide selection of fine liqueurs, brandies, and cordials, both domestic and imported. There was sparkling crystalware from which to sip and savor these excellent after-dinner libations. And there were fine German cigars, the General's private stock. Taggart couldn't believe it. Who could blame him? The change in circumstances of his three Stalag buddies was really not to be believed.

The Kriegies were all soon lying about like beached whales. They had gorged themselves on the exotic variety of delicious foods that had appeared before them. It would have been ungracious—and impossible—to decline any of those exquisite culinary offerings.

Hornstein, the man of Manhattan and self-proclaimed connoisseur of haute cuisine, had to admit, "I really haven't had a Friday night dinner like that since I moved out of my mother's house. And that was a long time ago!"

"Fit for bloomin' royalty, it was." Witherspoon was too relaxed and too satiated to say more.

Hyams cast his gaze approvingly about the room and its occupants. Who would have thought the previous night that things could have turned out like this? Good old Weisskopf! What a miracle worker! What a great guy! And what a bum deal life had handed him. The loss of his entire family. To be left all alone. But he would come out of it. He was tough . . . and smart. He would survive. But then all these girls, now working away so diligently in the kitchen, had all taken the same bum rap.

These people were truly special. No bitching, no griping, no feeling sorry for themselves. Hyams thought it was really a privilege to have been able to contribute somehow to making their lot a little easier, even if for just a couple of days. And, of course, to have been instrumental in bringing about the miraculous reunion of Marta and Weisskopf. That was a big break for her, and, of course, for him too.

Hyams felt good about the whole thing. And so did Hornstein and Witherspoon, who had been so reluctant at first to get involved. Witherspoon was really into the spirit of this new experience. He had even taken up cigar-smoking, like Hornstein. Free cigars are hard to turn down, and the General's cigars were *el supremo*.

Witherspoon, ever the gracious host, now offered Taggart his choice from a giant teakwood humidor. Anyone can get used to the good life.

Taggart accepted a slender panatella, bit off the tip and lit up.

"Thanks, mate. This will go perfect with the dinner. That meal, by the way, was definitely super. Hungarian-style cuisine, you say? Truly outstanding! I really appreciate you blokes including me in tonight." He was touched by the warmth and domesticity that pervaded the room and the entire house. There was a real family feeling about the whole thing, a nostalgic return to former times when life was normal. Taggart hadn't experienced that kind of warm domestic hospitality in a long time.

After a few drags on the panatella, Taggart thought to inquire about the "procurement" effort, which had produced such a bonanza of fresh provisions, reportedly enough to last for weeks. Witherspoon explained. "It was simple. The gals have this two-wheeled cart. We just took it out and went calling on a few of the more prosperous farms. These people didn't get cleaned out like the ones closer to the Stalag. These bloomin' farmers were down-right anxious to make a small contribution for the cause. The Russkies have really put the fear of God in 'em. We filled up the bloomin' cart in a half-hour. And the gals couldn't believe it when we got back!"

"Yeah, we even got a rise out of that Norma. And she never smiles! I can't figure her out. She could be sort of nice if she'd just loosen up sometimes!" Hyams and Norma just hadn't hit it off right from the beginning. Yet there was something about Norma that provoked a particular curiosity in him.

Perhaps it was because he could discern beneath her façade of stoic reserve a profound melancholy, and a vulnerability which held a strange allure for him. And he recognized in her a calm and serenity that he had never seen before in any human being.

Hornstein rose to Norma's defense. "Well, I shouldn't think she has too much reason to be smiling. She spent almost three years in that friggin' Nazi death camp. That had to be a real hell. Saw all her people destroyed, right in front of her eyes." This was surprising coming from Hornstein, who always eschewed depressing subjects. He hated anything that was depressing or aggravating. But he had gotten this story from Magda with whom he had established a remarkable degree of rapport considering that there was no common language between them to facilitate conversation.

It was true. Norma had put in the longest stint in Auschwitz of any of the girls. She had been taken there back in 1942, when the place was being built. She was just out of high school. Thousands of young Slovakian Jews were drafted there for "work." It was then billed as a "work camp." That part was true enough, but it soon became a straight-out "death camp." And she had seen it all. For almost three blood-drenched and terror-filled years.

Hyams steered the conversation into other channels. The tales of Auschwitz could not, and should not, be discussed on a full stomach. It was better to contemplate the blessings of the moment. "Nobody is going to believe this back home in Brooklyn!" Hyams crowed. "Look at us. Sprawled out in a godamn Jerry general's living room, drinking up his vintage brandy, smoking his cigars, and maybe even sleeping in his godamn bed tonite! Why the hell not?"

Taggart was enthralled with the whole situation. "You say that he has been unaccounted for since last October? Let's see, that's seven months! Long time. Commanding an infantry division, eh? Well, the bloke is either dead or in some Russkie *Offlag!*"

Witherspoon opted for a live general. "Generals have a way of surviving, you know, mate."

Billows of cigar smoke wafted across the room and hung in a thick haze against the panelled ceiling. Wouldn't the General be surprised if he were to walk in? Hyams, recently given to occasional flights of paranoia, was even preparing a cover story if the General, or his ghost, should happen to materialize. But nobody else thought that was a real possibility.

There was much in the room to forcefully remind the intruders that this was the home of a very important German personage, whose presence could still be felt in many ways. There were all these antiques and military artifacts, as well as the ancestral portraits which still adorned the walls. A man's home is his castle, and this was still definitely the General's castle.

And then the conversation turned to matters military, and how things were going in the war. Taggart, who had put in five tough years as a POW, since he was taken on the beach at Dunkirk in June of 1940, was naturally the one who most closely followed the BBC war news. He had managed to keep himself very well-informed as to all developments in the war through the clandestine radio that the British prisoners managed to maintain throughout this time. He reported that the fighting was practically over, except in a few isolated hot spots. Ironically, the last remaining German holdouts were in Czechoslovakia, in territory the girls would have to traverse on their way home.

Things were really moving. "There's been the broad link-up between the Yanks and the Russkies west of Berlin. Zhukov and Eisenhower exchanging victory toasts and all that. My guess is by this time next week we'll all be on our way home."

After five years in Kriegieland, Taggart had a right to be impatient. He was another one, like Weisskopf, who was not expecting to find his family waiting for him in an ivy-covered cottage. Five years was a long time in this fast moving and changing world, a long time to be cut off from a young wife and child. Taggart had lost much more than just the five years spent in captivity.

Refilling everyone's glasses from a decanter of French cognac, Witherspoon offered a toast to "Lance Corporal Taggart and the lads who held the bloody beach at Dunkirk. To those who made it off the beach, and to those lads who didn't!"

Taggart sipped slowly from his glass. Those dark days and nights of Dunkirk beach would never fade from his memory. He would never be far from Dunkirk, in space or in time. Dunkirk, where the Brits stood alone against the waves of German Panzers and dive-bombers, proving themselves in glorious defeat, and had then salvaged a broken army. Where they demonstrated to Hitler and the world that there would always be a Britain, no matter what the cost, no matter what the adversity. Taggart was there, and he and his comrades had paid the price, leaving their indelible footprints on that rocky beach.

Just as Taggart was setting his glass down, there was a loud knock on the massive front door.

And then Hyams admitted Tibor Weisskopf to a chorus of greetings. He was definitely the hero of the day. As he entered, he was handed a snifter of cognac by Witherspoon. This time

Weisskopf accepted. He was drained of vitality. The day had left its mark on him.

"Thank you. I am a bit weary."

And then Weisskopf, holding the drink, collapsed into one of the General's easy chairs. He looked drawn and very tired. His eyes, usually bright and alert, were dull and glazed over, his usually ruddy complexion now drained of color. The Kriegies lapsed into a respectful silence. Weisskopf appreciated that. He was in no mood for idle chatter.

Marta soon appeared in the room, brightening visibly at the sight of her brother-in-law. She rushed over to him, gave him a sisterly peck on the forehead, and then proceeded to deposit herself on the arm of his chair, never taking her eyes off him.

Weisskopf was warmed by Marta's presence. Reflecting on the years and what the years had wrought, he sighed. "Little Marta! The last time I saw her she was a snip of a girl, about thirteen, in pigtails so to speak! Now look at her . . . a grown woman who has suffered enough for a lifetime!"

It was a night for sad remembrances, yet it was a night for some joy and renewal of faith and hope for the future. For Marta it was a time of thanks and relief—that she had found someone from out of her past, and that she was now, after all the horrors, no longer alone in the world, and surrounded by friends both old and new.

And then Marta went into the kitchen and returned with a tray of food for Tibor. "It is a great Chicken Paprikash, Tibor! Would you believe it? Just like at home."

And Tibor brought himself to eat after insistent entreaties from Marta. He was refreshed by the exquisitely prepared food. And then Marta brought in a dish of fruit-filled crepes—*palachinta* she called them. And again Tibor ate. And by then he seemed much restored, and he commented about what a lucky thing it was that he should have been the one assigned to handle the Frau von Hesselmann's urgent complaint.

Hyams agreed wholeheartedly. "Without you, Tibor, we would have been in one hell of a mess!"

"Yes, I agree, my friend." Weisskopf couldn't deny it. "Of all the houses in Krondorf, you had to pick a general's house to take over. It is true you have very good taste, but . . ." and he shook his head in wonder and amazement, "these are very important people. They even have some influence with the Russian *Kommandatur!* But, of course, I . . . uh, I have more influence!"

It was the old Weisskopf again. That old beguiling gleam had reappeared in those baby blues. He could crack a smile, and see the humor in life again. Or so it appeared.

The party broke up around midnight. It had been another of those super-eventful days, with its tearful and wrenching reunions. Weisskopf went out into the night. He knew, as he climbed into his "Studebaker" jeep, that life for him would never be quite the same. (All American-made vehicles were called "Studebakers" by the Soviets, for some reason.) All his fears had been so tragically confirmed. Now, where there had earlier been some pretext of hope, however forlorn, there would now be only a bitter and aching emptiness. He was sick at heart as he leaned over wearily to turn the ignition switch and prepared to drive off into the night.

CHAPTER EIGHT

The *Pistolentasche*

THE NEXT DAY was Sunday, May 6th. This would be a day to kick back, to do nothing, maybe visit the cadet barracks, or just catch some sun on the General's spacious terrace. The Kriegies really needed this respite from the mad pace of events of the last two days.

The war was effectively over. The Third Reich, which was supposed to last a thousand years, had finally crumbled in ashes after twelve years of unmitigated terror and blood-letting. The last remnants of the once-vaunted German Army had been entirely liquidated except in those few remaining places where S.S. zealots were still in control and compelling a hopeless resistance by the ruthless intimidation of last-minute youthful conscripts, often accompanied by summary hangings and executions of their own exhausted and demoralized troops.

One such place where diehard fanatics would exact the last measure of pointless carnage was in Prague, the ancient capital of Czechoslovakia, lying some one hundred miles to the southeast. It was the only European capital still remaining under Nazi control. On the previous day, Czech partisans in the city had risen in a desperate revolt against the German occupation forces and the S.S. The streets of Prague were running red with the blood of Czech patriots as well as hundreds of innocent civilians caught in a last orgy of S.S. reprisal. The Nazis in Prague would not easily be brought down. The house-to-house fighting would continue for five days and nights, long past the formal surrender of the German High Command, to come on May 8, and the official end of hostilites between Germany and the Western Allies.

But in Krondorf and in the General's house, all was peaceful

and mellow on this early Sunday morning. The women woke early.
It was a big house and there was much to do. Frau von Hesselmann would no doubt be making her inspection visit some time in
the morning. There was cleaning and laundry and food preparation
to do. There was to be a visit later on to the Russian hospital to
check on Kati's condition, and also on Olga and Sari, who would
probably soon be ready for their release from the hospital. This
would be a busy day for the women.

Breakfast was to be ready when the Kriegies woke up. Marta
and Sonya were in the kitchen. Things were settling into a routine.
There were still a few pots and utensils to be cleaned from the
night before. Marta loved to putter and cook and prepare the food
for the "men guests" as she called them. It was all good clean fun.
And Sonya had calmed down considerably from her hysterical
condition of the recent past. She was eager to help out with the
chores. And now, as she sat in a kitchen alcove awaiting
instructions from Marta for setting the breakfast table, she
hummed softly to herself, perhaps a lullaby to the lost child.

But there was an unknown presence in the house, cold and
implacable like a gust of raw wind, rushing through the upstairs
rooms. Young Kurt von Hesselmann had come at an early hour at
the behest of his mother to retrieve a few valuables from the
master suite upstairs. That section was securely closed off from the
rest of the house. He had entered the house unnoticed through a
rear door and had proceeded stealthily upstairs. After only a few
minutes he came barrelling down the main staircase, ranting and
cursing wildly. He was livid with rage as he burst into the kitchen.

Catching sight of Marta, the young man rushed wildly at her,
shouting obscenities and flailing his fists. The startled girl managed
to elude his initial assault, but Kurt was determined to inflict some
telling blows as he spat out his accusations. "Filthy thieves . . . you
will not get away with this! You and the others! You will all pay for
this!"

The ashen-faced Marta recoiled in panic. "Keep away, you
lunatic! Keep away from us!"

Sonya, still unnoticed by the young man, was transfixed by the sight of the wild-eyed youth who had previously stirred up such violent agitation in her. She now withdrew further into the alcove and crouched down on her haunches like a frightened animal. Kurt's main focus remained on Marta.

"Lunatic, eh? You thieving bitch!" Kurt cornered Marta, grabbed her arms and started shaking her violently. "Where are my father's things? Who got into my father's study? I want every-thing—but everything—returned right now, or none of you scum will get out of here alive! I promise you that."

To underscore his freewheeling threat, Kurt released his hold momentarily on Marta, and hauled off with a clenched-fist blow to her face. Marta reeled back but remained on her feet. As Kurt rained still more blows upon her, she lunged forward clawing and scratching at her crazed assailant, shrieking frantically for help.

As the struggle continued, Sonya, wincing at the violent blows falling on Marta's face and head, rose silently from her corner and drew from the folds of her tattered frock an object that had earlier come into her possession, and which she sensed was the prize that Kurt was willing to kill for. This was a black leather pouch of exquisite hand-tooled quality. It was something of special significance for her, and it was as if she understood that this article was equally important to the raging Kurt. It was a highly burnished expand-a-pocket capable of holding a miniature deringer-type pistol or other hand-size objects or small weapon.

As she rose, Sonya's fear turned to defiance. She walked quite calmly to the center of the kitchen and tossed the leather pouch on the breakfast table. There was a muffled thud as of a weighty metallic object as it landed. Kurt's attention was diverted instantly to the pouch lying on the table. This was indeed the prize that he would kill for. He was vindicated. Turning on Sonya he sneered in a voice laden with contempt, "Aha, *die Pistolentasche!* You! Idiot! I'll teach you to steal!"

He snatched the pistol pouch and opened it. On one side there was a small jewelled dagger resting in a contoured pocket. The

pearl handle was inlaid with the infamous death's-head logo of the
S.S. A second pocket, shaped to hold a small pistol, was empty.
Kurt went completely berserk at the sight of the empty holster. He
had been defied and now taunted by this demented Jew-woman
who had so blithely invaded the sanctum of the family's private
quarters and appropriated a precious family memento. The pouch
had been a gift to the General from his deceased brother-in-law
and Kurt's favorite uncle. Uncle Klaus had commanded an elite
Panzer brigade in Russia and had died a hero's death in battle. The
pouch was drenched in rich memories, and it would someday belong to Kurt. It was holy. And now the pistol had been removed
and was missing!

Kurt advanced toward Sonya. He would teach her to play
games with him! She was a madwoman who could not be reasoned
with. He would have to use force to immediately recover the pistol
she had obviously stolen and secreted somewhere in the house.
And then he would file the appropriate criminal charges against
the entire cabal. That stupid Bürghermeister would have to act
now to get rid of this rabble, who had taken such cynical and calcu-
lating advantage of his mother's gentle nature.

Sonya was strangely unruffled. She stood her ground. She was
standing once again beside the open trench in the forest of Goraj.
And then she calmly drew the small pistol from her frock pocket.
And then, holding it steady, she took deliberate aim at Kurt who
was almost upon her at that moment. Sonya gently pressed the
trigger, just as she had seen the S.S. man do at that earlier time. As
the first shot reverberated in the kitchen, Sonya uttered a single
word: "Murderer!" There was a second and then a third shot in
rapid succession, as Sonya stood over the fallen Kurt. She was
killing the blue-eyed devil who, on an earlier Sabbath day not so
long ago, had calmly and deliberately shot her baby and then
turned his gun on her.

She remained deathly calm, as the other occupants of the
house came rushing into the room.

Marta was screaming hysterically. And then, before anyone

could reach her or grab the weapon, Sonya, quite serenely and without emotion, turned the pistol on herself, putting one shot into her right temple.

As Hyams and the others looked about the room in horror, both Kurt and Sonya were lying on the kitchen floor in widening pools of blood.

CHAPTER NINE

Frau Von Hesselmann's Lonely Vigil

Sonya died that afternoon in the same Russian hospital where two days earlier Kati had her leg amputated.

Wars don't really end. They only subside. They flare up and consume everything in sight, and then they subside. A land mine concealed under the dust of a country road, or a fancy little pistol fitted into a fancy leather pouch hidden in a desk drawer . . . all symptoms of man's addiction to violent "solutions." Times change and the instrumentalities of death change, but not human nature.

That afternoon as Frau Liesellote von Hesselmann waited in the same Russian hospital for Kurt to come out of surgery, she had time to reflect, in her anguish, on the unrelenting series of misfortunes that had torn her world asunder in the past few months. At forty-one, she was indeed at a sad and critical crossroads of her life, a life that had once been so orderly and structured and secure, even in wartime. But it was these past few months which had inflicted the unsettling wounds, the deep wounds. The very foundations of her world had been undermined. The crushing and humiliating defeat of Germany, with all that this portended for the future . . . the lingering mystery surrounding her husband's fate . . . the recent loss of her father and, earlier, her only brother . . . and now this ghastly episode that had come so close to claiming her son's life.

In this past year she had mourned the death of her father whom she had worshiped. A man of great character and distinction. Dr. Josef von Buhlow, professor emeritus of quantum physics at the University of Berlin, had succumbed to a heart attack shortly after receiving the tragic news of the battlefield death of his only son. As a young graduate student, Frau von Hesselmann had assisted her father in his laboratory and with his writings. He had strongly influenced her early thinking and her attitudes about life and people. He was for her the embodiment, an exemplar, of an earlier era when German culture and achievement had been at its zenith, when life in Germany was comfortable and natural, and when human dignity was a sacred right.

The shock of her father's passing had followed so closely the tragic loss of Klaus, her baby brother, whose life had been for so long irrevocably committed to the Nazis. Hitler had come to power when Klaus was only eighteen; even before that, as a high school student, Klaus had fallen completely under the spell of the Nazi movement. It was so fashionable at the time. His entire adult life had been spent under the Hitler influence. He had been imbued and vitalized by the Hitler syndrome, and the girl whom he would marry and who would bear him two sons was equally committed to the new Germany. The S.S. was his career, his life, his mistress. There came to be nothing else. So his loss, at the head of an elite Panzer unit, was probably inevitable, and it was surely the death that he would have chosen for himself.

It was painfully ironic that young Kurt who so idolized his Uncle Klaus, and who, since early childhood, held such unshakeable convictions on such esoteric matters as the dangers of racial contamination, and the rightness—indeed, the absolute necessity—of punitive policies against non-Aryans and other inferior races, that he should have been gunned down in his own home by a deranged Jewess wielding a weapon which had come as a gift from Klaus. Frau von Hesselmann would cringe inwardly when she recalled the fallen Klaus' apoplectic diatribes against the Jews. She had often wondered how a highly sensitive young man raised in a calm and tolerant home environment such as hers had been could embrace such rabid and inflexible racial views. And now, of course, her own son had chosen the hard and obdurate philosophy of the Hitlerites over her own more moderate leanings.

As for the Jews, Frau von Hesselmann had known many Jews in her earlier years. They had been among her close friends, fellow students, and associates of her father at the University. They had been almost uniformly bright and congenial people. No one could have doubted their character and patriotism. One night, many years earlier, in her father's house, she had met Professor Albert Einstein, and her father had welcomed him warmly and had spoken glowingly of him on many occasions. And then some years later, she remembered her father telling about the unsuccessful efforts of Professor Max Planck, the Nobel Laureate and Germany's foremost physicist, to intercede with Adolf Hitler personally to spare the Jewish scientists from the early Nazi exclusionary laws. She had been amazed to learn from her father that there had been a total of fourteen German Jewish Nobel Prize winners in literature, medicine, and the physical sciences. Hardly the sign of a moribund, parasitic race. And her father had said how remarkable that was, considering that the Jews represented only about one percent of the total German population at the time.

Of course she could agree that in many instances the Jews had brought the curse down on themselves. They were perhaps too successful, engendering envy and resentment, and set themselves up as an inviting scapegoat. "But," she reflected, "what had been gained by their persecution? The Jews are a hardy, indestructible race. It was a mistake to single them out as an adversary in a war where the whole world was against Germany. It had only gained powerful enemies for Germany, and had made the Reich look bad in the eyes of the Western world, the Judeo-Christian world."

Well, perhaps the great "persecution" had not been as vicious and inhumane as some people now represented. There were obviously goodly numbers of survivors still circulating about the land . . . witness the people who had so brazenly installed themselves in her home at that very moment.

And what was it that Ilse, her sister-in-law, had said on one occasion when they were discussing the Jewish situation and their forced resettlement to the Eastern territories? "Why shouldn't the

Jews accept sacrifices and some privation when our men are dying daily on the battlefronts? This is war, and everyone must suffer! Everyone in Germany is subject to the will of the Führer. Why should the Jews be any different?"

The last report on the progress of the surgery indicated that Kurt had been struck in the chest by two bullets, neither of which were life-threatening, while a third shot had inflicted only a flesh wound. The young man was not deemed to be in critical danger, but one bullet in the chest was deeply embedded and required delicate surgery. A highly rated Russian thoracic specialist was leading the surgical team. The Frau, though agitated and apprehensive of possible complications, had been strongly reassured.

This was a difficult situation for a woman alone. It was a time when she desperately needed the comfort and support of her husband, but unfortunately the fate of the General was itself very much in doubt. It was now many months since she had last received any letter or communication from her husband. There had been an inexplicable dearth of information from the War Ministry, only the usual vague reassurances. Not knowing made it so difficult. There could be no rest from the constant strain and worrying. All of this had exacerbated young Kurt's confusion and bitterness.

She knew only that the General's division had been ordered to stand firm in an all-but-hopeless rear-guard action against overwhelming Soviet forces. But she had always maintained her conviction that the General would personally survive the ordeals of battle or even capture by the enemy. He was a professional and he was tough, resolute, and resourceful. At forty-seven he was in his prime as a man and as a field commander.

Life lately had become so frought with ironies. The band of intruders in her home were all people returned from the "missing." Perhaps this was an omen to her that her own "missing" husband would also soon return to his loved ones. Perhaps if she had earlier been ready to discern this parallel she might have been able to soften Kurt's raging scorn for these people. But of course it was too late for that now.

She had last seen her husband in September 1944, some eight months earlier, on a few days' leave from the front. At that time they had celebrated their twentieth wedding anniversary and had travelled together to Berlin, where the General attended a conference at the War Ministry and she had been able to visit her father at his home in a Berlin suburb shortly before his death. But the General, back then in September, had seemed preoccupied and deeply troubled. He had confided to her that the overall military situation was in complete disarray—was in fact hopeless, beyond redemption.

He had also been greatly saddened by the suicide of his old mentor and patron, Field Marshal Gunther von Kluge. Her husband had once served as an aide to the Field Marshal, and revered him as one of the last of the "old lions" who could still possibly pull Germany from the edge of the precipice. The Kluge death, shrouded in some mystery, was thought to have been related to the Field Marshal's deep disillusionment with Hitler's conduct of the war. Coming so soon after the mass trials and executions of numerous high-ranking officers in the wake of the July 20 assassination attempt against the Führer, his death had been withering in its effect on many of the career professionals like her husband. During that September visit, the General had seemed full of new doubts and anxieties. This was starkly out of character for a man who was born and bred to the military life, and steeped in its highest codes and traditions. It had pained her to see him so disheartened. Their anniversary trip to Berlin had proven sombre and overlaid with numerous portents of looming disaster.

As the waiting hours dragged on, Frau von Hesselmann was joined in her vigil by an elderly couple, old family friends and neighbors, Herr Heinrich Schmidt and his wife, Gertrude. They were a delightful pair who, in normal times, always raised her spirits. Herr Schmidt asked if there was anything they could do for the Frau during this difficult time of waiting. She could only report that the doctors were very hopeful and they seemed very competent, and one could only pray.

Herr Schmidt had known young Kurt growing up. "He has a strong constitution, that Kurt. And he is young. He will recover fully and speedily, you will see, Liesl."

Frau Schmidt was incensed about the whole affair. "How horrible . . . poor young fellow . . . an innocent victim of a deranged woman!"

And then Frau von Hesselmann heard herself say, "Who is innocent . . . and who, dear Gertrude, is guilty? I honestly don't know anymore!"

CHAPTER TEN

Sonya At Rest

SONYA got a proper funeral. She exited the temporal world in a brief blaze of notoriety.

To some, her striking out in a final and seemingly irrational round of violence starkly illustrated the machinations of an unbalanced and tortured mind. To others, the shooting of Kurt and the taking of her own life could be understood as both logical and inevitable considering the immediate circumstances. The brutish manhandling of Marta by the enraged Kurt, as evidenced by the bruises and contusions that the girl bore, was proof of the violent passions that raged before Sonya's eyes as she cowered in fear. To have her young friend suddenly set upon so fiercely by this churlish youth, whom Sonya had come to see as the embodiment of evil, could have triggered the most extreme reaction in any normal person. Her shooting of the attacker was perfectly logical and understandable. It was the only way she could deter the savage onslaught at the moment when Kurt turned on her.

As to the taking of her own life after shooting the young man, that too was capable of explanation. In the world in which she had witnessed the slaughter of countless innocents, and the sadistic retributions levied for the most minor of infractions in the various hell camps which she had passed through, anyone who would commit any physical transgression against a member of the dominant race could most certainly look forward to the meanest of deaths. She had chosen death cleanly and by her own hand, not being able to imagine what the alternative might be. And fate had placed the instrument of escape so neatly in her hand. So what else could she have done?

So, was Sonya deranged or merely playing out the part fate had inexorably ordained for her? To those who mourned for her, Sonya had committed nothing more than an extreme act of passion, engendered by the monstrous wrongs she had endured at the hands of a succession of evil-doers.

The funeral was on the Monday, May 7, in the graveyard behind the Lutheran Reformed Church on the Dresdener Way. Weisskopf, the man for all seasons, had handled the arrangements. There was of course no Jewish synagogue nor cemetery in Krondorf, although there had once, before Hitler, been a thriving Jewish community in the town. No one knew where the Jewish cemetery might have been, or if indeed there had ever been one.

Weisskopf opted for the fashionable churchyard on the Dresdener Way even though the deceased was neither Lutheran nor Reformed. But this was obviously where all the "right" people in Krondorf came to their final resting place. The churchyard was generously shaded by beautiful old trees, and the grounds were meticulously tended. The place had peace and dignity and "class." It was hallowed ground where all are equal before their Creator, and Weisskopf demanded the best for his girls. But it was understood that this would be an interim burial. There was talk that Sonya would be re-interred at a later time in a more appropriate setting, considering that she was of the Orthodox Jewish persuasion. A final resting place would be a matter for a later decision, at an unspecified time, by some person or persons yet unknown. Weisskopf had struck a compromise, exactly as he had negotiated with the Frau von Hesselmann several days earlier about use of her house as a temporary way station.

So the pastor agreed, perhaps somewhat reluctantly, that the deceased might be buried in an obscure, little-used corner of the Lutheran graveyard reserved for charity cases. Sonya would thus remain in Krondorf for some indeterminate time, a continuing reminder to the townsfolk of what had occurred that fateful morning in the General's house when an impetuous and volatile youngster was brought down by a "deranged" interloper who took him to be the devil incarnate.

A sizable group of mourners came to pay their last respects to the unfortunate Sonya. At the graveside were all six girls, including Olga and Sari, both of whom had been released from the hospital that morning. As for Kati, it would be some weeks before she would be out of the hospital. There were the three original Krie-gies—Hyams, Hornstein, and Witherspoon—plus several others from the cadet barracks including Taggart. The saga of the girls, their histories, their misadventures, their exceptional culinary prowess, and the audacious Kriegie takeover of the General's well-stocked mansion—all this had gotten around among the Kriegies residing in the cadet barracks.

A religious burial service was conducted by Weisskopf, who in-toned the *Kaddish*, the Hebrew prayer for the dead. He humbly beseeched the Lord above to grant Sonya the peace and solace that had been denied to her here on earth.

The service was completed within a few minutes. As the pine coffin was lowered into the grave, there were flowers placed upon it. Of the men, only Weisskopf lingered at the graveside for a few private moments. It wasn't only Sonya he was saying goodbye to. It was his dearly beloved young wife and three small children, whose remains were intermingled with the ashes of millions of other vic-tims at a place called Auschwitz. There would be many moments of remembrance. This was one. Marta stood by. She understood; she was also saying goodbye to loved ones.

In the background, standing apart at a discreet distance, was a lone mourner. It was the young Russian girl-medic, Lieutenant Irina Svobodin. It was a rare off-duty appearance. In her early twenties and petite, she could almost pass for a teenager except for her military garb and serious demeanor. There was a girlish softness about her. She was very pretty, with brown hair and blue eyes, serious yet open. She had come to feel something for poor Sonya in the brief moments before her death, just as she had come to know most of the girls of Norma's "troupe." She had treated several of them in her hospital in addition to Kati. She knew the effects of the various traumata they had suffered. Her nation and her people had also been traumatized in this war.

At the completion of the service, as the lieutenant turned to go, her presence was discovered by the girls, who rushed toward her, swamping her in their tearful embraces. They expressed their appreciation for her kindness and that she would take the time from her duties to attend this memorial service. Jock Witherspoon now saw his chance to make some points. While the lieutenant talked to the girls about Kati's prognosis, Jock's eyes were glued to her. He revelled in the sight of her. The lieutenant was beginning to show some signs of uneasiness, but she continued to direct her attention to the girls' concerns.

"Kati is doing extremely well. We are very pleased with her progress. She will be able to dance the polka as well as any of us, maybe even better. She is young and has such a positive outlook. She will overcome any initial difficulties."

Much technical progress had been made in the field of prosthetics. The need for artificial limbs had skyrocketed on all sides in this war, and medical science had generally kept up with the demand in this field. The lieutenant felt confident that she could paint a bright picture for Kati's future.

The uplifting report on Kati was a tonic to the girls, and it helped to dispel the gloom over Sonya's fate. Soon there were smiles where moments before there were only tears and sorrow. Witherspoon hung in the background, searching for an opening to initiate some sort of dialogue with the lieutenant. He was trying to think of some appropriate medical question.

As the girls drifted off, leaving the lieutenant undistracted, Witherspoon offered to walk the lieutenant the hundred or so feet to where she had parked her bicycle. She accepted the offer of company. She was after all a young woman, freed for the moment from her weighty responsibilities, and Witherspoon was an engaging fellow, even if verbal communication with him was fragmented and labored. The two were seen walking out of the churchyard, with Witherspoon doing most of the talking and much gesturing. The jaunty little paratrooper had really polished up his jump boots for this long-awaited opportunity.

CHAPTER ELEVEN

The Man From Borodino

IT WAS on the Monday night, the seventh of May, at about 2100 hours. The occupants of the house were each resting quietly with their own thoughts and reflections about the wild succession of recent events, and the funeral of Sonya that morning and how Weisskopf had managed to provide that poor woman with such a dignified and respectful final salute and farewell.

Despite the fact of Sonya's tragic passing, the population in the house had actually increased this day with the arrival of the two young women, Olga and Sari, who had just been released from the hospital. The two were incredulous at the comfort and luxury of this grand home that was now theirs to share and enjoy for a restorative interlude of indeterminate duration. They received conducted tours through the place, were assigned sleeping accommodations, and then were introduced to the ample stocks of toiletries, cosmetics, and other civilized necessities with which the house abounded. They soon settled in and joined in with the others as appreciative guests.

Everyone was looking forward to a quiet and uneventful night at last, and hoping to catch up on some sleep and relief from the recent tensions. This despite the general sense of anticipation which hung in the air over the predicted final unconditional surrender of the German forces. It was understood that this happy event was very imminent, only a matter of days. Corporal Dennis Taggart had mentioned that it could come to pass as early as the next day. At any rate, everyone in the General's house was exhausted and ready for a good night's rest. Hyams and the Kriegies, collected in the drawing room, were beginning, one by one, to doze off in the comfortable chairs when there was suddenly a violent pounding on the front door. It was too late in the night for casual company, and from the intensity of the pounding it was evident that this might not be a friendly visit. What else could happen now? Hyams' paranoia burst forth in full flower. This was still a war zone, technically and actually. Could it be the Russians on official business, or maybe even Germans on war business? There could be some night-riding Nazi marauders who might decide in a last-minute symbolic action to reclaim the General's house, maybe even to punish the foreign interlopers who had taken over a German home. Nobody had given any serious thought to nighttime security considerations. There were no weapons at hand. They would be virtually defenseless against any armed intruders.

But after the initial spasm of alarm, Hyams decided that this loud banging on the door, rather than coming from a hostile source, was probably some juvenile horseplay by one or more of the Kriegies at the cadet barracks who might be out on the town celebrating victory somewhat prematurely. Finally the front door was unbolted and cautiously opened.

There on the portico stood a solitary but rather large and imposing figure; a Russian in full battle gear, armed to the teeth, gesturing and shouting angrily. His left arm, fist tightly clenched, was just coming into position to resume the heavy blows against the door. In his right hand he clutched a cocked machine pistol, with his trigger finger obviously ready for immediate action. A torrent of Russian oaths and denunciations roared forth as he clambered through the doorway into the entry foyer and challenged all the occupants to assemble immediately before him. Within another split second he had entered the sumptuous dining room where the remains of an ample meal still set on the table surrounded by a dozen empty chairs. The strange character was becoming more agitated by the second, and the way he bellowed, waved his arms, and shoved his weapon at one and then another, the Kriegies and everyone else within earshot knew they had a real problem on their hands. None of the men spoke the language well enough to converse with an over-excited and out-of-control bull of a Russian, who was totally confused and aghast at what he was seeing here in this grand house in the heart of what he considered enemy territory. The girls, on the other hand, those who could speak or understand Russian or any Slavic equivalent, were very reluctant to come center stage and engage this person in direct conversation. Their past experiences with freewheeling Russians had made them very skittish. They just seemed to want to fade away into the wall paper. Although he appeared to be a Russian trooper, his uniform was somewhat nondescript and consisted of several items seemingly of German origin, such as his black leather boots and some incongruous emblems and battle decorations that he might have acquired as trophies along his combat itinerary. He seemed to be driven by a frenzied anger that was clearly self-induced and at a level that one would expect to find only in close-quarter combat!

The fact that he was Russian, however, afforded some small measure of relief from the earlier dire misgivings of the return of the Nazis. But this was only a small blessing, for he was definitely a bad character with mayhem on his mind. He was assuming, perhaps reasonably, that this was a household of German people, enjoying an unimpaired ease, comfort, and luxury in this well-stocked mansion tucked away in this quiet corner where all had miraculously managed to escape the unpleasantness of war. So he was going to bring the war home to them! The sight of the wine bottles, the crystal stemware, the Dresden dinner plates, the heavenly aromas of all that Hungarian food still remaining in the kitchen—all this could drive him to exact some insane revenge. A total massacre was not out of the question, and would be all the more tragic because of the obvious case of mistaken identity!

As the Russian stepped into the bright glare of the dining room lights, one could see that he was a man of about forty, a bear in size, with a swarthy complexion and huge black moustaches. His snarling mouth was chock full of sparkling metallic teeth, and he was indeed clad in the attire of the Russian front-line combat infantry. He was definitely intent on making major trouble. The way he handled that submachine-gun showed that he had used it in anger on much more than one occasion. At this hour of the night he must already have had a full ration of alcohol coursing through his veins. His eyes were narrow, blood-shot slits in a leathery grizzled face. The Angel of Death incarnate!

For a moment there was a sort of silent stand-off. The Russian was probably wondering at the low level of hostility in the pallid faces that now surrounded him. These were not enemy faces; the men did not present a threat of any kind—while there was fear there was no palpable animus. Then one of the girls at the back of the group muttered a barely audible Yiddish oath. "May the devil take the swine!" He swung around, aiming his weapon in the direction of the oath, then suddenly it was as though he were struck by a bolt of lightning! Yiddish is the universal language of the Jews of Eastern Europe, be they Russian, Polish, Hungarian, or whatever. He heard those Yiddish words and was instantly transfixed. "Did I hear Yiddish spoken here?" he shouted with a golden grin that could warm the polar ice-caps. He almost jumped out of his fancy black leather boots. From that instant he became the embodiment of human love and kindness. He threw down his weapon and embraced one and all in a Russian bear hug. Tears of joy and recognition welled up in his eyes.

The table was reset for him. Platters of food were brought out. He ate, he drank, he laughed, he cried. He told funny stories, and he told gruesome tales of the war he had seen. He listened to the girls' sad histories. He cursed. He brandished his fists in the air. He was like a man who had crossed a raging river to a friendly shore. He embraced the Kriegies. They all, even the girls, even Olga and Sari, even Norma, drank some fine Kümmel from the General's locker, and they talked for hours. Everyone there had volumes to tell, and everyone's story was different, yet the same! The story of survivors who had seen the other side of hell and were still alive to tell about it.

Battalion Sgt. Moise Kagan declared, "I've been in the fighting from the start, since the bloody summer of 1941! I was wounded twice. Once I was left for dead on the battlefield. But I am here. We never knew about Auschwitz, Treblinka, Maidenek . . . until we advanced into Poland. But in Russia, in our country, they killed the people in their own homes, or they would collect them in the fields and in the forests and shoot them down with machine guns. In every city and in every village there were unspeakable Gehennas created by the Germans. In my own town of Borodino, every Jew is gone. My wife and daughter, gone, killed by the S.S. I left my family there in July of 1941, in the first summer of the war, when the Germans were invincible. I have been in battle ever since, except for the months in hospital. Now it is four years later. I ask myself, for what did I fight and suffer? For what? I have lost everything. Borodino, it is seventy miles from Moscow on the road from Smolensk. Napoleon was first stopped there in 1812 by the Russian Army of the Tsar. The Nazis were like vicious dogs when they entered the city that first summer. They destroyed all the ancient monuments on the old battlefields; they didn't want any reminders of Napoleon's fate!"

Kagan was like a man possessed. He had to relive the war, to re-tell his story again to people who would listen and understand. "In that first interminable summer, it was all defeat and retreat for us! In five months from June to November 1941, Hitler had devoured almost half of Russia! The speed of his Panzers and his slashing encirclements were incredible. There was no way to slow him down. Only one week after his invasion on June 21, Minsk had fallen. He took Smolensk in mid-July. By mid-September he had Kiev, in the very heart of the Ukraine, and by November he had all southern Russia including the Crimea, except for Sebastopol, our naval base. Rostov and Kharkov had fallen. Leningrad was besieged, and the German lines were twenty miles from Moscow."

"We ask ourselves, how did Russia survive? What saved us from total defeat and destruction? Was it the Russian winter? Was it the immense vastness of the land? Was it the unflinching attachment of the Russian people to their native soil, to their Mother Russia? Or the stoicism of a people determined to survive at all costs? That first summer was the ultimate test of Russia's destiny. Our strength flowed from many springs, including, of course, the strong hand of God! It was a miracle that we were able to deny Hitler his final victory that first summer. We learned to live not in the present but for the future. We fought tanks with bottles filled with gasoline. They sent dive-bombers against our horse-drawn carts, and still we survived and fought on. And then, mercifully, the winter came."

Kagan had been born to fight in this war, and to tell about it. "The frost and snowdrifts of December froze the Germans in their tracks. They had expected to be in Moscow by October, not on the open steppes, in their summer gear, in December. Now we counter-attacked with cavalry, infantry, and massed artillery; and the Germans, those who could still move, fled before us in panic. Our partisans inflicted grievous damage on them from the rear. It was bitter cold, the snow shone blue on the ground; the sun looked like a frozen shroud. The frost was so severe that the faces of the German dead were flushed and seemed alive, yet our Siberian troops grumbled that it was not yet cold enough for them! The sudden tide of victories came as a surprise to everyone. We could not imagine that the Germans would be so unprepared for our winter."

Kagan went on as if in a trance, often beating the air with his fists.

"But the ground that we recovered had been laid waste by the retreating Germans. Villages and farms burnt, cities levelled, people slaughtered. I was on the Moscow front; my unit was attacking in the direction of Smolensk. It was then that I came to Borodino again. What hadn't been blown up was burnt to the ground. They had set fire to the town center and the museum, and the fires were still blazing in the 35-degree-below-zero cold. I proceeded to my old neighborhood with anger and trepidation. I could find not a trace of my home. The entire area was burnt out and lay in ashes. On what had been my street, I met an old woman who looked at me with vacant eyes. When I attempted to question her about the whereabouts of the people, she mumbled dazedly that she was alone and knew nothing. On the walls that remained standing there were posters about the 'new normalization of life,' and announcements that for aiding the partisans or hiding Jews, the penalty was death by hanging!"

Kagan held his audience spellbound. He was chronicling with detail and passion those compelling chapters of history that the people in the General's house that night really had known very little if anything about. Yet these chapters were pivotal and critical in the strategic development of the victory they were on the threshhold of realizing. "While we were in a great hurry to continue our advance, and tired though we were, we took time out to dig up the graves of the Germans buried in the main squares of all the towns and villages. They had this custom, that first summer when they were swollen with confidence in their victory. They buried their dead in the town squares, perhaps as a memorial to the permanence of their conquest, and as a historic reminder to future generations that they had paid for this land with their lives. At any rate, this was a grievous affront to us of the Soviet Army, and everywhere we dug them out of their graves in the town squares and dumped them into mass burial pits. Thus we waged war even against the dead! In other places they had set up orderly cemeteries with graves in neat rows marked by wooden crosses bearing the names of the dead. These cemeteries we did not disturb. As a matter of fact, there was an unspoken envy of the degree of care accorded to their dead by the Germans. Damn them for their meticulous precision!"

Kagan went on to describe the battle at the gates of Moscow in the winter of 1941, where the Russians had decisively deployed masses of artillery against the overextended and weakened German forces. It was at Moscow in December 1941 that the tidal surge of German victories was turned back at the last crucial moment, and he was there. He had total recall, a photographic memory for places, sequences, and people, and was thoroughly imbued with the lore of Soviet military achievement. He was born to fight in this war, a war that cost him dearly in personal loss and the virtual destruction of his world. But here he was, in the heartland of the despised enemy, alive, vibrant, bellicose, blustering and drinking the Kümmel and the wine of one of their vanished generals.

The Kriegies and the women all were enthralled by Kagan's broad-ranging narrative. He was a man possessed by a past which both repelled him and held him in a deathless grip. After about midnight the girls started drifting off to bed, overcome by the deep sadness he had re-kindled in them, re-focusing on visions of death and despair that they had so recently themselves experienced; but not without extending an invitation to the grizzled soldier to return the next night for a real dinner. He accepted with alacrity and even indicated that he would like to bring along his commanding officer, who would, he felt, appreciate the opportunity to visit with the Anglo-American Kriegies and exchange some thoughts about the war and the future. The men remained under the spell of this strange magnetic character who could drink and expound on the war and its misery for endless hours.

After the girls retired, Kagan went on with tales of terror alternated with episodes of great heroism and self-sacrifice along his thousand-mile odyssey of war. He had seen mountains of corpses, he had talked with captured Germans, including many high-ranking officers, even generals. When the question was interposed as to the probable fate of the absent landlord, General von Hesselmann, he shot back "That poor gentleman is either dead or in one of our prisoner camps! At any rate, he won't be coming back to harass you."

Then in a somewhat softer vein he commented, "We have captured many German generals, even field marshals. We treat these people with respect, and according to international law. If they have not committed crimes against humanity they would have nothing to fear. It is the S.S. who are the butchers. They will all be tried. But if your General is regular *Wehrmacht*, and he is not charged with crimes against our people, he may now be safe and comfortable in a Soviet camp and possibly be coming home someday to this palatial home. Possibly even soon. Who knows? The war will soon be over, and life must go on. There must be a reckoning, but for the rest we must try to restore a normal, civilized world."

CHAPTER TWELVE

Peace, It's Wonderful

THE MORNING REPORT on the B.B.C. on Tuesday, May 8th brought the blockbuster news that the world had been waiting for. The war in Europe was officially ended! All the big brass had finally signed off as far as the Western Allies—Britain, France, and the United States—were concerned.

Allied generals had accepted the unconditional surrender of Germany at a little red schoolhouse in Reims, France. It was at General Eisenhower's headquarters, but Ike had shown his disdain by refusing to receive the German delegation personally until after all the surrender documents had been signed. The bloodiest conflict in history had begun in Europe almost six years earlier. An offshoot of that war was still raging unchecked in Asia and the islands of the Western Pacific; there the Japanese enemy was still very much alive. But on the ravaged continent of Europe the lights could at last come on again.

The Soviets would conduct their own signing ceremonies in Berlin on the following day, and May 9th would become for them the official date of the German surrender. They were also to succeed on this day in liquidating the major German holdouts inside Prague, the Czech capital, although there remained some pockets of Nazi resistance in several of the city's eastern suburbs. But the Third Reich had now finally been consigned to history.

May 9th was the day for gala victory celebrations by Russians everywhere. For the Soviets in Krondorf there was round-the-clock partying and dancing in the streets and continuous fireworks displays. Vodka flowed like water. The human spirit had been suddenly released from the bondage of war. Eyes could be lifted once again to the heavens without the fear of roaming killer craft raining death upon the earth below. For the first time in years blackout curtains could be removed and street lights turned on without inviting death from the skies. It was a magical transition out of darkness into the dazzling light of a world restored at horrendous cost to sanity and peace.

In Krondorf, the day and the night reverberated with random gunfire as weapons were emptied into the air by revelling Soviet troops. Anyone even remotely connected with the winning side had a carte-blanche license to raise hell.

The German populace, on the other hand, could best be described as being in a state of total shock. From the beginning and almost to the very end they had been repeatedly assured by their leaders and the controlled news media that the German nation remained invincible, that despite everything their ultimate victory was assured.

Indeed the early years, the *"Blitzkrieg"* years, had of course seen an endless succession of spectacular victories . . . in Poland . . . in the Low Countries, Holland and Belgium . . . in Norway . . . in France . . . in the Balkans and Greece . . . in Russia in the early months of that conflict . . . in the deserts of North Africa . . . and on innumerable far-off battlegrounds where the German military octopus had extended its spiny tentacles. Through the good years and the bad, the will and the fighting spirit of the German nation had never faltered. The nation and the people had obeyed and followed and sacrificed, just as the Führer had demanded of them. How then could the mighty Reich have been brought so low? Where now were those dynamic and omniscient leaders who had harangued and beguiled the masses with promises of glory and everlasting strength and ultimate victory?

With nightfall on the 9th of May, the citizens of Krondorf stayed indoors behind shuttered windows and bolted doors. It was not at all safe on the streets with all those carousing Russians celebrating their victory. For the German populace it was indeed a time of sad introspection, a time to mourn their lost heroes and to reflect and pray. For them the future was clouded and uncertain, the peace fraught with fear and apprehension. It was probably good that the war was finally over, but what now?

The General's house on this night was the scene of a quiet "family" celebration. There was a fine dinner for about a dozen diners . . . the usual group. There were the "charter members of the club" and a few Kriegie guests from the cadet barracks, including old Taggart, who was considered "family" by one and all.

Weisskopf, of all people, couldn't make it for dinner. He was understandably out with the boys, out celebrating with his comrades-in-arms. He was missed. He was still the main man, the protector, the father figure. But he could pop in at any moment. He'd show up when he ran out of steam, and got hungry for a home-cooked Hungarian dinner. Boys will be boys, especially on a night like this. Sergeant Kagan had also not re-visited the house, but he also knew that he was always welcome.

Moderate quantities of liquor were consumed in the General's house by the men guests, as were some mouth-watering desserts, befitting the momentous day. For the Kriegies, relaxing as usual after dinner in the easy chairs with their cigars and after-dinner drinks in hand, the prospects were totally bright and positive. There was an overpowering feeling of relief and satisfaction, a dreamy euphoria that at last all had been set right with the world. Justice and goodness had prevailed. The victory was theirs. Their collective efforts had been crowned with success. They were, in a sense, heroes. They felt like heroes. They had fought, they had survived, and their side had won. The dark clouds that had for so long lingered over their horizons were now dispelled. The bloody, fire-breathing dragon had been slain and dismembered. This was the dawn of a new and better time in the affairs of men. And they happened to have been placed by fate right at center stage just when it was all happening.

For the girls, for Norma and the others, the perspective was totally different. For them it was not possible to distill any dreamy
euphoria from this most historic turning point. Their wounds
would long outlast the war. Their wounds were still open and raw,
beyond healing. They were not mere physical wounds. They were
forever; wounds to the soul, to the psyche, to the core. They were
more than wounds. They were offenses and affronts to their dignity, to their humanity, to their integrity, and even to their sanity.
Yet they all knew that life demanded a forward momentum. There
would be life beyond the horrors and injuries of the past.

It was now five days since the General's house had become
home to the girls and the three "host" Kriegies. Five days of a new
life for the girls. They felt safe and secure here. Even the daily inspection visits by Frau von Hesselmann were not entirely unpleasant. They had developed some vague admiration for the lady. They
had expressed condolences about the son. They were relieved that
he would make a full recovery. The Frau understood. She had paid
a bitter price in this war. They respected her. She didn't raise any
complaints about their presence. She was a lady.

They could, in this house, do all the things that they couldn't
do as refugees on the road or as slave workers in the camps. They
could sleep in real beds, they could bathe, they could take their
leisure, they could enjoy the company of their new friends. They
could do all the domestic things, like cooking and baking and
housekeeping, that brought so much pleasure to their protectors.
It was a way to show their appreciation and affection for the three
Kriegies who had adopted them and were taking such loving and
respectful care of them. And they were free.

Apart from the terrible tragedy that had befallen Sonya, the
entire experience in the Hesselmann house had been a happy and
constructive one for the girls. In this short span of time they had
learned to relax, to laugh, to relate to new friends, to begin to
enjoy the world about them. And they no longer looked like
"Haftlinge," or victims. They were dressing like girls—and they
could sense that they once again looked like girls.

And then, of course, the Kriegies had begun to look upon them as girls rather than as "victims." There were the faint stirrings of the boy-girl syndrome.

Hyams was somewhat surprised to find himself at times thinking tenderly of Norma and eyeing her as a girl. He was noticing her hair, her eyes, her mouth, her demeanor, her gait as she walked. At first she had seemed so remote, so cold and untouchable. And then he found her responding more softly to his looks and occasional bits of mundane conversation.

On this night most of the girls drifted, one by one, into the drawing room after dinner, to relax and enjoy the mellow ambiance that pervaded the room. There was something delicious about having survived to this day after what they had been through. There was not even any need to talk. Just sitting quietly with friends who understood—that was delicious.

But Hyams noticed that Norma did not come out of the kitchen. Upon investigation he found her still working alone in the kitchen, surrounded by stacks of dishes and cooking utensils. She seemed to prefer the solitude. Hyams understood and withdrew quietly, returning to the warmth and cheer of the drawing room. But he soon found that her absence on this very special night bothered him. He realized that he wanted to share these special moments with her. This was a time for sharing, so he thought he would try again.

Hyams pushed open the kitchen door and approached her. She did not look up from her chores. Hyams cleared his throat hesitantly, trying to think of some opening remark. And then he remembered the Cinderella story, and he went with that. "Aha, Cinderella! I knew I would find you still in here, in the scullery!"

Norma looked up quizzically, "Scullery? What is a scullery?" A flicker of a smile played across her face as she continued at work.

"A scullery maid is one who must remain working in the kitchen when everyone else has gone into the drawing room to talk and enjoy this great holiday! But you are not a scullery maid. This can wait. Won't you come and join all of us and drink a toast to peace and victory? We would all like that."

Norma turned to him, speaking softly, and for the first time she called him by name. "For me, Zeke, there is no victory . . . and no peace. It is unfortunate. There is too much to remember."

"Yes, but the others seem happy. This is a time to be thankful . . . " Hyams began.

"That is true, Zeke. We are all relieved that the killing has finally ended." She continued her dishwashing. She was rinsing the last of the large platters. Hyams picked up a towel and began drying the dishes. It brought him closer to Norma.

They worked there in the kitchen together for the better part of an hour. It gave them an opportunity, their first opportunity, to be alone and to talk and to get to know each other. He noticed the sheen in her hair. The color was a dark reddish brunette. Her complexion, despite the exposure to the elements, was very fair. Her eyes were large and expressive. They were an unusual gray-green. As he observed her, he began to suspect, in wrenching disbelief, that he was in love with her. But that was crazy. How could that be? They had always, from the very beginning, been so totally unappealing to each other. Even hostile.

But there was a softness, a serenity about her that held him spellbound. He took in all her features. The soft angles and curvey lines of her figure. He noticed, with a jab of pain, the faint tattoo on her left forearm. It was a stark reminder of her ordeal. Some sort of six-digit serial number with which she had been branded like an animal.

"Isn't it possible that some of your family survived and that you will find them alive? Couldn't they have survived, just as you have survived?" Hyams knew that there was always hope in life. He also remembered that he had once used those same hopeful words with Tibor Weisskopf, in the Stalag.

Norma knew that there was sometimes no hope. "My parents are gone . . . killed in the camp. I was the eldest of five children. Five children, Zeke." She paused for a long time. Then she continued. She didn't look up. "I am twenty-one. None of my brothers and sisters are alive. It is very hard for me to say this, or even think of it. It must be impossible to comprehend. But young children had absolutely no chance whatsoever. They were the first. My mother went together with my brothers and sisters. My father lasted a few weeks. Then he died. It is a tale from Dante's *Inferno*. It was an inferno."

Hyams had never heard such a horrible story. "Can you know this for certain?" It didn't sound possible. He challenged Norma. Was she serious?

This was the very first time that Norma had spoken of her losses to anyone who did not share the first-hand knowledge of the holocaust. How could she portray the horror, the incredible lunacy that had stripped her bare, had destroyed her entire world? How could anyone believe it if they were not there? Hyams was the first outside person she had met that she could talk to about it. It did not make pleasant conversation. It was best to pass more lightly over the past. But Hyams wanted to know. Perhaps it was because he wanted a deeper understanding of her, her burdens, her trials, her pain.

He repeated his question. It sounded very naive. "Couldn't they have survived? Maybe the older ones were put to work, like you were?"

A sad smile passed fleetingly across her face and then was gone. But she was touched by this young man—so sincere, so compassionate, so resourceful and yet so innocent. She turned slightly toward him, "You do not know how I survived, Zeke."

Hyams hesitated. "I can imagine," he said.

"No, Zeke. You could not imagine it," Norma didn't want to pursue the subject. "It is not a subject for now, Zeke. You are right. This should be, as you say, a happy time." She touched his arm as he continued wiping. It was a casual, almost accidental touching but it was enough to redirect the focus of the conversation.

She continued now in a new vein, "Zeke . . . I really owe you and your friends an apology . . . a belated apology . . . for some of my earlier behavior. Like when you first offered us your help. I know that I have been cold and rude and, one could say, insufferable at times. Especially in the beginning. I am ashamed for it. And I have never really expressed my appreciation for all that you have done for us . . . for all of us. I will never forget it; neither will the others. We are so lucky that we met you. We were in such a desperate situation."

Hyams had never considered that he and his friends had done anything particularly heroic or noteworthy. It was no more than anyone would do. "We really did nothing special. Things just worked out where we could help."

His unassuming attitude now only served to ennoble Hyams in Norma's perception. She realized more than ever the unusual gentility and goodness of the man. "Zeke, you really saved us. You did so much. You brought us back to life. After Kati received those terrible injuries we were completely demoralized and panic-stricken. We were beside ourselves. We thought we would lose her. You changed everything for us."

As she put away the last of the dishes, she turned hesitantly towards Hyams, her eyes reflecting warmth, affection, approval, and curiosity. She brought her face close to his. Hyams drew her to him. She did not resist as he kissed her gently on the lips. It was a sweet, lingering, unhurried kiss, full of tenderness and feeling. When it was over she looked up at him, studying his face. She was silent, then she moved away.

"Perhaps it is to the good that we must leave soon, Zeke, or there could be other problems to face. It would be foolish to become too close. Our time is so short."

Hyams couldn't disagree. "Yes, I know."

"It is very sad, the circumstances. It would be so fine to rest a while longer in this safe place . . . to spend another Sabbath here with you and be surrounded by friendship. But it is not to be. I and the others, we must continue on our way. We must return to where was once home to us, even though we don't know what we will find. But we must go back."

"And where is that, Norma?" asked Hyams softly.

"My home?" mused the girl softly as in a trance, "My home was once—it seems like in a dream that has faded—my home was in a beautiful old city called Bratislava, on the beautiful Danube River. Have you ever heard of it, Zeke? It is not famous, like Chicago, but it is very old. That was once my home, dear Zeke. A long time ago." And with this Norma gave Hyams a playful peck on the cheek, and proceeded to remove her apron. She was ready to rejoin the others.

"I will miss you, Norma." Hyams was a bit choked up. The entire interlude in the kitchen had come as a total surprise to him. He had not been prepared for the depth of feeling he had for the girl. It was different. It was deep. And it was serious. He hadn't bargained for this.

Norma led him out of the kitchen and into the drawing room, where Hornstein was organizing some parlor games and introducing the girls to "spin the bottle." There was no point in letting the empty bottles go to waste. And the girls were so eager and excited about learning American games. It was all good, clean fun.

CHAPTER THIRTEEN

A Walk In The Park

IT WAS EARLY AFTERNOON of a perfect spring day, the kind of day when time stands still and the senses rejoice in the splendors of nature. The kind of day that should be spent away from the mundane cares of daily life, somewhere where there are trees and grassy meadows under the open dome of heaven, perhaps in a park, possibly near a rushing stream, and definitely in the company of one with whom there is a tender, loving attachment.

Thursday, the 10th of May, was that kind of a day. And Hyams knew exactly where there was such a *Naturpark* on the outskirts of town, about a two-kilometer walk from the house on the Bismarck-strasse. Norma was willing. She had not stepped out of the house during the time that they had set themselves up in it as temporary, though uninvited, guests, except for the trips to the hospital and to the funeral for poor Sonya. Now it would be good to be out in the open, away from the house and away from the cooking and house-keeping chores that had occupied all of her time. It would be good to spend a few carefree moments, to ventilate the lungs and the mind.

They strolled through the town, past the spot where less than a week earlier Hyams and his cohorts had chanced upon Marta and Eva in that fateful meeting. During that fleeting and incredible in-terval everything had changed—for everybody. They talked about it. Norma chuckled as she was reminded of her initial diffidence and distrust of the would-be Samaritans. Soon they were in the park.

A soft breeze herded wispy white clouds across an azure sky. They followed a long, winding pathway sloping gently down toward a bubbling stream driven by the melting snows of winter on distant mountaintops. Lush grassy meadows on both sides of the walk were dotted by majestic old oaks interspersed with alder and birch. Hyams was enthralled by the idyllic setting. "I never knew that Germany could be so peaceful. I never really thought of it as having a quiet and peaceful side to it."

Norma was walking beside him. They had done much talking since the previous night. Norma had gone into considerable detail about her experiences with the Nazis. Those years had etched themselves into her soul. Yet she remained strong, defiant, true to her faith and her ideals. The Nazis had not broken her spirit, even as they had robbed her of everything on this Earth that she had held dear. But she had emerged whole and undiminished and, in a sense, victorious. Hyams marveled at her resilience and inner strength.

And now she smiled and laughed easily. It was so uncharacteristic for her. She was happy and relaxed as she walked briskly with a rolling gait. "Europe was not always ugly and sick and torn apart by hatred and war. My country, which lies probably less than 200 kilometers from here, has magnificent mountains covered with pine forests, and there are splendid lakes and valleys and rivers, and of course the famous Danube. It was very beautiful, Zeke. And I am sure those places are still very beautiful. And people could live out their lives in dignity and peace and contentment. Only for me, I am afraid much of that beauty has been ruined. It will not be easy to go home again. How will I cope with the memories?"

She stopped suddenly in her tracks and turned to face Hyams. "Oh, Zeke, how shall I ever erase all the cruelty and the horrors? Shall I be haunted the rest of my days? Is there any hope for me?" She had been struck by a sudden panic. She needed help, the reassuring words and the touch of the man she had come to admire and to love. Hyams slipped his arm about her waist and drew her gently to him. They kissed, right there, standing on the pathway in the park. Despite a few scattered passers-by, they were alone in their own world. They drank an exquisite nectar from each other's lips, and slowly her panic subsided.

She was soft and yielding in his arms, yet their love transcended physical passion. They were two people who had found each other for only a fleeting moment at this improbable crossroads of history. They came from separate worlds, and were destined soon to be torn apart by centrifugal forces beyond their control. Yet in that instant of time there was an indissoluble communion of their souls.

Her face was flushed with the excitement of the moment. She withdrew, composing herself quickly as she rearranged her frock and dabbed at her hair. She had made the most sparing use of the Frau's ample supply of fragrances and cosmetics.

Hyams took her hand. "You are strong, Norma. You will come through this." And then mischievously he added, "You have already changed quite a bit since we met!"

She looked into his eyes approvingly. "You are right, Zeke."

They continued down the pathway leading to the stream. Hyams' presence and love had indeed enabled Norma to better face both the past and the future. She felt stronger. "Zeke, you are the only person that I have been able to talk to like this. It has been good for me. I needed it. I have been so alone."

Norma desperately needed this catharsis. There were three years of hell that she now had to place in a new perspective. Talking about it was the only way to relieve the pressure of the past. Hyams was a good listener. He had so recently worked as a chronicler, as a reporter for the Stalag newspaper. He was conditioned to receive facts and information. He listened, and he posed questions. Norma was anxious to regurgitate everything. Nothing was too painful for her to talk about. She never took refuge from any question. No details were too sordid.

She had been inside Auschwitz for almost three years. She was sent there in the early spring of 1942, when the camp was just being set up. She was eighteen at the time, drafted by the Slovak government into what was euphemistically called "war service." She and several thousand other young Jews had literally built the death camp for the Germans, never knowing at the time what its ultimate purpose was to be. Of these first "draftees," very few would survive the hunger, disease, and brutality. Those few that survived would soon see their neighbors, friends, and relatives brought into the camp in cattle-cars and systematically gassed and cremated. This went on without interruption for over thirty months until the end of 1944, when the Russian advance came within striking distance of the camp. During those months, somewhere between two and three million men, women, and children were killed and disposed of in the ovens. And Norma had seen it all.

They came to a grassy knoll partially shaded by a gnarled old oak. Hyams removed his jacket and spread it on the ground as a blanket for them to sit on. What he was hearing defied all credulity, yet he knew that it was all true. The Germans had set up death factories. Old Andreas, the kindly Jerry guard on the march from Schoenberg on that first morning of Hyams' captivity, he knew of this monstrous illness and perversion of the Nazi crusade. That's why he had almost pleaded with Hyams to cast off his dogtags. "They shoot Jewish prisoners!" he had warned. "Throw away any letters or papers, anything, especially your dogtags, that will give you away to them."

But Hyams still couldn't accept that able-bodied men should let themselves be led like sheep to the slaughter. "What about the men, Norma? Couldn't they put up some resistance?" But of course he knew. Hadn't he once been a prisoner, beaten down and at the mercy of his captors? Why hadn't any Kriegie attempted escape in the confused aftermath of the Limburg bombing, when the German guards were cowering in their air-raid shelters, and when there might have been some momentary opportunity of freedom? And what sort of resistance were the Kriegies capable of after a few days of being locked in the cattle cars without food or water?

"There was no resistance possible, Zeke. Once inside the gates of Aushchwitz there was no way to change your destiny. There was once a group of about 200 Russian military prisoners, young men like you and your friends, Zeke. The Germans would sometimes even send military prisoners to Auschwitz when they wanted to exterminate a large number for some reason without leaving any trace. These were young men in their prime. We who were working near the gas chambers alerted them to their fate. We were hoping they would join us in some kind of uprising, even if it meant death for all of us. But they refused to believe us. They thought we were mad. They all went quietly to their death, like sheep."

"But why? Why would they accept certain death without putting up a struggle?" Hyams knew the question was puerile; he hadn't forgotten that earlier incident with the S.S. executioner on the road to Gerolstein on his second night of captivity, when his own knees were buckling and his throat parched. But he had to ask. Norma smiled patiently. "Dear Zeke, whoever arrived in that camp in those sealed cattle-cars was already half-dead from hunger and dehydration. It was all planned that way."

Hyams also knew about hunger and dehydration and being locked up for a week or longer in a sealed cattle-car. "Yes, I know," he said. "They pulled that on us. Eleven days in a cattle car to go three hundred miles. That was after we were captured. Of course they weren't going to do us in, but if they were, we couldn't have put up too much resistance after a train ride like that."

"And consider, Zeke, when the cars are filled with entire families, with babies and little children. Many people died in the cars. Every wagon held a few corpses when the trains pulled into Auschwitz. And, Zeke, the S.S. kept up the charade that the gas chambers were nothing more than bath houses for hot showers and delousing. That is why those young Russian soldiers went so willingly. As did everybody."

Hyams stretched out on his back. He had heard enough. He studied the cloud formations, the peaceful skies. It was hard to believe that perhaps a couple of hundred miles from this idyllic place there had been such a cesspool of evil, conceived and operated by men who might have been born and gone to school and lived here in this very same lovely town or in some nearby village under this same magnificent sky.

"Do you still have your faith? Do you still believe, Norma? After all that you have seen?" It was a rhetorical question. He knew that Norma's faith was unshaken. If anything, it had been strengthened and reinforced, although he wasn't sure that he himself could muster that kind of abiding faith.

"But of course. I have the faith in God that I was raised with. That is what kept me alive, what gave me the will and capacity to survive and a reason to survive. Without faith, Zeke, there was no reason to survive. Everything else was gone. There were people who never believed, who found God inside Auschwitz."

"Yeah, I guess that's true. They say there are no atheists in the foxholes, and I can attest to that!" Hyams had prayed the hardest when death had been breathing down his neck. When there's nothing else, what else is there?

They lolled there under the oak tree, alternating between quiet conversation and peaceful moments of reflection. Despite the chronicle of horror which Norma had related, she was, to his continuing amazement, relatively free of rancor. She was at peace. There was a serene harmony between them. Hyams marveled at the resiliency and depth of her nature. And after a while, Hyams leaned towards her and kissed her gently on the lips. She responded warmly. They had found each other in this unlikely place, where they were both transients in a foreign land, like ships passing in the night.

"I love you, Norma," he whispered.

She was pleased, but a bit skeptical. "That is good . . . but how can it be? You hardly know me. But it is good . . . that you think you love me. I am thankful."

"I know you enough to know that I love you, Norma." It was awkwardly put, but they both understood.

She was deeply affected. "Zeke, I have never before been spoken to of love. Until I was taken to Auschwitz I led a very sheltered life. My family was very strictly orthodox. I could never sit with a young man as we are sitting now. It would be unheard of to be alone with a young man. The only young men I ever spoke to were the students at my father's seminary. In normal times I would have been married at eighteen to a man chosen by my father. And now, having met you and come to know you, I also think that I love you. You are a very kind and gentle man, and the time that we spend together is very precious to me. I have never been in love before. But if this is love then I like it." She broke into a beaming radiant smile that lit up her delicate features. She had found happiness, however fleeting it might be.

Hyams pressed on. He took her hands in his. "I want to go with you, Norma . . . wherever you are going."

She smiled tenderly, "Ah, if it were only possible . . ."

But a man driven by love doesn't give up. "Why not, Norma? Why do we have to separate like this, now that we have found each other?"

Torn between emotion and reality, she searched for words. It was difficult for her. "Zeke, you must return to your home and your loved ones. You really have no choice in this. And I . . . though I no longer have a home, I must also return. Even though there is no one there, I must return to what was once my world. I also have no choice in this."

"But we belong together now. There must be a place for us! I want to marry you!" Hyams had never thought of marriage before, with anyone. But this girl stirred the tenderest protective passions in him.

She studied his face. She was touched. "You are a very good man. In so many ways you remind me of the world which is now lost . . . where people cared deeply, were compassionate . . . and wise." There was a long silence and then she continued. "We can write to each other, Zeke. I would really like that. This doesn't have to be the end. It can be the beginning for us."

Hyams knew she was right, but he did not want to lose her. His face mirrored his anguish. He started to remonstrate as Norma placed her hand to his mouth and silenced him. "It was fate . . .

a mysterious fate . . . that brought us together. We cannot know what the future holds for us . . . but I will never forget you, Zeke. I do love you."

The sun was beginning to sink in the west, as they embraced.

Soon they were on their feet preparing to return to the General's house. Hyams was experiencing both the joy and the exquisite pain of love.

CHAPTER FOURTEEN

Sergeant Kagan Returns

PEACE, when one has known only war for a long time, is synonymous with life—health—good fortune—love—great rejoicing—sudden freedom from fear and anxieties—a return to light from darkness—and above all, a return to sanity from a legalized madness. Zeke had often thought that if more people knew how difficult it is to turn off a war once it has developed, then perhaps there would be a greater reluctance to accept the teaching of war. One just can't hardly terminate a war once it has begun! Wars almost always begin suddenly and end slowly. One must stay with it to the very bitter end, no matter how long it takes and whatever the awesome costs. War is a bestial and ravenous devourer of men, ideals, sanity, and reason. It is a deep dark pit from whence no light appears until the entire devastating course is run!

Peace came to Europe during this early May. In the time immediately following there was a noticeable lowering of tension levels, an easing of apprehension and fears of the return of the past. Now the people in the General's house could take walks in the countryside and do all the other things that travelers at rest in a land at peace can do. They joked, they picnicked, they laughed, they enjoyed every minute more, they fantasized, they talked about the future with greater assurance.

While the war was in fact over, the military bureaucracies had not yet completed the necessary procedures and logistics for returning the multitudes of refugees, displaced persons, and ex-prisoners across newly delineated borders. Indeed, the new boundaries had not been re-aligned between the Western Allies and the Soviet zones. So while some technical confusion reigned between the friendly titans, the wayfarers in Krondorf remained in place, making the most of a very comfortable and pleasant situation. The men would go forth at regular intervals to somehow obtain the necessary provisions; the girls would happily do the domestic chores. There was undeniably some considerable depletion of the food stores in the General's large cellar, but those were the fortunes of war, and of peace. The dinners at the house became justly famous among Zeke's buddies at the cadet barracks; they had nightly visitations by appreciative friends. They had created a veritable salon of fine cuisine and serious discourse here in this most unlikely place. One would listen attentively to conversations in which the most vivid stories of recent history would be just commonplace.

On the evening of Friday, May 11, the group was again favored—much to their pleasure this time—by a surprise visit from Battalion Sgt. Kagan. He appeared in time for dinner. He was accompanied by two young Soviet officers, whom he introduced as Major Vassily Gruenfeld and Captain Yuri Konstantin. They were all warmly welcomed, the sergeant being an old friend, the other two adding some meaningful rank to the Kriegies' humble group. It was truly a festive meal, the Soviet guests furnishing all the authentic news about the great surrender, the spectacular deaths of Hitler and Eva Braun, the exploits of the Red Army in the reduction of Berlin, the capture of Budapest and Prague, and their success against the final fanatic hold-outs. The major wore the green collar tabs of the occupation forces, and he was in an excellent position to know and describe the emerging general situation, although at first he appeared somewhat shy and reticent. He listened to the girls' conversation, having considerable fluency in their languages. As the evening progressed he heard them describe the deportations, the infamous extermination camps, the losses of parents, husbands, sisters, brothers, and children. Frequently he would curse and shake his head in disbelief. This even though he had spent years in the war and had seen it all.

Unlike the sergeant, he was naturally a quiet man, not particularly of a military bearing, although he wore numerous combat decorations including the coveted Order of the Red Star. Before the war he had been an architect in Kiev. He was married and had a three-year-old son whom he had never seen. In the summer of 1941, his wife, a student of Western literature at Kiev University and five months pregnant at the time, had been evacuated with thousands of other women and children just days before the city fell to the Germans. They were taken to a distant city in Siberia, where the child was born and his wife worked as a schoolteacher all during the war years.

He had photographs of the two and was looking forward to an early reunion. Kiev, the ancient capital of Ukraine, that city of one million inhabitants, famous among other things for its old Jewish district, the Podol, had been held by the Germans for over two years and the city had suffered great tragedy and destruction, but it was retaken in November 1943. Now that the war was over, the major and his wife and child could return to their native city from a separation of thousands of miles and pick up the shattered pieces of their lives.

The major was remarkably free of overt bitterness or acrimony towards the Germans, in spite of the fact that the Nazis had killed his parents and most of his relatives along with millions of his fellow Jews. In his capacity as administrative officer with the occupation forces, it had been his duty since the Soviet Army had entered the German homeland to protect the enemy population against violent and illegal acts of vengeance and retribution. Everyone had to smile at this, all heads turning in unison towards the embarrassed Sergeant Kagan.

The major would not have chosen this assignment for himself, but he accepted it without reservation. He had extended his protection to unrepentant Nazis as well as to those Germans who were totally demoralized and crushed. He had felt at times the irrepressible urge for "sacred vengeance" but he had not permitted himself to fail in his assigned mission. He had even served for a while as a commandant of an occupied town in East Prussia that was notorious as a hotbed of unreconstructed Nazism. In other places he had found the German population docile and abjectly humbled.

Gruenfeld also described the unexpected and exotic range of people imprisoned or enslaved within Germany whom his unit had liberated over the past few months. There were of course prisoners-of-war of all nationalities ranging from Norwegian to Greek and everything in between, even including many from countries formerly allied with Germany, such as Italy. Then there were priests, nuns, clergymen of all the Protestant denominations, foreign students, merchant seamen of all nations, and so on ad infinitum.

There were also many hundreds, possibly even thousands, of Polish girls pressed into institutionalized military prostitution to serve the needs of the German forces on the Russian front. Hyams himself could incidentally confirm the existence of such female contingents on the Western Front, having observed, as a newly taken prisoner, an entire Pullman train on a siding in the Ardennes, close behind the German front lines. It was brimming over with bumptious young females who appeared neither starved nor deprived. It was indeed a plush rolling bordello for maintaining the morale of deserving German troops. Sort of a front-line cheering section. The girls there had been Polish, or at least so he had been told. It seemed that only the most flaxen-haired and blue-eyed Polish girls were suitable for these purposes because, of all the subjugated nationalities, they came closest to the stringent Aryan racial and physiological standards for womanhood.

Captain Yuri Konstantin, Kagan's other guest, it turned out, was a military writer on the staff of *Red Star*, the Soviet Army newspaper. His purpose in visiting had been twofold: to have an opportunity to converse with the Americans, and to meet the girls and obtain some lucid, in-depth material from recent victims of the Polish death camps for a forthcoming book on Nazi atrocities. However, he himself soon became the center of attention. He was a very interesting man of considerable erudition, fluent in English as well as the Czech language, which several of the girls spoke. Before the war he had been a news correspondent in Paris and other European capitals, and he had a very broad perspective of the war and the interrelation of Russia with its Western Allies.

After dinner, over some drinks, he allowed himself to reminisce about the war years in Russia. His English was Oxonian, his syntax measured and poetic. He used a phrase in particular that would always remain with Zeke. He spoke of "deep war."

"One hears of deep love, deep hate, deep passions; but when I think back to the climactic stages of the war inside Russia, I must call that 'deep war'! It was a war of unmitigated rancor and malice, carried on by an aggressor whose one aim was total demoralization and destruction—destruction of a people, their system, their culture, their heritage, unto the last traces. And on the other side, defenders who would absorb the greatest military punishment ever conceived by man and rebound again and again after the criminals had grown weary and exhausted of their slaughters."

"In Russia, beside the war against our troops and the general population there was indeed war against the very land itself. The Germans, even while in full retreat in 1943 and 1944, would take the time to gratuitously burn down whole villages and farms, to kill the livestock, cut down fruit orchards, and systematically destroy growing crops. The Germans came to the Russian War with, as you say in English law, 'great malice aforethought'! The Russian is by nature mild; he has to be very badly hurt to be goaded to fury; but we in Russia came to know fury as never before. Fury was our constant companion, feeding and nourishing our resolve from summer to winter and from autumn to spring."

The captain's thesis of anger and fury would help to explain that initial image of Sergeant Kagan as he stormed into the General's house that recent night.

"This war was the ultimate test of our nation and our people. Today we stand with our allies as strong partners. For every tank we possessed in 1941, we have today fifteen! For every artillery piece, we have today five! For every aircraft, we have today five!

We acknowledge the great material assistance from the United States, but it was our own factories within the Soviet Union and our own people who produced the mountains of war material that were needed to expel the invaders."

There was a hushed silence in the Hesselmann dining room as the captain concluded his remarks. He had spoken mainly in English for the benefit of the Americans present, but the others could divine the thoughts and messages conveyed. The captain was an eloquent reporter of the Russian people and their story. He had dispelled much of the mystic aura that hung about his people in the minds of these few Westerners.

The party broke up soon afterward. As Zeke lay in bed that night, warmed by the General's cognac, he went over the short history recounted by Captain Konstantin of the long war in his country. The young captain had conveyed the essence of the Russian experience. Zeke was really grateful to him, for he could now better understand the varied and contrasting images that he had of the Russians since Stalag days. He was also thankful that they were allies. He did not meet again with his Russian friends. Business would take them all off in separate directions.

CHAPTER FIFTEEN

Going Home

"IT'S ABOUT TIME we get the hell out of here! It's all turning to shit!" Hornstein was in another of his ugly moods. And who could blame him? At this grand moment in history, when there were parades and parties and welcoming ceremonies everywhere in the States, when Manhattan was alive with jubilation, and G.I.s everywhere were being lionized as heroes, and reaping the pleasurable harvest of a nation's gratitude, he was still stuck here in this jerkwater Jerry town, waiting for some Army bureaucrats and the Russkies to get their act together and send him home where he rightfully belonged.

Witherspoon commiserated. He was down too. "Gee, Maury, here we are in a house full of booze and food and those bloody cigars that you so dearly love . . . and why the bloomin' hell do we feel so miserable? Of course we all want to get home, but there's more to it. It's more than just the bloody homesickness. I just can't figure it out."

"It's those women. We never should have gotten involved with them. We didn't need it. It was a friggin' mistake, right from the beginning. And I knew it!" Hornstein was sprawled out on the General's divan, nursing a quart of the world's finest Kümmel. But nothing could cheer him up. "Things just got too complicated. Let's face it, we're in no shape for friggin' complications. Look at Hyams. He's got this crazy notion about being in love. The poor sonofabitch. Then just imagine if that Kurt kid had gotten himself killed by that Sonya. He came very close. Just imagine. The shit really would have hit the fan. We'd all wind up in Siberia as accessories. And Weisskopf would be back in the candy business, only in Siberia! Godamn!"

"Yeah, Maury, you're absolutely right. But it was a kind of beautiful thing we did for them. They said we turned their whole life around—gave them a new lease on life. They were really in bad shape. We just couldn't walk away and leave them. We had to get involved. And this bloody Kurt kid is going to recover, and I admit that is a very good thing. It's all bloody fate, Maury. And we've had some great times here in this bloody house, what with their cooking and us inviting our pals over for some home cooking. And Maury, think of the satisfaction we got out of doing something for a fellow human being. Look at the bright side, Maury."

"Yeah, I know. But I'm glad they left. Things were getting too sticky. I think that Magda really had her eye on me. She was a good-looking woman, got to admit it. And a great cook! Another few days and we'd all be what you call romantically involved with them. Like that poor boob, Hyams. Who needs that?"

Witherspoon had to agree. He was nursing his own bruised ego. He had lost his heart to that perky Leftenant who, it now appeared, was not destined to play a major role, nor even a minor role, in his life. Another case of fickle fate, of unfulfilled love. But it helped to talk about someone else's problems. "Poor Zeke . . . he's got it real bad."

"He'll get over it. What does the kid know about women? And love, yet? They were nice girls, and they were really great people in their own way. There's no denying that. But love? The poor sap says he wants to marry her. Wait 'til he hits Paris or Brussels with his pockets full of Yankee currency. Then he'll find out what love is all about. The poor sap."

"Maury, you're priceless. Tell me, have you ever really been in love? Like full-bore, in love?"

"Are you kidding? Dozens of times, kid. It's nice; I recommend it. But . . ." and Hornstein paused for emphasis while taking a short swig from the decanter, "you must not take it too seriously, and it'll go away."

It was late afternoon on this Sunday, May 13th. It was the time of day when the house would be filled with brisk activity and anticipation as the girls would be preparing a full-course dinner. Now, on this fifth day after "V-E" Day, the General's house was suddenly empty, silent, and forlorn. These two were trying to console themselves by looking forward to their own hoped-for departure from this cold and empty house. But the place held sentimental memories for them. There was no denying that it had become home.

The girls had left that morning. The leave-taking had been very sad. There had been real bonds of friendship and more that had to be severed abruptly and probably forever. There had been promises to write and that sort of thing, but the roads out of Krondorf would be radiating out in a thousand different directions. Such parting is usually forever, despite the best of intentions.

And now Witherspoon had to unburden himself. He had it bad for the Leftenant. "I know how Zeke feels, Maury. Because I think I'm in love with Irina. Really in love, believe it or not, Maury."

Hornstein waved the bottle, "I think the whole friggin' world has gone bananas!"

"I know how Hyams feels, Maury. I've never had it like this. The Leftenant—I mean Irina—she's really different. So kind and sweet, and really beautiful. I think she really cares about me, but she said that we should not see each other again. She says it just wouldn't work. I think she has asked for a transfer. So, Maury, maybe you're right. There's no bloomin' percentage in it."

"The quicker we can get the hell out of Krondorf the better off we'll all be. We just don't belong here. There's too many lousy memories." Hornstein was right. They didn't belong there anymore.

And then Hyams appeared. He was out of sorts and listless, his face unshaven, and the Kriegie pallor had all but returned. He threw himself into a chair without a word to the others. Hornstein snickered, "There, Jock, that's what love can do for you." Then he offered his bottle to Hyams, "Here, my young buckeroo, this will put the bloom back in your cheeks."

"Thanks, Maury, I could probably do with a drink, but maybe later. I wonder where the gals are by now."

Witherspoon estimated that they would be somewhere in the vicinity of Dresden. And Hornstein figured that with the safe-conduct pass they had received from Weisskopf's commanding officer, their homeward journey would be smooth and uneventful.

Hyams agreed, "Yeah, Tibor said that they'll have priority even for military transport. So they'll be riding rather than walking. That's a break." Hyams now took a deep draught from the bottle. He was not a drinker, but tonight he would drink. "Damn, if I was any kind of a man, I'd have gone with them."

Hornstein winced. "Yeah, real smart! Then instead of being just 'missing in action' you could up-grade yourself automatically to 'desertion.' That makes a lot of sense. From the Stalag to the stockade! And what the hell could you do for her out there in Russkieland? You'd be a godamn burden to her. You'd be a fish out of water. Wake up, kid; you're living in friggin' dreamland!"

"Did it slip your mind, mate, that you are still officially in the United States Army? And they're gonna want to be seeing you again—like real soon?" Witherspoon had a point there, and Hyams knew the little paratrooper was thinking more clearly than he was. But the pain was still there.

Hornstein poured the last of his bottle into a crystal goblet. He thought he knew how to cheer up his young friend. "Pretty soon, maybe in a couple of days, maybe even sooner, Zeke old chum, we are going to collect a big fat paycheck from Uncle Sam for all that hard time that we did. That will come to quite a few bucks. You know, money . . . moola . . . greenbacks . . . the folding stuff that buys anything and everything—in such places as Paree, Brussels, even London, like in Picadilly Circus, right, Jock? Tell the boy, Jock!"

And about then, the front door creaked open and in strode Tibor Weisskopf. Having Tibor around always raised Hyams' spirits. Here was a man who never let trouble get him down. And Tibor's face was wreathed in smiles. "Cheer up, all of you. I have good news for you!"

Hyams perked up, "You've heard from the girls!"

"No, my good friend, we haven't heard from the girls. But not to worry. With that passport with my colonel's signature they will be under the protection of every Soviet headquarters along the way. I assure you that I have taken care of things. Don't forget my little Marta is traveling with them. And besides, did you forget? The war is over!" Weisskopf really had the juice. He was practically on a first-name basis with his colonel. He was still the "candy-man" who could pull the rabbits out of any hat. "They'll be home within a couple of days."

And then his expression turned somber, "Of course, my friend, what they will find at home, or rather, what they won't find . . . that is another story."

But Hornstein was impatient. "Okay, so what's the good news, Tibor?" The portly little sergeant had mixed feelings about the "good news."

"The good news, gentlemen, is that you can very soon say good-bye to Krondorf, and to Germany . . . and to me . . . and to everything that happened here." He wasn't smiling any more. He was slightly choked up. "Tomorrow morning you will be homeward bound!"

There was a heavy silence in the room as Weisskopf continued. "An American truck convoy will arrive in the morning to pick up all the British and American ex-prisoners. You will be departing tomorrow morning from the cadet barracks. It's official." With this, Weisskopf poured himself a glass of cognac and downed it. The man of iron had become attached to his Kriegie friends. He had spent many months in the Stalag with the Anglo-Americans, and he had come to know them and admire their open style, their sense of fair play. He had actually become "westernized" in the Stalag, and now he would be losing that last remaining link to a world that he had glimpsed and which had so impressed him.

The Kriegies now individually and collectively expressed their appreciation for all that Weisskopf had been to them. Good friend, protector, defender and staunch ally. He had been an unfailing beacon in a strange and sometimes mystifying swirl of events, which no one but Weisskopf could influence or control. There was much toasting and hand-pumping. And in this parting with Weisskopf, Hyams was likewise losing a last link to a world that had seen so much suffering but had survived victorious in its humanity and age-old wisdom; and also a link to Norma's world. The General's fine liquors could not dispel the hurt and the sadness.

Weisskopf was a man who would not easily be forgotten. And then Witherspoon came up with a question that had apparently long intrigued him. "Tibor, there is one thing that I must ask you. I can't leave Germany without knowing how the devil you managed to come by all those luscious Viennese bonbons inside that bloody Stalag! And all the bloody business you did inside Starvation Acres! Weren't the bloody Germans on to you, man? How the bloody hell did you do that, man?"

Weisskopf assumed that inscrutable smile, his eyes crinkled around the edges. "My friend, that was a long time ago, and perhaps too complicated a story for now. It is perhaps for the next time we meet."

"The next time we meet . . ." Hyams repeated those words to himself in a soft whisper. "Where and when?" he wondered.

The American truck convoy showed up at the cadet barracks at 1000 hours on the Monday, May 14th. It was good to see the old Stars and Stripes again, and that long cavalcade of mud-caked trucks just like the one that only a half year ago, in early December 1944, had carried Hyams and his buddies over the mountain roads of Luxembourg and into the winter wonderland of the Belgian Ardennes, where the German Panzer divisions lay so craftily concealed. It had felt like a Boy Scout outing then. They had been so innocent, so naive.

A misty-eyed Weisskopf was there to wave goodbye as the Kriegies boarded and the trucks started rolling westward. The route took them by the *Bismarckstrasse*, and Hyams thought he could see the Frau von Hesselmann entering her deserted house. Somehow she seemed like an old friend. It had been only about ten days since he had first laid eyes on that lady when she had materialized so imperiously through that oaken portal with her son at her side.

Requiem for Father and Son

Requiem for Father and Son

THE YEAR was 1944. It was the fifth year of all-out war. It was a year of agony and death across the entire European continent; from the beaches and along the hedgerows of Normandie, to the ovens of Auschwitz, to the broad, tank-strewn killing fields of Russia. Death was everywhere in Europe that year. There was death for the soldier. Death rained down from the skies over shattered cities. Death awaited the daily trainloads of new arrivals at Auschwitz-Birkenau in the southwestern corner of Nazi-occupied Poland.

People like Viktor Wulf, the untold numbers like him, all lived from minute to minute in a dark, sunless world of unrelieved gloom and despair, a world devoid of laughter or friendship or the faintest flicker of hope beyond the next bread ration. It was a world without clocks or calendars, where time was frozen in space, without news or any shred of information other than what might be gleaned in the snarling commands of the S.S. slavemasters.

For the people like Viktor Wulf—to be assigned to work—and to be physically able to work—and to endure twelve-hour workdays—under the harshest conditions, without adequate food or rest—this was the only tenuous key to survival, albeit a short-term survival at best. Life expectancy could be measured in days or weeks. Anything beyond that could not be realistically contemplated.

The only chance of real survival, however remote, lay perhaps in an Allied victory—or the eventual downfall of the demonic Nazi regime by whatever circumstance. Any of this could only come about through a major miracle. But even if such an unlikely miracle should come to pass, who would be alive to see it? Hitler and his Nazis were cunning, cruel, and seemingly invincible—devils in men's habit.

In fact, in the autumn of 1944, Adolf Hitler's Reich was still functioning internally like a fine precision watch, ticking away silently and smoothly. Despite the historic success of the Anglo-American landings on the fortified beaches of Normandy early that summer, and the subsequent victories of the Allied forces during the late summer pursuit of the German Army through France and Holland and Belgium, plus the smashing Russian breakthroughs on the Eastern Front, Hitler had survived. And now he had some reasons for optimism as the blood-soaked summer of 1944 faded into autumn with its clouded skies and muddy, rutted roads, which would impede the expected Allied assaults by land or from the air. He could sense a steady recovery of the German military equilibrium on the Western Front as the Anglo-American legions began to outrun their supply lines.

Despite the massive reverses, Hitler could still count on a finely honed military and security machine numbering some nine million men under arms, all buttressed by a powerful and still functioning industrial base, only marginally affected by the round-the-clock aerial poundings by Allied bombers. He would continually exhort his generals and inner circle of sycophants that the war, then entering its sixth year, could yet be won despite the losses and heavy casualties taken. It would certainly yet be won, he stormed, if only the craven defeatists and traitors could be identified and combed out of the military staffs. The German people, that indefatigable master race, could then be rallied to its full potential.

The ethos of the "master race" was part and parcel of the basic war strategy. Only the purest of Aryans, those of total dedication, could be entrusted with the destiny of Adolf Hitler's Third Reich and with the ultimate destiny of mankind on this earth. The "Aryan supermen" were the privileged instruments who would spearhead Germany's wars and gain the eventual victories worldwide. The shining objective to be achieved at all costs was a thoroughly Aryanized world, cleansed of Jews, Gypsies, and all such other inferior races that an Aryanized world could not live with.

Meanwhile, at the base of the societal scale, the millions of faceless and soulless drones needed to power the support engines of war—whether on the farms, in the factories, or deep in the mines all across the bomb-battered Fatherland—would be drawn from the motley tribes of expendable non-Aryans that proliferated across the European continent.

From mid-1941, some three years earlier, with the launching of the attack on Russia, Hitler's Reich would process untold millions of foreign prisoners and non-Aryan slaves through its concentration camps and forced-labor system. It was institutionalized wholesale slavery of a kind and on a scale hardly seen or imagined since the days of pagan Rome; the purpose being not merely the exploitation of these extraneous masses, but the short-term coincidental destruction of the exhausted slaves, who were plentiful, cheap, and readily disposable.

Hitler had declared, back when his armies held most of Europe in their grip and were still advancing across the Russian plains, "The area working directly for us now embraces more than 250 million people! We must succeed, we shall succeed, in involving every last one of these millions in our labor process!" Hitlerdom, then at the zenith of its power, controlled a total population pool that was four times Germany's pre-war population. An inexhaustible labor supply was assured despite the drain of the war upon German Aryan manpower.

These faceless masses whose lives were forfeit to the German war effort were mainly from the conquered lands . . . Poland, Russia, all the Balkan countries including Greece, and even from Hungary and Italy, two erstwhile partners with Germany in the Axis alliance. There was also slave labor from France, Belgium, and Holland, and political prisoners and dissidents from every corner of Europe, including Germany itself—men and women and children—both with and without their parents. All went into the giant hopper, names and pasts irrelevant, to be accounted for by an impersonal, numbering system such as might be used to inventory fungible goods in a gigantic stockpile.

A contrived code of concocted legalities covered every aspect of the immense slavery operation. The slave masters were punctilious in their record-keeping and in their adherence to book-balancing procedures. Ironically, the numbers had to check out perfectly. Not one slave could remain unaccounted for, dead or alive. The euphemistically detailed train manifests and the frequent roll calls and body counts were all part of the unflagging official record-keeping, with copies going out to various S.S. administrative headquarters. At the top of the pyramid, Berlin was always kept meticulously informed of the most insignificant minutiae.

The "legal" status of these interchangeable and replaceable human chattels was officially that of *Haftlinge,* meaning "persons in custody" or "Wards of the Government." To ease any fleeting qualms about their treatment or condition, they could all be thought of simply as "Enemies of the State" and consequently devoid of any human value or dignity, and unworthy of any sympathy or consideration in these times of total national commitment to war.

With the total combat casualties then approaching four million, and the millions of fresh recruits, including the very young and the elderly, now required to man Germany's beleaguered armies on both the Western and Eastern Fronts, the Third Reich in the fall of 1944 could rationalize that it indeed required a vast army of slave labor to ensure an adequate labor supply at home and the continued viability of the war economy.

Thus the *Haftlinge,* the slaves, thankful for a temporary reprieve from death, were shipped off to munition factories, steel mills, farms, mines, quarries, railroad gangs, construction sites, oil refineries . . . wherever men and women could be profitably put to work in furtherance of the war effort. It all made excellent economic sense. The private firms which employed them would hire the slave workers in wholesale blocks of hundreds or even thousands, negotiating with and paying the S.S. Financial Administrative Bureau in Berlin "sweetheart contract" rates that would both yield handsome profits to the corporate employers and fill the private coffers of the S.S. hierarchy.

Major industrial firms with the right political connections had their pipelines set up into the concentration camps to siphon off this cheap and plentiful labor supply. Indeed, several firms had actually created vast "industrial parks" inside the electrified perimeters of some death camps so that those inmates fortunate enough to be selected for work could be marched daily from their barracks directly to their workplaces, thus eliminating the need for long distance rail hauls.

The slaves were very easily motivated, for they lived in constant terror and were immensely grateful to survive each day. They needed nothing more than a single ration of soup and bread per twelve-hour work day, supplemented by what food scraps they could scavenge from nearby garbage dumps. The only investment in each individual was the negligible cost of transportation in packed cattle cars from the "processing centers" in the East to the particular work site, plus the issuance of such minimal gratuities as a thin blanket and a tin cup to receive the daily soup ration.

Replacement necessities like shoes or clothing came from the mountains of personal belongings left behind by the hapless victims of the gas chambers in those very same processing centers.

And in the mass extermination camps in the Polish backwaters, the S.S. in 1944 switched gears from the automatic killing of all new arrivals to the selection and temporary reprieve of all workable individuals, deferring their destruction so long as they remained capable of hard work. A valuable national resource was thus no longer to be frivolously frittered away. Conservation was the new password.

The Führer's prize industrial property remained, in late 1944, the Ruhr District in the northwest corner of Germany tucked in close to the Dutch border. This was the factory-filled wonderland which, since the early days of the Industrial Revolution in the nineteenth century, had been the main source spring of German wealth and power. The district comprises a total area of about two thousand square miles, about the size of the state of Delaware, and was home to about five million Germans. It was certainly at the time the richest industrialized region in the entire world.

At the heart of the Ruhr lay the venerable and prosperous city of Essen, with its 600,000 hard-working *Bürghers,* its magnificent thousand-year-old Gothic cathedral, the sprawling Krupp steel and armaments works with the nearby Villa Hugel, ancestral home of the legendary Krupp family, set among baronial woods and parks.

All manner of heavy industry proliferated in and around Essen, including, in addition to the great armaments plant, several other important iron and steel works, locomotive and truck assembly plants, chemical factories, oil refineries, glass, furniture, and instrument manufacturing, and an incredible number of mining operations. And as for the coal mining, the Ruhr coal fields, which lay just to the north of Essen around the grimy suburb of Gelsenkirchen, comprised the second-largest known coal deposits in the world, representing over three-quarters of the total German coal production. Likewise, the coke ovens and blast furnaces of the Ruhr yielded over 70 percent of Germany's entire iron and steel production.

The belching smokestacks of the Ruhr had served as guiding beacons for Anglo-American bomber fleets since early 1943. The entire region was the top priority target of the American Strategic Air Command by day, and the Royal Air Force Bomber Command by night. They had unloaded massive tonnages of high explosive against the cities, towns, industrial installations, railroads, and refineries that filled the Ruhr landscape. It was saturation bombing with a vengeance, but at a fearful toll in Allied planes and their crews, who ran the deadly gauntlet of Luftwaffe fighter squadrons and the most concentrated anti-aircraft defenses in the world. Despite all, the Ruhr miraculously survived, rising daily from its ashes like a mythical Phoenix, and its smokestacks continued to pour out the black acrid smoke that hung in an unmoving blanket as if to conceal its wounds from its tormentors.

By the late summer of 1944, four out of every five buildings in and around the city of Essen had been leveled by Allied bombings. As in so many other German cities at this time, one could stand at the center of the city and look out at an unending vista of flattened structures and desolate, bomb-scarred streets.

In the brief interludes between the bombings, however, the streets would fill up with numerous work gangs called *Arbeitskommandos,* whose function it was to hurriedly clear away the collapsed walls, broken masonry, fallen timbers, chunks of cement, twisted steel girders, and whatever debris the high-explosive bombs would splatter about, including, of course, the dead and the wounded buried in the rubble. The keynote was as always, *"Schnell!"*—"On the double! Move it!"

The casualty rate from the air raids was staggering among these same work gangs, for they were housed for the most part in the open, mainly in tent compounds or barracks in the shadows of the very targets themselves. The crews were in constant rotation because of the high casualty rates and the decimation by hunger, exhaustion, and disease.

The rail lines that threaded through the Ruhr region were handy and available for shipping these human cargoes, in packed freight cars, or even on open flat cars, back to the processing stations like Auschwitz, where worn-out slaves could be speedily disposed of in the gas chambers. New arrivals came in, and the exhausted and depleted were shipped back to the East from whence they came.

The city of Gelsenkirchen, about ten miles due north of Essen, was in reality an extension of Essen's coal mining and industrial concentrations. The place could best be described as Essen's cluttered and dismal backyard, where the mines, refineries, coking plants, and railroad yards seemed to blend together and stretch endlessly.

On the main highway between Essen and Gelsenkirchen was situated the largest petroleum refinery in Germany, operating on a feverish 24-hour basis. The plant was capable of producing fully a third of the total German requirements of motor fuels and lubricants, and almost all of the gasoline for the Panzer forces on the Western Front. The sprawling refinery had been converted earlier in the war to use brown coal or lignite—which was locally in plentiful supply—in a secret process to produce gasoline. This one momentous technological breakthrough, which substituted cheap, plentiful soft coal for hard-to-come-by petroleum in the manufacture of motor fuels, had enabled the Reich to withstand both the impenetrable Allied naval blockade and later the loss of the Russian and Rumanian oil fields. The formulas and technology involved in this process have always held a fatal fascination for chemical engineers, statesmen, and the financiers of all nations both before, and since, the war.

The Führer had ordered that this vital facility must be kept in operation at all costs. The Allies would bomb and destroy, while the Germans and their slave contingents would immediately patch up and restore the plant, only to have it knocked out again as soon as production resumed. This was obviously a situation that called for the presence of large numbers of expendable slave labor, and the S.S. would not flinch from this challenge. The barracks and tent cities within the refinery perimeter were kept full to capacity with *Haftlinge*—holding about eight thousand slave workers, with new contingents and replacements arriving on a weekly basis.

Among the new arrivals one gray morning were some six hundred male prisoners, Czech and Hungarian Jews from the processing center at Auschwitz in Poland. One of these people was Viktor Wulf. As they detrained at a rail siding, the shuffling skeletons, in baggy pajama-like raiment, were blinded by the daylight. They were confused and disoriented after five days locked in the freight cars, tightly packed in more than a hundred men to a car without food or water. Yet whatever their fate or assignment in this new place, it had to be a vast improvement over their former circumstances.

A squad of grim-faced S.S. troopers quickly took charge of the prisoners. They were counted off, tallied against shipping documents, and then hustled off on the double to a row of large tents inside a broad meadow enclosed by multiple redundant coils of barbed-wire that would preclude any thoughts of wandering about.

"*Schnell! Schnell! Fünf! Fünf!*" It was still the same S.S. slave masters who were giving the orders here, but for these *Haftlinge* it was a tremendous relief to find themselves in a place where the first order of business might be something other than death and abject degradation. At least here they were apparently wanted and needed. "*Arbeit Macht Frei*"—"Freedom through Work." Work was normal, desirable, essential—and especially so if a *Haftlinge* was to live through the day in Hitler's Germany.

That evening, after the prisoner formation and additional head counts, Viktor Wulf, formerly of Berehovo, Czechoslovakia, walked slowly back toward the giant circus tent, one of perhaps twenty set up in the open field, that was to house him and hundreds of his comrades.

Wulf was one of the more elderly of that morning's arrivals. He had survived the original Auschwitz selections because of his youthful bearing when he had first arrived at the Polish death camp some four months earlier. Then he had been a robust and handsome middle-aged man with just a trace of gray around the temples. But now he could feel every one of his fifty-six years in his emaciated arms and legs and in his shrunken muscles and bones.

In his home town of Berehovo he had been, just months earlier, a prosperous lumber merchant, one of the town's leading citizens. He had settled there with his young bride after his service in the Austro-Hungarian Imperial Army in the First War. He had served with distinction in that long-ago conflict, attaining the non-commissioned rank of brigade sergeant, a rare achievement for a Jew, even in that relatively benign old empire.

Berehovo, a bustling market town of some twenty thousand souls, lay at the center of a broad, fertile valley surrounded by verdant hills covered with small and medium-sized vineyards. The entire region was sheltered from the cold winds of the North by the semi-circular sweep of the Carpathian mountain range. Viktor and his family had skied the mountains and had frolicked in the gently flowing rivers and the crystal waters of the mountain lakes. The decades had been kind to him and his family in Berehovo. He had lived in a large brick house in the center of town, and had earned the respect and esteem of his neighbors, Jew and Gentile alike. His wife had borne him two handsome children. He had all the blessings that a man could hope for.

This war, this evil war that began in September 1939 and raged across Poland and finally into Russia was not directly felt in Berehovo in the early years.

True, the map of central Europe had undergone many revisions and transformations. The Republic of Czechoslovakia had been dismembered, and his town of Berehovo had gone under Hungarian rule. But other than governmental changes in such things as the official language and currency and the like, the tone and quality of life were not radically altered. In those early years the war seemed like nothing more than a distant thundercloud on a dark horizon.

The Hungarian government, though allied with Hitler in the war against Russia, had sought to maintain some semblance of integrity and independence. The elderly Hungarian regent, Miklos Horthy, had managed to steer a moderate course in the internal affairs of the nation.

But on March 20, 1944, German legions had suddenly swooped down upon Hungary like a plague of locusts. And with them came the dreaded S.S. and the Gestapo, who brought unmitigated hostility and menace. Within the short span of two months, Viktor's business was closed down, his life savings and all his property, including his home, were confiscated, and he and his family were compelled to move into a congested and confined Jewish ghetto as a preliminary phase prior to the "resettlement," which was soon to follow.

Resettlement?—Deportation?—Expulsion? Jews in Hitler's

world had to be prepared for such unkind and peremptory treatment. Soon Viktor's entire family was delivered by cattle car across the Polish border, in a several-days-long hell journey to the infamous death camp at Auschwitz.

It was on that dark day, May 17th, 1944, a day etched in Viktor's soul, that he had last seen his wife and eighteen-year-old daughter. Families were separated at the train dock, with men and women being marched off separately in opposite directions.

To think now of his family's probable fate was to sink into the depths of hell and despair. "Resettlement" and "deportation," it turned out, were cynical euphemisms for murder, extermination, and incineration, with only a "lucky" few selected for work and short-term survival. Viktor's seventeen-year-old son, Peter, had been able to remain in the same work group with him; the fate of his wife and daughter remained unknown.

Through the intervening months the father and son had managed to stay together, although always maintaining an outward separation. Certainly if the S.S. had known of the father-son relationship, a final separation would have long since occurred.

Peter had arrived on the same train that morning at the Gelsenkirchen refinery, but with a different batch of prisoners, and had been assigned to a different work *Kommando*.

Viktor Wulf's arrival at the Gelsenkirchen refinery was on a Saturday. By a stroke of kind Providence, the following day, Sunday, turned out to be a day of blessed rest for Viktor and his comrades. Lengthy studies conducted by the ever-scientific S.S. Labor Office in Berlin had concluded that six 12-hour work days per week were the most that could be extracted from the slave gangs without causing immediate breakdown of these underfed and exhausted wretches. They might have remembered that even horses do better with an occasional day's rest.

Early on that Sunday morning, seeking a breath of fresh air after a night inside the foul and congested tent, Viktor and his young son ventured together into the open yard, where they discovered a place of quiet refuge in a shallow trench about a hundred yards from the perimeter fence. They rested there for a while, savoring the solitude and safety of the cool, silent earth. This was indeed a rare moment, this opportunity to be together and converse fully and freely without bringing down the wrath of an overseer.

They embraced, shed some tears together, and gained strength, one from the other. They soon fell silent when reflecting on what their life had become. There were no answers, there were no questions. Their thoughts and fears focused on the possible fate of the mother and daughter still unaccounted for. The haunting image of those two loved ones being hustled off by bellowing S.S. ruffians and camp orderlies in the reception yard at the killing factory that was Auschwitz some four months ago . . . that image tore at their vitals. Neither man could break the mournful spell that hung over them like a suffocating blanket.

Then they sought to exchange a few scraps of rumour that might offer some solace. There were reports of numbers of survivors who had been spared the fate of the gas chambers; of female Jewish workers who had been seen toiling in *Arbeitskommandos* at various work sites; but the reports were all so vague and ephemeral when weighed against the known horrors.

Yet in spite of the new dangers that they were now exposed to, they took heart from the destructive evidence all about and the massive damage to the refinery complex that they could observe from their resting place. Since that first arrival of their death train at Auschwitz some months earlier, the Germans had always been perceived as the omniscient, invincible super-men, immune to death and danger. Their only concern had been the meticulous selections of their victims—which of them would live for a while, and which must die immediately. They had always been so impervious to any doubt or pain or defeat. There had earlier been no such scenes as these to suggest that Germany itself was indeed caught in a crippling pincer and was being dragged down to ultimate defeat as it was subjected to God's wrath from the skies.

Viktor now charged his son to remain alert for any chance

word, of rumour or speculation, that might shed some light on the fate of their loved ones. There had been word that within the various sub-camps in the Gelsenkirchen area there were several that held women prisoners from Auschwitz. There could possibly be a ray of hope.

The possibility of escape fleetingly occurred to them, and was dismissed almost automatically. Despite that at the moment the perimeter fence was not being patrolled; there were no guards in sight; even the guard dogs were momentarily absent. A sudden wild urge to break away struck Viktor. Why not? Why couldn't an escape effort be made? The security here appeared to be less stringent and lethal than the multi-layered electrical fences and guard towers of Auschwitz.

Ironically, the thought of escape hardly ever occurred to these condemned men. Escape from these omniscient masters was rarely attempted and rarely even thought of, except in such circumstances as these when external conditions appeared to alter the odds ever so slightly.

But escape involved great imponderables and even greater risk of immediate death in event of failure or recapture. It would also require some reserves of physical strength and stamina. The system was so all-pervasive. There were no safe harbors, no friends on the outside, no rescuers willing to assume the great hazards and the dire consequences of failure. There were no real chances for successful escape. The world was perhaps even more hostile and unmitigating on the outside of that fence than it was within.

Before Viktor could continue with his half-hearted analysis of escape prospects, two Schmeisser-toting guards sauntered into view and ordered the two *Haftlinge* back to their quarters. The father and son complied instantly. It would soon be time for the morning head-count, a formation that could, incredibly, take two to three hours to complete.

The morning head-count. This was yet another psychological tactic to crush the spirit and drain the already depleted resources of these people. The daily hours-long head-count was an essential ritual for the Germans. If a prisoner were to fall out of formation, to crumble or collapse, this meant immediate expulsion from the work corps, with its usually fatal consequences.

As the day wore on, on this blessed day of rest, Viktor and the others became aware of the frequent overflights of flotillas of "enemy" bombers. Like flocks of migrating geese, the aircraft flew at great altitudes in chevron formations, trailing hundreds of white contrails in the gray sky. All the planes were heading on the same course, eastward and deeper into Germany.

Viktor had never before imagined that there could be such concentrations of air power. At home in Hungary and then over the Auschwitz death camp, the skies had usually been empty and placid and peaceful, the only refuge for troubled spirits. He marveled now at the majestic movement of these armadas, seemingly immune to the deadly puffs of anti-aircraft fire reaching out to them.

The penetration of these air fleets into the German airspace suggested that the Germans had been thrown on the defensive, at least relative to the air war. To the *Haftlinge*, who knew little or nothing about the Allied ground operations in Western Europe, and the presence of massive British and American armies then poised within a scant hundred miles of the Ruhr, these high-flying formations suggested some hope for their future. They were things of beauty, even if their cargoes could rain death down upon them who were now situated so close to the prime targets. The sight of something that could even remotely be considered beautiful triggered an hallucinatory reaction in Viktor as he sat on the bare ground in the shadow of the great canvas asylum.

Reveries of a former life infused Viktor, faint memories revived of his close-knit family, of a calm and ordered home life, of happy and beautiful times. And he who had forgotten how to pray now formed a silent prayer for his deliverance, and for the deliverance of his loved ones. He dreamed of home, of his vineyard of six hectares of gently sloping land in the foothills above Berehovo. He had planted that vineyard at an earlier and happier time, selecting the young plants, laying out the rows, the spacing, the drainage patterns. He would visit the vineyard almost every afternoon in all seasons, stealing time from his regular work to keep checking on the vines, the shoots, the pruning and the shaping.

In those times he had been in close harmony with nature. He could sniff the air and know what kind of a summer or fall was in the offing, when to delay the harvest for three or four days, and when to hurry the taking of the fruit. His vineyard, which had started out as an adventure, had become a labor of love, and then an avocation, requiring commitment and attention to wide-ranging and absorbing detail.

As the vines matured and the grapes became locally renowned, Viktor had built his winery, the cellar, the presses, and the great hogshead storage tanks and barrels made from the finest kiln-dried Carpathian white oak.

That Sunday afternoon, in the lifeless camp close to the refinery and the grimy railyards of Gelsenkirchen, Viktor could sense that those long-cherished vines that he had so lovingly tended for so many years on that distant Carpathian slope, were now, through the neglect and drought of the long summer and the cold and wet of autumn, shriveled and dying. It was yet another dagger thrust into his burdened heart.

Seeking to avert that pain, his thoughts next drifted off to the varied and bountiful fruit orchard behind the fine stone house where his children were born and where life had been so full and rewarding. He had experimented in those years with the crossbreeding and grafting of exotic strains of various fruit trees. He saw the walnut tree that his little Rachel had planted when she was only two, when he had handed the child a walnut and she solemnly embedded it in the rich black soil. That was to be her tree, and through the years she had remembered and nurtured it, and taken pride in its growth and development. His orchard was veritably a Garden of Eden and, like the vineyard, had been a confirmation of nature's munificence and of God's unstinting design for all living things.

Viktor had hardly thought of home or of those remembrances of peace and safety and goodness since coming to Auschwitz. That place of horrors had filled his entire consciousness and had totally eclipsed all memories of a normal life. Now, in the yard at Gelsen-kirchen, he gave thanks that he could summon again some recall of the beautiful days of his life.

While the memories brought sadness and pain and wrenching fears for the wife and daughter who had been so cruelly cast into the cauldrons, Viktor realized that to remember and to feel were of themselves benefactions to be treasured.

Somewhat refreshed in spirit, he thought now that perhaps he might find the strength to cope with the ordeals that lay ahead. He was humbly thankful that he had his young son by his side, and was determined to survive to ensure the lad's survival. The two were now very dependent on each other, which also caused Viktor some grave misgivings. He knew that at his age he might at any moment fail the ongoing test of endurance and will, and young Peter seemed unprepared for the loss of his father. But they would look to Almighty God for sustenance and protection.

The distant rumble of heavy guns and bombing continued all day without drawing much attention other than some rueful com-ments by the *Haftlinge* that there would surely be mountains of rubble to be cleared on the morrow.

For the men of the slave-labor gangs, the ensuing days would be full of back-breaking work, often exposed to the elements in the most inclement weather. Viktor, at fifty-six, was now suffering from rheumatoid arthritis; the joints of his arms and legs swollen and painful, yet he dared not complain or falter. On those days when the sun shone and warmed the air, Viktor was thankful for any re-lief and the chance to be working close by his son.

Peter was seventeen, at an age when he would soon be coming into full manhood. Despite the nightmare existence, he was gaining strength and maturity. With the buoyant sanguinity of youth, Peter soon managed to find a small group of female prisoners in a neighboring work camp with whom he established a surreptitious acquaintanceship. Any sort of contact between members of the opposite sex, even the slightest, was strictly forbidden and subject to severe punishment, but in spite of the rules and the constant surveillance, Peter and one of the girls did strike up a tacit friendship. The women's duties involved food preparation for the German guard personnel, and, as in all European armies, there were mountains of potatoes to be peeled.

Peter's secret friend always made sure that there were a few whole potatoes cast out with the mounds of peelings at the garbage dump, to be retrieved by Peter as he passed by in the evening from work.

To have been apprehended in this "crime" would have had the direst consequences for the girl. To Peter, his father, and a few trusted friends, the occasional bonanza provided by the shaven-headed young potato-peeler meant life itself.

Viktor existed from day to day, keeping up with the work and pulling his weight along with the younger men, but he could feel his strength slipping steadily. He lived only to ensure the survival of his son. Within the deepest recesses of his soul, there now arose a new anguish, the torture of guilt and self-reproach.

He began to blame himself for the loss of his wife and daughter, and even for the death in Auschwitz of his eighty-three-year-old mother, along with his brothers and most of their families. But how could he have foreseen the black wave of cold and unrelenting anti-Semitism and the unimaginable crimes carried out by a "civilized and cultured" nation against innocent victims, the programmed extermination of entire families and populations?

Now he and any others who might have escaped early death in Auschwitz were really on borrowed time. Viktor was well aware that there was no future for them; even if Germany were to be defeated eventually, it would come too late. It was impossible to survive under these conditions for very long. None who had seen and experienced the death camps would be allowed to remain alive to see the war's end.

If only he could have had some measure of foresight, of

wisdom, to sense what was coming. There were plenty of tell-tale signs, omens that should have alerted him!

Since the war began in 1939 there had been a virtual black-out of hard news in his country. However, he had heard some of what had happened to the Jews in the neighboring countries such as Austria and Poland during that time—particularly in Poland, with its three million Jews. But he had rejected those reports. He couldn't accept them. There was really no solid verification. He couldn't credit them.

Why had he felt so safe and secure in Hungary? Was it because of his distinguished military record in the last war, when he had served in the army of Emperor Franz Josef? Was it because his own life had been so idyllic and rewarding that he could not face up to the jolting truth?

Why had he not, at the very least, sought safety for his children while there was yet time? As late as 1940, it might have been possible to send the children away to America or to England, where there were relatives, and where they would have been safe. Why hadn't he done that? It would have been so simple. His two children could have been saved. But how could he have known?

The torment was unending and unanswerable. Even when he slept there was no rest. There was no escape, not even in the deepest sanctuaries of his mind, nor in the fantasies of the past, nor of the future.

Gelsenkirchen remained a beckoning bull's eye for the Allied bomber fleets based only forty-five minutes away at their British bases. The only way to choke off the petrol for the lumbering Panzer forces on the Western Front was to destroy the sprawling refinery once and for all. Yet this vital strategic objective was to be denied to the Allied Air Command. Despite the unstinting tonnage of high explosives and incendiary bombs dumped on the place during the critical autumn of 1944, the refinery incredibly arose anew from the ashes every time. As winter laid its icy grip on the European continent in late 1944, the Allied strategic bombers were

grounded by the weather much of the time. The refinery soon resumed full uninterrupted production. And then the gangs of depleted *Haftlinge* became superfluous. They became extra baggage.

The ovens of Auschwitz could readily dispose of all the non-es-
sential slaves, unless of course other work assignments for them
were to come down from Berlin. And there was indeed to be yet
another work assignment for Viktor's group, further to the East,
further away from the advancing Allied forces, deeper inside the
belly of Germany, in a place called Eisenach, in the forested mountains of Thuringia. There was a factory there that needed a fresh
supply of slaves. And there Viktor and Peter would, for a brief interval, benefit from the good deeds of a new friend, a man called
Menachem Levin.

Hitler's Germany was shrinking rapidly, turning in on itself
from the relentless advances of Allied forces on both the Western
and Eastern Fronts. Still, in the declining winter of early 1945 it
remained a very busy and tightly compartmented universe. Life
progressed on vastly different planes where individuals and groups
traveled lonely and separate tracks.

On such a solitary and separate track, traveled one Menachem
Levin—Latvian, Jew, engineer, and mathematical genius. Levin
was a rare bird, an anomaly. His story was very sad, and very
unique. Despite his crushing racial baggage he was, in this dark
world of slavery and killing camps, tolerably well treated and even
deferred to. In fact he was sought after and highly prized by some
of the most hardened people in the S.S. industrial complex.

Diminutive, hawk-nosed, and sad-eyed, the very caricature of
Jewishness, Levin was yet a very important man at the newly commissioned factory in Eisenach, which was producing, in the early
winter months of 1945, electronic components and parts for the V-
2 rockets, Hitler's secret vengeance weapon. This was top security
and very high priority work, and Levin's professional capability was
deemed important, if not crucial, in the plant.

Eisenach lay cradled in the dense forests of Thuringia, in the heart of Central Germany, where a new hi-tech industrial concentration was being created. Here the natural camouflage of mountains and forests would conceal the factories and test facilities from enemy spy planes, as a last-ditch German technological leap forward was to be made while massive American forces were poised for the final assault less than two hundred miles away.

Legions of slave workers had been employed for months digging the excavations for the subterranean factories, some of which were hidden in abandoned mines hundreds of feet below the forest floor.

Years earlier, as a young man in Riga, Latvia, Levin had opted for a secular career despite that he was the scion of an ancient rabbinical family. This had been a radical departure from his ancient heritage. In his father's eyes he had disgraced himself and his family by forsaking the path of traditional Talmudic studies in which he had been immersed from early childhood. But Levin had other ideas about life, and he went on to graduate from the Riga Polytechnic Institute with the highest honors and won his baccalaureate both in mathematics and in mechanical engineering.

Mechanical engineering and machine work were for the Gentiles, for the infidels, not for the sons of the Torah. Levin, however, had persisted in his chosen profession, and soon after graduation achieved considerable prominence as an industrial designer and innovator in his native country. That was in pre-war Latvia, before the Nazi tide swept in. Then in 1943 history would write the final chapter for the Jews of Riga, and soon Levin and his entire family were on a cattle car headed for Auschwitz.

In a selection at Auschwitz where the rest of his family was liquidated, Levin was pulled out of a line-up when a civilian official on a headhunting mission for technically qualified inmates learned of his technical education and credentials in the field of engineering design. Germany at that moment desperately needed a "few good Jews."

Levin was immediately transferred out of the death barracks, and from that day on he was kept working as an engineer and designer at several key industrial facilities in Germany. It was that or the gas chamber. After an odyssey of various assignments where he proved his genius for solving complex design problems, he was placed in a sort of consultative capacity in the high-priority machine shop at *Fabrik* Number Twelve at Eisenach, where hundreds of *Haftlinge* slaves were employed around the clock.

Levin had no illusions about his own ultimate fate. He knew that, despite everything, he was surrounded by hatred and contempt, and was marked for death at any moment when his usefulness were to be questioned. The Germans would never allow him to survive in any case, for he had gained intimate knowledge of classified technologies and of the building of various prototypes of key rocket components. Furthermore, there was the envy and unmitigated resentment of many rabid S.S. functionaries, who had to endure the presence of this diminutive Jew who was so far ahead in a technical area where absolute German supremacy had always been taken for granted.

So, over the months, Levin had to continue to play the fool. Any hint or suspicion of betrayal would have instantly propelled him into a Gestapo torture chamber.

Whatever Levin had learned as a young man at the Polytechnic Institute of Riga now ensured his day-to-day survival in this nightmare world. But the slightest misstep would be his last. When alone in the darkness and still of the night, he was sick with remorse and guilt. Wouldn't it have been better if he had perished along with his parents and brothers and sisters? What value was there now to his life if its only purpose was to serve these monsters in their war against humanity?

In the various factories where he had been assigned, perhaps as a penance, Levin always sought out those among the slave workers who seemed most worthy of help and sustenance. It was the least he could do. He made it his personal mission to save whatever few Jewish lives he could.

It was to *Fabrik* Number Twelve that a transport of over one thousand slave workers was shipped from Gelsenkirchen in early

January 1945. And in that shipment were Viktor Wulf and his son Peter. After one hundred and fifty miles and five days in the cattle cars, most of the passengers were more fit for the death barracks than for work.

Viktor and his son were both assigned to the machine shop, Levin's bailiwick. It was indoor assembly line work. In spite of the twelve-hour work days, one could live with it. Viktor and Peter were soon to benefit from Levin's benevolence: extra bread rations, extra soup. The father and son, here in humiliation and bondage together, struck a special chord with Levin, and he was determined to help them survive. He responded to a special quality and grace that he perceived in both father and son, a dignity and unyielding devotion between them. They reminded him of his own father and a young brother of his own. There would be some survivors . . . there had to be.

The concern and care emanating from Levin was the only significant instance of friendship or kindness that Viktor Wulf had experienced since falling into the Nazi clutches some eight months earlier, except for that brave gesture in Peter's behalf by that nameless young potato peeler in Gelsenkirchen. It did much to restore Viktor's spirit and hopes during this short-lived hiatus. But as the weeks progressed and the general German situation became daily more desperate and hopeless, the work load at *Fabrik* Number Twelve began to dwindle. Rockets were no longer considered essential to the German war effort, the launching sites having been largely destroyed by Allied airpower. The dynamics of the German situation were changing daily. The great new industrial order that was to be activated in the forests of Thuringia was coming unglued. Nothing was working out as they had planned. There were no raw materials or parts to work with; no fuel; no supplies; no orders; no transportation; no direction; and ultimately no purpose.

The winter had turned bitter and merciless. The German taskmasters became daily more confused, anxious, and desperate. The Führer's dream was about to come crashing down on them, as yesterday's supermen now found themselves with thousands of enfeebled and starving prisoners on their hands, with no orders or instructions from any responsible headquarters, and no facilities at hand for their discreet and speedy destruction as in times past.

It was at this time of chaos and desperation that Menachem Levin's special engineering team was to be reassigned to another plant some distance to the north near the city of Magdeburg, a factory that was still actively engaged in the production of truck and tank parts.

Levin knew that the war was all but lost for the Germans. So why was he now being moved to yet another work-site? Was this in reality a thinly veiled charade to conceal the truth, that he was now marked for the inevitable liquidation that he knew awaited him before the final curtain came down for the Nazis? Perhaps death would be a welcome release. The Germans must surely understand that no amount of factory production, be it trucks, tanks, or roller bearings, could possibly alter the balance at this late date. Hitler's final grand assault in the Belgian Ardennes, though taking the Allies by surprise, had eventually been thrown back with heavy casualties. Only the Rhine River now remained as a last line of defense against an unstoppable Allied juggernaut. Hitler had played his last card. The Russians were pressing in from the East with a momentum that would likewise not be denied. Poland had been overrun. Even Auschwitz, that focal point of evil and death, had been taken by the advancing Russians. Levin knew all this from illicit news sources, which, though fragmentary, clearly outlined the accelerating collapse of the German position.

Levin went a last time to see Viktor and Peter in their freezing barrack. The elder man had aged and shriveled; the cold, the hunger, and the rheumatism destroying him day by day. Young Peter was lying death-like in his bunk. He had been running a high fever for several days. Excuses had been made for him every morning at roll-call, for if the Germans suspected any sort of infectious illness they would have turned him over immediately to the S.S. for execution and cremation. They were deathly afraid of epidemic.

Levin knew that he would never again see this father and son whom he had so recently come to know and deeply admire. For some days, as the work ran down, he had tried to look after them, getting occasional extra rations for them. Even now he knew that he could prolong the old man's life by obtaining a reassignment for him to another work-site, a play for time. But with the young man sick and wasting away, there really was not much hope for their survival. The boy was too sick to move, and the father would not abandon him. The bitter cold, the lack of vitality, the malnutrition, the hopelessness, and the mounting desperation of the Nazis . . . Levin knew there was no way out.

With feeble choked-up words of encouragement and with tears in his eyes, Levin took a final leave of Viktor, Peter, and their barrack-mates. Most were too weak to respond in any way. Viktor embraced him weakly, muttered some words of benediction and turned away. Peter waved glassy-eyed as Levin departed on yet another leg of his pain-wracked odyssey through a sick and tortured land.

At the slave factories near Eisenach, production ground to a complete halt during the first week of February. While there was still some residual need for the military goods, the production system had just collapsed. The *Haftlinge*, who only a few short months ago were being touted by Berlin as a valuable national resource, had now become an acute and embarrassing nuisance to their wardens. Frantic calls were made to S.S. headquarters in Berlin. In mid-February the requested orders came. All Jewish workers not deemed essential for continued production were immediately to be relieved of their work assignments and were to be removed, by whatever means available, eastward to the city of Chemnitz, a distance of some hundred miles, where a special facility was available for their final handling.

A move of such distance was indicated in order not to overload the facilities at nearby Buchenwald Concentration Camp where there were already preliminary contingency plans in the works to self-destruct the camp, lest any surviving inmates or operating personnel fall into Allied hands.

Chemnitz was deep inside Eastern Germany, hard by the Czechoslovak border. It would be a secure place for cleaning up the last surviving remnants of the slave labor force. Rail transportation was to be provided for the evacuation of a total of several thousand individuals, but in the event that there should be any delay in obtaining the necessary transport for each *Kommando,* they were ordered to be taken out on foot, under close guard, and marched at maximum speed in the direction of Chemnitz.

When word reached the inmate barracks, a hush of doom descended. Everyone understood the full import of the new edict. Within minutes there were squads of S.S. men with their snapping guard dogs rousting everyone out and stampeding the lethargic prisoners. The various encampments were cleared in short order, with long lines of shivering skeletons in their pajama-like garb preparing to take to the road—in freezing weather—without adequate clothing or footgear to keep out the cold, the slush, and the ice.

Peter had only recently begun a slow recovery from his mysterious fever, and he was almost too weak to stand up, let alone join a march on the open road in weather and conditions like these. But to fail to join the straggling column would mean immediate death by bullet. Viktor, himself totally depleted, supported his son in his faltering steps, as did some of their barrack-mates, but the column was being driven along by the S.S. men and their dogs at a rate of over three miles per hour—a normal speed of march for healthy troops, not for men who were more dead than alive.

With the approach of night, the temperature dropped precipitously and it became plain to both the slaves and their guards that not one prisoner would survive until the next morning.

The S.S. officer in charge of the column decided around midnight to give the marchers a few hours rest. As they passed a large barn-like structure he ordered the column to take shelter for what remained of the night. The benumbed and dazed men stumbled toward the shelter of the building and collapsed in heaps, huddled together for warmth. They fell on the snow-covered ground, or inside on the dirt floor, in a stupor of utter exhaustion.

Of the two thousand men originally in Viktor's labor *Kommando* at the refinery in Gelsenkirchen back in September, some five months earlier, there remained less than five hundred barely alive here on this frozen Thuringian field. Before dawn the next morning, the column was roused and again ordered back to the road. The guard dogs were let loose among the collapsed forms. Most of the men wearily regained their feet and moved into formation, but some of the lifeless bodies had by now turned cold and stiff. Almost a hundred men had perished during the night from the cold and exhaustion. It had been a merciful death in sleep. One of those that did not return to the march that morning was young Peter. The father stood over the lifeless form of his son, and had to be dragged off by several of his fellows.

Viktor was beyond tears, and beyond feeling. His world had ended. He rejoined the column, plodding along silently with this tragic column of men who were about to die. His body and legs were there, but his mind was gone, and his spirit was dead.

All day they marched. The traffic on the road moved by in both directions; military and civilians, trucks, combat vehicles, and horse-drawn carts in a never ending stream. Nobody in those passing vehicles could have believed Viktor's story. Viktor himself would never have believed it. A story of incredible collective madness.

The S.S. had their orders: "Get those damned swine to Chemnitz!" Toward night, the pathetic column reached a railroad yard where a train of open flat cars awaited them for the final leg of their journey. Some of the cars were already piled high with prostrate and barely moving human forms. Other cars were only half full. Viktor's group was ordered to climb aboard the cars, wherever space could be found. Viktor, by now limp and moribund, was carried and dragged onto one of the open cars by his fellow prisoners.

The train slowly pulled out of the yard that night headed east for an unknown destination. Viktor would expire within the passage of a few hours.

Bibliography

Because of the rather wide-ranging historical research that the author undertook in preparation for the writing of these stories, he also felt that it might be helpful to share with the reader this partial list of reference sources available to broaden and amplify one's perspective on the period and the events that are touched upon in this work.

Baldwin, Hanson. *Battles Lost and Won*. New York: Harper & Row, 1966.

Ball, Adrian. *The Last Day of the Old World*. New York: Doubleday & Co., 1963.

Bernadac, Christian. *The Naked Puppets*. Geneva: Ferni Publishers, 1978.

Bradley, General Omar N. *A Soldier's Story*. New York: Henry Holt & Co., 1951.

Cohn, Norman. *Warrant for Genocide*. New York: Harper & Row, 1967.

Conot, Robert E. *Justice at Nurenberg*. New York: Harper & Row, 1983.

Craig, Gordon A. *The Germans*. New York: G.P. Putnam & Sons, 1982.

Crankshaw, Edward. *Gestapo*. New York: Viking Press, 1956.

Crookenden, General Napier. *Battle of the Bulge—1944*. New York: Chas. Scribner's Sons, 1980.

Dawidowicz, Lucy S. *The War Against the Jews*. New York: Holt Rinehart & Winston, 1975.

Davidson, Eugene. *The Trial of the Germans*. New York: Macmillan Co., 1967.

Davies, W.J.K. *German Army Handbook—1939–45*. New York: Arco Publishing Co., 1977.

Downing, David. *The Devil's Virtuosos: German Generals at War 1940–45*. New York: St. Martin's Press, 1977.

Eisenhower, Dwight D. *Crusade in Europe*. New York: Doubleday & Co., 1948.

Encyclopedia Judaica: "The Holocaust." Vol. 8. Jerusalem: Keter Publishing House, 1972.

Fest, Joachim C. *The Face of the Third Reich.* New York: Pantheon Books, 1970.

Fleming, Gerald. *Hitler and the Final Solution.* London: University of California Press, 1984.

FitzGibbon, Constantine. *20 July.* New York: W.W. Norton, 1956.

Gilbert, G.M. *Nuremberg Diary.* New York: Farrar, Strauss & Co., 1947.

Gilbert, Martin. *Final Journey.* New York: Mayflower Books, 1979.

Graber, G.S. The History of the S.S. New York: David McKay Co., 1978.

Hart, Liddell. *The German Generals Talk.* New York: William Morrow & Co., 1948.

Hilberg, Raul. *Documents of Destruction.* London: W.H. Allen & Co., 1971.

——. *Destruction of the European Jews.* Chicago: Quadrangle Books, 1961.

Hohne, Heinz. *The Order of the Death's Head.* New York: Coward, McCann & Geoghegan, 1970.

Hoffman, Peter. *History of the German Resistance.* Cambridge, Mass.: MIT Press, 1977.

Humble, Richard. *Hitler's Generals.* New York: Doubleday & Co., 1974.

Infield, Glenn. *Skorzeny, Hitler's Commando.* New York: St. Martin's Press, 1981.

Irving, David. *The Secret Diaries of Hitler's Doctor.* New York: Macmillan Publishing Co., 1983.

Jackson, Robert H. *The Nurnberg Case.* New York: Alfred A. Knopf, 1947.

Kenrick and Puxon. *The Destiny of Europe's Gypsies.* New York: Basic Books, 1972.

Keitel, Field Marshal Wilhelm. *The Memoirs of Field Marshal Keitel.* New York: Stein and Day, 1966.

Lengyel, Olga. *Five Chimneys.* New York: Ziff-Davis Publishing Co., 1947.

MacDonald, Charles B. *The Mighty Endeavor.* New York: Oxford University Press, 1969.

——. *The Battle of the Huertgen Forest.* New York: Jove Books/Lippincott, 1963-1983.

Manchester, William. *The Arms of Krupp.* Boston: Little-Brown, 1968.

Maschman, Melita. *Account Rendered.* London: Abelard-Schuman, 1964.

Manvell, Roger, and Fraenkel, Heinrich. *The Incomparable Crime.* New York: G.P. Putnam & Sons, 1967.

Merriam, Robert E. *Dark December.* New York: Ziff-Davis Publishing Co., 1947.

Michel, Jean. *Dora—A Concentration Camp.* New York: Holt, Reinhart & Winston, 1979.

Moorehead, Alan. *Eclipse.* New York: Coward-McCann, Inc. 1945.

Mosley, Leonard. *On Borrowed Time.* New York: Random House, 1969.

Muller, Filip. *Eyewitness Auschwitz: Three Years in the Gas Chambers.* New York: Stein and Day, 1979.

Nyiszli, Dr. M. *Auschwitz: A Doctor's Eyewitness Account.* New York: Crest/Fawcett World Library, 1961.

Pawelczynska, Anna. *Values and Violence in Auschwitz.* London: University of California Press, 1979.

Peis, Gunter. *The Man Who Started the War.* London/New York: Oldham's Press/Popular Library, 1960/62.

Reck-Malleczewen, Friedrich. *Diary of a Man in Despair.* London: Macmillan & Co., 1970.

Shirer, William L. *The Rise and Fall of the Third Reich.* New York: Simon and Schuster, 1960.

Speer, Albert. *Infiltration.* New York: Macmillan Publishing Co., 1981.

——. *Inside the Third Reich.* New York: Avon Books, 1971.

——. *Spandau—The Secret Diaries.* New York: Macmillan Publishing Co., 1976.

Taylor, A.J.P. *The Origins of the Second World War.* London: Hamish-Hamilton, 1961.

Toland, John. *Battle: The Story of the Bulge.* New York: Random House, 1959.

——. *The Last 100 Days.* New York: Random House, 1966.

Trunk, Isaiah. *Judenrat.* New York: Macmillan Co., 1972.

——. *Jewish Response to the Nazi Persecution.* New York: Stein and Day, 1979.

U.S. Army, Office of the Chief of Military History, European Theater of Operations: Cole, Hugh M., *The Ardennes: Battle of the Bulge.* MacDonald, Chas. B., *The Siegfried Line Campaign,* and *The Last Offensive.*

Vogt, Hannah. *The Burden of Guilt.* New York: Oxford University Press, 1964.

Whiting, Charles. *Death of a Division.* New York: Stein and Day, 1981.

——. *Bloody Aachen.* New York: Stein and Day, 1976.

Deborah Gibbons
705 - 3399

Philip Albaum
805 969 - 1481

Mike + Seal

Printed in the United States
51654LVS00004B/85-213